"KERR

HARMFUL INTENT IS

"TERRIFIC."

—RICHARD NORTH PATTERSON

HARMFUL INTENT IS

"QUICK-PACED."

—SCOTT TUROW

HARMFUL INTENT IS

"COMPELLING."

—*KIRKUS REVIEWS

Praise for
Harmful Intent

"This straight ahead debut thriller [is a] strong first novel. . . .
Kerr handles the courtroom scenes with savvy. It would be a
shame if suspense fans overlooked this one."

—*Chicago Tribune*

"From its opening page, the story demanded my attention and
never let me go. Stylish and convincing, *Harmful Intent* shows
Baine Kerr to be a talented writer with a terrific feel for the
courtroom."

—Richard North Patterson

"*Harmful Intent* is so good that you hope the author gives up
law to write full-time. . . . Kerr shores up the plot with switch-
backs and fascinating medicalese."

—*Texas Monthly*

"The story grabs, the plot is believable, and the characters are
human."

—*Booklist*

"[Laced] with suspenseful twists and turns . . . for insight into
the inner circles of law and medicine, *Harmful Intent* delivers.
It's a fun, fast, and often poetic read {with} an inside scoop on
legal wrangling."

—*Rocky Mountain News*

"*Harmful Intent* is full of passion and urgency, a brilliantly plot-
ted courtroom drama that flares, occasionally but irresistibly,
into poetry. Terry Winter is a touching and profoundly authentic character. In some ways, she speaks for us all."

—Juliet Wittman

"*Harmful Intent* should put Boulder on the map for mystery
lovers, right next to Stephen White's Alan Gregory books."

—*The Denver Post*

continued . . .

HARMFUL INTENT

Baine Kerr

JOVE BOOKS, NEW YORK

Lines from "Because One is Always Forgotten" by Carolyn Forché (from *The Country Between Us*, Harper and Row, 1981) are quoted with permission.

HARMFUL INTENT

A Jove Book / published by arrangement with
Scribner

PRINTING HISTORY
Scribner hardcover edition / April 1999
Jove advance reading edition / June 2000
Jove edition / October 2000

All rights reserved.
Copyright © 1999 by Baine Kerr.
This book, or parts thereof, may not be reproduced
in any form without permission.
For information address: Scribner, an imprint of Simon & Schuster, Inc.,
1230 Avenue of the Americas, New York, New York 10020.

The Penguin Putnam Inc. World Wide Web site address is
http://www.penguinputnam.com

ISBN 0-515-12924-0

A JOVE BOOK®
Jove Books are published by The Berkley Publishing Group,
a division of Penguin Putnam Inc.,
375 Hudson Street, New York, New York 10014.
JOVE and the "J" design
are trademarks belonging to Penguin Putnam Inc.

PRINTED IN THE UNITED STATES OF AMERICA
10 9 8 7 6 5 4 3 2 1

For Cindy

The heart is the toughest part of the body.
Tenderness is in the hands.

—*Carolyn Forché, "Because One is*
Always Forgotten"

Part One

THE CASE

ONE

$\mathbf{T}$*erry Winter twisted* the wand to level the conference room blinds. Glittery cold on the street outside, November on the Front Range. She glanced both ways then took a chair across from Moss at the black teak table, a rippled blaze of light at her back.

She'd brought her daughter to the interview, a twelve-year-old in blond dog's ears and jeans with iron-on stickers, friendship pins on Nike knockoffs. Moss demurred to the girl's request to remain in the conference room with them. He had *People* magazines brought in, a Pepsi, and jellybeans from the paralegal's jar.

"This is Emmy." She indicated her daughter with a toss of her head. "As in M. E., as in Mary Eliza." Her black hair shook and shone.

"Are you our lawyer?" Emmy considered him skeptically.

Peter Moss tightened his Jerry Garcia neckware. "Could be." They might take some convincing. So might he.

Moss negotiated the introductory pleasantries alert for false notes, weak links. Practiced in the evaluation of suffering, he sensed only a suggestion of reserve, purposeful rather than diffident. Terry Winter was holding something back, but not necessarily from him.

"So tell me what happened to bring you here."

She thought a moment. "What I say to Emmy is you take your knocks and you keep going. You could say, why me? Or you can say, why *not* me? Who else *is* there?" She rolled a thumb along her palm. "The idea that you overcome things. That's what got us to you."

It was what Peter Moss needed to hear.

He was three months back from a half-year sabbatical in Costa Rica, in the cloud forest of the Cordillera de Tilarán. Like a million other lawyers he'd felt the urge to quit shudder through him like a fever chill. He'd looked with dismay on the decline of his profession, the rapacity, rancor, and deceit of an adversary system in extremis, ever less up to the tasks of justice. He'd seen the red flags flying in his marriage. Not since Vietnam had imponderables of such magnitude confronted him. What am I doing here? What is the point?

In the six months off Moss aimed at nothing dramatic— Spanish studies and neotropical biology in the Quaker colony of Monteverde. Detox, recharge, and reflect. Reflection had led to resolution: No more medical malpractice. He wrote it on Post-it notes and stuck them everywhere. MAL-PRÁCTICA NO MÁS.

You can get some distance, some perspective, from the Cordillera de Tilarán. When the misty jungle rings with bell birds, and howler monkeys roar at dawn, it can occur that suing doctors is too much grief.

After fifteen years of his doing little else, malpractice cases remained too hard to win; they cost too much; and winning meant too little. Settlements were confidential, the client was still as maimed or dead, and the practice and malpractice of medicine would proceed unedified. The epic contest of lawyer against doctor faded away in a quarrel over money. You have it and I want it. I got it and you can't have it. The dust that settled was swept under the rug.

Do such labors, Moss had given pause to reflect, make a better world?

He vowed to return to less anguished stuff. The bloodless combat of commercial disputes. Businesses for clients instead of damaged human beings. Patent infringement for excitement.

Yet here he was, eye-to-eye with Terry Winter, sizing up her case.

Moss had found the reflective life by itself insufficient. He had an incorrigibly Western outlook. Virtue was acquired by deeds, not contemplation. He'd always succumb to the suffering born of desire. Still, the cumulative glow from spending each day for six months apart from the world and in the company of his wife felt something like enlightenment.

On Earthwatch projects in Monteverde he and Sally recorded the mating dance of long-tailed mannikins and inventoried golden toads. Sally drew and etched. He reread Shakespeare and the court romances. He rarely brought up cases. Life's too short, Sally would say, when the subject turned to past disappointments. Her miscarriages; his bad verdicts. When he thought of getting older, and of his wife's forest beauty in the Cordillera de Tilarán, Moss agreed. Life's too short. *Malpráctica no más.*

Three months back and already it wasn't working. Part was boredom. Moss was restless, and restless lawyers cause trouble. Maybe patent infringement wasn't quite the answer. Maybe leaking underground storage tanks would better suit a somber turn of mind. He caught himself weighing whether to take on a guy brain-injured by a water balloon at the Flatirons County Fair. Could he find fulfillment proving which of those manning the catapult was to blame— the clown, the cowboy, or the commissioner's son?

Then Lata rang him with a cold call. Lata, the Junker and Wylie receptionist, a high-boned beauty from the Orange Free State with a prized African Oxbridge telephone voice, had a sixth sense for good work. Mother and daughter had walked in off the street. May I be of assistance?

Lata inquired. I think I need a lawyer, mother replied. Daughter added, I want to meet him too.

"How's she look?" Moss had asked.

"Talk to this lady," Lata said.

That was another part, the novelty of Terry Winter.

But the main part was the doctor, the reason to breach his sabbatical treaty for one more clash of arms. It had been Bondurant. Again. No way could he tell her no. But no way, either, could he tell her why.

Terry Winter looked maybe midthirties but had to be older, with clear skin, black eyes, features reminiscent of Maria on *Sesame Street*, but not so tall. She was dressed like a ranch hand and lived in the mountains west of Boulder. The boots and tight jeans had turned Junker's head as she stood at the reception desk talking to Lata. She could pass, Moss judged, as a *sabanera*, a cowgirl, in the Cordillera de Tilarán. She appeared unrelated to the blond kid reading about the princess in *People*.

Terry had breast cancer. Large tumor, positive nodes. The afflicted breast was gone. No visible effects of chemo though he observed a subtle stiffness, left arm extension a little short, from the axillary dissection of her armpit. Otherwise, she said with emphasis, healthy and cancer free. In Moss's assessment she gave off strength. But a bad prognosis for recurrence. She knew what that would mean.

"It means you're toast," she said. "*I'm* toast."

"How did Bondurant miss it?"

"I was fixing to ask you that."

Moss outlined what needed to be done. He'd want an authorization signed that day for the release of records and film. He'd get her charts from Bondurant and the cancer center, have the mammograms independently read, have her parafin tissue blocks recut and slides sent out. When all the information was in place it would be forwarded for review by a family medicine specialist, probably out of state. Moss may need to meet with her other doctors, if they were cooperative. Then he'd tell her whether he thought she had a case.

"Always remember," Moss said, as he always did, "your health is more important than any lawsuit. Go to your doctors regularly. Comply with their directions. Bondurant can use it against you if you don't. Trust me," he said. "I'm a lawyer." His self-deprecating joke.

The daughter rolled her eyes.

"Trust is the issue, isn't it?" Terry shifted uncomfortably in her chair. "I'm trying to be proactive about it." She crossed her arms. "My health," she said, as though health were an abstraction in which she tried to place faith. The way people say, my country.

The twelve-year-old peered at her mother from behind the cover photograph of Princess Di.

"These are hard cases," he said frowning and leaning her way. Moss was somewhat slow of speech, with a bearing obscurely Lincolnesque—careworn and distantly countrified enough to earn raised eyebrows from the teasippers in the state capital when he deposed their physician clients in splendid rooms with wraparound views of the Rockies. His vivid, pale eyes, set in lines, could be read as expressing the correspondence of desire and, if not suffering, a standing discontent. He had the air of a passionate man with too little to be passionate about.

Moss had a spiel that came next, as much for himself as the client. Malpractice cases, he explained, settle late or never and can cost a fortune. You'll be personally, perhaps viciously, attacked. You'll contend with tough, even brutal adversaries, special rules that treat medical negligence far more leniently than any other kind, and blind biases in favor of the defendant. Bondurant's colleagues of course will be biased, and now he's president of the state medical society. But so will jurors who tend, with some justification, to respect physicians so uncritically they forgive them even terrible wrongs. Suing one is major brain damage.

"Brain damage is relative," she said. "And a doctor's still a human being."

"A family doctor, like Wallace Bondurant, is a human

being dedicated to the prevention of illness." They were all so different. The action-oriented surgeon, the crisis-oriented ER doc, the internal medicine sleuth, the cloistered pathologist, the jock orthopedist, the cerebral shrink. Judging medical care, he explained, meant judging judgment— dozens of subtle factors synthesized in complex professional decisions. And medicine involved sick people. Some wouldn't get well, some would die, and there would be nothing the doctor could have done.

"The family doctor is your guardian against disease," he said. "The question is, why did the disease get past him?"

"Something about the man."

It was the kind of doubtful musing Moss might have engaged in himself. He ran a finger along his lower lip. Check the eyes, he thought. The eyes and hands, for shifts and shakes. Her left hand had an erratic little tremor and she kept it balled, contributing to a fierce and guarded carriage. Napoleonic. Her dark eyes were steady and uncompromising. The woman, by and large, seemed settled and clear and capable of intensifying.

"We'll find out," Moss said. "Good news, bad news, we'll figure it out."

He was struck by what she hadn't asked. She didn't ask about his fees—one third of settlement or judgment, plus costs. She didn't ask about her chances of winning, Moss's won/lost record, or how much her case was worth. His won/lost record, had she asked, was excellent—except against Bondurant.

Instead she said, "I'm in. I like what you say about figuring it out."

He sought to wind things up. At a later meeting, after he'd studied the records, they'd address facts programmatically and search for skeletons in closets. At the outset the objective was rapport. In a confidential relationship the client should feel comfortable confiding. He began a wrap-up round of sympathy and assurances but she cut him off.

"Hey," she said. "I like having cancer." She smiled falsely, leaning now his way. "You get cancer and you can drop the shit, you know what I mean? Be who you are. Say I have this boss. I find out I have cancer, doesn't look good. 'Bye, boss. I care less what men think anymore." She laughed off at the sunny window, pedestrian shapes beyond the blinds shuffling along the snow-blown sidewalk. "That's right. I love my cancer. Mind if I smoke?"

"*Mom.*" Emmy wrinkled her nose. Smoking was yucky. It occurred then to Moss what was withheld: She doesn't return her daughter's eye; her scrutiny is all on him.

"Truth is," Terry Winter said, "why I came to see you is sort of like Thoreau, why he went in the woods." She paused. "To find out about myself."

"Let's find out first about your case."

"You like the lady," Lata observed when Moss returned from escorting them out. Many troubled souls had come and gone through the glass doors with the gold-leaf stencil of the scales of justice. This one went with brandished fist, leading the way for her child.

"The lady will take some breaking in," Moss said. "The defendant's what I like."

Upstairs to sell the name partners as the firm's screening rules required. Junker, head of litigation, gave it a green light and Wylie, the managing partner, went along. Bad doc, bad miss, big harm. Go for it. Then Moss took to the halls. Everybody liked the case—even Crutchfield, rabbi of the risk-averse. Directly a mood took hold in Junker and Wylie, LLC—the invigorating tonic of a promising contingent fee, the bracing feeling of litigation in the air. Junker would consent to advancing thirty K if she panned out. Don't buy in, he cautioned, but this time kill the son of a bitch.

Moss returned to his desk to map out an investigation, for the first time since his sabbatical fully engaged.

Back at it. Chasing the docs.

Chasing Bondurant.

TWO

The *North Pavilion* of University Hospital had been a psychiatric asylum that went bankrupt in the latest wave of insurance cost containment. Respectable hospital departments remained across the street. The North Pavilion housed odds and ends and two floors of long-gone AIDS victims.

Moss, an outsized manila envelope under his arm, got his bearings. It had been a year or so. Failure to diagnose breast cancer now topped all other filings in medical malpractice litigation, and was second only to obstetrics in average size of settlement. Moss had prosecuted a half-dozen cancer cases—one colon, one chondrosarcoma, and four breasts. He liked to begin an investigation with Borkin at the North Pavilion.

Emaciated patients loitered at the latte bar in the hospital lobby. It was a smoke-free facility. A handful of backsliders puffed and hugged themselves outside, inspecting passing nursing students with the caged stares of the seriously ill.

Around the latte bar folks at various levels of sedation socialized. A trio in cowboy hats conversed in Spanish. A couple with matching oxygen bottles sat together breathing rhythmically. A youth, cap backward, motored a wheelchair across the terrazzo floor, IV rack swaying wildly.

Down a worn but well-swabbed hall solicitations for clinical trials alternated with motivational signs on the tiled walls:

WHEN LIFE HANDS YOU LEMONS MAKE LEMONADE!
SUCCESS IS A JOURNEY NOT A DESTINATION!

Moss weaved through mopper and buffer traffic past doors posted Transplant, Blood, Pastoral Care. He cocked his head at the open entrance to the Prosthesis Plant, busy as Santa's workshop with the sawing, hammering, and gluing of limbs.

A series of steel security doors yielded to him. A head nurse enclosed in Plexiglas tracked his progress down a row of tiny cells that were formerly padded. He became aware of an elaborate network of alarms, intercoms, buzzers, and bells. The hallway ended at the metal door to what Moss had come to think of as the Chapel of Breasts.

Dr. Borkin greeted him with vigorous bonhomie. A small tidy radiologist in spectacles, Borkin ran the breast imaging department. Beside him stood a skeleton, like a physician's assistant. All four walls, floor to ceiling, were of backlit glass bathing Borkin, Moss, the skeleton, in circumambient light. Festooning the walls, confronting Moss whichever way he turned, were hundreds of luminescent breasts.

"Coffee? Sweetener?" A chrome coffee press stood at hand, looking, like everything in the room, mystically utilitarian.

Moss declined.

"What have we here?" Dr. Borkin was a man of roving attentions. He took the envelope of Terry Winter's mammograms and slid them out in an array. He beamed.

Doctors, Moss reflected, as he had in the Cordillera de Tilarán, inhabit a different world than you and I.

"I need to know what these tell me," Moss said. "I need to know what I need to know to help this woman."

A lawyer's world is self-referential, client-referential at

most. A lawyer indulges a single but shifting point of view, passing from subject to subject like a flashlight. Doctors prefer well-lit rooms, with fixed reference points of objective realities. Lawyers are less boxed in. Truth and honor are things in motion.

"Nobody can help this woman." Borkin drew back from a close inspection of the most recent films. He organized the rest chronologically, starting with a baseline study from before she started seeing Bondurant. "Very tough. Very tough," he said. "Occult"—the tumor, if it was there at all, was hidden in the white whorls of young, dense tissue. He snapped the film from 1989 under a bar on the lighted wall. Terry Winter's left breast glowed against a black background, larger than life, exceedingly shapely—an artifact of compression by the plates.

"Know why they're called X rays?" Borkin's manner had become confidential.

"No idea."

"When Roentgen discovered them their nature was unknown. Mysterious rays of light that pass *through* matter. The X ray, the unknown ray. Invisible light. *Passing through matter.*"

Borkin's voice dropped, his tone sepulchral, his illuminated face beatific.

"Passing through flesh as though it wasn't there. . . ." Borkin pushed softly at the air before him. "What you see are shadows of what to an X ray is opaque."

"The evidence of things not seen," Moss contributed reverently, a communicant in the Chapel of Breasts. The substance of things hoped for.

Borkin looked at him skeptically. "What has your client been told?"

Moss was unsure.

"You've got to give it to them straight from the shoulder. Lots of docs won't."

Dr. Borkin was a man of abrupt transitions.

"Lots of docs have problems with women and cancer. Women and cancer make guys nervous. I've had colleagues describe nightmares. How would you like this line of work?"

Moss considered the question as generously as he could.

"Don't worry. You wouldn't. Me, I'm the guy who writes up the news. Telling the truth comes with the job. But," Borkin raised a finger. "Never tell a woman she has cancer on a Friday. Sure way to ruin the weekend. Now let's see what we can see."

He snapped views from the next four years under the bar in a row. He ran a fingertip over the images, pausing here and there to tap or to trace little circlets. Moss stared at the line of well-turned breasts, stared into them, their fibrous cottony patterns, galaxies against a black sky. The secret constellations of flesh revealed by invisible light.

Borkin popped the rightmost film with a fingernail. "Mr. Magoo could find this tumor." Moss peered at the crazed lines of light. He saw nothing.

"Watch." Borkin crossed his hands, forming an *A*. He held them against the film creating a triangular window he slowly moved like a Ouija master. He stopped and there it was. A black-and-white bull's eye of concentric streaks and dots occupying the space entirely, as sinister as the pistol in Antonioni's *Blow-Up* resolving from the foliage.

"That's your girl, last year. Architectural distortion, microcalcifications in clustered patterns. In hindsight you can see it forming over the last few years, but very dim, soft. No cause for alarm except in hindsight. Roentgen himself would have missed it on the earlier films. Not me, but Roentgen and everybody else."

Moss studied the bad place on the films. He could sense the tumor lurking there, like a lethal presence in the dark.

"There it was, year after year, taking shape. Look, here's the thing. It was there to be found, not on film, but clinically. It was big and mean, for three, four years. Who was feeling this woman's breasts?"

"Family doc."

"She's a dead woman, isn't she?"

"Healthy and cancer free." That was how his client had put it.

Borkin shook his head, as if rejecting an argument. "She's a goner and the family doc's your man."

THREE

I*n the beginning* is the patient chart. From the chart proceed all things good and evil.

The first reading never failed to get Moss's juices pumping. Charts were his Dead Sea scrolls, encrypted with SOAP notes, mandarin abbreviations, lab glyphs, pregnant omissions, coded euphemisms, the illegible flourish at a critical point. *Taber's Cyclopedic Medical Dictionary* and highlighter in hand, Moss crept along letter by letter raveling out human meanings from medical ideography.

More often than not it was in the psychology of events that things went awry. The intrusion upon professional relations of things like pride, power, resentment, jealousy, sometimes greed, and more than you would like to think, revenge. Of course, personality mattered with lawyers and clients as well as doctors and patients. Revenge remained the unspoken reason Moss had taken the case, and it risked corrupting the undivided loyalty he now owed Terry Winter.

Moss had sent Morlock to Bondurant's office with a copy of the medical records authorization Terry signed. Morlock was not possessed of a subtle and ranging intellect, but, process server by day and bouncer by night, he worked effectively within his limitations. His subluxed jaw from an episode in the line of duty gave Morlock a permanently doubtful, on-the-verge-of-getting-pissed-off look. It made people want to keep him happy. He was instructed not to leave Bondurant's office without the complete chart.

Moss took the predictable call from Bondurant's front-office "girl." Doctor will not release the records without reviewing them first. The man is acting rude. Moss faxed her a copy of the statute, starring the criminal sanctions. The girl called back. No photocopier was available. We'll wait till one is, Moss said. At five-thirty Morlock dropped off the copies of the chart. It was soon apparent Moss would have to see the originals, one page in particular, and one visit, November 12, 1989, four years ago to the day.

He drove to the Wellness Clinic northeast of town at the end of the following day. Northeast Boulder was in transition from rootcrop farms and jerkwater crossroads to city open space and gated developments surrounding a golf course and Flatirons Community Hospital. To the west, the Front Range was ashen from a thin cover of new snow. Rough-legged hawks manned the power poles, conning for prairie dogs. A redtail quartered and soared. On the radio a talk-show host, an autodidact with an attitude, stammered and sputtered about socialized medicine. The sky ran with the heartbreaking pastels of late fall in the Rockies— lavender, lime, and Viking blue.

Moss gave the girl his card and another copy of the medical records authorization. Same one who'd called him, Patti, a gum smacker. This time she didn't argue. The color drained from her face and she reeled away from her chair.

He browsed the magazines and brochures. *Sports Illustrated, Time, NRA Insights, News for Young Shooters.* Know the Symptoms of Diabetes. When Is Aspirin Safe? Facts About Bedwetting. The How and Why of Breast Self-Examination. He slipped a couple of the latter in his jacket pocket and took up a months-old *Time.* Rangers were after warlords in the Horn of Africa.

From the photocopied set Moss had recognized Bondurant's peculiar charting style, SOAP notes typed then edited by hand. By now he should have learned in some risk-management seminar how to keep clean charts.

He tossed the *Time* on the coffee table. Thing about doctors—creatures of habit. He contemplated his surroundings. Chairs that matched the carpet and walls that were arranged in three-unit groups. A mom in a Boulder Panthers sweatshirt and her sunken-eyed kid looked at him like he didn't belong. An aquarium gurgled under a black light. A Norfolk pine in a wicker basket heeled in his direction.

In the first lawsuit against Bondurant Moss had never gotten around to visiting the Wellness Clinic. His clients were the parents of a young gymnast, junior high kid, with rotator cuff tendinitis from the rings. Bondurant had been the Fisher family doctor for years. To relieve the tendinitis he injected Jessie Fisher's AC joint with cortisone. She remained a little sore the week before the next meet and he reinjected her and scheduled monthly follow-ups. When the pain returned he put her on ten days of Tandearil—oxyphenbutazone, the most powerful and toxic of the anti-inflammatories, banned in Europe and being withdrawn from the U.S. market, contraindicated in children. The morbidity and mortality from adverse reactions were staggering. Nobody gave Tandearil anymore and certainly not for tendinitis. Bondurant couldn't find an expert anywhere in the country who admitted to using it.

Jessie Fisher had a severe reaction and an exceptionally gruesome death. A bodywide rash progressed to toxic epidermal necrolysis, an immune system breakdown in which she sloughed all her skin, was grafted from cadavers, but died after two weeks in the burn unit of overwhelming sepsis. It was unimaginably horrifying to everyone but Bondurant who, in deposition, but not at trial, said her death hadn't bothered him a bit. Sometimes you get bad outcomes. He even snuffled out an awkward laugh.

On that case Moss had bought in. He had so identified with the parents' grief he fooled himself into thinking winning could compensate in some real way for their loss. He began believing it was his job to avenge Jessie Fisher's death and the case became a mission. Because in a way he came to think he could bring the girl back for her parents, when he lost at trial it was as though he'd let her die again. It took him over a year to drink his way past it and he was still salving the wound on sabbatical.

Patti, the front-office girl, was standing in front of him, looking now a little saucy. She was holding Terry Winter's original chart in its jacket in both hands. She dropped it on the coffee table with some force. "You can't take it out of here," she said, emboldened by something. "It's got all originals. I'll be watching you."

"Bet you will."

Patti popped her gum. With exaggerated propriety she took up her front desk station among snapshots and flowers and a tray of leftover candy corn.

The Boulder Panther and the fish were watching him too.

The original entry for November 12, 1989, raised even more questions than the photocopy had. The handwritten interlineations were in three different colors of ink. "Non," of "nonmobile" was scratched out, as was "ir" of "irregular." "Tender" was written in, as was "comes and goes." On the bottom right a large section had been scribbled over in black. Patterns of parallel lines ran several different directions across each other, so heavily inked they bossed out the other side of the page. He ran a finger over the ballpoint impressions. This is one for the document examiner, he thought, one for Moschetti. He began envisioning a color blow-up for trial.

Moss felt a hot glare coming his way and glanced up. Bondurant himself stood staring from a partly open door down the hall behind the front desk. Their eyes met and Moss at once could see it was more complicated than simple revenge. You know me, he thought. But who are you? Same cropped gray hair; same blue Dacron short-sleeved shirt. Short sleeves on a cold day; that was Bondurant, but what else was there? He stood transfixed, lips parted, gray eyes wide as if in fright.

I'm what you've been waiting for. Moss sent a thought message. I'm the other shoe dropping.

Bondurant's face ticked and the door shut swiftly across it.

FOUR

That *evening in* his office Moss methodically worked back through his copy of the chart. The substance of the case was plain. Terry Winter had taken all of her regular care to Bondurant for over five years. There were epigastric upsets, minor infections, sore throats (don't strep checks get boring? and where does boredom lead?), pap smears, and, increasingly, breast exams. Each office visit was recorded, each record matched by a bill designated "self pay." More than three years before diagnosis a lump was first charted, under *S* of SOAP for subjective, meaning reported by the patient. There were no findings under *O*, objective. *A*, for assessment, was fibrocystic breast disease—a descriptor, not a diagnosis—for the lumpy breasts most women have. The plan, *P*, was mammography and return in three months.

Subsequent visits were similar. They increased in frequency. The patient's reports under *S* became gently insistent, then mildly alarmed. "Pt. returns for br. ck." "Pt. concerned with lump in left upper outer quadrant." There was a handwritten note from Terry that it felt bigger and asking if she should come back in. But *O* would always read "no masses present." *A* remained fibrocystic disease even after the dimpling of the skin called *peau d'orange*.

Still Bondurant prescribed vitamin E and asked her to return in a month. Finally he sent her to Anita Greenwood, an oncologist in the capital. Terry hadn't seen him since.

The son of a bitch was dead meat on the face of it, but so had he been the time before. The tumor was eight centimeters across when they got it, the size of a small lemon, fixed to both chest wall and skin. Ten lymph nodes were malignant. No distant metastases but every other ominous staging criterion in the book.

Bondurant had flagrantly violated the standard of care for following breast lumps: If a questionable mass is felt it may be watched through one menstrual period. If it persists, whether it's cystic or solid must be determined at once by needle aspiration or ultrasonography. If ultrasound shows a hollow lesion, the needle expresses cystic fluid, and the lump deflates, the problem, a benign cyst, is gone. If these results are at all equivocal, proceed to biopsy. Remove and analyze the lump for malignancy. If malignant, definitive treatment is in order: Mastectomy or, if the breast can be preserved, lumpectomy, then radiation and chemo—slash, burn, and poison. Prognosis depends on how fast you've moved. You want to nail the tumor when it's small and before cancer penetrates the lymph nodes or reaches the blood. If you do you can save the breast and usually eradicate the disease. But disease let go three years to Terry's stage sooner or later comes knocking again and when it does, it's terminal.

In breast cancer, Moss told his juries, there is a magic day. There is a day when a woman goes to sleep with a treatable illness and wakes up with incurable cancer. The outcome of a cancer case should turn on a fundamentally simple calculation: Did the doctor's negligence in failing to find detectable cancer happen while the patient's magic day still lay ahead of her? If so, the doctor is responsible for all the harm the cancer will cause.

Terry Winter's magic day came and went long past when Bondurant should have acted. His negligence was ultimately going to cost her life.

How can he get out of this one? Moss mused. Let me count the ways.

They were sure to see the Judgment Call Defense, a.k.a. Hindsight Is 20/20, a.k.a. Medicine-Is-an-Art-Not-a-Science: Distinguishing cysts and lumps is tricky in a dense-breasted woman Terry's age, thirty-nine at the first mention of the lump in the chart. Her lump behaved like a cyst. In hindsight mistaking the tumor for a benign process was perhaps an error in judgment but not a deviation from the standard of care.

And the related Low Index of Suspicion Defense: There was little to alert Bondurant to follow this lady, given her relative youth, negative family history of cancer, her child-bearing history (as pregnancy and breast feeding lower risk), and the negative mammogram reports (not a defense in itself; mammography can find cancer but not rule it out).

Or the Respectable Minority Defense: While most family doctors might have thought of needle aspiration and biopsy, a respectable minority would have followed Terry as Bondurant had. In other words, because there are probably other doctors who would commit the same malpractice it is not below the standard of care.

The Noncompliant Patient would be sure to surface, perhaps through the Phantom Phone Call, unrecorded in the chart. Smart defendants don't alter records; they fabricate phone calls they claim to have forgotten to write down. Bondurant is likely to remember having told Terry over the telephone to get a biopsy opinion from a surgeon, which his lawyer would claim she blew off.

Bondurant's pals would be sure to advance the Circular Argument: Bondurant must have had a clinical basis for what he did or he wouldn't have done it; Bondurant's decisions couldn't have been below acceptable standards or he wouldn't have made them.

Then there were the causation defenses peculiar to cancer litigation, pseudoscientific sophistry ironically the last redoubt of doctors. Here Moss was sure to encounter once again the Doubler and the Carcinoma Angel, courthouse doctors made wealthy by breast cancer lawsuits. They would argue, as they always did, that this tumor was fated to kill decades before Bondurant missed it. Early detection is a hoax. There is no magic day. The die is cast with bad DNA and there is nothing a family doctor can do about it. Tricked out in technical jargon they would subtly promote the metaphor of cancer as moral flaw, disease as retributive. Breast cancer a pox visited on a wayward woman for a reckless youth.

In closing Moss would ridicule it all as the Three Dog Defense: Bondurant doesn't have a dog. But if he did have a dog he wouldn't bite anyone. But if he did bite someone he must have been crazy.

The problem is jurors crave to believe in doctors. They'll even swallow the Circular Argument. They're putty in the Carcinoma Angel's hands.

The jurors in the Jessie Fisher case deliberated for six days. On the seventh they returned a verdict for Bondurant. Those partial to the plaintiff left quickly, two in tears. The others said they just hadn't thought guilt was proven beyond a reasonable doubt, confusing medical negligence with crime. The trial had been a birdwatching trip for the blind.

For over a year Moss beat himself up for the hundred little things he might have done differently, but he never put his finger on why he lost. Bondurant's lawyer, Freeman Stackley, had done a credible but workaday job. Judge Becky Gonzales was, if anything, sympathetic to the Fishers. Bondurant projected an air of umbrage, of privilege put upon. He was a medical doctor. He had influential colleagues, and better things to do, and different rules applied. He lied outright on the stand, his thirteen-year-old patient not there to contradict him. But the reckless prescription remained an established fact, and the jurors chose to ignore it. Moss had failed to bring them to feel the complex animus he held for the man, his imbedded conviction Bondurant was a bad doctor. The jurors must have liked the guy.

Bondurant wasn't satisfied just with a win. He turned his indignation at being sued into a crusade to save medicine from law. He became a tort reformer, a player with an oped profile and influence at the capital, and grateful colleagues elevated him to the top of the medical society. Moss, meanwhile, went his unreformed way, filing and settling lawsuits, occasionally cleaning up at trials, but chewing on his loss.

On balance, he had to admit, he hadn't learned a damn thing from suing Bondurant before.

He made a note this time to strike prospective jurors who like to listen to talk-show windbags. He returned to Terry Winter's chart. It told much, but not what Moss wanted to know. He wanted to know *why*.

He took another look at Bondurant's scribble at the lower right of the page for November 12, 1989. It had been unsettling meeting his eyes. Fear was not what Moss had expected to see there. It was *his* office, after all, his home territory. If Jessie Fisher's death hadn't bothered Bondurant a bit, what was bothering him now?

Moss got the vodka bottle from the bottom drawer. The office bottle—a Philip Marlowe convention of the hardboiled. And of those whose wives had poured the house bottle out. It was time for serious cogitating.

He sloshed a few fingers of Gilbey's in his almost empty coffee cup. Tan streaks swirled in the clear fluid like old blood. He rotated his cup, dissolving the swirls, then tipped it to his lips. He liked the mingling of tastes.

Moss sipped and stared at the photocopied wedge of cross-hatched lines. He thought he could make out a pattern of sorts, prism shapes stacked lengthwise and vigorously effaced with many-directional lines. It resembled a doodle the Richard Dreyfuss character in *Close Encounters* might compulsively create. There was nothing whimsical to it, nothing quickly scratched off. These were marks of some deliberation.

It would be interesting to Rorschach this guy, Moss said out loud.

He poured more Gilbey's and started back through the chart from the beginning. He quickly got loaded and began to mumble. What goes around comes around, big guy, he mumbled. What stays around sticks around.

Thinking of Bondurant suddenly enraged him. His pals at the state medical society, his fraudulent experts. Assholes to a man. And men to a man, except the Carcinoma Angel, the son of a bitch.

Moss stood, overly resolute. He planted his feet and took a mighty two-handed swipe with an imaginary broadsword. He lay about his office smiting enemies one by one with the blinding sword of justice. He stopped, limp, breathing heavy.

You killed her, Moss muttered. Isn't that enough? You fucking shit-sucking *el médico* swine.

Fuck this shit.

Moss staggered off to brush his teeth, chug an orange pop, and join Sally at home.

FIVE

D*on't go with* a virgin is my advice."

Junker reclined in his oversized calfskin Ralph Lauren chair, hands behind his head, knees splayed. Junker's belly could not help but catch the eye. On his walls were diplomas and an O'Keeffe cow skull knock-off. Polished black bowls, ersatz Marias, lined the aspenwood credenza. A Two Gray Hills rug with yei dancers lay atop the carpet. On the corner of the desk a kachina doll brandished a gourd. The rain-maker.

"Virgins are pussies. Virgins are cavers."

"I'm thinking of a local doc for the screen," Moss said. "Not an expert for testimony necessarily. I want someone objective to start with, to spot issues in a way I can depend on."

"Objective? You got an NIH grant to research this case, son? I'm not spending money on objective."

Moss struggled with a feeling of diminishment. Not an unfamiliar feeling in Junker's office. Junker and Wylie had been subdivided democratically into a perimeter of 225-square-foot allotments, identical except for Junker's. Junker tore a wall out for a double space suitable to his bulk and station. Over the years Moss had advanced square by square, like a Monopoly player, finally to the southwest corner with postcard views of downtown and the Front Range. Park Place to Junker's Boardwalk. Still, and always, Junker would tell him how to run a case.

Junker swiveled on little thrusts of tasseled toes. His vast butcherblock desk, meant to imply the handhewn, looked seaworthy. Moss sank further in an overstuffed couch. He took Junker's point.

The statute required prefiling merit screening by a doctor of the same specialty, family medicine, as the defendant. Likewise at trial, Bondurant's professional negligence, unlike ordinary negligence, could be proven only through the testimony of another family physician. Have the case screened, Junker was telling him, by the same family doc you want to use in court. An advocate, that is. Someone who's been there before, who knows his job is to help you win. Screw objective.

Junker was an ironist run to fat, and for Moss a moral exemplum. He'd been fast out of the Harvard blocks, with a nose for high-profile causes that endeared him to the establishment left. But the higher calling, in Junker's case, was the acquisition of money. He pursued serial brides, a condo in Santa Fe, a black 400SEL, the table by the fireplace at the Rattlesnake Club. He traveled the continuing legal education circuit elaborating on how to win gigantic verdicts from the big boys on Seventeenth Street in the capital. He settled into the roles of client-getter and captain of litigation, which meant he no longer worked on cases, he oversaw them. He might be available to dazzle juries when a trial rolled around, but he was long past mucking through the tedious preliminaries. His charm, in the process, had gotten smirky.

Moss was first drawn to the firm by Junker's reputation for courtroom skills and public interest cases. Only five years older than Moss, Junker continued to exact an almost filial deference long after Moss could tell his hero had clay up to the eyeballs. Six-foot-five and once an all-Ivy guard, Junker had grown ponderous and huge. He reeled down the

halls like an incarnation of mortal sins—sloth, pride, glut-
tony, lust, greed—rolled into a fleshy composite. Anger and
envy he derogated as the unproductive failings of associ-
ates.

While he was lavish and overextended in personal in-
dulgences, at the firm Junker practiced austerity on others.
With Neil Wylie, the managing partner and Junker's com-
plement from the political right, they worried the books like
IMF auditors demanding structural adjustments in the Third
World.

But there was one thing about Junker: he thought big. If
a jackpot was on the table, he'd say roll 'em.

This case was big enough, in Moss's view, to do right.
Moss would always prefer a first-time expert, chaste of the
racket, and someone in-state. Someone with the guts to take
the witness stand and criticize a colleague in the same community. That stood for something to Moss, whether jurors
caught on or not. It was his nostalgia for honesty, why he
became a lawyer. But that entailed a long and costly search,
Demosthenes looking for an honest expert, and Moss had
no choice in this particular matter. Junker controlled
contingent-fee cost allowances. For now, Moss would have
to skip the objective review and shelve his sentimentality
for unvarnished truth. He'd defer cost showdowns with Junker until the case was up and running and he had a little
leverage.

"So who do you know?" Moss asked.

"Family doc type? Nobody in-state, that's for sure. Forget in-state with Bondurant running the goddamn medical
society. Forget anybody insured by ROMPIC." Insured by
Rocky Mountain Physicians' Insurance Company, that is,
which provided medical malpractice coverage for Bondurant and the majority of doctors in a five-state area. Its approach to risk management when it came to one insured
testifying against another resembled the informer network
of the East German STASI.

"I will not stoop," Moss declared, "to a mail-order
expert."

"You want a no-name? A no-name'll cut your nuts off."

"No dial-a-docs."

"O.K." Junker frowned. "Make it tough." He wheeled on tippytoes toward the window, a jowly profile against the framed diplomas, the Courageous Advocate Award, the ACLU Lawyer of the Year, the Inner Circle of Barristers certification, his seventies' glory. In places Junker looked inappropriately thin, at the shoulders, knees, the delicate wrists. One could envision the three-point guard hidden within his flesh.

Outside the window Flagstaff Mountain dissembled in lightly falling snow. Junker nodded once and swiveled back toward Moss. "Try Margolis," he said. Junker's pal from the Inner Circle.

Like most trial lawyers Moss had love/hate feelings about experts. The parasites he hated, the $600-an-hour courthouse whores who'd abandoned practicing medicine in favor of testifying about it. The jury-friendly folksy frauds with their dog-and-pony shows. He loved the intellectual part, brainstorming with someone in the know, the sheer learning involved, and the occasional ethical stand that blows you away. Ethically, you'd get *High Noon* every now and then, experts who did the right thing, downsides be damned.

But Lord did he fear cavers. Cavers filled him with existential dread. When your standard-of-care expert collapses, your case ontology is up in smoke, you've lost your text, and your client is going down. Among the firm's sixty grand in out-of-pocket losses on the Fisher case was nearly $40,000 Moss spent on medical testimony, some of it by virgins, one of whom caved royally. Moss could still see him waffling in the witness box, eyes darting for help.

"I heard about this family-doc-type guy Margolis used from New Hampshire," Junker continued. "And Margolis has handled a lot of breasts."

Moss didn't laugh.

"Supposed to be an in-the-trenches guy. You want in-the-trenches or ivory tower? Optimal care or real world, down and dirty?"

"Med school's not right for this one."

"Med school's cheaper. Whatever. I don't know anything about the guy but Margolis used him in federal court in Cheyenne. Cleaned up. Call Margolis. Go with the tried and true."

Moss called Margolis. For standard of care Margolis would recommend Ray Hoover without qualification. He's reasonable and he does what he's told. Testifies a lot, knows the ropes, and has a practice like Bondurant's. Same size town, similar background. Not long on credentials, but a couple of boards. Strong convictions about bad medicine.

"So, hey," Margolis said. "Sounds like you got a case. Give 'em hell."

Outside Moss's window a siren wailed, some emergency vehicle on Broadway. "What's that?" Margolis asked. "Are they playing our song?"

A few days later Moss's secretary put him through to Dr. Hoover in Manchester, New Hampshire. He was taken with the man's courtesies. Hoover would be pleased to review the materials. Moss liked his sound, the clipped Yankee emphases, the hesitancy and understatement, reserve suggesting a well-considered viewpoint. He began thinking covered bridges, rectitude and principle, heading out with a black bag on a snowy night for house calls.

"Keep an open mind," Moss told him. "Stay within your expertise. When you've formed impressions call me. Don't write a report. Be as frank with me as you can."

Dr. Hoover called back the following week. He'd reviewed the records. He'd identified five deviations from standards of care. None were defensible. He found it a tragic case and deeply troubling. The length of Bondurant's neglect, the harm that was done. It is the physician's first obligation to do no harm. Dr. Hoover's obligation, as a matter of conscience, is to testify to these findings.

After hanging up Moss whipped off a big check by the liability expert item on his to do list. It's time to file, he thought. He put in a call to his client. It's live-free-or-die time.

SIX

Moss *had begun* his sabbatical in a condition of nervous exhaustion after five trials in nine months, innumerable sixteen-hour days, increasingly alcoholic. His previous jungle experience had been with the Americal Division south of Danang. He sought an innocent's view this time and so was searching for birds. Birds recalled his childhood. He had stood in the sand at Point Bolivar, Texas, and watched warblers rain from the sky after crossing the gulf. He'd seen whooping cranes. He had a feel, as a boy, for spirits and myth.

In Costa Rica Moss was looking again for the uncorrupted experience of wonder, simple miracles, beauty, flight. *The thin waist of the Americas* . . . a good place to set off with Sally and get straight.

One night they found in the same preindustrial sky both the North Star and the Southern Cross, the measure of the visible universe. They passed another night with a leatherback laying eggs. Formations of scarlet macaws shot overhead at dusk like Apollo's arrows. A harpy eagle chivied a sloth. A laughing falcon beheaded a snake. One dawn they approached a wild avocado in fruit. Toucanets swarmed like bees. Keel-billed toucans ornamented the crown. The interior was arranged with resplendent quetzals, a bird so gorgeous for centuries European scientists thought it was a hoax. An emerald male, the Mayan Adonis, flashed scarlet from a branch, flourishing tail feathers a yard long.

Once, by a waterfall, they watched great jacamars feed on butterflies in a space of wind-driven light.

Their cloud-forest journeys were metaphorical, Keatsian. Beauty and truth were reciprocal, and beauty its own reward, and truth found by searching for it, but rarely where it was sought. Clichéd but revelatory, like other lessons— that family is life, more than life and, certainly, than work.

The sabbatical became a domestic and an aesthetic enterprise, a time to seek the truths of the heart. His professional self receded; he disrobed from its protective conceits—to crusade for underdogs, seek justice for all, speak Truth to Power—too simplistic pieties. Truth was phenomenal. Truth was tricky. Truth was lowercase. It came and went like a jacamar; it did not keep long to any perch.

On his office wall he'd framed a photograph of a waterfall high in jaguar country called Salto de Perro, Dog's Leap, after some forgotten, remarkable event. Blue morpho butterflies had circulated delicately in its misty drafts. He and Sally had bathed there and there had seen the jacamars, dazzling rarities birders spend fortunes to find. A blinding storm passed and sunlight moved through as shadows do in temperate forests. Suddenly above the shimmering pool a green-orange fury of feathers snatched a huge blue morpho in a convulsion of iridescence. The jacamar looped to a bough beside the falls to share the gaudy insect with its mate.

Crutchfield entered Moss's office as he was reflecting on the Salto de Perro. The month after he and Sally were there a deadfall dam upstream broke on a sunny afternoon, drowning three children swimming in the pool.

"How's the new case?" Crutchfield asked. Crutchfield's career had never fully kicked in. He was everyone's first choice for second chair, a mild passive/aggressive, even with voice mail. He'd say something sarcastic then tell the machine good-bye.

"Just finished the complaint," Moss said.

"Good. Good." Crutchfield stayed on his feet. "Wallace Bondurant, the good doctor. You trying to make some kind of point?" Crutchfield's expression registered something possibly comical.

"Fuck off."

"This puppy worth it?" Crutchfield moved across the room to the second-story window and peered down on the street. "Apart from making points?" Crutchfield had fallen into the role of office poor mouth, a half-empty-glass type who reality-checked Moss from a certain querulous salient. He counterbalanced Junker's guts-ball way of winging it.

Moss said nothing. Hadn't he determined in the Cordillera de Tilarán that med mal was never worth it? He occupied himself with a photograph in a little stand of Sally in an old-fashioned pose, unsmiling, looking off in quarter-profile. There was another shot of the two of them, fists raised on Longs Peak summit. And her intaglio print of a holy monkey, turbaned and seated cross-legged on a flowered rug.

"Give me the math," Crutchfield persisted.

"It's a big one, Crutch." Moss smacked his lips lightly. "Less than twenty percent chance of surviving five years when it would have been ninety-plus for total cure if Bondurant had caught it when he should have."

"Differential of. . . ."

"Seventy, eighty percent."

"Age?"

"Forty-three. Doesn't look it."

"What kind of a plaintiff?"

"Different."

Crutchfield grimaced. "A flake, in other words."

"Not a flake. Unconventional. Dégagé."

"French for flake."

"And tough. Tough as whang."

"Socioeconomic profile?"

"Working mom. Major mom points. Outdoorsy type. Qualifies for Medicaid. Negative equity in the family home."

Crutchfield considered the ceiling a while, calculating. "You've got future earnings capacity of probably near zip. Twenty-two-year worklife tubed. Medicaid lien knocks out your past meds but lots of future meds when the cancer comes back. Cancerphobia until then."

"Disfigurement."

"Mastectomy?"

"Bondurant could have saved the breast."

"So." Crutchfield nodded slowly. "Huge future damages." He was actually impressed.

"Very huge."

"Where'd you get your survival probabilities?"

"Literature."

"You'll have to do better than that." Crutchfield's cautionary notes could get annoying.

"For this case I'm getting the best."

"Treating oncologist not good enough?"

"Anita Greenwood. So far she's not talking, according to the office manager at the cancer center. Know anything about her? Bondurant made the referral."

"She's talking to Bondurant then. She'll skewer your client for sure." Crutchfield watched the street life out the window. Lots of Patagonia wear down there, a season of purple and teal. "Who will talk to you?"

"The best, like I say. Lewis Epstein at M. D. Anderson. Mr. Breast Cancer himself."

"Sounds pricey. Better Junker doesn't know."

"In due time." Moss had to sign off, work to do.

"O.K. O.K." Crutchfield said. "But do us a favor, Peter. Keep some perspective this time. Don't buy in."

Moss waved him off.

"Better hope you don't draw Judge Langworthy." Crutchfield tossed a final caution from the door. "Goodbye."

Get a life, Moss thought. He reviewed again the elliptical

catchwords of the complaint. He trailed back to thoughts of colleagues and careers. Get a life; too cold. Who had a life? What could be said of his own? Of the Dewar's Profile of Peter Moss—Age: 48. Profession: Chaser of docs. Secret for Success: Facts are your friends. Credo: For a better world. Drink: Gilbey's 90 with a splash of French Roast.

It may be too late to get a life.

Moss was raised on the saltgrass Gulf Coast prairie, the only child of high school teachers in the refinery town of La Marque. In 1963 they packed him off to Cal-Berkeley. They believed in education, and didn't have a clue what lay in store. College began with Kennedy's assassination, Mario Savio and Free Speech, and ended with the jihad for the Oakland Induction Center and the panic conferred by 1-A draft status. Moss remained culturally awkward. He retained what was, for the times, an atypical capacity for ambivalence. In an age of movements he felt apart. He did reach the conclusion that new-left politicos were grandstanding solipsists incapable of life outside their petri dish, and the sure knowledge that if he slipped the draft some other even more sorry-assed son of a bitch wouldn't.

In a badly focused moment Moss enlisted. He teetered between approach and avoidance, then lunged for the service with desperate enthusiasm.

After a damp winter in coal-fired barracks in Fort Benning, Georgia, basic then infantry training, Moss got orders for Vietnam. Combat ops out of Duc Pho on the coast. Within ninety days his company lost seventy men to booby traps, trip-wire grenades, and mines. With four officers down, Moss, an E4 radio operator, was third in command because of his degree. A buddy had also gone to college. Kenyon. Moss was standing next to him when he took a rocket in the chest.

Captain Haas made Moss an E5 and got him a pistol. He sent the company into free-fire zones with Hobart, the remaining lieutenant, then Moss in charge. Heading down-country in an APC convoy, crushing paddy dikes as they went. A figure had stood silhouetted on a hillside leaning on a hoe. The hoe twice as tall as he was. A kid. At first he waited for their approach as he was supposed to, then, maybe two hundred meters off, he dropped the hoe and ran. Lieutenant Hobart gave the order. The rule of engagement was clear. They'd been warned; leaflets had been dropped. The kid was brought down with the .50-caliber gun. Seven or eight years old, Hobart had him draped over the hood of the APC and taken to base camp so his family wouldn't know.

And the only ones there who liked them were the children.

Moss paid a furtive call on the division-level Inspector General at Chu Lai. His commanding officer had been putting the company into known mined areas. The company was down to half strength. Unarmed civilians had been hit. Captain Haas was running up the body count, looking for a field promotion. Moss was told he was pissing in the wind.

Near the hamlet of Phu Quan, Hobart got out by Medi-Vac with a round in the knee and Moss was left in command. From the firebase at LZ Believer Captain Haas called in orders to take the hamlet. A full Fort Benning night line sweep, though they hadn't received fire. At Phu Quan Moss made a stand. He saved a hamlet the captain thought he'd burned to the ground. For something that never took place he won the first of three Bronze Stars. Moss knew he had to leave line infantry.

He volunteered for ranger training with an Americal LRRP detachment out of Chu Lai. Long-range recon patrol. Lurps: crazy men, renegades. But the assignment was re-connaissance, not search and destroy. Forbidden even to use your weapon, since gunfire could give your team away. Primo rations and the sole mission was to observe.

Moss managed not to wash out of training and soon was rappelling from choppers at dawn at insertion sites fifty klicks into enemy territory. Painted up and stripped down for night travel, never on trails. Counting moving lines of North Vietnamese regulars. Whispering situation reports

into a handset. Praying for monkeys not to chatter overhead.

Moss craved the jungle. He loved the night. He lived for
the illusion of not being seen.

The problem was what he could not help seeing. A row
of kids hit from behind with M-60 fire. Village girls plant-
ing mines like a game. A teammate kicking open a hooch
and blasting a baby in his grandmother's arms. A fourteen-
year-old, released for interrogation to South Vietnamese police, butted to death with an M-1 carbine. Villages in flames
from tracers. The crimes against children.

What jarred it all loose was an extraction, swinging on
a McGuire rig above the jungle canopy, canvas loop on a
steel-reinforced rope hanging from a Huey. He looked up
to see the Huey bank into an incoming Chinook. Both blew,
bodies flying like sparks from the fireball. There was a
wretched weightless moment, like the time between the
flash and the thunder, nothing pulling at his armpits. Then
the sling jumped like a yo-yo and he fell. He somehow
missed hitting branches and came to in a paddy, mostly
unharmed but not the same. He couldn't bring himself to
touch a weapon again.

Though Moss was down to three months on his tour, he
filed for a conscientious objector discharge. He was required to describe it as a religious conversion, but it wasn't.
It went in fact deeper than that. He spent a half year in the
stockade. Incarceration came to suit his ascetic turn. He
fudged the question on the use of force but not what he
thought about the children, the boy with the hoe, the others.
Eventually the Army was done with him.

It had been a renunciation, a fiercely idealistic act, but a
withdrawal from events. It shamed his parents and some of
his buddies. It was agonizing but cleansing, a cutting wind
that swept away the smokes of ambivalence. He had taken
another stand. He had exercised a discipline of decisions
and deeds the like of which he'd not summoned since.

Acts of renunciation clear the air but don't maintain well.

The problem is going on to lead the just life, an issue with which he struggled still.

Nobody had been welcomed home from that war and certainly not Moss, a pariah shunned by one side as a killer and the other as a traitor. He went through a couple of bad years, stoned and drifting toward a crack-up. What saved him was meeting Sally through American Friends counseling for vets. Sally was finishing her M.F.A. at the San Francisco Art Institute. She was an unusual Quaker, outwardly irreligious and apolitical. Her art—stylized and allegorical—contrasted with her philosophy of personal relations. She placed belief in people before ideas, and certainly before institutions, governments, or gods.

Renunciation had left Moss bitter, cynical, and alone. Sally forced him to engage the world again. He cleared rehab, appealed to the Discharge Review Board for an upgrade from general to honorable, applied to the V.A. for reinstatement of benefits, and won a waiver of his military prison record to attend law school and take the bar. He followed Sally to Boulder when she joined the art faculty. Through her diplomacy at their wedding, he made a clumsy peace with his parents. Sally combined right-brain insight with exacting standards, a tough lover back when loving was easy. Moss never forgot that Sally saved his silly ass.

There were many lessons from those times, among them that seemingly caring and responsible people are capable of horrible deeds, of lying and killing without compunction. That in the big picture we will keep having draft-dodger epithets in presidential campaigns, denials of Agent Orange claims, and no reconciliation. That being somebody—a lawyer, a doctor, a criminal, a saint—isn't what matters. Who we are and how we matter are the results of what we do. That's what counts—what we do.

The night sweep that saved Phu Quan had proven it.

Vietnam seemed not a place to him now but a mood, the one you get when something bad is about to happen. Instead of true memories he had frozen moments—the fireball, the boy with the hoe, a bicycle in the bamboo, men bleeding on a bridge. He carried them in his mind like broken pieces jangling in a box he clutched without knowing why.

Ever since he went down with the choppers Moss had suffered a fear of flying. When he boarded a plane he entered a derealized state, channeled and hyperaware. The fact of being alive could overwhelm him suddenly from the air. His eyes could fill with tears.

The feeling of not belonging also never really left. Melodramatically Moss conceived himself wandering a DMZ, disowning opposing armies, peaceniks and vets, the trial lawyers and the medical society, petri-dish academics and mad-as-hell talk-show hosts. To live with ambivalence is not to live without conviction but he felt a strong inclination to break loose. To return to the jungle to sort things out. Make some decisions. Take a stand again. The sabbatical had suggested another way.

SEVEN

A *few days* after it was filed, a conformed copy of the complaint in *Teresa S. Winter v. Wallace W. Bondurant, M.D.*, was left in the firm relay box at the courthouse, stamped to Judge Langworthy's division. The defendant's answer arrived a few days later.

"Who's defending him?" Crutchfield appeared at Moss's door like the office imp. "Stackley again?"

"I wish. It's Jerome Basteen." Moss wondered about the change in lawyers. Had Bondurant fired Stackley, or vice versa, or had ROMPIC shuffled the deck?

"Jerome 'Don't Call Me Jerry' Basteen?"

"Fucking A."

"I feel your pain."

Moss had crossed swords with Basteen before, a bad baby case that settled for too little when the parents finally wearied of Basteen's vilifying them for trying to milk money from their son's cerebral palsy. Basteen believed, with a vengeance, that an unrelenting offense was the best defense. His assignment to Bondurant would mean an unpleasant escalation of hostilities.

Basteen favored preemptive strikes to turn the opposition's stomach for war: requests for health records back to infancy; a hundred written interrogatories invading marital, sexual, medical, and legal privacies; the grueling, humiliating deposition to rob the plaintiff of her heart for battle.

Moss had his client in. It was time to explain the phenomenonology of lawsuits and poke through the closet for skeletons. He started by summarizing what he'd learned so far and what was coming up. He gave Terry the bad news about Judge Langworthy—gave it straight from the shoulder—and prepared her for Jerome Basteen.

Langworthy was the worst possible draw, a judicial sadist who'd abused Moss in a number of hearings though not yet a full jury trial. The problem was he detested Moss's line of work. He'd been appointed by the governor from a med mal defense firm as a payback to health care interests for campaign contributions. The bulk of his fees in private practice had come straight from ROMPIC. He'd adjusted poorly to the pay cut on the bench. And Langworthy remained a believer, intellectually unable to accept the possibility that, short of overt criminal acts, there was such a thing as substandard medical care. He retained alliances among physicians, time-shared a Vail townhouse with a group of orthopods, addressed forensic issues at medical society conventions. He was also a bird colonel in the Army reserves. He'd served in Nam as a JAG officer prosecuting fraggers, AWOLS, and resisters like Moss.

There was a plus. Langworthy detested Basteen, a former rival from defense bar days, even more than he detested Moss.

"This would not have been the judge," Terry Winter mentioned, "if it were up to me." She wore a button reading FUR IS DEAD.

"I could move to recuse him. It's never worked before."

"It might make him mad."

"Madder."

"So play with what you're dealt?"

"Agreed," Moss said. "Forget the judge."

He turned to the coming encounter with Basteen. He gave a practiced introduction to the art of parrying a deposition. He needed to know before Basteen did what he had to worry about.

"Tell me about you." All he'd learned was that she lived in the Boulder foothills and tried to make ends meet with a pet care business. "I hate surprises."

Terry glanced at Emmy then back at Moss. The kid slouched across the table reading a library book. *Are You There, God? It's Me, Margaret.*

"She can stay or not," Moss said. "It's up to you. We'll be talking about the past."

"What does Emmy know about the past? She thinks Woodstock was a bird. Emmy, beat it."

"Mom."

"Out in the lobby. Go."

The kid rolled her eyes. "So retarded." She left heavy of foot.

"O.K.," Moss continued. "Police, prison, tax evasion, other lawsuits, I need to know it all."

"None of those." She kept her left fist clenched, forearm shielding torso like a boxer.

"You tell me. Husbands, wives, felonies, car wrecks, anything."

"Where to start?"

"Parents. Start there."

"Deceased."

"Died of what?"

"My dad was killed in a ranch accident when I was twelve. My mom died when I was eighteen."

"How?"

"Is it important?"

"Possibly, if there was a family history Bondurant failed to take."

"About all I can tell you is she got sick and died."

"Sick with what?"

"Not sure and nobody told me. She was just sick and then the hospital and then she was dead. Cancer, yeah, it could have been. That bothers me some, not knowing."

"Any brothers? Sisters?"

"Nope. Nope."

"Children other than Emmy?"

As a matter of fact there was a son she'd given up for adoption—something Emmy didn't know. It happened a long time ago when she was a different person and she wasn't interested in talking about it.

Moss let it go but warned her Basteen might not.

"Why would he? It's got nothing to do with this."

"A lot of his questions won't."

"It's none of his business." She had a meaningful look.

"Agreed," Moss said. "Moving on to, let's see. Drug use?"

"Nonmedicinal? Nothing serious."

"Meaning?"

"No street drugs."

"Meaning?"

"Meaning lying in bed all day smoking dope and listening to *Blonde on Blonde*. Meaning three months getting sick on peyote buttons in Mexico when I tried to be a hippie."

"Inhaled, I suppose?"

"Can't say I didn't but I don't eat meat."

"Convictions? Rehab?"

"No, sir. None at all, sir."

"Just a little youthful experimentation you've long since put behind you?"

"I'd like to see Mexico again. These Seri Indians I stayed with on the coast, they have this—respect, I guess it is. They think dogs are shamans and God is a dirty little guy with a bag of cactus fruit and everything is funny. There's something about the ocean in the desert. The light. It's *pura vida*, pure life, but eventually you need a bath."

"All gone, I bet. All fairways. Jet Skis and Para-Sails."

"Not my Mexico."

"Moving on from your Mexico we've got, let's see. Husbands. Dads. They're out there, evidently."

"Out there, is correct."

"Tell me about them."

"That's kind of involved."

"Give me the brief version."

"Brief version is husband Tom was the seventies, no kids. Husband Warren was the eighties, one kid. Sixties was no husband, one kid, forget about it. I have. Doesn't exist. Never happened."

"Nineties?"

"I'm past men. No offense. The child-producing variety anyhow."

"What about Tom?"

"Probation officer in the Springs. Good guy, to put up with me. The *Blonde on Blonde* days, the college days, the barmaid days and nights. Maybe the one flat-out good guy in my whole checkered career. But, you know, short on vision. Short on reach."

"Short on conversation?"

"Very short. It got to, is the rest of my existence going to be like this? Tommy knew. He helped me pack. He'd married a notch too, what? Not too high." She illustrated with her hand. "Too far apart." She extended an arm.

"What about Emmy's dad?"

"Tommy's opposite. You wouldn't like him."

"Whereabouts?"

"Hereabouts."

"Name?"

"Warren Winter. Never did like winters, should have been a give-away. Next life, I'll fall for Mr. Spring."

"Or vice versa. Tell me about Mr. Winter."

"A piece of work, Warren is." Her knee began to jiggle. The left fist tightened.

"What does Warren do?"

"Do for kicks? Do for jobs?"

"Start with jobs."

"Different stuff."

"Yeah?" Moss affected impatience.

"Buys things, sells things. This is a man with a short attention span. He gets around. I'm not sure anymore."

"I see. Licit things or illicit?"

"Like I say, he gets around."

"You living together?"

"Not on your life. It's just Emmy and me, forty acres and a dog. And the best view of the range in Flatirons County."

"Warren support Emmy?"

"That's a matter of opinion. He thinks so."

"Still married?"

"I didn't get around to getting unmarried."

"That could be a problem. Down the road."

She became thoughtful. She chewed at a lip. "As you can see, I messed up my life some. I don't want to mess this up."

"This?"

"This part."

"What part?"

"Emmy. This is an important time."

"Of course it is." He'd thought she meant the case, money, the usual, but something else had made her pensive.

"People tell me I got cancer because of bad forces in my life, like Warren. Or I'm a bad person, or chlorinated pesticides, whatever, Richard Nixon, who knows. What do you think?"

"I think that's bullshit."

"What do you think is the meaning of illness?"

Moss was nonplussed. He tried to come up with a Confucian response. "Got me," he said.

"Got me too."

He refocused. "Your husband, as I say, is a bit of a concern. We're going to have to deal with Warren Winter at some point. He might claim an interest, depending."

"Depending how?"

Moss temporized. It was not presently opportune to spin worst-case scenarios. "On how the case goes."

"Well, we are going to have to deal with Warren Winter," she said. "You are very right about that."

EIGHT

$M_{oss\ met\ with}$ his client again the morning of her deposition. Emmy was in school. Terry looked good, like a working mom, in a plaid jacket and gabardine skirt, not especially stylish, no shoulder pads, lustrous hair swept back and held by a wooden band. No buttons with slogans. Moss himself was less disheveled than usual. For luck he wore a rubber band on his right wrist as he always had for trials, client depositions, and combat patrols in the Republic of Vietnam.

Crutchfield joined them to play the part of Basteen. The prep was a waste. The woman was uncoachable. She took Crutchfield's corrections as insistence that she lie. Moss observed a categorical imperative at work. She would act according to the principles she would have govern everyone. She had no trouble discarding Moss's admonitions not to volunteer, nor to guess, to pause and think before answering, to keep her cool. Likewise his suggestions for artfully skirting sensitive issues.

"Here's the thing," Terry said. "I intend to tell the truth *truthfully*. Meaning not your words and nothing planned."

"Great. Spontaneity will please Basteen."

"I'm who I am," she insisted. "Who else is this about but me?"

"Jerome Basteen is who. Your mortal enemy. He'll trap you. He'll twist what you say."

"I won't descend to his level." She smiled. "Why should I? Life is short."

"Yes." His wife had mentioned something similar.

"So I may as well be, what? *Authentic*."

She was.

In the Junker and Wylie conference room Jerome Basteen was passing time with his court reporter, a young woman with short blond hair, dark eyebrows, a prominent labial mole, a slit skirt. He greeted Moss cavalierly, as though he were tangential to the business at hand. He gave Terry, when introduced, a brief inspection and curt nod. "You know Dr. Bondurant," Basteen remarked to them both. Moss turned to the far end of the black table where the defendant sat, fingers locked in front of him, as if presiding.

Their eyes met and stayed. It was different this time.

"Terry," Bondurant said. "You look *good*. And Peter." He stood and extended his hand.

Moss walked the length of the table to shake it. Peter? They never made it to first-name familiarities in the Fisher case. Some risk-management tip on how to condescend to a plaintiff's lawyer?

"It's been a long time," Bondurant said without obvious irony.

"Too long." Moss smiled.

He explained the self-serve coffee pots on the warming plate. "I'll pass," Terry said. "Me neither," said the court reporter. Bondurant asked for a Coke. "Bottled water," Basteen said. "If you have it." Moss let his secretary know.

Presence was important to Basteen's style of lawyering. Presence required a coordinated effect. The effect included a dove gray BMW 750iL, a pearl Armani suit, a tie with twilit patterns of tropical vegetation, and woven Italian loafers. It included close-cut hair and mustache, nailhead cufflinks, long manicured fingers, a calculating grin. To be sure it included his great height, taller than Moss, and the trim physique to which the suits were tailored. In Basteen, everything—color, shape, pattern, size—meshed to maximize the capacity to control. There was a unifying theme, a tone and richness—muted gold, in the burnish in the swirling tie, the woof of the threads of his socks, all the places he quietly gleamed. Muted, in the suggestion rather than the declaration of opulence. Muted, not in the sense of discretion but of reserve. Of withheld threat.

Jerome Basteen conducted a highly tight-assed deposition. He never strayed from his initial mind-set. Every question was leading, closed. He interrupted if he was failing to get the answer he wanted. He asked a question again and again. Consequently he rarely appeared to learn anything, but he could beat you down and make you say what he wanted.

Some trial lawyers are effective because they're imaginative. Some are effective at power trips. Basteen belonged with the latter. Crutchfield called him three times a bully. A Seventeenth Street bully. A ROMPIC bully. And a big black bully. His combination of statuses had tricked him into thinking he could get away with anything—lying to judges, hiding evidence, humiliating witnesses. Basteen had come to adore status. In the glare of status he'd gone ethically blind.

But there were ways to rattle him. Sitting slightly to his rear and side when he was examining could lead him to suspect you were trying to read his notes. A few cranings of the neck and fake bored look-arounds could get him actively paranoid and losing his thread. Another technique, a grave taunt best held in reserve, was to refer to him as Jerry.

Moss seated Terry and himself with the windows at their backs. Bondurant joined his counsel opposite them. The court reporter positioned her machines at the head of the gleaming table. She put a finger to a lip and inclined Basteen's way. He nodded for her to begin. Terry was sworn, and Basteen's picked and filed fingernails converged.

"Ms. Winter, you were diagnosed with breast cancer—"

"October 28, 1992," she said. "I know it better than my daughter's birthday."

"You are suing my client because you got cancer."

"No."

"What are you suing him for?"

She thought a while. "It's a process of working things through. Figuring things out."

"You are in fact suing Dr. Bondurant for money, isn't that it?"

"Objection," Moss said. Moss was restricted to a passive role. He could object but not intervene unless it got truly out of hand.

"I don't know. I'm not suing him for money."

"You've had, what, three failed marriages?"

"You could say that."

"How has that affected your feelings toward men?"

"For crying out loud," she muttered to Moss.

"Do you hate my client because he's a man?"

"I don't think I hate your client. I don't understand your client."

Bondurant rolled a shoulder. He squinted hard into the winter light silhouetting his former patient. Terry held his look until it dropped.

Bondurant was a burly ex-ballplayer at Brigham Young who might have been intimidating, Moss observed, but for a certain lack of definition. Rounded and sloped, domed on top, oval face, dull gray eyes. Compared to his counsel, not a natty guy. Short sleeves again, permanent press, discount tie. Off line, off era. He could pass for an airline pilot. A hell of a grip, however. Big, pink, hairy hands, as though blistered by the cold.

"Can we agree," Basteen quietly continued, "you are suing Dr. Bondurant because you got sick and you blame him for it?"

"No," Terry said. "It's because I trusted him."

"Oh?" Basteen cracked a satiric smile. "You're being coy. Now answer my question."

"Objection. Asked and answered."

"Because I trusted him. And for my daughter."

An eyebrow went up. "So you want money for her?"

"No. Because I want to teach her."

"Teach her what? How to scam the system?"

Bondurant grunted approval. As a party he could attend any deposition but was not allowed to take part in the colloquy, the on-the-record exchange.

"How to stand up for yourself," Terry said slowly, and to Moss, "You were right about this guy."

"How old were you at menarche?"

"What?"

"When did you first begin menstruating?"

"What are you asking me? Can he ask me that?"

"When did you begin having periods? Monthly periods?"

"I have to answer this?"

Moss frowned and nodded. Early menarche was a breast cancer risk factor.

She leaned her forearms against the table edge. "I don't know. Twelve, fourteen, somewhere in there."

"Be more exact."

"Can't."

"When did you first engage in sexual intercourse?"

"Fuck you, asshole."

Basteen's smile broadened. He shot his cuffs and repeated the question.

"That one don't answer," Moss said.

"Nikki, please mark the transcript." Basteen had a conniving familiarity with the court reporter. She played back to him, mole-side forward, in the way she crossed her leg, arched her back. How she watched his mouth as she popped the keys.

"Ms. Winter, how many abortions have you had?"

"Good Lord."

"Keep it up," Moss said, "and I'll terminate this sucker."

Basteen appraised Moss a few moments. He expressed

disapproval. "Are you instructing your client not to answer my question?"

"Damn straight I am."

"Mark it please, Nikki. Ms. Winter, answer the question."

"I instruct my client not to answer," Moss said.

"Ms. Winter, your complaint alleges my client's negligence has harmed your sexuality. Do you masturbate?"

"Instruct not to answer. One more and we adjourn."

"Would you like my husband to know about the questions you're asking?" Terry asked. She gave Basteen a vivid look.

"In this deposition I ask the questions, Ms. Winter. You don't ask the questions. You answer the questions."

"I'll answer *my* question," she said. "You would not like my husband to know what you're asking. No, you would not."

Bondurant had tensed, Moss noticed, massaging a fist as he tracked question and response. With a feeling of revulsion Moss understood that this was what he had come for. It was what Bondurant expected from his lawyer. He'd come for spectator sport.

NINE

The examination turned to the harm caused Terry by the failure to diagnose her cancer. This was less a subject of interest to the defendant. He sat, chin on palm distorting his features in a loose grimace, dreaming off at the sidewalk traffic beyond the blinds. He looked inert as a model on a set between shoots, but he did not look like a model.

"Are you presently unable to work," Basteen asked, "as a result of my client's alleged negligence?"

Terry collected her thoughts. "Can't make a living dancing at the Bustop."

"Have you worked in the past as an exotic dancer?"

She sighed. "No, no."

"What do you do for a living?"

"I work with animals."

"You work with animals?" Basteen looked her up and down with amused and prurient incredulity.

She smiled back. "Dogs are people too."

"Summarize your prior work history."

"Prior? First job after high school was clerk at the Walsenburg DMV. Driver's license tests, eye tests, took their pictures, toes on the line. Rolled their thumbs in the ink. Want more?"

Basteen shook his head as he made a bored pass through his notes, pencil eraser tapping his tongue. "What next?"

"DMV was followed by a run of waiting tables, time behind the bar. Some college if you're interested. This and that."

"And?"

"College wasn't too helpful as it developed. You know how that is."

Basteen didn't seem to. Nor, from his expression, did Bondurant.

"And then?"

"Ranch hand on and off a couple years. A little rodeo. Barrels. Three-jump cowgirl in my day."

"What else?"

"Livery work. Farrier's helper. Trucker's helper. That was Bud's Horse and Mule Transport. Dashing Through the Snow Sleighrides was one winter. Tack shop. Horse Of Course. Wild horse rescue, off and on, which was my passion, actually."

"Continue, Ms. Winter."

"That brings us up to last year and the pet grooming business. Putting on the Dog Curbside Pet Salon. Animal sitter on the side. You got a dog? I'll do your coat, trim your nails, express your anal glands, and throw in a blow dry for nineteen bucks."

He stared at her, pencil aloft.

"How about it? Any takers?"

"Shall we proceed, Ms. Winter?"

"Special rates for lawyers."

Moss was starting to feel proud of his client but on break she told him she was fired up, ready to tell it like it was. A bad sign. Wait for the question, Moss cautioned. Think about it before you tell it.

In the hallway Bondurant passed, carrying a glass with ice and a can of Diet Coke.

"What happened to Freeman Stackley?" Moss asked him. "Too much the gentleman for a case like this?"

Bondurant shrugged. "Freeman has his reasons, I guess. I'm in good hands."

"Right. It's important to love your lawyer."

"I wouldn't know about that."

As the day wore on Basteen kept his suit jacket on though the conference room was warming in the southern light. He had begun marching toward the heart of the case. Why did Terry choose his client as her doctor? he asked.

"He was into this whole wellness approach," Terry said. "I wanted to do it right this time."

"Do what right?"

"My kid. My goal has been the best for my kid."

Basteen had a way of tilting his head and grimacing when he disapproved. Bondurant glanced up from doodling on his pad. "I'm asking about you, Ms. Winter. Did you understand my question?"

"There was this thing in my breast. That was mainly it with me. I told you that."

"This thing?" He laughed aloud. "What did this thing feel like?"

"Funny."

"Funny?" He fixed her with bright suspicious eyes. "Are you trying to be funny?"

"I can't explain it. Like a knot, I guess."

"You guess?"

"It felt like a knot."

"Did you bring this thing to Dr. Bondurant's attention?"

"Sure."

"What did you tell him?"

"I don't remember. I pointed it out."

"What did he tell you?"

"Not to worry. Keep an eye on it. Come back."

"Did you worry?"

"Who was I to argue? He was the one with the diplomas and the clothes on."

Basteen grimaced and tilted his head. "Did you worry?"

"I don't really remember."

"Did you come back?"

"Sure."

"Because you were worried about this thing in your breast?" He shaped the question with long, thin hands. His fingers curled with irony.

"And for Emmy's wellness checks."

"How often?"

"A lot. Every few months."

"Was this thing always there?"

"I don't know. I guess. He said not to worry. That's what I remember."

On it went, Terry less positive the more detail he sought, Bondurant smiling openly from time to time. Harm was being done not from Basteen's overbearing interrogation but Terry's offhand vagueness. Moss winced inwardly. This was telling it like it was? It was time for Plan B.

Moss stood up, pretending to stretch. "Back trouble," he explained, "Please continue." He paced a bit as the petulant questions continued. He made his way behind Basteen and to one side. He leaned against a wall. He could tell Basteen was creeping up to the Phantom Phone Call; she had to deny it unequivocally.

Basteen's frown sank deeper. He shielded his papers. His head twitched in Moss's direction behind him. He called Terry by the name of another plaintiff from another case. Bondurant pursed his lips.

"Objection," Moss said. He was feeling a little impetuous.

Basteen reinflated. Here it comes. "Ms. Winter," he said, "isn't it true that you and Dr. Bondurant spoke on occasion by telephone?"

"I don't remember that."

Moss silently cheered. He edged up a bit in back of Basteen.

"Are you saying you're absolutely sure you never spoke with him by telephone?"

"No."

"So you may have spoken by telephone?"

"No."

"Yes? It's possible?"

"It's possible, but—"

"Assuming you did speak by telephone, isn't it the case that you don't now remember whether in any telephone conversation Dr. Bondurant discussed his recommendation that you see a surgeon for biopsy?"

"Object to the interruption," Moss said.

"What are you saying? He never did that. He said it was benign."

"You're unable to remember the conversation, is that what you mean?"

"I'm not sure I'm—"

"Who is Dr. Mayhew?"

"Object to the interruption," Moss repeated. Basteen was going off his game. It was time to press some buttons.

"Ms. Winter, my question was very simple. My question was this. At this point you cannot say whether or not you were referred to Dr. Mayhew?"

"That wasn't your question," Moss said. He was feeling increasingly off the wall.

"Thank you, Mr. Moss, for telling me what my question was."

"The record," Moss added, "will reflect that Mr. Basteen has just described as his previous question a question he in fact never asked. The record should also reflect that when Mr. Basteen thanked me for pointing that out he did so with an expression of ravening, fang-bared sarcasm."

"Well said," Terry commented.

"Words," Moss replied, "is my life." He turned to the scowling Basteen. "The record should also show that when Mr. Basteen said 'Thank you,' his ear-to-ear grin actually meant the opposite of 'Thank you.' It meant 'Fuck you.'"

Basteen was on his feet, shouting. The court reporter threw up her hands. Bondurant looked confused and Terry looked disgusted. Basteen demanded they get Judge Langworthy on the phone, a threat so hollow he fell further in disarray. He began to jabber senselessly. Control was down the toilet and he stood spent, towering, huffing, and glaring, jabbing an elegant finger at Moss.

"Mr. Basteen," Moss said quietly. "Put your finger in your mouth and sit down." He shook his head sympathetically.

"Jerry, you're hyperventilating."

The ultimate affront.

"Jerry," Moss said again. "Are you all right?"

It struck the man dumb.

Moss looked at Nikki, the court reporter, which made her flinch. "We recently celebrated Thanksgiving," Moss said.

"Is this on the record?" Nikki was near hysteria.

Moss nodded. "We recently celebrated Thanksgiving and I have a question. What do they do with Jerry at Thanksgiving," Moss gestured at the speechless Basteen, "to keep him from being stuffed, basted, roasted, and eaten?"

Basteen swept up his things, stuffed and snapped his litigator's bag. "Let's go," he said. He took his client's elbow and left the room with a hissed envoi: "I'll grieve your ass."

Before they resumed the following day Moss was informed by his client, in a reversal of roles, how to behave at a deposition. Moss was informed that this was serious, this was her life, stop farting around.

The defendant elected not to attend again. Both Moss and Basteen were subdued when they got back under way. There was even an attitude afoot of deference to the witness.

"How was it finding out you had cancer?" Basteen was wrapping up a line of questions on the impacts of Terry's illness on her life.

She thought a minute. "Like a bad marriage," she said.

"A marriage?"

"A husband you don't want anything to do with, only this one lives inside you."

Basteen was loading his bag. The questions were throwaways. He was done.

"He can stay a while," Terry continued, "but down the road it's him or me."

"I see." Basteen looked up. "And what do you think you've learned from this experience? Having cancer?"

"To value your life," she said without hesitation. "Shitty as it is." She took a deep breath. "To value your life and your children."

TEN

The *deposition finished,* Moss called home about picking up something for dinner. He looked forward to an undemanding evening, unwinding with Sally and a video—something feel-good, or science fiction, or both. A glowing hearth and a liter or so of middle-brow West Coast wine. Moss needed a brain dump. He needed to get away from the case.

When he called about these arrangements he thought he'd gotten a bad connection, a fluttering static, a periodic roar. His wife, he realized, was beating about the house with a cordless phone in one hand, Dustbuster in the other, sucking up box elder bugs, hair on the bathroom tiles. She raised and lowered her voice with the noise levels, the wake-the-dead wail of the Dustbuster, the telephone static like spatters of rain.

God, I love that woman, Moss thought. Fiery woman. Mustang Sally, salty as country ham.

They wound up not watching *Star Trek IV* again. He wound up not getting away from the case.

Sally was responsible. "Here we go again," she observed. They were finishing ribs and vegetables he'd grilled in the cold and dark. Sally still wore an ink-spattered work shirt and black jeans from a day at the double-cylinder press when she hadn't been busting dust. Though she had an office and studio on campus, Sally preferred to work in a converted garage on the irrigation ditch behind their poptop fifties bungalow. The garage's west wall of floor-to-ceiling glass gave on a green bower of cottonwoods and willows in the summer, and, in winter, the shapely red slabs of the Flatirons. Here she spent most afternoons alone carving and stippling intaglio plates and listening to NPR. Her miniatures were well-collected, from the MoMA to the deMenil. Work clothes suited her lean frame, setting off intense, intelligent features that grew more intriguing with age.

"Again?" Moss feigned puzzlement, suspending a rib over his plate in the chrome and maplewood kitchen—the remodeled part of the house.

"Your promise to stop doing these cases was sincere," Sally said. "I acknowledge that. I know why it didn't work. I could have predicted." She sat back and let her commentary settle over her husband like a mist.

"Why?" He resumed gnawing.

"Unfinished business."

Moss nodded. "All right."

"Why do you have to make it personal? Work's supposed to be professional, not personal."

"This was *gross* negligence, Sally. This woman is eventually going to die because of the bastard. He came to her deposition to get his rocks off when Basteen beat her up."

"It may not be a good idea to pour your whole self into your cases, you know. I mean your whole wee emotional being."

"You sound like Junker."

"I do not sound like Junker."

"Like Crutch."

"I sound like the one who knows and you know it. The voice of inner truth."

"Inner truth?"

"You and I are what's supposed to be personal."

"Sally, please," Moss said abjectly. "Help me. I've got no feel for this case." Actually the case felt decidedly different, peculiar, but just how or why he wasn't yet sure.

"Remember the phone calls?" She sighed. "I still think it was him."

"Not likely." Moss was a little abashed. "Not nuts enough."

"I just don't want this messing us up."

The Fisher trial had been a sensation, followed in the paper every day, on the front page of Section C. The phone calls began the first night, a man's voice muffled by a sock or something. Sally stopped getting the phone when it rang and messages were left, escalating threats, to bulldoze their house, to rape Moss's wife and rub him out. Moss disconnected the answering machine and a letter was delivered with clichéd cut-and-paste lettering that he had framed and still kept on his office wall, a truer certificate of professional status than any diploma: I HOPE YOU GET HIT BY A TRUCK AND YOUR CAR BURSTS IN FLAMES AND YOU SLOWLY BURN TO DEATH. I ALSO HOPE YOU CONTRACT AIDS.

"What's Bondurant been up to since he kicked your butt?"

"I launched his career in medical politics," Moss said. After the trial Bondurant filed a spate of lawsuits of his own, against the Fishers for abuse of process, against the newspaper for defamation. He filed a grievance against Moss. Nothing went anywhere but his institutional clout began to grow. He lobbied for damages caps and against health care alliances. He took a place on ROMPIC's board and put out the word no insured should help Moss on any case. Now that he presided over the medical society, insurance executives, health bureaucrats, legislators, and pundits all paid sober attention when he told them lawyers were ruining medicine.

"He started a victim support group for doctors who've been sued. They bitch about lawyers and backslap each other for being an inadequately worshiped elite. In the name of risk management they hold 'Defendants' FACs' at country clubs with speakers and open bars. Basteen no doubt hands out cards."

"Not a bad idea." Sally was clearing the table. "You should start a support group for victims of lawyer jokes. Happy Hours for ambulance chasers."

"How come they think being sued is the end of the world?" Moss had been sued for malpractice by an ex-client who thought her thirty-thousand-dollar claim should have been worth millions. Defending it had been an aggravation for a while, a drain on his time. But he was insured and that's what insurance was for. It qualified as an interesting experience. Few doctors find being sued interesting.

Sally doffed the lid of the Ecocycle bin. An empty green bottle rang out against its fellows. She sat back down, wanting to hear more about Bondurant. Was he like he was before?

"We'll see," Moss said. The chart was revealing to a point. He brushed off what a deft physician would puzzle out. He discredited what his patient told him. There was a proprietary tone and, inferentially, a reluctance to refer the patient for specialty care. Probably a concern less for loss of business than of control. All that was the essential Bondurant, well behind the cutting edge, stiff-necked, unreflective, dead certain when he's dead wrong. "But there may be something different here. What I saw at his office in his eyes. Fear, I never saw before." What in the case, Moss continued to wonder, did Bondurant fear?

At the Fisher trial he had come across as bluff and a little coarse, miffed at having to be there though as outwardly unconcerned as he'd seemed that morning at Terry's deposition. But Moss always thought there were hidden levels to the man. Moss couldn't still the feeling that he'd never grubbed out the gross truth of what had happened to the Fishers, and it ate at him like a parasitic worm.

Bondurant hadn't offered a dime in settlement. Never, he declared, would he agree to settle any malpractice claim.

"So," Moss said, "what does the voice of inner truth think happened?"

"Maybe he's just—I don't know—not very bright?"

Moss shook his head. "It's not like he's stupid. And it's not like he's loathsome."

"What's it like?"

"Like something's missing."

"Then what you need to do," she said, "is figure out what's missing."

Moss valued Sally's brainstorming more than any colleague's. After all, he owed her his mental health, such as it was. Their marriage had not been without tension, over drinking, the miscarriages. There had been three. The last time she'd hemorrhaged and nearly died and it scared him shitless. He realized losing her would be worse than anything, worse than Vietnam, the one thing he could not survive. Forget assisted pregnancy. Forget children. Cauterize the vas deferens and cleave to each other like the lovers of "Dover Beach." But for Sally, after that, without the hope of there being more than two of them, life was a diminished thing. The loss was something she would never resolve, like her husband about the war.

"Give me your take on it, Sally. Give me vision." Moss decorked a second sauvignon blanc. "I'm trying to get into the psychology of this. I only get so far. It's not one bad decision, a single transaction with a bad result. It's a whole course of care. Years. It's like system failure, the failure of early detection, of prevention, what family medicine is supposed to be about."

He explained that Borkin told him the tumor was palpably there for over three years, waiting to be found. Bondurant examined her breasts nine times in that period and recorded nothing overtly suspicious for cancer. But it *was* there and the patient was telling him so and the doctor kept bringing her back.

"Go figure." Sally shook her head. "The man's got a rotten touch. Or he doesn't see what he doesn't want to see. Feel, that is."

"That's it, I think. That's my hypothesis."

Moss laid out his provisional theory of the case. Early on Bondurant makes his judgment call. Fibrocystic disease.

Benign breast lumps. From then on it's, I'm the man. Don't tell me what to do.

"He gets more and more entrenched." Sally glommed to the notion. "He responds perversely to contrary evidence. He takes her reports about a growing lump personally. She's questioning him. The man. He gets in deeper and deeper. He can't let go."

"My guy in New Hampshire, Hoover, says you can fall in love with your diagnosis."

She was shaking her head again. "But still, why did he?"

They were quiet a while. Moss was feeling winey and dull, unmoored. He was ready for the stairs.

"Look," Sally said abruptly. "He's a family doctor, right?" Moss observed that she was pointing at him. "*Family* doctor. The answer's in his *family*."

It was one of her sheeringly illogical statements that had cracked cases before. In Terry's deposition she'd said something provocative. How did Dr. Bondurant respond, Basteen wanted to know, when she mentioned her fear of cancer? "He said he understood how concerned I was. His own mother died of breast cancer. He said it was a terrible way to go."

"There you have it," Sally said. "His mother. What was their relationship? How did he act when she was dying? Is breast cancer something he can't deal with because of his mother? Is that the source of his fears?"

Moss frowned and nodded. "You think—in his family?"

"That, or there may be a money angle."

"Money? How?"

"How do I know? Kickback? Insurance scam?"

"She paid cash."

"Deep Throat said follow the money." She was quiet a while longer, at the end of her speculation. "Think, Peter. What do the two cases have in common? What pattern is there in his behavior?"

"None. He killed a young girl with a reckless prescription. He let a woman's cancer go for years. Just bad doctoring, twice. This time a mother, not a daughter, will be dead because of his negligence." He shuddered. The strength of the wave of bitterness that rolled through him was disorienting. His heart went to these families past where judgment should allow.

"There's got to be something in common." She was pacing the kitchen, putting things away. She turned, hands on the hips of her black jeans. Sally was a turn-on when she worried a thought, biting a lip, cocking a long leg. "You're just not going to understand this case," she said, "until you dig into the man's personal life. Something blinded him to evidence under his nose. Something compelled him to keep this patient coming back again and again to be reassured she had no disease. We're talking a compulsion, Peter. We're talking a deep-down psyche thing."

Love that woman, Moss thought. Ride, Sally, ride.

ELEVEN

In boasting to Crutchfield he'd gotten the best breast oncologist on the planet Moss overstated things. Epstein in fact
was the best, but Moss didn't have him. Yet.

The trip to Houston, to the M.D. Anderson Cancer Center where the honored Epstein held sway, was an exercise
in brinksmanship. Lewis Epstein chaired the Department of
Breast Carcinoma Medical Oncology at this most presti-
gious institution. Perhaps only he could speak with the authority Moss would require to discredit the probable
defense experts, the Doubler, Dr. Krishnan Irizarry Singh,
and the Carcinoma Angel, Dr. Angelika Franzblau, who
were sure to testify that the three-year delay in diagnosis
had been immaterial.

This was not an insignificant issue in the case. The problem was, while Moss had studied Dr. Epstein's articles,
he'd never in fact communicated with the man.

Moss had been able to sweet-talk an hour's appointment
out of Epstein's secretary without fully disclosing his purposes. He bought a nonrefundable, same-day, round-trip
ticket to Houston, packed a trial bag with medical records,
tissue slides, and film, and caught the Airporter for Stapleton. Once aloft and leveling out of the bank, he snapped

down the windowshade and tried a little meditation. The GTE Airfone in the seatback was distracting. It seemed as though it might ring. Above a flight attendant's backward-facing fold-up seat a flashlight was set in wall mounts. Its red LED battery-life indicator lit up every three seconds. And what were the purposes of flashlights on airplanes? Power failures? Search and rescue? More meditation was in order.

Eventually Moss was able to relax, hit the seat-recline button, take some stock en route. A wound had been opened by Basteen during Terry's deposition. Bondurant's notes implied his patient repeatedly reported a lump that he was unable to confirm. He would undoubtedly assert there was no palpable mass to be found. But if that were so, how had his patient, on self-examination, found it so consistently? Confident testimony from her of the existence of the lump was critical to undermining Bondurant's expected defense.

She hadn't given it. Her self-examination had been sporadic. She remembered a "thing" at times, at other times not. Maybe it was in a different place. Maybe, she volunteered at one point, a different breast?

Fuck me, Moss had thought, smiling casually at Basteen.

As Basteen pounded, Terry got progressively equivocal. She was giving Bondurant his out: I could never find anything. Half the time she couldn't either. There was nothing definitive on mammogram. How can you biopsy what can't be felt or seen?

Moss had been pissed. He assailed his client during one of the breaks. All she had to do was confirm Bondurant's own notes of her reports of a lump. She backed away as though just noticing he was radioactive. "What are you asking me to do, man? That was years ago. I don't remember, O.K.?"

The woman didn't woodshed well. "Look, Terry. You win a case with facts. Remembering facts, not forgetting them."

"Fact is I don't remember."

"I'm not asking you to lie."

"Not lying's different from being truthful," she had said. "What more can I tell you? Cancer makes you truthful."

Moss had sighed and embarked on Plan B, to disrupt Basteen.

The wound was not necessarily mortal but the weakness of Terry's recall meant Moss had to blow Bondurant's version sky high. In effect, he now had to catch Bondurant in a very healthy lie.

The Texas Medical Center in Houston is a city unto itself. It suggests the futuristic vision of an entire metropolis populated by the seriously ill, a *Star Trek* episode—*City of the Terminal*. Moss moved uneasily from a parking lot toward Building 55 among a slow-moving parade of the assisted, with their canes, walkers, wheelchairs, oxygen, and IVs, their flowing escort of family members bearing flowers, fists tethering shiny foil balloons with cartoon faces bobbing and grinning brightly in the gray mists of Houston in December.

Portents, Moss thought. A fear momentarily pinched his breath—*we're going down*. He cleared it away. Anxiety about being turned back.

Dr. Epstein was at the moment engaged by a CNN camera crew, Moss was informed by the sweet-talked secretary, Dana. Come on in and wait in his office.

It's another spot about the epidemic, Dana explained. Dr. Epstein found it tiresome. But somebody had to do it, and the doctor, after all, was Mr. Breast Cancer. So there he was again patiently running through the stats, one woman in eight now likely to contract the disease, explaining the genetic breakthroughs for which they were poised and the research funding contests with Mr. AIDS, Mr. Diabetes, and Mr. Heart, and with the cigarette cancers, so obvious but so lethal.

Moss thanked her and took a seat opposite Epstein's reef fish screensaver. He had three hours before airport time. One went by. On swam the colorful fish, then Lewis Epstein was at the door.

Moss did a double take. Epstein had an awfully wild look. His white frock was festooned with buttons, gadgets, geegaws, and labels, among them, DESPERATELY SEEKING SUSHI; Nixon-Agnew '72; I'M PROUD TO BE A KICKER; I'm Not a Dirty Old Man, Just a Sexy Senior Citizen; What's Ft. Worth? It's Worth the World to Me; YO AMO A MI MÉDICO with pins, pendants, buzzers, bells, cups and saucers, little tin cowboy boots and lone stars, happy faces galore. How, Moss wondered, is this guy going to sell on the stand?

Dr. Epstein was also taken aback. "Who the hell are you?" he said.

Watch this, Moss thought. "A lawyer."

Epstein stared in disbelief. Yes, Moss noted, I know the reaction. Give this man a balloon and send him back to his patients. I'm going home.

Instead Moss implored. "I've read your work. It is very important that I consult with you. Please hear me out."

The doctor did, then explained his problem. He got nothing out of legal consultations. No fee whatsoever, by policy of the center and university. Consulting with a lawyer was nothing more than an unpaid burden on his time. Something had to be worked out with the legal department but nothing went to him. The legal department knew how to discourage legal consultations. They had this funny idea that his time was better spent saving lives and trying to eradicate disease than helping lawyers sue doctors.

"I'm sorry," he said. "I'm really busy enough."

Moss pricked up a bit at the apologetic tone. "You're saying you're unwilling to be involved under *any* conditions?"

"I'm unwilling to be involved." He nodded briskly, regalia shimmying on his frock.

"Unless?"

"Unless truly grave injustice could not otherwise be avoided."

Ah-hah, Moss thought. Gotcha. "That is precisely our

circumstance, Dr. Epstein." It was fawn-and-grovel time in the doctor's office.

Moss expounded on the needs of the case. They reviewed together the medical records and film. Dr. Epstein popped a slide in the microscope. Moss was almost there. "Let me tell you about the other side's experts," he said.

Moss described Dr. Irizarry Singh, the Doubler, who in every case ran the same calculations. He measured replacement volumes of malignant lymph nodes, assumed a "doubling time" for the primary tumor—the number of days it takes to double in volume—assumed the same growth rate held for the nodes, then divided the nodes' volume backward in time at that rate to prove the cancer had already metastasized beyond the breast to the nodes by the time the misdiagnosis occurred. No harm, in other words, no foul. The magic day had already come and gone.

"But that fails to take account of Gompertzian growth."

"Exactly." Moss had no idea what Epstein was talking about but he liked the sound of it. He next described Dr. Franzblau, the Carcinoma Angel. The Angel clinched the deal. If it meant discrediting junk science, Dr. Epstein thought he could help.

What Epstein might be able to say at trial was this: Ms. Winter's was long an indolent tumor. It persisted harmlessly for years, the kind of slow-growing cancer most amenable to intervention and cure. It was by its nature frankly diagnosable. But it was let go tragically long. It is harmless no more. It is going to kill Ms. Winter. Sometime in the not-distant future, almost surely within five years, the cancer will recur, mutated and drug-resistant. A bone scan will heat up along her spine or signals show on CT-scan in the liver or lungs or brain. This time chemotherapy may shrink and slow the malignant growth somewhat and extend her life. But remission is impossible and the outcome is certain. She has a killing disease. The only question is when the dying process starts.

"These can be humiliating deaths, Mr. Moss, especially if several organs fail. Her flesh will waste. Bleeding is a

concern. Transfusions may be required. Breathing becomes
a worsening struggle. She'll be too exhausted to cross a
room. If the brain also is involved there are additional effects as you may imagine. And all we can do is tap her
lungs and run her through mineral oil enemas, and pump
her full of so much morphine it obliterates consciousness,
and hope she dies unaware of the enormity of her prostra-
tion.

"Ms. Winter has no chance of reaching her forty-eighth
year. And hers will have been a needless death. This was
a cancer that could have been stopped."

Moss walked back through the medical center to his
rented Tempo under grimy *Blade Runner* skies. On the runway, as would happen when he waited for takeoff, a spir-
itless melancholy descended despite his success in signing
Epstein. The jet began to taxi and Moss's fists clenched on
the rests. He was compelled to witness a phenomenon
through the scratched oval window. Some packing crates
had split and spilled. Tens of thousands of lime-colored
Styrofoam popcorn balls were bounding across the tarmac,
following the drafts of the plane in a dense, dancing pack,
closing in from an angle. Moss thought of a heartless parent
abandoning its young as they futilely clamored after. The
taxi speed increased, sweeping the balls within cover of the
wing. The jet blast began and Moss's fingers marbled. With
a whining, shuddering roar the plane surged forward. The
balls leapt and swirled in violent eddies, spiraled ecstati-
cally into the sky, stripped away by the jets, atomized in
takeoff.

The plane sheered over a sodden, pine-forested plain.
The image assumed a meaning, the fatalism of maternal
love. The end is always separation, children thrown upon
the winds. Suddenly Moss also understood Epstein's buttons and bells and pins, gifts from patients he wore to keep
their spirits up, playing the fool for the dying.

TWELVE

He *was stunned* by the statutory offer of settlement. Junker too, and Wylie, the managing partner, a tax lawyer who couldn't figure litigation but kept a keen interest in the ripening of contingent fees. And Crutchfield, of course. Crutchfield suffered the double cross of favorable developments with judiciously deferred dismay.

The offer arrived the same day as other good news, Basteen's motion to disqualify the judge on grounds of bias from the days when both worked malpractice defense. A decade earlier Basteen had courted and won away Langworthy's meal-ticket client, Kaiser. Before two lean years were out Langworthy had sent the governor his application for the bench and suffered a civil servant's income since.

The motion was a win/win for Moss—if Basteen succeeded he'd be rid of Langworthy; if Basteen were denied the judge would make the big guy suffer. Regardless, Moss meant to keep the September 1994 trial setting. The setting was optimal, time to prepare but not so distant his client might not make it.

It was the offer of settlement, though, that blew him away.

Not its amount, $60,000, insult-level, or the accompanying disparagement of Moss's case, or the tactic. Basteen presented the offer under the costs statute that provided that if not accepted within ten days all defense costs from that point forward would be assessed against the plaintiff and her attorney if she fared more poorly at trial. It was a standard Basteen ploy that forced plaintiff's lawyers to explain to clients the statute's mighty downsides, driving a wedge in their relationship and intimidating fainter hearts, colder feet, or weaker knees than Terry Winter's.

What blew Moss away was Bondurant's having authorized any settlement at all.

The ROMPIC policy allows the holder a veto over settlement of claims. In this, the ROMPIC policy, like all medical malpractice policies, diverges widely from the car-wreck norm where the adjuster calls the shots. Moss had neglected to mention to his partners Bondurant's vow at the time of the Fisher case that he'd never consent to settle a malpractice claim. To Bondurant, settlement implied an admission of professional unworthiness. Never would he authorize a dime.

But Basteen could not have faxed the offer without Bondurant's consent. Moss thought again of the look in his eyes at his office. The timing was also telling, eleven days before his deposition. What did he not want to talk about?

Moss was ethically required to run through with his client the offer and the risks of the statutory costs award if they did worse than sixty grand with a jury. Terry Winter's telephone number, Moss was informed, was disconnected or no longer in service. He called Emmy's school. Mary Eliza had been absent from school. The school was also looking for Mary Eliza. Social services had been informed.

Moss told Lata at the front desk to run him down as soon as Terry called. A few days later she did.

"Hey, what's up?" The brightness seemed a touch forced.

"Where've you been?"

"Friends."

"Where are you living, Terry? I have to know how to reach you."

"Kind of catch as catch can at the moment."

"What's going on?" he demanded. Her vagueness set him on edge.

"I guess you could call it money problems. Husband problems."

Moss remained mystified. It must have registered.

"Slow season for groomers, but wait till those winter coats start to shed."

"Terry?"

"Bank got our mountain place."

"Your house?"

"And I've been a little preoccupied."

"Where are you living?"

"Redemption time came and went and we lost it all, so we had to hit the road, but the mobile dog unit broke down. Tranny. Bank can have her too. Don't tell Basteen."

"Why isn't Emmy in school?"

"That mostly has to do with Warren. I'm a little concerned about Warren. He's a bubble off plumb, if you know what I mean. Not sure where it's headed."

"Are you all right?" There was a strain in her voice.

"Sure. Under the circumstances."

"Circumstances?"

"Adiós la vida cómodo. Adiós la vida."

Moss stared at the receiver. "Why are you speaking Spanish?"

"New me. Air of mystery. I've been feeling in a Mexico mood."

"Look, Terry. There are things we need to talk about. You need to come in. It's important to check in regularly."

"That's sweet."

"Terry." His frustration was genuine. "This is *important*. What's your address?"

"It's kind of complicated," she said. "I'm not alone." She was at Safehouse, an emergency shelter for women, she didn't know for how long.

"So. You're homeless," Moss said stupidly.

"That's us. Lost the ranch. Lost the dog unit. Freedom's just another word . . ."

Singing over the telephone made Moss squirm.

"A Christmas-time tearjerker, I want to tell you, and it's gotten worse since. Warren's been bullshitting the school and the county too. Caseworker's talking about foster care."

"Terry?" The phone had gone seemingly dead.

"I was thinking you might represent me? Us? Her? Something."

"That's kind of outside the contract."

"We'll watch it a while."

"Sure."

"Monitor the situation."

"Right." Moss groaned. He blew through his teeth. With the gusto of a back patient getting out of bed he grudgingly committed. "Terry, listen, nobody's taking your daughter away from you. I'll make sure of that."

"You are my lawyer."

"So it seems."

"I respect that."

"Well, back to the case."

"I don't want things to just happen to me anymore," she said earnestly. It appeared he'd lifted her spirits. "I don't want just to go with it. I want to *surf the flow*. You know what I mean?"

"Surf the flow?"

"There are lessons in experience."

"You bet."

"You got to gut up and get on."

"Terry. Bondurant wants to settle."

"Settle what?"

"Your case. He will pay you money if you dismiss your lawsuit against him."

It was a formulation that apparently had not occurred to her. "Is that good news?"

Moss explained the offer, the sixty thousand, the requirement of confidentiality, that the ball was in their court, he needed to respond, and quickly. He gave her the rap about the statute and potential defense costs award. "What do I tell him?"

"You're the lawyer."

"I can't make this call. Ethical rule. I make recommendations only. You have to decide. It needs to be an informed decision, so I explain the facts and the tactics, give you my opinion, and you tell me what to do."

"*I* tell *you* what to do?"

"I advise. You decide."

"You are shitting me." There was a period of contemplation that made Moss a little nervous. "You do all this work for which I'm paying nothing and I still call the shots?"

"Some shots. The big ones. I shit you not."

"Wow."

"But I'm not working for free, Terry. Payday comes at settlement time. One third plus costs are reimbursed, which would leave you barely half of this, maybe thirty-five thousand. So you need to reject it. It's an opener. There's much more money there."

"O.K. Tell him to stick it."

"How about a counter?"

"I don't know. What do you think?"

"Something big, round, and fat."

"Tell him I'll walk away for a cool million. Hear that, girls?"

"My recommendation exactly."

"And tell him nothing's confidential."

Moss hesitated. Confidentiality was invariably a condition of a med mal settlement, but he might use secrecy as a bargaining chip. Bondurant would not have forgotten the media coverage of the Jessie Fisher trial. In his faxed response Moss put confidentiality in play.

THIRTEEN

P*eter?" Lata was* ringing. "We have an awkward situation. Downstairs." There was an accelerated clip to her Oxbridge locution, something between impatience and hysteria. "A gentleman would like to see you."

"Friend or foe?"

"He's having a bad day," she whispered.

"Name?"

"Watch out. He's coming up."

The man immediately was at Moss's office. He let himself in and closed the door. He stood a mini-cassette recorder on the desk and punched Record. "O.K., shyster," he said. "Where is she?"

"Who the hell are you?"

"I think you know."

Warren Winter had a pricked blond ponytail and a pharmaceutically enhanced vulpine look. Leather jacket over a tight T-shirt. A lot of Y-time on the free weights. On the T-shirt was a winged skull in a squared-off cap with a bayonet in its teeth and the words DEATH FROM ABOVE.

So they had something in common.

Moss knew the type. The ones who volunteered for tunnels, fragged lieutenants, broke into survival kits for Dex and amyl nitrite. The ones who loved it over there.

"Last time I saw her she wouldn't talk with me. Said, 'Talk to my lawyer.' Here I am."

"Here you are."

Winter had a high-pitched voice you wouldn't want to get caught imitating. He had seemingly unlidded eyes.

"So where is she?"

"Why do you want to see her?"

"She has my kid. She's running up bills. I got a right."

Moss imagined Winter's lidless eyes do a split-second Roger Rabbit whirligig. Something highly lipid-soluble shooting past the blood-brain barrier.

"Caseworker says she took my baby out of school. That's not right. I want my kid. Get the picture?"

Moss said nothing.

"You think I'm stupid?"

"No, I don't think you're stupid." Moss looked him over. "Airborne? Ranger unit?"

Winter evaluated Moss. "You in Nam?"

Moss nodded.

"Let me hear it."

"Americal, one-ninety-sixth. Infantry."

"Pussy outfit."

"Followed by LLRP. Followed by stockade." Let him wonder why. "You?"

"Same as you."

Hell of a note, both of them Lurps. What to make of that? Nothing he could think of.

"I knew Calley," Moss said.

"Yeah?"

"Sawed-off little racist punk."

"I was Calley," Winter said.

A joke, Moss surmised. He smiled.

"That's the difference between you and me. You're a relativist. I'm an absolutist."

"Maybe that's the difference."

"I am a fucking purist." Winter began to chuckle. He clicked off the recorder and put it in a pocket. "You understand I'm married to the bitch. I got a stake in this operation. My esquire tells me I got claims already. Consortium loss."

"You have a lawyer?"

"When your wife won't sleep with you, that's consortium loss, correct?"

"Not in your case."

"Hey, don't get personal on me, snakehead. You sleeping with her now?" He winked, eyelid after all.

Moss accosted Emmy when they showed up a week later. "You should be in school. What are you doing here?" He turned to Terry. "What the hell is going on?"

"You've seen Warren." Her button read BAN BLOOD-SPORT.

Moss shook his head. He was dumbfounded. "Why *him*?"

She shrugged. "I'm a fool for a pretty face." She touched Emmy's shoulder. "Where she got her good looks. Her good sense she got from me."

"Yeah, right." Winter's beautiful daughter twisted away and plumped an armload of books and notes on the teak table. She wore a Pearl Jam sweatshirt, a colorful silkscreen of a sad marionette.

Moss shook his head again. *"Why?"*

"Warren used to be a somewhat well-heeled guy," Terry said. "Ran into a little trouble, developed some habits. Put a few holes in his screen door, if you follow."

Moss wasn't sure he did.

"To answer your question, I pretended who he was. I made him up. He could do anything. He could ride the rough string." She turned to Emmy. "See the mistake, making somebody up? The real one comes around in the end."

"I know." Emmy frowned like the sad marionette.

"What do you know?"

"I know he will. I see the future," Emmy said, glum and matter-of-fact. "I wish I was never born."

"Oh, brother." Terry glanced knowingly at Moss—see what I have to deal with?

What Moss saw, he thought, was a subtle shift in mother/daughter relations. "Terry, help me. What's this guy after?"

She opened her hands. "Story of my life. Men not the high points. I said that already." She told Emmy it had come time to wait in the reception area again. Emmy gave a what-a-dork roll of the eyes and stomped out, hugging her books against her sweatshirt.

"So what's Warren's story?"

"Small businessman of a sort."

"Business?"

"Firearms, primarily."

"Don't tell me. Antiques, right? Black powder muskets."

"I don't think so. Tec-9's, Glocks, Grizzly Windmags, Kalashnikovs. Like that."

"Jesus." Moss could forgive a vet a fondness for guns and drugs, but it looked like Warren was over the top. He pondered the magnitude of the risks. It must have showed.

"Get a grip," she told him. "You're my lawyer."

"So far."

"You can't quit on me."

"Watch."

"We need you."

Her earnestness took him aback. "I can handle Warren," he said. "I think."

"Maybe he pays Mr. Basteen a call?"

"Not like that." The time had come to spin worst-case scenarios. Terry needed to face the fact that her cancer could recur and she might die. Sooner, not later. There were no adjudicated limits on Warren's parental rights. She dies and he gets Emmy. She dies before trial and he also gets the case. It becomes a wrongful death claim worth a fraction of her claims while alive. A surviving spouse has rights prior to a daughter's. Warren Winter would become the client.

Moss allowed he didn't want Warren Winter to become his client.

"You have to divorce this guy. Now. Right now. You have to plan for a guardianship for Emmy. You have to sever this guy from your life." He gave her names and numbers at legal services.

She nodded dutifully. "I'll get right on it, sir."

They didn't speak again until Moss chased her down at Safehouse to show her Basteen's next fax. It arrived the day before Bondurant's deposition, surprisingly gracious, complimenting Terry on her deposition performance, expressing sympathy about her illness, and upping the offer under the cost award statute to $400,000 if she would settle her claims in confidence. The amount and terms were nonnegotiable. The offer would expire the following day.

This was way wrong. Way weird. Way too early. Experts hadn't even been disclosed. It was too damn much money, too damn soon. It shook Crutchfield's core belief structures. It loosed from Junker a run of high-five, kick-ass sports metaphors. It sent Wylie to his Lotus 1-2-3.

Moss told Terry this was a deal she had to think about real hard.

"I'm the one's got to pull the trigger, right?"

"Right."

"Supposed to be like you said, informed?"

"An informed decision. Ask me anything you need to know."

"I can't believe this falls on me."

"Well. I want to help."

"What do you think?"

"I think four hundred thousand dollars is a very substantial offer. The threat to withdraw it tomorrow may be serious. These are hard cases to win. Your share of four hundred thousand would cover your income and housing problems and leave a substantial trust for Emmy. I can set it up so Warren can't touch it. We could counter and call their bluff. You could just accept the offer. Either would be an entirely reasonable decision."

"This doesn't really make sense to me," she said. She

flashed her fingers. "Moves too fast." She put her left hand in her jeans pocket, looking more confused than pleased. "What's wrong with this picture? Something's wrong."

"What can I say?" It was true. It did not feel right at all. It made him itchy for Bondurant's deposition. But he couldn't recommend against settlement, not with her needs.

"The money means nothing to me personally, you understand."

Moss nodded. He was starting to understand. She sought neither money nor vengeance, the common motivators. She sought knowledge. She wanted to assign meaning, and she wanted to invest her daughter with strength. Not the purposes lawsuits were designed for.

"Don't get me wrong. It would be nice for Emmy. But money's only money, right?"

"Squeezing insurance companies, that is my job."

Moss tried to say this without irony. He had an ethical duty to settle disputes to his client's best advantage. Best advantage means most money. The client's material interest has to remain paramount whether or not truth and justice shake out in the process. Still, duty aside, like every other lawyer on earth what Moss truly longed for was the rare, sweet convergence of truth and justice and victory.

But what he said was, "Money's everything to me, so let's talk money." Crude self-deprecation to get the client's attention. It only made her feisty.

"Money's nothing next to learning how to live your life," she said. "And what's supposed to be secret? Why should anything be secret about the lives we've led?"

"It's a thing with doctors. It's a big deal. It's standard in settlements."

"What's he want secret?"

"Everything."

"Everything what?"

"Everything about the case, about you, about him, all the facts as well as the settlement."

"Well, I guess I got to think that's bullshit."

"Standard bullshit."

"Then what's the point? He did harm us. He *damaged* us. From what you tell me he did wrong."

"The point is compensation for those damages. This isn't journalism, Terry. This is money damages. We're not in church either. Sorry." Moss in fact believed in the idea of compensation, not as in pay through the nose, but in the sense of moral balance. Restitution and retribution. Although in practice the moral dimension tended to get lost. Moss would find himself instead just managing a minor transfer of wealth nobody but the litigants cared about.

"My job," he said, "is not to prove to the world that he's bad and you're good. My job is to make him responsible for the harm he caused you."

"No hush money. There's a principle involved."

"Sometimes you have to put aside your principles and do the right thing."

"Sometimes lawyers aren't as funny as they think."

"It's a fact of life, Terry. A malpractice case has to settle in secret."

Moss patiently explained that doctors insisted on confidential settlements because of the impact on professional reputations. Bondurant would be especially sensitive. ROMPIC as a matter of policy demanded confidentiality without exception. He was going to be trying the case if she didn't agree to this term.

"Sorry, Peter," she said. "I think you need to try it."

Junker was pissed, Wylie furious, Crutchfield comforted the world was as it seemed. Wylie had already calculated the early-settlement premium off bookkeeping's computer memoranda. At 108 lawyer hours a $133K fee brought a return of $1,234 per hour worked. What they lived for, a true piece of good work, booted away. He gnashed and fumed like Wile E. Coyote, as he was known behind his back.

Easy money, Moss replied, is not the same as good work.

"Easy money's the best kind, Moss. Hard money I have problems with."

Moss was dismissive. "You should try a contingent fee

some time, Neil. Walk a mile in your client's moccasins. Do you good. Put a little more, you know, adventure in the old practice."

Wylie's expression advised him he did not practice for the adventure of it. How many times had he apologized for his partners' cases to other boardmembers at the bank, the Mountain States Legal Foundation, the Council on Commerce and Industry? He'd stopped trying to defend them. They were indefensible except when they paid.

Junker informed Moss he'd employed the strategic brilliance of Saddam Hussein. "What derring-do have we here, amigo? You God? Can God create a rock He can't lift? Have you?"

"I'm building this thing, Junker. Wait and see. This is just starting to get hot."

"Get your goddamn client in line."

"She needs to digest this stuff. She'll come around."

"*Bring* her around. Play the kid card hard, what she can do for her kid."

Moss nodded. That would take some diplomacy.

Wylie reminded Moss of his duties to the firm exchequer. "I'll be watching this one, Moss. Like a hawk."

Junker smiled in a fatherly way. "I control the purse strings, Peter. Keep me happy."

"Guys. I'll do what I can."

Truth to tell, Moss was well past exasperation at his client's mulishness. Now he'd get a chance to lock eyes with Bondurant again, to try to chase out some answers before another case was shoveled over.

FOURTEEN

F*ew white-shoe firms* soil their spats with garden-variety insurance defense. Carriers cheapskate their trial work, restlessly shopping bottom-dollar fees. There's no good way to get rich except by padding time, double billing, overstaffing, and churning files. Such practices contribute not only to the deteriorating repute of the profession but to the defense lawyer's anxiety: The carrier will tumble and you'll be canned.

But you could get rich defending doctors. Malpractice defense baited in the silk-stockinged boys down in the capital city. Physician-owned insurance companies were the most generous. When it comes to lawyers, doctors pay what's asked and demand the best. Lawyers are that way about doctors too.

Basteen, and Judge Langworthy as well, were grown from this culture. In Boulder there were no defense firms. Plaintiffs' lawyers proliferated instead, like graduate students, coffee bars, and alternative FM.

Moss was shown down the mahogany-paneled Edwardian hall of Basteen's offices high above the capital. Irene, Moss's longtime court reporter, followed after him, hobbled with her gear. Through a glass wall Bondurant could be seen sitting pensively in a golfer's cardigan at the far end of a long table. Heinz, the top adjuster from ROMPIC, sat a few chairs to Bondurant's right. Basteen stood at parade rest in front of a forty-foot view. From Seventeeth Street four hundred feet below to the foothills encrusted in the distance with coralline subdivisions, the city rolled away toward the range. The range rose from the smog like a shore from the sea, fourteen-thousand-foot peaks finally striking blue sky on stage right and stage left.

Basteen motioned to his guests; he offered them chairs. "Hey, Jerome," Irene said. "You looking good." Basteen smiled uncomfortably. He inquired after Terry. Terry had declined to come. A lot was going on in her life. No one spoke of the settlement offer, now expired.

Many times Moss had tunneled through the smogbanks toward the shirtboard-gray skyline to examine a doctor at a Seventeeth Street defense firm. He'd never seen Heinz sitting in on a deposition before, but he'd heard tales.

Heinz remained motionless. He said nothing. Heinz did and said almost nothing ever, a trait for which he was celebrated. By his very brevity of word and deed he was known to still a roomful of garrulous poseurs, bring prima donna plaintiff's lawyers at settlement conferences truckling to heel. He could convey contempt simply by being alive.

Heinz adjusted the big ones for ROMPIC. Uncompromising burr cut notwithstanding, he did not have necessarily commanding features—grayish pock-marked skin, black-rimmed glasses so thick they magnified and deflected his gaze like a diver's mask. The effect was a disconcerting combination of indifference and huge-eyed hostility, as though he found the subject of his scrutiny both boring and despicable. Without lifting a finger or making a sound, Heinz gave the impression of toying with one, of cruel play.

"Ready, Doctor?" Moss drew a vertical line down the front of his legal pad.

"You bet." Bondurant stood to remove his sweater and hitch his pants, display pager clipped to his waist. He faced

Irene and raised his palm. Moss valued Irene as much for character judgments as her technical skills in court reporting. An old hand from Basteen's long-ago neighborhood in Five Points, she'd been swearing scoundrels to tell the truth for over thirty years. Despite Basteen's adornments, the silk and gold, *JB* monograms, handkerchief fountaining from breast pocket, he was just another homeboy to her.

Moss began with a little background. He worked down the curriculum vitae, Bondurant's journal subscriptions, civic and LDS church activities—the Family Learning Center, the Attention Home for runaways. A little bio, his three grown daughters, Caroline, Gennifer, and Rose, the prior claims against him, the medical society posts and presidency.

"Your board certification," Moss asked. "It's lapsed, correct?" A weak spot he wanted to probe without ado.

"That's right. Not needed."

"Does a family practice board certification have a value in the marketplace?"

"If you're starting out, sure. Want an HMO gatekeeper practice, you may have to recertify."

"Can a family physician be recertified without examination?"

"Meet their experience criteria, you can."

"What do you have to show?"

"Certain number of patients, certain number of years, certain range of demographic categories."

"Some patients, then, you might want to hang on to if you wanted recertification."

"Hey, call me old-fashioned." He threw up his hands. "Corporate medicine's not going to dictate my patient profile, Peter, if that's what you're driving at. The Wellness Clinic's doing just fine."

Moss favored a nonlinear, digressive inquisition, wandering and circling back, tarrying for what approached moments of revery, but he was not beyond chiropractic manipulations of a witness's points of tension. He let lines of inquiry drift to subcortical depths. He played instinctual rather than logical games of give-and-take. Like a jacamar in the cloud forest, truth could burst in view when least expected.

Moss handed the defendant a document marked by Irene as deposition Exhibit 1.

"Recognize this, Doctor?"

"I can read it, Peter, and see what it is. I don't recall having seen it before."

"What is it?"

"ROMPIC Risk Management Guideline 113, adopted as Flatirons Community Hospital's Breast Carcinoma Protocol."

"At what hospital do you have staff privileges?"

"Community. Courtesy staff at Methodist."

"So you practice under the Exhibit One protocol?"

"After a fashion."

"What does Exhibit One recommend?"

"Well, this is what we call an algorithm, Peter, a kind of decision tree, if you will. If clinical examinations confirm a suspicious breast mass that persists as long as six weeks, fine needle aspiration is recommended by this document. If the results on needle biopsy are equivocal, excisional biopsy is then suggested."

Moss retrieved the flyer. The patronizing Peter shtick was starting to wear thin. "Do you endorse Exhibit One as setting forth the applicable minimum standard of care for differential diagnosis of breast lesions as of 1989?"

"Peter, you need to understand that I don't practice corporate medicine."

"How is that?"

"I am no one's employee. I don't take orders from a hospital administrator or a managed care plan. I don't practice medicine according to what an insurance adjuster tells me."

Heinz was unmoved.

"Are you saying no standards apply to the differential diagnosis of breast carcinoma?"

"Of course not, Peter." Bondurant became earnest. He

looked steadily at his questioner, eyes blunt as nailheads. "Let me tell you where I'm coming from. I think of myself as a patient advocate. I exercise clinical judgment in the best interests of my patient in light of her complete clinical setting. Guidelines are fine but they don't tell you how to practice medicine. You don't follow a recipe to make a medical diagnosis. You don't practice medicine according to a cookbook."

How many times had Moss heard that one?

"Wouldn't you agree, Doctor, that if a suspicious breast lesion persists six weeks definitive diagnostic procedures should be undertaken?"

"That's a hypothetical question, Peter."

"Not really, Wallace," Moss said. "I'm just interested in your standards." He got up and poured a cup of coffee from the Krups console while Bondurant calculated a response. The witness had acquired a kind of crude élan, a long way from the answering machine death threats and cut-and-paste hate mail Sally suspected him of, though his oily familiarity made the skin crawl.

"I practice in the real world," Bondurant at length replied. "I'm interested in health as well as disease. Wellness rather than illness. That's my focus. When someone walks in my office I don't see *disease* to differentially diagnose. I see a *patient*. How about you, Moss? When a person walks in your office what do you see?"

Moss took the doctor's measure. The doctor held his eye.

"Do you see a *case*? Or do you see a *client*? Is all you see a fee, a way to get money out of somebody? Or do you see a human being who needs your help?"

"Let's break," Moss said, their eyes still joined. Bondurant smiled and stretched. He helped himself to a Coke.

"You got trouble," Irene told Moss on the break. She was snitching a Parliament down a felted corridor past the ladies' john. She tamped a chunk of ash in the water fountain. "White folks might buy this man."

FIFTEEN

The senior litigator in Moss's firm hung it up early a few years back. A recovering lawyer, he still met Moss for lunch, Tennessee-burgers at Fred's, the last honest cafe on the toney downtown mall. Talk would turn to the sorry state of the practice. To TV advertising, 1-800-4-DINERO, tort reform dismantling the elegance of the common law, the hardball tactics, the mendacity, the demise of collegial professionalism. Until the seventies the firm operated as it had for a hundred years. No one tallied time. Saturdays partners met to figure out fees for the past week's work. Files were kept according to client. One name might have thirty subfiles spanning fifty years—a home purchase, a business capitalization, a personal injury, an audit, a water adjudication, a criminal defense, a divorce, a will, probate. A complex human narrative, losses and triumphs and threads of meaning in the accumulating pages of a client file. A life. Now files were kept by case or matter. That is, by lawsuit or deal. As in, *Winter v. Bondurant*, 15217.002. Cost Lim. $30,000. Fee contin. Opp. Coun. Basteen, J.

So Bondurant had struck a nerve.

Bondurant had deflected Moss from the objective to the subjective, from standards to individual human needs. *Go with it*, Moss thought. He asked the doctor about his mother.

Basteen failed to object. Basteen was not well-suited to deposition defense; these weren't his questions; he was not in control. Aggressor by nature, as protector Basteen sat uneasy. He could be seen dreaming off, giving his nails a ladylike inspection.

His mother, Bondurant acknowledged, succumbed to breast cancer five years ago. Although the tumor was small it recurred within two years.

Was he there for her last months?

"Actually no."

"Objection." Basteen woke up. "Not calculated to lead to the introduction of admissible evidence."

"Where were you?" Moss asked Bondurant.

"Instruct not to answer," Basteen snapped.

"How did your mother's death from breast cancer affect how you followed your own patients?"

"Not at all." Bondurant's eyes were on the Front Range blanching in the rising light.

"How did you change your algorithm?"

"No change."

"It remained as set forth in Exhibit One?"

"Yes."

"Does Exhibit One in your opinion continue to set forth the applicable minimum standard for differential diagnosis of breast cancer?"

"Yes. Yes. But there's more to it."

The defendant had just endorsed the plaintiff's proposed standard of care. "What more is there to it? What *other* considerations could keep you following a patient with a suspicious lump without doing anything about it? For *years*?"

There again it possibly was. A glint of the inscrutable fear.

"Dr. Bondurant?"

"I need a break." Heinz had spoken. Speech, from Heinz, had a seismic quality. Like Mount Pinatubo, the atmospheric effects were lasting. Even Irene lost her bearings. Her fingers fluttered up from the keys of her machine and settled on her cheeks.

"First an answer to the pending question."

Heinz stood. The building seemed to sway.

"Dr. Bondurant?"

"I didn't cause her cancer, for Christ's sake. What's the question?"

"The definitive diagnostic procedures to which one must proceed after following a lump a maximum of six weeks are needle biopsy, or ultrasound, then lumpectomy. Correct?"

"Yes."

"What is the purpose of following a breast lump in this manner?"

"To catch the disease early."

"Why does that matter?"

"*Hey*," Heinz said, a drill sergeant mustering recruits.

"Why do you think? The earlier it's diagnosed the greater the chance of cure."

Unexpectedly the truth burst into view. Moss was getting confirmation not only of the standard of care but of causation, that delayed diagnosis reduced chances of survival. Would Bondurant next blurt out a confession that he'd blown Terry Winter's cancer and her hope to survive it? He glanced Basteen's way. Basteen failed to look crestfallen. In fact, a lip was rising, fang starting to show.

"Hey," Heinz repeated.

They broke.

As Moss saw it, he had two potentially profitable approaches. Hit the man hard enough to jar loose some basic assumptions, or give him enough rope. It was time to play it out.

What had the doctor found on examination of Terry Winter? Why was her lump ignored? Why was it never biopsied? "Couldn't you have proceeded to biopsy," Moss asked, "in 1989 or even before?"

"Sure I could have biopsied this woman. I could biopsy every gal who comes in with lumpy breasts." After the towelings in his corner Bondurant was jaunty self-confidence again. "But that's what's called defensive medicine. That's what's wrecking this country."

National security comes into play? "Wrecking the country? How's that?"

"No offense, Moss, but when we start looking at every patient as a potential lawsuit, when I biopsy a girl just because I don't want you in my waiting room with a summons, we as a people have lost our moral bearings."

You get sued and society has lost its moral bearings? "What was Terry Winter's diagnosis in 1989?"

"You need to understand. Terry Winter, Mary Eliza Winter, these were my patients. Patients are people, people with problems. My approach is, I try my damnedest to help people deal with their problems."

Bondurant was mastering the arts of casuistry. Winning a medical deposition depended on whose definitions prevailed. He was not exactly smooth and too confrontational, but this faintly wounded manner could be dangerous. There was an implied rhetorical complaint behind the heartfelt evasions, the dissimulations of reasonable concerns. Who is the real victim? Isn't it the caring physician who did his best but still gets sued for a million bucks? Whose career and reputation are on the line?

"Did you help Terry Winter deal with her problems by waiting to refer her for biopsy until she had a breast tumor the size of a lemon?"

Bondurant manufactured a thoughtful pause. Basteen remained opaque. Moss felt Heinz's skewed gaze tracking him, like the eyes of El Greco's Grand Inquisitor when Moss had crossed the gallery of the Prado.

"This woman was impossible to examine. She had extremely dense, lumpy breasts. You can't tell what's going on in breast tissue like that. You look to your mammograms, and they were negative. I never found *a* lump, I found lumpiness, everywhere. She didn't either. She'd think there was some change, but couldn't say where, and then say it had gone away. I'd locate what might feel like something one time but not the next. It came and went with menstruation. It behaved like cysts behave, very regular, tender, mobile, smooth." He had just ticked off every hand-written interlineation on the November 12, 1989, page of the chart.

"But even if seemingly cystic," Moss asked, "if an abnormal-feeling area persisted why not needle it?" It was so easy.

"Because it didn't. It went away. You can't stick a needle in something that's not there."

"If a cyst, lump, whatever, you found on one visit had still been there in the same place on the next, what would you have done?"

"Object to the form."

"That never happened."

"What would you have done if it had?"

"Objection."

"What I always do."

"Which is?"

"Object."

"Measure it, diagram it, describe objective signs. Needle it. Take it from there."

"According to the Exhibit One protocol?"

"If you want to put it that way. Point is, that never happened."

"How do you know?"

Bondurant let out a how-dumb-do-you-think-I-am? chuckle. "I can read. I can remember."

"Read what?"

Bondurant looked doubtfully at Basteen. Where'd they get this ying-yang? He settled a watery glare on Moss. He expelled a tactical sigh. "SOAPnotes, histories. Counselor, you've seen this girl's chart. All there are are scattered references to a cyst that came and went. Rubbery little fellow. Here today, gone tomorrow."

Moss asked about the chart, the interlineations, redactions, the scribble, the different-colored inks. Bondurant confessed to mumbling at times. His front-office girl Patti does her best typing but syllables get dropped, words run on. He goes back and corrects by hand. "All my charts look that way."

"When is the editing done?"

"Same day. Never later than following day. Chart needs to be accurate. Chart needs to be current."

"Chart shows *she* was concerned about a lump. She even sent you notes."

"Yes, she was. That's why I referred her to Dr. Mayhew."

Moss braced, nausea rising at the coming falsehoods, lawyer-scripted and video-rehearsed.

"I gave her Dr. Mayhew's name and number. Although I never found a lump, she was concerned, so I called Bob and asked if he would see her as a favor to me."

"None of which you charted."

"Phone calls I don't usually chart. It was her responsibility to follow up. Bob tells me she never did."

"You've talked with Dr. Mayhew?"

"Oh yes."

Moss rested his eyes. He shook his head and opened them.

"You and Dr. Mayhew have any economic ties?"

"Economic? No. We're on a couple of boards."

"Like?"

"Legislation task force. Junius Foundation."

"What's that?"

"Physician-owned capitated health care is the concept."

"Whatever that means."

"Yeah. Whatever that means."

"You and Dr. Mayhew going into business?"

"No, no. Med society project, down the road. What's this got to do with anything?"

"Your referral of Ms. Winter to Dr. Mayhew. I suppose he has no record of it in his chart either?"

"How could he? She never made the appointment."

"But he remembers an undocumented telephone call from you three years ago?"

Bondurant cleared his throat with a tight smile. "He recalls our conversation well."

"As do you."

"Vividly."

"Is this like a recovered memory?"

"A what?"

"You know, like incest victims. Blocked memories of sex abuse your therapist brings to the surface. Or your lawyer."

"Whose therapist? What the hell is he talking about?" Bondurant's élan turned ugly. "I'm a physician. I don't have to take this crap."

"I don't care," Moss said evenly, "if you're the Grand Dragon of the Ku Klux Klan."

Basteen was on his feet jabbing his finger and jabbering about grievances.

"Hold it, brother." Irene spoke. Basteen stopped. Heinz took note. "Can't have you both going at once."

"Forget it, Doctor," Moss said wearily. It was depressingly predictable—the phantom phone call, the noncompliant patient, the patient's to blame for her disease. The odor of false testimony pervaded the room. It clung to Moss's professional dress like cigarette smoke.

"Tell me," he said. "Did you and she have a good relationship?"

"She?" Bondurant asked distractedly.

"Your patient."

"Oh, I see what you mean. I thought so. I thought so." He reengaged. "And that's the tragedy, Moss." He contrived an expression of sincere concern. "I thought she was a compliant patient. But why didn't this girl go on to Dr. Mayhew? You know, he might have found her cancer. That's his specialty, general surgery, breast biopsy. I like this girl, and Mary Eliza, her little daughter, what a charmer. They were like family. That's how I practice, like patients are family. It's really too bad. It's tragic, but she was terribly irresponsible."

At the next break Basteen lingered at the coffee console as Moss blearily approached.

"No surprises there," Moss commented.

Basteen smirked.

"Run-of-the-mill doctor perjury, suborned by counsel."

Basteen winked.

SIXTEEN

Langworthy *enjoyed putting* lawyers out. The 7:00 A.M. status conference was a favorite discipline. Moss busted a knuckle de-icing the windshield in the dark and motored east toward court. In the cold gloom of the car he suffered a moment of doubt. Bondurant was almost certainly lying but he could still be essentially right. Maybe Terry had been as vague and difficult with her doctor as she could be with her lawyer. Maybe she'd minimized the worry hardening inside her because she couldn't face it. With no gift for subtlety, Bondurant then failed to detect her denial. Or could it be something even worse for the case—some need *Terry* had to keep returning to Bondurant? And what needs were driving Moss? Was he waging a vendetta to avenge his defeat?

The moment passed. Vendettas are the price of a profession's reluctance to police itself. And there was the Jessie Fisher case, the callous perjury, the stupid loss of life. To hell with doubt.

Moss's breath bloomed on the glass. He scribbled a dashboard note to order Bondurant's public records—civil, criminal, real estate, corporate. What the hell, dom rel, traffic, and auto registration. And to check into the Junius Foundation. There's always something, as Willy Stark told

Jack Burden, if you dig deep enough and string it together right.

His destination, the notoriously ugly, livid green, circular courthouse, graced not Boulder but Sand Creek, the blue-collar hub of east Flatirons County. In Boulder latte bars outnumbered ATMs and all the cars were foreign. Nubile young women were disconcertingly abundant. Athleticism was a defining spiritual concern. Sand Creek produced a different sort of juror—Hispanics, bikers, turkey processors, and the hardy holdouts still digging beets and cursing the government that propped up their sugar prices while their land was lost to development and the laws of descent and distribution. Looking west toward Boulder and the Front Range, the farmers saw a land of Oz, wild with liberal academics, yuppie professionals, mountain hippies, and death-rouged anarchist youth. When it came time to empanel citizens to mete out justice in the round Moss would challenge for west and Boulder while Basteen would shoot for beetdiggers from Sand Creek. Flatirons County had the highest hung-jury rate in the state.

Through an irregular oval Moss watched a breaking dawn silhouette Butler silos and Harvestors and many-fingered cottonwoods following draws. A horse, a goat, and a dog stood together at a dooryard still as a crèche. He passed a boarded-over landmark on the outskirts of Sand Creek. Simon Warp's Pioneer Village, "Showing Man's Progress Since 1855." Magpies on mullein stalks, convict-colored, beaks apart, faced the wind like weathercocks. A crew of box makers took a smoke break at the loading dock of Golden Poultry.

Moss rolled through the silent town following the tracks and the trailer courts. Sand Creek was the heartland. The heartland had discovered salad bars. Jake's Cafe and 24-Hour Salad Bar was bright and lively. Then there the courthouse stood, capping an ice-glazed shelf above the black Platte, the yucca-studded plains glowing coldly beyond, like a huge green Warhol tunafish can.

Above the basement jail, above the ground-level municipal courts, and the next circle, the county courts, and the highest circle of the district courts, were the chambers Judge Langworthy affected to call his robing room, to which the lawyers were escorted by a muscle-bound bailiff.

The judge appraised them in different ways. The look he shot Basteen in his two-thousand-dollar Brioni suit, red silk erupting from breast pocket, was floridly envious. Of Moss Langworthy seemed indifferent. He settled into a studded leather chair at the head of the glass-topped walnut table.

Langworthy had a compact stature, shadowed jaw, de-curved posture, and gabled jut of mustache and brow that recalled G. Gordon Liddy, or one of Kipling's gentlemen rankers. He was born to be uniformed. He wore the robe like evening clothes.

Langworthy's chambers were carefully appointed. A crossed West Point sword and scabbard hung from the wall behind him. A triangle-folded flag was positioned on a console between an eagle figurine and a mounted artillery shell. The bare gleaming table invited no disorderly briefs and pads, the straight chairs no slouching. A Judge Advocate General commission competed with a Michigan law diploma and the governor's certificate of appointment to the bench. Langworthy could be seen in snapshots skiing with children and a wife. Wall art ran to war and cowboy themes, the trail ride, the branding, the round-up, the Battle of Malvern Hill. The severity of walnut, leather, glass-cased shelves, was relieved here and there by a humorous touch, a Gonzo muppet in a barrister's wig. A robed Smurf.

Moss contemplated the sword. Langworthy had spent his tour in court-martials, not combat, prosecuting people like him.

A stack of motions had been piling up. Langworthy informed the lawyers he meant to cut through them in one hearing like a grizzly tearing into a salmon run. This was a judge who, alone with lawyers in chambers, could lash out unpredictably. He had good days and bad days and Moss liked neither. Good days were characterized by cunning, bad days by ire.

Ire, this status conference, turned out to be the portion of Basteen.

"So, gentlemen. We've got a med mal trial." The judge rubbed his hands energetically. "I love a med mal trial. Explain for me, Mr. Basteen, why I am incapable of presiding over a med mal trial fair to your client."

"I would not suggest that, Your Honor." Groveling disoriented Basteen. His cognitive dissonance surfaced; the facial twitch returned. "It is simply that with your and my history of zealous competition a division transfer may be in everyone's interest."

"Your position, Mr. Moss?"

"I completely disagree."

"Basteen wants to bump the trial date, doesn't he?" The judge shot a cock-eyed grin at Moss. "Basteen's hoping your client dies before trial. Do you realize that?"

Moss didn't know what to say.

"Mr. Basteen, for the sake of argument, assume I've got a stinger out for you. You have no basis to argue I would let that harm your client."

"I am concerned, Your Honor."

"Every litigant gets a fair trial in my court. Fair trial does not mean being nice to lawyers. Motion to recuse denied."

Langworthy retained from private practice an adversarial style, but his adversaries now were his former colleagues. Taking no further argument he abruptly announced the rest of his decisions. Each was plausible by its terms, though where discretion was available it was exercised to the hilt, punitively, against one side, then the other. Thus was justice blind.

Moss's motion for production of the ROMPIC policy rider by which policyholder physicians were fined $25,000 for testifying in a malpractice case against another policyholder was denied. ROMPIC was not a party, Judge Langworthy opined. Moss's motion amounted to an allegation of criminal obstruction of justice, defamatory in any other forum. Any mention of ROMPIC in the jury's presence would earn an automatic mistrial.

Basteen's motion for a continuance of trial was summarily denied.

Moss's motion for a documents examination of the original November 12, 1989, entry in Bondurant's chart was granted. While the exam would entail destructive testing, Basteen and his expert could be present. The examined documents should be reproduced before and after testing, and the examination videotaped.

Moss's motion for discovery of Bondurant's board of medical examiners file was denied. A fishing expedition, the judge concluded, unless and until Moss could show cause under *Martinelli v. District Court* why the narrow discovery needs of his case should overcome Dr. Bondurant's presumptive privacy interests.

Last, and provoking a little joke as the conference was concluding, was Basteen's motion for redeposition of the plaintiff. In light of the Affidavit of Dr. Angelika Franzblau, the judge ordered Ms. Winter to sit for resumed deposition and respond to Mr. Basteen's questions regarding terminations of pregnancies, sexual activity during and post-puberty, and birth control history.

"Now I understand your defense, Mr. Basteen." The judge gave Moss a familiar leer. "Safe sex prevents breast cancer."

Some light tittering was obligatory. The judicial humorist, he's surely on the list.

SEVENTEEN

From *leather chairs,* beneath the frowning aspect of early jurists and firm founders, a glaring gallery of dead white guys, Crutchfield's multicultural clientele waited impatiently in braces and casts. Crutchfield was a settler, not a trier, of cases. He trafficked in rear-ends and comp, whiplash and sore backs. He didn't promise the moon, just triple your specials and quick turnaround. He thrived on volume and speed.

Tina did his intakes. A buxom paralegal who couldn't type, Tina was a client pleaser. She had an exciting way with a steno pad, licking the pencil tip ceremoniously, looking up sympathetically while crossing a knee. Willingly would clients hobble up the stairs behind her as she led the way to Crutchfield's office, papered with diplomas and citations. "Hello, hello!" He forced high spirits and fellow feeling. He welcomed them gamely. "Friends call me Crutch."

Learned Hand, Holmes, Jr., John Marshall, Cardozo, the firm's original Gardner Giles continued to disapprove.

Moss had stopped in to ask Crutchfield to cover the Doubler's deposition in L.A. Moss was getting busy and it would save his having to fly. Crutchfield was of two minds about helping out, he said. If Moss was going to score on Bondurant he'd like some of the hours for premium compensation points. But Moss might not score. But the responsibility level was about ankle-high. So what the hell.

"Well?" Moss asked. Tina, in Crutchfield's office when Moss interrupted, crossed her knee. Ankle-high was over her head.

"I vacillate," Crutchfield said. "Therefore I am."

He opened his window that gave on an alley. A draft of ice-laden air sailed through the room. He had switched to Merit Ultra Lights after his second heart attack. To Crutchfield a cigarette was an expression of resignation, his life's theme. He lit one.

"Tell me what to do."

"Depose him. Krishnan Irizarry Singh."

"Jewish guy?"

"We got the book on him. You could do it sleepwalking. I'll take the Angel."

Moss ultimately forewent deposing Dr. Angelika Franzblau, the Carcinoma Angel, as the trial bar knew her. He'd deposed her enough before; her act never varied. Might as well catch her cold at trial and save a little dough by skipping the depo. That should please Junker.

The act entailed the moving story of Dr. Franzblau as a pioneering woman scientist, toughing out med school while raising her children, rising to colonel and chief of the pathology service at Fitzsimons Army Hospital, and there reflecting on her gender's scourge. Breast cancer. For all the screening mammograms, the showerhead placards illustrating self-examination, the earlier and earlier diagnoses of smaller and smaller tumors, still the incidence and the mortality rose. Why? Why would one woman with a tiny tumor recur and die while others with advanced primary cancer live on disease-free for decades? What was medicine missing?

Medicine was infatuated with the clinical. The realm of the clinical would not yield cancer's secrets. The realm of the cellular would.

Late into the night in her home laboratory, Dr. Franzblau paced with her cane, shaking her head of snowy hair, pondering the psychosis of cells. There at length she achieved what no one in medicine had. She decoded breast cancer's rosetta stone.

A noncancerous cell has a fixed eight picograms of DNA. A true malignant cell has either more than that or less. It is therefore unstable and can split away, travel the blood or the lymphatics, alight elsewhere. The worst of them—"bandit cells"—survive, divide, flourish. Some are indestructible. Like Jurassic Park blood in amber, like cockroaches surviving atomic blasts, like Dracula, bad cancer predicates the immortality of evil.

"Bandit cells are mean as the dickens," she'd explain to lawyers, offering foil-wrapped candies around the deposition table. "They're born to kill."

Whether a cancer kills depends on the instability of tumor DNA, a quality the Angel can precisely measure with her flow cytometry machine. She pares off a slice of tumor tissue, isolates ten thousand cells or so, strips down the cell walls, stains the nuclei with fluorescent dye, and runs them through a particle counter keyed to DNA volumes. Terry Winter's findings are regrettable, she was sure to report at trial. Her tumor is aneuploid, with abnormal DNA. Its low S-phase, or percent of cells in mitotic synthesis, shows it was slow growing. It has been there for years, mitosing away, spitting out rogue cells to course the vascular circuits and eventually effloresce in fatal bursts throughout her body.

Dr. Bondurant, she'd inform the jury, was an innocent bystander at a drive-by shooting. There was nothing he could have done. Terry Winter's fate was sealed decades before she had a lump, when the bandits first skulked forth.

What produces such assassins? Normal, hormonally stimulated growth that is either prematurely arrested or artificially enhanced. For example, accelerating the sexual activity of still-pubertal girls. In puberty hormones produce dramatic body-wide changes, especially in breasts. When estrogen-based birth control medications exaggerate this naturally stimulated state, abnormal cells form with super-capabilities to detach and multiply and ultimately kill.

Dr. Franzblau's affidavit therefore had averred to the critical need to question Ms. Winter about sexual activity and birth control measures in her young womanhood. Likewise any abortions. With abortions mammary tissues hypersti-mulated by pregnancy suddenly lose their signal. The hormone-driven process is dammed full-flood. Bandit cells spill out in a lather, geared for growth with nothing now to grow for, wanderers in a dysfunctional system.

Like Crips and Bloods looking for trouble in the dark alleyways of the female body.

No reputable medical study corroborated the Angel's constructs but juries were easily sold. She exalted what many longed to believe: Bad women are punished for their sins.

Crutchfield returned from L.A. predictably morose. "This town," he explained to Moss, "can be tough on dreams."

Dr. Irizarry Singh had sat for deposition in the Beverly Hilton, temporary quarters while rebuilding a house lost in the Malibu fires. He outshone Basteen—gold chain draped on chest hair, gold link bracelet loose at his wrist, no socks, embroidered slippers, brushed eyebrows and a richly scented pomade.

Therapeutic nihilism was Singh's bag—debunking the power to heal. He proselytized against early detection. He sang of the futility of treatment. There are no cures, only palliatives. We may prolong your life but still you sicken and die. Medicine is vanity. He mocked it in defense of doctors, by whom, when sued, he was highly sought.

Crutchfield was quite taken in. "My kind of guy. Tells it like it is."

"Surely you scored some points."

"I made it out of L.A. with my Nikes on."

For cancer misdiagnosis cases, Singh's racket was proving early mestastasis to lymph nodes outside the breast.

Like all closed systems, like talk-show versions of the free market, or David Koresh's theology, it was flawless on its own terms. He calculated a total volume of 5.6 cm^3 of Terry Winter's lymph nodes had been replaced by cancer as of diagnosis, then halved that volume backward in time every 150 days, the average time he assumed it took her carcinoma to double in volume. One cm^3 contains roughly a billion cells. Irrefutably, then, five years before, when Terry's primary tumor was too small to be detectable by Dr. Bondurant or by anyone else clinically, millions of cancer cells had already lodged outside the breast in the nodes. "Your client already was, as you say, history." He twinkled. Metastasis had taken place. There was nothing Bondurant could later do to change things.

"Bottom line?" Moss asked.

"Guy's slicker'n owl shit."

"Beverly Hills gonna fly in Marlboro Country?"

Ever suggestible, Crutchfield opened a window and tapped out a Merit, a passive/aggressive trespass in Moss's smoke-free wing.

"Guy's got facts. Guy's got math. Math don't lie."

"Math lie like a dog." A quantity can be halved an infinite number of times, always with half its previous volume remaining. "He could prove Terry Winter had lymph node metastasis before she was in utero."

"Breast cancer begins at conception? Right-to-lifers could use this guy."

"They do. The Angel too."

"Guy's still got facts."

"Don't be scared of facts. Facts"—it bore repeating—"are your friends." Facts and feelings—fear and pity—were the stuff verdicts were made of.

EIGHTEEN

March 5 and fat flakes were dropping. Eight cottony inches. Macho commuters on cross-country skis. Lights, bells, and a favorite chestnut, sung to "Winter Wonderland."

I'm walking 'round in women's underwear . . .

Moss was feeling a little off-kilter again. His car churned the unplowed drift. He honked at a skier in his lane.

*Lacy things, she's been missing,
Didn't ask . . . her permission.*

He had to trudge in a quarter mile to Moschetti's survivalist outpost in the foothills. Basteen and his expert were to meet them there directly. On our turf, Moss thought, as he passed the warnings posted on the ponderosas, the surveillance cameras in the branches.

Moschetti, formerly Lieutenant Moschetti, welcomed Moss at the doublewide addition to an abandoned silver mill that was his lab. A lot of unusual hardware was to be seen, illuminated in pools by hanging bulbs. Swinging a portable kerosene heater, Moschetti led Moss along narrow passageways made difficult by cables, wires, surge protectors. There were aromatic sinks and beakers. There were stockpiled chemicals the EPA would be interested in. A darkroom with a violet glow. It was a place to watch your step. Keep your hands in your pockets.

"Want to tell me what it is about doctors?" Moschetti was saying, swinging the heater. Moschetti was a little guy, in a bright blue cap with ear covers flapping, and a kind of amazed sidelong grin that gave him an Art Carney doofus look.

Like folks of any walk who spend all their time in labs, Moschetti was a little different, his sensibilities a little rare for lack of human contact. The usual social inhibitions and courtesies were not fully stocked.

He ticked off the medical profession's venial flaws.

"They drive shitty, write illegible, evade taxes, and alter records. They have like courses in this stuff at medical school? How to drive bad? Hey, I'm not complaining. I'm nothing without altered records. That and assignations. The rest is just cop-shop hack work. Forgery. Theft. Nowhere. Me, I live for civil deceit."

"So do I," Moss said. "But I'm nothing without you, buddy."

Moschetti had a habit of nodding forcefully while he spoke, less a positive expression, it seemed, than a neurological sign. He had run the sheriff's crime lab until the commissioners drove him from the force. Media relations were an area that had come in for criticism. Loose lips sink investigations.

They reached the table where Terry Winter's original chart lay spotlit and open to November 12, 1989, the page with the interlineations and the cross-over in the corner, the cross-hatched prisms. The place had a Delphic feel.

"So far, what have you got?"

"On casual observation, I see a lot of pens here. Red, blue, several different blacks, ballpoints all."

"So what?"

He shrugged. "And there's something under this." He tapped the scribble in the corner.

A buzzer rang. Moschetti left Moss with the heater and the chart. Basteen, brooding and seigneurial in double-breasted gray, soggy about the cuffs, followed Moschetti back to Moss. He surveyed the lab with disdain. Behind Basteen was a kid in a ponytail with a camcorder, and a reedy fellow, totally bald, hunched under an oversized overcoat. The kid set up a foil lighting umbrella and tripod.

They exchanged pro forma courtesies. Moss confirmed the game plan. Moschetti was to examine the document, explaining what he was doing as he went so the mike could pick it up. He was not to comment on what he found.

"What's bulbhead doing here?" Moschetti stage-whispered to Moss.

"Judge says Basteen can bring an expert to observe."

"Bulbhead couldn't observe his own fucking signature," Moschetti added, sotto voce fortamente.

He produced a scalpel and several syringes. "Everything's ballpoint, right," he spoke to the camera. "Gonna take some samples for ink analysis. Destructive testing but I got the go-ahead, right?"

Basteen nodded gravely.

"I need it verbal, buddy. For the record."

"Do it," Basteen said.

Moschetti sliced a half-dozen tiny blocks of ink from the edges of the writing, drawing each into a numerically labeled syringe. "Gonna mail these to BATF," Moschetti advised Basteen. He addressed the camera. "Bureau of Alcohol Tobacco and Firearms has an ink lab. Has samples of every pen ink ever made, when it was marketed, ingredients. They'll identify and date each sample. I've got samples here of blue and red, and three kinds of black. Unless this doc used like all Bic pens, we'll get at least like the year each one was brought to market, in what order, like that."

"No commentary," Moss reminded him. "Just tell them what you're doing."

"Gotcha." Moschetti nodded.

"I'll need a set." The reedy fellow had an unexpected baritone.

Moschetti looked at Moss, who assented. "You bet, buddyboy." He located another set of syringes and offered them to the opposing expert, along with his floppy blue hat. "Chilly up there?"

The bulbhead declined.

Basteen affected boredom laced with contempt as Moschetti laboriously photographed each centimeter of the chart page through a stereomicroscope according to a numbered grid. He set the microscopy equipment aside.

"O.K. Now we're gonna pull up the cross-outs. See if they mean anything."

He opened a metal box and removed a stack of white cards. "Finger-printing cards we treat with triazenetrione dehydrate and alcohol. We're gonna press 'em on your boy's page. They'll lift impressions of the topmost layer of ink only, not what's underneath." He positioned numbered cards over the page and rolled them with a cylinder, removed and rearranged them in order, and placed a sticky backing on top. He held it to a mirror and all peered forward. The interlineations to the typed text were clearly legible: "tender" and "comes and goes" written in between lines; delete marks through "non" and "ir." The scribble still looked like a scribble, three prisms and crossed lines.

"So that tells you a whole lot of nothing. Except he scribbled on top of something trying like hell to mark it out."

"No commentary."

"Right, right, right."

"On to the original writing." Moschetti winked at the bulbhead. "The holy fucking writ, as she were. We'll go at her two different ways."

Moschetti led them to something like a photocopier. "Electrostatic detection apparatus, ESDA. One of the few west of the Pecos. This should pull it out by indentations."

The bulbhead had acquired a closer interest.

Moschetti lay a cellophane film over the backside of the

chart page and placed it in a cage on the surface of the machine. He hit a button, explaining, as a bar swept the film and page from top to bottom, that an electric element was laying down a charge. He worked the charged page with a nozzle, lightly spraying carbon particles. He swung a camera in place along a track and took a series of photographs that, when developed, would reveal images of the placement of negative particles that should reproduce the lines of original indentations. No one said a word.

Moschetti removed and discarded the cellophane, vacuumed the page, and took it to another machine, a projector of sorts. The bulbhead whispered something to Basteen. Basteen frowned.

"Down here," Moschetti indicated the scribble, "what the cop cards picked up was rollerball, is my hunch." Moss let him go. "Pentel rollerball. Recent vintage. We'll see. If it's rollerball, it doesn't reflect infrared." Moschetti started to cackle; Moss thought of Ross Perot. "If what we got underneath is older basic ballpoint—and the ESDA indentations sure look like basic ballpoint to me—then we're down to the nutcutting. So here we go."

Moschetti slipped the page under a glass plate on the projector. He lowered a screen and pulled the lightcord. He leaned over the projector, clicked a switch, and was ghoulishly illuminated from below. He spun the focus knob. The white rectangle on the screen consolidated as a picture of the page from the chart.

"We got a series of filters on this, ultraviolet to infrared. We'll pull 'em one by one. What inks don't shine back bit by bit won't show at all."

He slipped a filter out with no effect on the screen, then another. When he removed a third the prisms began to fade. After a fourth, the interlineations were too faint to read. The prisms were gone. The cross-hatching had begun to efface. Parts of lines, invisible before, could begin to be made out. Curving penstrokes excited by the infrared rays.

Moschetti paused with some drama before removing the final filter. "This'll leave us pure infrared, folks." The ponytailed cameraman was wide-eyed in the weird light. "If what we're about to see is the same thing the ESDA indent shots are gonna show, you'll be looking right at it. The revealed Word. The Book of Mormon. The cat's asshole itself. What your dead duck doctor took up his Uniball and drew on this page the very first time he touched it."

Moschetti slowly slid the final filter out. The typed text was rendered clean. The last of the cross-overs entirely evanesced. The scribbling receded like a wave from the shore as the filter edged toward the bottom of the projector field.

"Jesus Lord."

On the lower right of the image of the page, like faces rising from the bottom of a pool, an immediately recognizable drawing was revealed. Two breasts, with a dark oval blotch.

The bulbhead turned on the heel of his galoshes to pack his briefcase. Basteen maintained a poker-faced frown.

"I get it." Moschetti was speaking to Basteen. "Your man a gynecologist?"

Basteen followed out his team without responding.

Ten days later Moschetti reached Moss at his office. "Got the ESDA photos. Got the ink-dating from BATF."

"And?"

"They confirm. Doctor drew pictures on a clean page. Pictures of titties."

"Same diagram?"

"Same two titties. Fucking pervert doodles pictures of titties. This a sex crime? I thought we were civil."

"Did the indentations track the same diagram we saw?"

"Yeah. Very simple. Nipple and tit. One with a mole."

"So that's the first thing he drew?"

"You got it."

"How big is the black oval when you measure the indentations?"

"A very big mole."

"Which breast?"

"Let's see. We photographed the back, so we rephotographed a mirror image to reverse it. And that put it on the right."

"You mean right side of the page?"

"Yeah."

"So left breast, because she's facing you."

"Breasts're facing you. So left breast. Right."

"If it were actual size, the mole, how big would it be, the black mark?"

"Like a nickel."

Two centimeters or so, Moss thought. Perfect. "Same place as the infrared?"

"Yep. Top right. An inch from the nipple."

Supra-areolar. Upper outer quadrant. The exact place Terry testified she felt the lump and the same quadrant where, three years later, the big tumor was found.

"Were the diagram and black mark all in the same ink?"

"You bet. EF Uniball #2603. ATF says they stopped selling it in 1989. The cross-overs weren't done until 1991 or later. All new Pentel models on those, like I thought. Weren't on the market before 1991."

"And the interlineations?"

"All added two years or more after the notes were typed."

"I love you, Bobby."

"Better you don't. Just nail this pervert, whatever he did."

Moss hung up, kicked back and smiled. Outside, Broadway was dense with shoppers. Snow was falling again. Crutchfield would hate the news, so good it portended catastrophe, but it filled Moss with cheer. He'd celebrate with Sally. The case was over.

> *I've been wearing her clothes,*
> *Silk pantyhose,*
> *Walking 'round in women's underwear.*

We've got the pervert nailed.

Part Two

THE CLIENT

ONE

Moss *ignored the* insistent green message light. Some other client, tired of being ignored. Or Junker. He was too hung over to handle Junker's telling him how to run his practice. He did want to talk to Terry. She should know they'd cracked her case.

Bondurant had testified in deposition that if a lump persisted he would have diagrammed it. But, "I never found a lump." Oh yes he had, and he diagrammed it too. With a diagrammed lump he never treated there was now proof Bondurant had violated his own standards. And it got Moss not only negligence but the pure poetry of perjury exposed, with attempted destruction of evidence. Dead meat. Slam dunk. In his sans souci hungover state the metaphors mixed, road kill crammed through the hoop.

Errors in judgment were no cause to visit professional ruin on anyone, but perjurers were fair game. Perjurers, in Moss's view, belonged under the jail with George Wallace's recidivists, or, next best thing, under a crushing judgment. He amended the complaint to add a punitive damages claim. This was certainly conduct attended by fraud, in the words of the statute. Still, the final goal was not punitive.

To the extent he could he'd advance his client's quest for truth, for meaning as well as winning.

In this heady spirit Moss wanted Terry to know what he'd learned. He wanted his client to appreciate what his work was coming to.

His client was not to be found. He called the Safehouse; she was two weeks gone. He called the school. Emmy hadn't been in school since winter break over two months ago. Briefly he considered calling the husband. He called the cancer center where Dr. Greenwood, Terry's oncologist, officed. They hadn't seen Terry there for five months. Five *months?* She should have been in for regular rechecks. Nothing's regular, the office manager said, about this patient. The office manager wanted a lien for unpaid bills. Moss temporized. Dr. Greenwood had not returned any of his calls. Moss had no recent records. Could the records be updated and a meeting scheduled? Only if Moss would sign the lien.

Nine-thirty one night Terry finally phoned him. The office bottle stood breathing on the credenza. Outside, a Broadway nocturne of soughing tires and muttering exhausts. Moss had drifted off highlighting journal articles on monoclonal antibodies. The burr of the phone startled and annoyed him. His mood took a surly turn.

"What's shaking?" She was checking in from a roadhouse in the east county where she'd taken a job. The Sugar Beat. Moss said she had to come in that week. Say what? Terry yelled over pounding country percussion. The music broke.

"You've got to come see me."

"God, you sound like Warren!"

The band was on an amphetamine tear. It did not pause long.

"Hey. That's me. *Bah bah bah living on Tulsa time....*"

Moss hung up.

A few days later there she was. Jeans, check blouse, boots, half-yard of shiny black hair. Emmy in tow with a yellow

Walkman and a Big Gulp. An appliqué sweatshirt.

"New button?" RETURN THE WOLF. RESTORE THE BALANCE.

"You bet. Bring 'em back."

"Sit down," Moss said. He wasted no time setting in on her for blowing off her oncologist, a crucial witness predisposed to protect Bondurant and no one to alienate.

"Sorry. I'm past doctors."

"You can't be past doctors."

She gave her serious head of hair a toss and shake. "Allopathy. Thing of the past."

"They'll think you're a flake."

"They who?"

"Jurors."

"Jurors are just people."

"Precisely the problem."

"Sorry. I'm becoming myself. That's the concept. Not somebody's patient."

"You're still somebody's client."

"Hey, cowboy!" She was pointing.

Moss had on that day his oft-soled wore-out Luccheses, cracked and crazed across the vamps, rimed from waterstains.

"Bet I know where you got them boots," Terry said. Emmy put a fist to her mouth.

The Luccheses had been a graduation present, law school, from Moss's in-laws in Wichita. "Where?"

"You got 'em on your feet."

Emmy yelped and stamped her sneakers.

"As a matter of fact," Moss said, "I got these boots in Central America."

"Central America? What part of Central America?"

"Central Kansas."

Emmy hit the floor stricken with giggles.

"Girl, you get in my dope again? Just kidding, Counselor."

"Better be kidding."

"Just a little laugh therapy, according to Cousins."

"Well," Moss puffed up some. "My job's not therapy. My job is to try cases. Want to know about your case?"

She studied him critically. "I like having a lawyer," she said at length. "You hear people say my lawyer this, my lawyer that. But it in fact is kind of cool having one."

Moss shook his head in some amazement. "Do you want to know about your case?" This woman had a lot to learn.

"Good news only."

He explained Moschetti's results. Good news was not how she took it. She took it hard.

"What are you telling me? I just thought he was dumb." Her clenched fist loosened. The fingers danced.

"He did not miss your tumor. He *found* your tumor three years before biopsy. He knew it was there all along. We've got him by the short ones."

"Bullshit." He was shocked to see her eyes filling with tears. "What was he doing to me? Did he want me to die?"

Emmy stared queerly at her mother. She seemed to go pale.

Moss was shocked further by his realization then that he was no closer to understanding the case. Motivation ought to be irrelevant. The legal question is whether there were deviations from standard care, not why. But in this case motivation figured large. Motivation had to be known for truth to cohere, for meaning. What, like Holmes's dog that did not bark at night, was Moss still missing? *He* had a lot to learn.

"Mom." Emmy's pallor persisted, tears welling also, though her expression was rigid and fearful and unlike that of a sobbing child. *"I want to go,"* she pleaded.

"We're gone. Sorry, Peter. I can't deal with this on top of everything." She stood. "Let me know when you figure it out." She strained a smile.

"Hold it." Moss felt a surge of annoyance. Terry Winter was beginning to look like a problem client. Hard to reach, out of touch, life falling to pieces. No home, truant daughter, sociopathic husband on her trail. Refusing medical treatment. Hanging out at the Sugar Beat Saloon. Irrational,

ungrateful, demanding, uncooperative. No, they could not go yet. "You've got to get a hold of yourself. You've got to pull together."

"I have been pulling, brother. Believe me."

"For Emmy's sake." Playing the kid card, for client control. The kid card blew up in his face.

"You're over the line," she flashed.

Those were real sparks he'd struck. "No, Terry. I'm doing my job."

"He's stupid. Stupid, stupid," Emmy muttered, face instantly flushed, staring at her feet. "Mr. Lawyer. Mr. Sue People and Go to Jail."

Moss sighed. These women had him coming and going. "Look, Terry. You have a strong case, that's all. We caught Bondurant lying. Big-time lie. You should know that. Focus on the big picture. Strong claim. Good settlement for you and your daughter. This other stuff, what goes on in the case, is not what matters. Schoolyard posturing. Doesn't mean anything."

"What matters?"

Moss paused then went ahead. "Your life."

"You don't mean *my life*. You mean *whether I live*. Or not. Or die."

"Yes. That does matter."

"How are you going to help me with that one? Visualization exercises? Groucho Marx videos? Boost my beta-carotene?"

Moss shook his head. "Not my job."

"Job again. What's the job exactly?"

"I prepare lawsuits and I try them. I squeeze insurance companies for money."

"That." She considered him almost compassionately. "Want to know what I think matters?"

He did.

"Not life, not death, but what you do. Not what happens to you, not who you are. *But what you do with what you got.*"

She had his attention. He'd felt that way once.

"You need to understand. I am a wild goose. Every morning is a brand-new day."

She watched him with a mixture of conviction and apology. She smiled.

"So you're my lawyer. Go get 'em." She actually gripped his shoulder. "Kill 'em, cowboy. For me."

Coming and going, and scratching his head.

Terry gathered up her things. Emmy's anger had retracted into a pout. She got up to follow her mom. Moss caught them.

"What do you mean, this on top of everything? What everything?"

She looked at him forthrightly. "Warren. The county. How I'm doing."

"What Warren wants is money, right?"

She laughed. "He wants his daughter." Now she spoke freely; it was something she and Emmy had discussed. "And I think he wants to hurt me."

"Physically?"

"Nobody's taking my kid while I'm still around to stop them."

"Terry?"

"That's the priority." She turned and took her daughter in her arms. She pulled back and smiled and looked openly at Emmy in a way Moss had not seen before. Emmy melted against her.

"Emmy is an empath. You wouldn't know, her sitting there like a kid. She takes it in. *All* of it. But she's toughening up. Emmy may not be real big but she's got some sand. Right, girl?"

"Right, Mom."

She takes it all in? Maybe Emmy was the one to discredit the phony defense of the disappearing lump. "Did anybody go with you to Bondurant's office? A friend, Emmy, anybody?"

"Yeah, Emmy did, like when I come here. We got twofers at the clinic. Nobody else I can think of."

"Twofers?"

"We got the family plan since I was paying cash. Only one charge when you schedule two family members, so we'd go together."

"Emmy," Moss turned. "We need to talk."

"Wait a minute."

"I'd like to talk with Emmy one-on-one." Moss had worked with child witnesses before. Tough witnesses, and untrustworthy unless influential adults were banished from their presence. He had as well a question he wanted to ask in private.

Terry grudgingly agreed and left them. Moss rang his secretary as an afterthought to prepare an authorization for Terry to sign permitting Emmy to talk with him about medical issues and allowing the release of records.

"This is really stupid," Emmy observed when they were alone. She had moved to the far end of the conference table. Moss came around to her and she moved again. Her lip protruded. She put the Walkman headphones on. Moss asked her to remove them. "I can't help your mom," he said, playing the mom card, "if you don't help me. Please talk with me a little."

She took his measure.

"Can you keep secrets, Emmy?"

"Yes," she said through her teeth. "I hate secrets."

"I want you to tell me something and I'll keep it secret, but I want you to tell me the truth."

"Tell me the truth first."

"What do you want to know?"

"Is Mom going to die?"

Oh, shit. Moss could interpret the question broadly—everybody was going to die. Or narrowly—Terry was in remission now, so she wasn't dying. He was a lawyer, after all.

"Your mom's doing fine," he said. He registered her expression: not good enough. "Of course she isn't dying," he added.

"How do you know?"

"Well, I can't really say medically. I'm just a lawyer."

She shook her head. Nowhere good enough.

"It's your turn to tell me something, Emmy, and I'll keep it secret. You haven't tried marijuana, have you?"

She was scandalized. "*I'm* not sick."

"O.K. Great. Now you can really help your mom if you answer some other questions for me. Do you want to help your mom?"

She nodded.

"Do you remember Dr. Bondurant?"

"Duh."

"Was he nice?"

"Yeah, right."

"Tell me about him."

"He's mean. He wants Mom to die."

"How was he when you went with your mother to see him?"

"Just like a doctor is. He's all Emmy do this and Emmy do that. And I'm like, that's retarded. That's stupid. That's all."

"Were you ever in the room when he examined your mother?"

She nodded. "He let me watch sometimes."

"How was he with your mother?"

"Just regular. Like a stupid doctor." Outside of her mother, it was a stupid, stupid world.

"Did he ever draw any pictures?"

"Yeah, he drew pictures and played games and acted that way."

"What way?"

"Nice but he's not. He gave me a bear and I threw it away."

"Why?"

To show Moss was being stupid Emmy exhaled, then inhaled, then spoke as though to someone younger than she. "He wants Mom to die. He made Mom sick."

"Did he ever draw a picture of something on your mom's breast?"

She nodded. "She told him and he felt it and he like did

a picture of it. And he's all, you need to come back, O.K., and now he goes across the hall with me. They always talked about it and he goes like, come back and we'll see and we'll do some more and see, so let's go now. And I'm like, yeah, right."

"Did you see the picture?"

"I saw it."

"What was it a picture of?"

She blushed and touched her chest. "Here, with the thing."

This was something. The daughter if not the mother corroborated Moschetti. But pretty frail; no barkless dog. "Thanks, Emmy. That helps. Is there anything else you can think of?"

She shook her head.

Moss smiled and gave her a clap on the back. What one does with children? She flinched.

"How's your mom handling everything?"

"My dad's going to kidnap me so she's scared."

"Are you scared too?"

"He wants to hurt my mom."

"We won't let that happen, Emmy."

"Yes you will, but she'll be O.K."

"What do you mean?"

"My mom is a force."

"You mean—like a superhero?"

Emmy considered the concept. She scratched a fingertip against the raised design of her sweatshirt, Planet Hollywood star bursting from a blue globe. She nodded. "Like that."

"She cares about you."

"She's a worrywart."

"She loves you."

"Duh."

Emmy gathered up her Walkman and tapes and dropped the Big Gulp in a wastebasket. "Will the doctor go to jail?" she asked.

"I don't think so."

She frowned at him and he understood her look: You big phony. He threw up his hands. "Sorry." Neither of them got it. The lawsuit was about money.

TWO

The case puzzled Moss the way women puzzled Freud. He ought to have it by now. Three years of inaction after finding a dangerous lump. Perjured testimony, altered records. Rock-solid Granite State doc on deviations from the standard of care. World-class oncologist Epstein who'll blow Basteen's snake oil vendors out of the water. Attractive plaintiff facing terminal disease somewhere down the road. The judge was even slamming the defense. Still the great question slipped his grasp. The core enigma. What did the doctor want?

The backfires around the edges preoccupied him. He drove discourteously in the Friday afternoon traffic, late for the appointment in the capital it had taken weeks to set. He'd forgotten to tell Terry she'd been ordered to be re-deposed. He left a message at the Sugar Beat Saloon, as she had instructed. She wouldn't go for it. Had to be done. For the sake of thoroughness he sent Morlock to the Wellness Clinic again with the new release for Emmy's chart. Bondurant's public records came in. They all looked innocuous. He struck out on the Junius Foundation. Nobody had ever heard of it. He served a request for production of Bondurant's applications for board recertification.

Moss had been getting unsettling calls from lawyer friends. "Guy came in this morning, said some pretty unpleasant things about you, Peter." That Moss was turning his family against him, helping hide his kid, sleeping with his wife. "Wanted to know his legal rights. Not a happy camper. Thought you'd want to know. The threat-level was pretty elevated. Not a real nice guy."

The winter of '94 was finally over. Freeways were rebuilt in L.A. Jeff Gilooly had fingered Tonya Harding. Everywhere had been cold. Winter of mean energies, unnecessary complications. Discontent, indeed. Moss cut off a Firebird passing a UPS van. The Firebird honked. Moss flipped him off. All three came to a stop alongside, idling uneasily before a flagperson smoking a cigarette, bored out of her mind. Like a cheerleader for a losing team on a stalled drive, listlessly flipping a pompon. In back of her a highway crew in hi-vis yellow vests dribbled tar from an asphalt plant, sloppy and slow.

Everybody these days got a chip on their shoulder.

Not just him.

Free Lorena.

Free Erik and Lyle.

And the cancer center office manager kept him waiting for Dr. Greenwood going on an hour.

One of Moss's sabbatical projects had been to struggle through the early court romances, from the Pearl poet to *The Faerie Queene*. He'd given some thought to the question of chivalric love. Whether in these times of relationships and enlightened sex love could be a matter of honor. Of great deeds. Self-sacrifice. Of life and death. He entertained the conceit of such devotion for Sally. He contemplated *storge*, the celebrated love of mother and child. He once had a client, Lester, who sacrificed for love. Lester adored Debbie, a lesbian. Debbie rejected Lester sexually. To qualify as her partner Lester made the change in Trinidad. He bobbed it for love. Lester became Leslie. His last male act had been to father their child.

What the poets had in mind?

In the waiting room Moss went over notes, medical records, journal articles. His most recent records were six months old. He highlighted an article, trying to grasp the Log Cell Kill Hypothesis. He'd grasp it. He'd lose it. He readied himself to talk Cathepsin-D and genetic deletion, to rule out a role for Hpr epitopes. Got to break the ice. Rap a little Gompertzian growth. He'd finally gotten an appointment with the treating *médico*, and a premeeting meeting with her office manager to discuss the lien. Bondurant had referred Terry to Dr. Greenwood. When you sue the referral source it can get touchy. Got to be engagingly servile. Moss screwed his servility to the sticking place.

Something about medical waiting rooms retards the passage of time. Moss picked up a doctor magazine. He was the only one kicking his heels in the fabric-bound place, a dead chamber of neutral tones, beige, khaki, cream. A window cleaner was tethered precariously outside. He swiped and curled his squeegee with a matador's flare as his rig banged in the wind. A receptionist was engrossed in telephones and calendars. A diminutive woman, in full control, her voice carried the room. "No, hon. No, I'm sorry. I'll have Doctor call you. That's the best I can do, hon. I'll have Doctor call." Now and then a slow-moving patient was emitted from the back to transact a billing and reappointment and trudge away.

The magazine offered tips on tax-free municipals and convertible debentures, pharmaceutical broadsides and a spread on the Lincoln Mark VIII. Canadian queues were editorialized about, as was legal reform.

A kid came out from the back, glancing furtively around. Beneath a Rockies cap he had no hair. Moss smiled his way. The kid pulled down the brim shielding his eyes. *They flee from me that sometime did me seek*, Moss thought. An image of the boy with the hoe intruded, his panicked flight cut down by a .50-caliber gun. Moss quelled a piston-push of nausea. "Toss your cookies?" Lieutenant Hobart had commented at the time. "Ain't life a gutfuck in the Land of the Little People."

The office manager of the clinic might have been a pretty nice person. In other circumstances. A few decades back.

Past-due charges were to be addressed. "You represent this patient? Terry Winter?" Moss nodded. She beetled over him like a teacher.

"Cancer center's got a boatload of chemo in this girl. Forty-five liters. Twenty thousand bucks. Forty days of radiation. That's seven thousand more. Surgeon and hospital were eight total. Dr. Greenwood five. That's forty thousand dollars. Forty thousand dollars, forty percent paid for by the American people. As in us." The office manager then did something funny with her mouth. Projectile vomiting? But she was only turning up the volume. *"What about the other twenty-four thousand?"*

"What about it?"

"Not a penny from your client is what."

"My client has no legal duty to pay in excess of Medicaid coverage because she has no assets." Having lost the forty-acre ranch.

"But I want first cut at settlement. What do you say to that?"

"Well, nothing."

"I'll say something. I'll say Medicaid don't pay overhead." She indicated overhead with a gesture that took in the plush colorless room, the receptionist at the other end turning away another supplicant.

"I wouldn't know about that," Moss said.

The woman crossed her arms. She studied him critically. "I need a lien on settlement for the full twenty-four."

"That shouldn't be a problem."

"You need to sign it before you meet with Dr. Greenwood."

"I'll have to discuss it with my client, of course."

"No lien, no meeting, no records."

"Look. Under the Patient Records Act and the Interprofessional Code—" He stopped. The office manager had positioned her hands on her hips. She was slowly shaking her head.

"Listen. We do charity. Half the medical staff was gone to Romania last year. Treating orphans. Orphans. In Romania. That's the caliber of professional we got. Meanwhile, back in America, Medicaid Mama works the system. Stops treatment, walks the bill, sues her own doctor."

She studied him with accumulated distaste. "Lawyers," she said, an epithet. "I know your game. Still want to see Dr. Greenwood?"

Moss in fact was losing interest. *Malpráctica no más.*

"You sign the lien. Twenty-four thousand off the top comes to me. You sign, attorney and agent."

Moss caved.

When he knocked he was told in a small voice to come in. He did. He sat down though he had not been invited to.

"That's some troll guarding the bridge." He smiled. Forget servile, he needed sympathy. He needed help. The doctor wasn't buying.

Anita Greenwood was small, pretty, pert, nervous. Moss recognized the look in her eyes. The terror and revulsion of the barricaded traveler as the living dead clamor at a window. The physician peering at a malpractice lawyer.

As Moss tried to float a little Q & A, Anita Greenwood kept her guard up. She answered in five words or fewer, pathologically circumspect.

This was not one to soften up with Log Cell Kill small talk. Moss dove in. What was Terry's current status?

Dr. Greenwood didn't know.

"How was she on her last visit?"

"Well."

"Her prognosis?"

Dr. Greenwood looked like she thought Moss was trying to trick her. "How do you mean, Mr. Moss?"

"How likely is her cancer to recur?"

In the following silence Moss surveyed the office. Three diplomas from Cornell, an Albert Einstein residency, three board certifications—oncology, hematology, internal medicine—bound volumes of *Cancer*, Goodman and Gilman's, Lewis Thomas, Robert Frost's collected poems—snapshots of family, the doctor with children, the doctor's husband in a medical gown, the doctor's bay horse, the doctor and the kid in the Rockies cap on bicycles, in riding shorts and Courage Classic T-shirts, looking proud and determined. When life hands you lemons . . .

"I don't understand," Dr. Greenwood said at length.

"The statistical probability of metastasis, if you can tell me."

"Perhaps you mean, how much time does she have?"

"Time?"

Dr. Greenwood studied him. "Have you had other clients like Terry?"

"With cancer? Yes."

"With breast cancer, Stage IV."

"IIIB," Moss corrected her. He couldn't tell if he'd given offense.

"Mr. Moss. Are you familiar with the American Joint Committee on Cancer?"

"Yes. I know the AJCC staging criteria. My understanding is Terry was staged T4 N1 at diagnosis. Isn't that Stage IIIB?"

"Yes, but at diagnosis she was MO. She became M1."

"M1? Are you saying her cancer metastasized?"

"You didn't know Terry was Stage IV?" She observed him almost clinically. "Your client is terminally ill, Mr. Moss. Your client is dying."

Something about his reaction caused Dr. Greenwood to open a crack. The first signs the cancer had spread, she explained, were signals on brain MRI. A row of hot spots showed up later on the bone scan of her lumbar spine, and an equivocal sign in a lung. Where these had gone the last five months the doctor didn't know. Terry declined treatment. She called to thank Dr. Greenwood. She wouldn't be coming back. Terry was Terry. Like her reaction to the bad news.

"Which was?"

"Which was, now I'll never get my AARP-card."

Moss tried to let it sink in. It didn't. He couldn't accept it. "She doesn't seem sick."

"She wouldn't. Terry is very strong. She'll stay on top of this for a while, but it will break even Terry." She glanced down. "The brain, the first signs will be there." She looked up. "Your client is an exceptional person."

If he could persuade her to return to treatment, how might that help?

"She'd get tumor shrinkage but not cure. A marginally longer life, some palliation of symptoms, but at a cost."

The cost was long-term, high-dose toxic therapies until the disease overwhelmed. There was no alternative, except firestorm chemo with bone marrow transplantation or stem cell rescue, but Terry wasn't eligible and it probably wouldn't work.

"So she went off everything. Saved taxpayers a lot of money."

"You felt comfortable letting her do that?"

"Mr. Moss," she said. "Chemotherapy is my life. But this was Terry's call."

"My God." He shook his head. "When did you find the metastases?"

Dr. Greenwood looked through the chart. "October last year."

"Terry came to my office in November."

"She decided to stop seeing me and to start seeing you." The thought seemed to pain her. "I know what your case is about." Dr. Greenwood sighed. "Wally—Dr. Bondurant—called a couple of times, and his lawyer. Who is his lawyer?"

"Basteen." The ethically challenged Jerome Basteen, in a prohibited ex parte contact with a plaintiff's treating physician as Crutchfield had predicted.

"Yes. Mr. Basteen. I never had reason to think Wally Bondurant was anything other than a capable doctor. He is the president of the medical society."

"He is that." Moss hated asking what he had to next.

"Terry's trial is set for September. Can you tell me if she's likely to be alive?"

She gave the question sober consideration. "Multiple metastases are an ominous sign. The brain worries me most. She had indications of a brachial-plexus syndrome, a left-sided palsy down her arm and hand. If there's meningeal infiltration the outlook is very grim. What Terry needed was whole brain irradiation. You can imagine her reaction."

Indeed Moss could. "Will she live through September?"

"It might be possible with brain irradiation and VATH or stronger chemo. I can say with some assurance Terry won't be alive this time next year." Dr. Greenwood glanced down again. Dr. Greenwood had one tough job. "Regardless."

"And if she refuses further treatment?"

"Terry was in big trouble last October. Can she make it six months more without reducing the tumor burden? Unlikely."

"How unlikely?"

"I hate to say very. But, very."

"I need an affidavit from you," Moss said apologetically, but firmly. "I have to accelerate the trial."

Dr. Greenwood considered the request. "All right," she said quietly.

An uncomfortable silence resumed. Dr. Greenwood was looking at him in a portentous way. "I don't want to be involved," she said.

"I understand," Moss said.

"Except for Terry."

He looked back in surprise.

"Is Terry noncompliant? Totally. Do I defend her decision? Totally."

She touched her hair in distraction. She spoke softly. "It would have been a curable cancer if it had been detected a couple years earlier. It was a killing cancer when we finally found it. Is that what you want said, Mr. Moss?"

Dr. Greenwood exhaled through her teeth, watching him, wary and searching.

"At trial? Yes, it is."

"All right."

"All right?"

"I will testify if you like, for Terry. Please give her my love."

THREE

A *spring storm* was brawling at the windshield. Cattle huddled with frosted asses. A bald eagle brooded on a cottonwood branch, a fatalist ensphered by snow, pondering a black lake hooped with ditched tires. Ice formed at underpasses. The Friday traffic grew halting and anxious. The whirling white thinned to a pale Puritan blue.

Moss passed a sign. Two miles of turnpike had been adopted by the Sugar Beat Saloon. He fishtailed off the freeway.

Ordinarily Moss would file a motion to withdraw. His client had been lying to him, what every lawyer dreads. When you've relied on what you're told and it's important and it's false—ordinarily it's adiós. The mission is awry.

You are a lawyer. You draw the blinding blade of justice for those you serve. To make way for the frail enterprise you've pledged to champion, you will stand down any foe. You will harm others if required. You are a paladin, righting wrongs and slaying dragons for the honor of another.

Let clients rave and weep, cringe and crumble. Let them trash reason and goodness and order and still will you fight their every battle. But let them not lie to their lawyer.

Quixotelike, Moss confronted the Stop-a-Minit MiniMart

parking lot phone booth. He dismounted, tucking the door shut behind him.

At exactly this juncture, standing square to the world, alone at a bleak and empty spot on its wintry rim, Moss wondered if he'd made a mistake. Why not have a cell phone? A little fold-up number like Basteen had, and a portable fax modem for wireless messaging from a touch-screen on the turnpike, and God knew what else—global positioning systems, smart-bomb radar evaders—that Basteen kept in the dove gray BMW with discreet gold pin-striping.

But Moss held his ground. Cell phones were for sissies. He would drive, *then* talk, not talk and drive. He advanced across the treacherous asphalt. The directory had been ripped off. Information had no listing for the bar. On he drove by dead reckoning, deeper upon the guttering plains.

The lie was big. She'd led him to think she was in re-mission. The implications for the case of her metastases were disastrous. On Terry's death the case would instantly lose three-fourths of its value. And Warren would run things.

Warren.

The thematic decor of the Sugar Beat Saloon and Salad Bar unexpectedly favored the nautical over the vegetable. Inauspiciously, the Sugar Beat had begun as the High Plains Lobster Pot and frayed hawsers still fringed the bar. Japanese glass buoys were hanging in macramé bags. Be-hind the bar, cracking sail across a massive smoked-glass mirror, a majestic illuminated plastic replica of the *Golden Hind* ran down a darkened sea.

Adjoining the bar were a plank dance-floor and drinking area scattered with cheap tables and chairs. Along a wall the salad bar lay wilting under a glass hood incongruously etched with likenesses of cows. There were complimentary beer signs, beer posters, beer clocks, and bubbling beer mo-biles and lamps. From the poolrooms in the back came sounds of cracking balls and measured low deprecations and taunts. Arenas for decorous, ritualized surrogate com-

bat. Like courtrooms. Moss was warned away from the
poolrooms, Lakota country, where mean drunk bottle
smashers in shoulder-length braids would gut you over a
quarter game. Terry had given the warning. She worked the
bar in a sleeveless, fuchsia Sugar Beat blouse. The *Golden
Hind* in full sail behind her lent drama to her words.

"Lakotas're my buds," she said. "Not yours. They're why
Warren won't come in. He sits in the lot in his blue truck
waiting and we slip out back while my buddies keep him
occupied. That is getting old, I want to tell you. Time to
move on."

Moss said nothing.

"Lightning's the other reason he stays outside." A tail
thumped behind her. "Meet Lightning." A brindled gray
dingo named not for his speed, she explained, but because
he looks like he got struck by a bolt.

Moss nodded.

"So how about a beer? On the house?"

He shook his head.

"How come you looking at me like that?"

He frowned.

"There you go again."

"Jesus." He glanced away, eyes coming to rest on a
tacked-up broadside for the house band. Sugar Daddy and
the Beetniks.

"So you figure it out yet?" she asked.

"What?"

"Which cow ate the cabbage." She matched his blank
look. "Why the good doctor kept my tumor secret."

Moss shook his head. He reached deep for professional
distance but he just felt tired.

"Remember when I first came in, that's what you said
you'd do. Figure it out."

Moss didn't really remember.

"I remain interested," she smiled. She didn't look like
someone who was dying. Moss became self-conscious and
shook off his stare.

A door shut to some chamber off the bar. "Emmy," Terry

explained. "What do you call homework when you're already home schooling?"

"Just work, I guess."

"Report due on *Call of the Wild*."

"Good story."

"Great story. Now tell me what you think about my doctor."

"I don't know," Moss said. "What I think's not what matters."

"Yeah?" He got an irked and speculative look. "Then what brings you out to the honky-tonk, cowboy? Friday dance don't start till nine."

He exhaled impatiently. "Let me be frank. I'm worried about you, Terry."

"Let me be Terry. I'm worried about you, Frank."

He sighed.

"Forget it. Laugh therapy. Don't worry about me, though. Worry about the case."

Did she not grasp the connection?

He looked at her like that again.

"Why didn't you tell me you were dying?"

Terry stiffened. She tried to sound annoyed. "Come all the way out here to rag me out?"

"Terry?"

"Some things I don't even tell myself," she said quietly. "I don't want Emmy in on this." She glanced down the bar toward the shut door.

"You haven't told her either?"

"I can't. I mean, I want to do it right but I just can't yet."

Moss looked away. He must have carried a hurt expression.

"I was going to tell you when the time came," she said.

"Emmy ought to know."

"My mother never talked to me and I was nearly grown."

"Nobody much talked about cancer then."

"Cancer makes you truthful, huh. Got to be my little joke."

"How are you doing? Honestly. Seriously."

"Scared shitless when I think about it. Scared shitless but I don't want my kid to know so I don't think about it. And my kid doesn't know."

"How're you doing physically?"

She shook her head again. "As a matter of fact I happen to be getting sicker, on top of everything else."

"Else?"

"Things are coming to a kind of head. Warren," she stopped to contemplate what she was about to say, "has become capable of extreme acts. He calls the county with such bullshit. I neglect his child, I abuse his child. Tells the caseworker we're out here doing God knows what all, making porn videos, who knows what he says, what he'll do next."

There was a skirl of panic in her voice.

"See the irony? Bastard uses the government against me. The woman said she's forced to investigate."

"I'll call. I know the director."

"Too late. Caseworker's coming out Monday. I get to explain how a bar's a nurturing environment." She summoned up a credible smile. "But thanks."

They stood a while facing each other across the bar. He twiddled at the hawser.

"This shouldn't have happened to you," he said.

"I'm interested in why it did."

"I just can't believe you're dying."

She looked at her lawyer as if he were God's own idiot.

"Your doctor wants me to give you her love."

That produced a wry, retrospective lift of her lips. She was pleased but unmoved.

"Anita wanted me to join a support group called Bosom Buddies."

"Jesus."

"Peter, listen, I *am* sorry I didn't keep you *abreast* of my condition."

"Terry."

"What a *boob* I was!"

"For Christ's sake, Terry."

"Enough breast-beating."

"Jesus."

"How come everything I say, you say Jesus?"

"I don't know."

"It's like so original."

"No."

"Isn't it?"

"God."

Moss appraised his client with branching ambivalence. He supposed he was getting nowhere. He would like the beer, he said, vodka back.

She pulled the Coors tapcock to a tilted glass and set it on a drain. Chrome nozzle high above the rim, she struck a double shot glass brimful with clear liquor. She reached around to hand him the drinks and her left hand flew away. The shot sprayed and splashed his sleeve, the glass bounced and shattered.

"Well, goddang." She cleaned up, got him another. "Like a stump-tailed bull switching at a fly."

"*Terry*." He was becoming agitated; this is why he'd come. "*You need treatment*. You need to extend your life." Not for Emmy's sake. The kid card, he'd learned, wasn't a winner. Not for money—another loser. "For the case. For truth and justice. For you."

"I am a dying person, Peter, like you said." She put her hand in her jeans pocket. "I accept that. Treatment means a longer death. Sicker sooner, sicker longer, and doctors in charge. That's all it means."

"It means a longer *life*. It means you're there for trial. It means we get to tell your story. A jury gets to decide."

"They want to nuke my brain." She let the stark iambics sink in. "This is me we're talking about and I'm just not interested."

"If you don't get treatment I have to try to move the trial date."

"You do what you need to in your department," she said. "And I will in mine."

Moss glumly took a couple of swallows. He gave it a
last lame shot.

"It's crazy. You're giving up."

"On medicine maybe. Hell I am on me."

"It's not safe. You need medical care."

"Ship's are safest when they stay in port."

The *Golden Hind* reinforced her point. Moss threw in the
towel.

"Peter, listen. Life's not measured by time. Thoreau was
right."

"By what is life measured?"

"By how awake you are."

A couple of dusty Agro-Americans in Allis-Chalmers
signature attire had shambled up to the bar. Terry drew
them glasses of Coors.

"What kind of life is this?" He indicated the roadhouse,
gradually filling.

"It's just a stage. They'll say, that was Terry's beetdigger
phase. Phases don't last. Emmy wanted to be a cardiologist
at one point in time. Shuttle astronaut. Lawyer for a while.
Harpist currently, which I encourage. Ch-ch-changes. Don't
worry about it."

"Stage IV is your stage."

"Oh, yeah. I forgot. What's yours?"

"Kind of stuck in a rut."

"Well, hell, cowboy. Head for the wagon yard."

"What phase you got coming up?"

"I think it's time for the real me. Leave this phony me
behind. But you stay here and figure it out."

"Doing what? Where?"

"Somewhere west, over the range, south of the border,
who knows. Try a little cowboy poetry, sign on for the
Biosphere, do something crazy. Show my kid some stuff,
figure it out. I'll send you a card."

"You do that." He fingered his glass.

"You can spend your life asking if people want paper or
plastic or you can live deep, like the man said."

"The man?"

"Thoreau. My man Henry. The light that puts out our eyes is darkness to us. Think about it."

"Well." Moss lifted his beer glass. "To the light."

"The light."

Moss drank down half the glass, then he finished off the shot. Then he finished the glass. Then he asked for refills. He was getting the hang of the Sugar Beat.

At the jukebox some Agro-Americans were having words with a couple of pachucos from the turkey works. A Lakota warrior with an orthopedic corset and a 22-ounce cue looked on frowning.

"Hey, Yellowhorse," Terry hollered to the warrior. She shuffleboarded a half-dollar the length of the bar. "Play one for me. 'Sweet Rosie Jones'."

Moss went through another sequence of swallows. Here goes. He informed her of the judge's order reopening her deposition for questions about her sexual and childbearing history.

"Tell the judge he's dreaming."

It was an *order*, Moss explained. Langworthy could dismiss the case if she didn't comply. And he would, the goddamn JAG-ass courtroom captain.

"That's not how I'm spending my time."

"One last tête-à-tête with Don't Call Me Jerry. Has to be done. You'll rip him anew."

"Has to be done. Ain't gonna happen." Terry smiled. "I'm past it, Peter. I mean it. *I am past wasting my time*."

He examined her like a failed experiment. "You're irrational."

"Postrational."

"Jesus."

"God."

"I want to show you something." She worked a little leather pouch out of her pocket and laid it on the bar in front of him. She loosened the drawstring and brought out of the pouch a small black eagle, carved jet with coral eyes, a bundle tied to its back with sinew.

"O.K. What is it?"

"Obviously it is an eagle. My fetish. You've got six directions—up, down, and the points of the compass. Eagle's for the direction up. Skyward. The idea is that you overcome things."

That he did remember from when she first came in.

"How you overcome things is by living your beliefs. Call it whatever. Satyagraha. Live aloha. Love in action. But that's my direction now. Skyward."

"I wish you'd help me overcome some things."

"It doesn't work if you feel sorry for yourself."

"Right. The hell with it." He was getting hotheaded from the boilermakers. Screw love in action, what he wanted was Bondurant's balls for breakfast. "It's your case, Terry. Once you decide what you're going to do about it, drop me a line."

So much for professional distance.

Time to go.

In the parking area, a blue pickup was parked across the motorcycles-only slots. The storm had separated and drawn away and last light broke through. The driver-side window lowered in jerks.

"Hey, snakehead."

Moss winced. The blurred image unified—the fried eyes and ponytail, the left arm extended, middle finger erect.

"You Calley?"

"Keep off what's mine, chump."

Moss found himself bearing down on the blue truck, too stewed for exit strategies. "She's my client, ranger. Leave her alone." Smaller than he was but probably stronger and a whole lot meaner. Everybody left Lurps alone, stepped off the trail to let you by as soon as they saw your beret. So once it had been for Moss.

"I got rights. Husband and father, don't forget it."

"Stay away from her."

"I claim what's mine."

"Hurt her," Moss caught a hand on the door handle and readied to press a thumb, "I cut your nuts off myself." His head was roaring and aflame. Winter's tooled briefcase lay beside him on the seat, a blued barrel-cooler propping the lid ajar.

Winter smiled. "Tell your client I'll be waiting."

The truck reeled backward then spooled out of the lot. Moss massaged his pulsing temples and turned toward the Sugar Beat. A three-man war party stood on the stoop with longnecks loosely in hand, Lightning, the dingo, at their side. A cue stick fell across the crook of the middle warrior's arm like a buffalo lance. "Way it goes in America anymore," Yellowhorse called to Moss. He lashed the softening air with the cue. "Cavalry sends for the redskins."

Heading home for a weekend with Sally, Moss reconned in the rearview mirror until the road behind was straight and empty. He looped back on the turnpike and picked up speed, muttering as he drove. Of himself he muttered epithets like jerk, dope, drunk. He passed west through a big open country strewn about with stuff. Industrial parks, pastures caked with snow. Green Burlington Northern engines parked on a spur. Tractorless trailers arranged in a lot. Cottonwoods strung along washes, apart and ramiform against an orange sunset, complex black images of strength. The backlit rolling ridge line and dark denticled folds of the range, and above the range, splitting a seemingly colorfast sky, twisted contrails—simulacra of disaster.

FOUR

Sally wasn't happy. His showing up after boilermakers seldom pleased her.

Moss pleaded extenuating circumstances and crisscrossed lines of duty. That day his client's death had been announced.

"And the bell tolls for thee?"

"She refuses treatment," Moss said with an inappropriate note of self-pity. "She won't obey the judge's order." And airtight case was swelling at a seam and starting to hiss.

"Cut me a break, Sally. I might lose Bondurant again."

Memories, memories.

Then along comes Warren, stalking his wife and menacing her lawyer.

Sally was shaking her head in a way that meant, enough. Her artistic dinner pasta sat cold and out of bounds.

"Hanging out in a bar with your client," she observed. It was a judgmental observation. "You even smell. Your clothes smell. Have you gotten a little too close to this one?"

"This one's important."

She surveyed him coolly. God help him, he loved that look.

"Last time Bondurant or his brother or somebody threatened us. This time your own client's husband does?"

"We should assume he's serious."

"Shall I lower the blinds?"

She entered the front room hitting a switch. He stood at the doorway watching her move through the darkened space, window to window, dimly visible from streetlight outside. Give me a tall, good-looking woman, he thought, with a regal bearing, in bluejeans, shirttail out, lowering blinds and snubbing curtains closed. Then is my home my castle.

At the last window Sally paused. She turned to look at Moss in the kitchen doorway. How did he seem to her? She turned back for a moment at the window then pulled the curtain to. He switched the front lights back on as she joined him in their bright, remodeled kitchen.

"Warren drive a blue pickup?"

Moss was out the front door with a short-handled maul grabbed from the woodbox. He found himself in the empty street pivoting about like spastic tai chi. Nothing but a skirt of leaves behind him. He stumbled slope-shouldered back up the porch steps inside.

I am losing it, Moss realized.

From the way she regarded the maul in his hand Sally seemed to concur.

"What is going on, Peter? This isn't how it was supposed to be when you went back to work."

Moss hated having no answers. "It's the right thing to do. It's an important case. It's different. I can feel it."

"You need to get your shit together." She offered this advice in a just possibly, someday-maybe playful way that gave his spirits a tentative bump. "Why is it consuming you?"

"Bondurant. I just don't get it. I can't let it drop."

"Maybe you drank too much to get it."

Sally's look was not totally unsympathetic but quite disheartened. Why? her look inquired, and, will it ever change?

There had been changes from time to time, four, six
months on the wagon. But abstinent, he got continually
pissed off at himself for letting his life become so truncated.
A half year of enlightened togetherness on sabbatical had
failed to liberate a marriage oppressed by career. That he
was a good lawyer, and sometimes made money at it, and
got money now and then for people who could use it, was
just not enough, it became increasingly obvious. The more
obvious it became the more he wanted to drink. The more
he drank the more ironically wistful he was for the awful
long-ago experiences that had wrenched virtue out of him—
physical courage, self-sacrifice, taking a stand, ice-clear
acts of conscience to make a better world.

Something's missing when you're nostalgic for combat
and prison.

Virtue kept receding into the moral ambiguities of professional life, the false clarities of vodka, idealism finally
telescoped into something quaint and self-deceiving—folk-
songs by sensitives who later killed themselves.

"Peter." Sally's soft voice was as penetrating as a hyp-
notist's. "Something's torturing you." She took him by the
shoulder, inquiring deeply. "Is it this case?"

"No." Who was speaking? From what level? "The case
is the way out."

And where had that come from?

Moss shook her off, filled and swilled a tall glass of tap
water, rubbed his eyes and smiled. He eyed the bowl of
pasta coyly, angling for an invitation. Andouille sausage
with chanterelles she'd foraged and dried herself.

"I need your help with Bondurant," he said. "Over dinner. I'm at a dead end."

She still had that blunt deep look.

"This is work," Sally said with a gesture signifying every
square inch of their lives was drenched in it. "Your life has
got," the gesture flew off helplessly, "to be larger than your
work." She had a pleading and a scolding tone.

"Right." Lawyering was just a way to make a living, as
had been combat ops at the time. It is important to step

back and question the value of your work, the meaning of your acts. He'd been stuck in a rut too long.

Swaying a little, Moss tried to step back and question. He'd had a bad Friday. He defended his home from a scatter of leaves with a short-handled maul. His wife backed him into facing who and where he was. He had a fading noseflush from Sugar Beat boilermakers, "Sweet Rosie Jones" yearning like a God in pain from behind a distant door. Apparently he smelled. A swell of energy tumbled over him. He got overdecisive.

"Sally. It's time."

She raised an eyebrow.

"*It's time to make the swerve.*"

The swerve of which Moss spoke was nothing less than the great swerve itself. The D. H. Lawrence swerve. The wild swerve in the onward-going life course. *Skyward*.

For an instant, like a power surge, everything around him was charged with possibility, the processor, pastamaker, toaster, juicer, the cappuccino nozzle, the marble pastry board, the slotted spoons and spatulas, pans, pots, woks, and forks dangling from ceiling hooks, glowing in aureoles, trailing ribbons of afterimage, starred and shadowless, immanent with purpose.

Moss squinted and blinked. His rheostat dimmed as quickly as it flared.

"The swerve?" Sally said. "I think I'll make some coffee."

They sat face-to-face at the scarred oak table. Her look was analytical, distant. She drank hers black; he sweetened his with a spoon and a half.

"Tell me about this woman," Sally said at length. "*Ban Bloodsport* marries *Death from Above?*"

"She believes in love in action."

"Yeah? Party girl?"

"A spiritual thing. Commitment. Living what you believe." The coffee was starting to help.

"I know. As a Cuaquero," she said—Spanish for Quaker, "I appreciate moral stands. I *expect* them."

"She has a good sense of humor for a dying person."

"Yes, Peter. But who is she really?"

To see Terry Winter for herself, and not as his client, leading lady in his case, was, Moss realized, probably beyond him. In every case, but especially this one, lawyer and client inhabited separate realities. Moss's world was beset by perjuring defendants and unethical adversaries, autocratic judges and undependable partners. Terry lived with more malevolent threats. Moss in truth knew little about what Bondurant's negligence had really wrought, or of Terry's struggle to make of her short life something of worth. Except that in her own way Terry's quest for answers more than matched his own.

"All I can say is how she comes across to me," Moss said. "I like her. She's gutsy. Headstrong, naive, hard as nails sometimes. She can act like I owe her."

"The aggressor defense." Sally was an artist, not a shrink. What did she know? "This woman's got things to be afraid of, right? Like dying in a matter of months. Like her husband. Like doing the wrong thing in front of her kid. *Losing* her kid. She projects her fears and attacks the projection. Stay out of her way. She's been getting sicker and you never noticed. Her time's running out. She's past doctors. Lawyers may be next."

As usual Moss was all ears.

"But hard as nails she isn't, Peter. She's coming to pieces and can't let it show, especially to her daughter."

Moss recalled Terry's odd ambivalence with Emmy, how she seemed both detached and complicit. It could be seen as a deliberate process, an acceleration of independence. Lifting Emmy out of the world of kids, girding her for separation. "I've come to appreciate that she's not as self-centered as she can seem."

"Child-centered," Sally said. "It's all about her kid."

"Then why not settle to provide for her daughter? Why not add to the time she has left with Emmy, smooth it out with methadone and nerve blocks?"

Sally looked off at the blinds lowered against Warren

and the Warrens of the world. "You underestimate women, Peter. Pain can be pleasure."

"This is no masochist."

"I don't mean that. Pain can be fulfilling because it gives things value. What if giving birth weren't painful?"

Rhetorical questions answer themselves but hers became a riddle. In their kitchen of bright things, comforts, appetites, routine, it swept in like some Old Testament voice blended from the wind: If a mother values a child more for the pain of bearing her, to what does the greater pain of childlessness give value?

To us. Moss came around the table. He bent blindly down to kiss his wife. "I ever tell you you saved my silly ass?"

Her soft worry facing back at him was easy enough to interpret: Don't make me have to again.

FIVE

Silver Mormon light welled the length of Spanish Valley and the warming air stirred. Terry pinched the reefer butt into bits to be taken on the wind. A pad of orange clouds took shape, then waves of fiery orange. Then all color drained away before the blinding golden ball that crowned the triple peaks of the La Sal.

Sunrise struck her as a struggle. Everything was a struggle. Day against night. Future against past. There, here—then, now—inside, without. Coming and going with her suspended between.

She shut her eyes, stabbed by the sun, photophobic from dope and disease.

The light that puts out our eyes is darkness to us.

She stood and steadied on the metal chair, sweating in the cold. Her eyes watered. Her lush black hair luffed on a breeze. No traffic, no patrol cars, no blue truck. Just the Sugar Beat panel van in the Moab Motel parking lot. Couple of rental cars with passionate Utah! tags. Sunday morning, two days gone, and no one was after them yet.

Maybe the boss wouldn't mind after all, borrowing his transportation, under the circumstances.

Inside she turned the dead bolt and sliplocked the chain.

Lightning's eyes followed her across the room, tail thumping softly. As always at this hour Emmy was asleep.

Terry put her luggage on the bed and fished through for her things—Dr. Bonner's soap, spirolina, wobemogus tablets, aloe vera powder, mistletoe oil.

In better days Warren built a raised bath for her at the ranch above Boulder. From the clawfoot tub could be seen their meadow, the line of fenceposts with bluebird boxes vanishing in the firs, the back range wavering in the air. After *Walden*, a brass plate on the tub was engraved with the bathing orison of King Tching-Thang:

> Renew thyself completely each day;
> Do it again and again and forever again.

She stood before the motel bathroom mirror in a green robe and gray hiking socks.

Henry. You're the man.

She clawed into the hair above her forehead, loosened and pulled it away with a flourish, shook it out twice and hung it on a rack. She examined her appearance, a spiky-headed tough, and pressed her sore eyes.

Henry knew pain was something to experience, to get the whole and genuine meanness of. But the phantom breast phenomenon he lacked.

Henry lacked a phantom breast.

Terry giggled, lit a stick of Five Hills incense, disrobed and showered.

After drying, she observed herself further. Gnarly little broad. Scarred like a warrior. Amputee. Cyclops. Amazon. She liked what she saw, except for the trembling hand. She looked kind of awesome.

If you don't like my peaches don't shake my tree.

She began working in the oil along the diagonal slash and hollow of her chest, and from there behind her neck, her low back and down a leg, the places she hurt. She massaged her aching missing breast.

Some of the medicines had sounded interesting, the

methadone suppositories, and the morphine button had done wonders for daytime TV in the hospital. But after nine courses of hard chemo, whoa Nelly! Pink piss? Mouth pitted with cold sores? Twists of hair slipping down the drain. Dry heaves and drizzling shits and fevers. The end of several decades' pleasure in sex. Her fingernails, a vanity, clubbed and broken like a bricklayer's.

Those guys could do a number on the feminine mystique. Surgery for the maternal part, oncology to wrap up the rest of your sexuality.

First we cut off a breast. Next we poison you. Then we fry your brain.

Hey, I'm outta here!

Terry reconsidered her reflection. Gouged eyes, grunge hair, the rope vein across her temple like forked lightning. The warrior slash glistening with oil. Half woman, half ragged breastless beast. So I'm something else. Why not something better? Selected for some mission, to slay some fattened foe.

She worked on her bra and fitted the foam I'm Me Again! prosthesis. Robed and wigged, she went to her daughter's side. Above the knotty pine bedstead, on the knotty pine wall, was a photographic print of Delicate Arch. She rocked Emmy's shoulder softly. The dog stretched and pulled at the single pile. Light was coursing in.

Wake up, girl. Hit the deck. It's morning in America.

To be awake is to be alive.

"Where are we going *now?*"

Terry shot Emmy a look, sitting arms crossed in the front seat in her Pearl Jam sweatshirt with the marionette. "Home," Terry said. A red-tail labored up from the bar ditch alongside the highway. A kangaroo rat, tail whipping, twisted in its talons. From the back seat Lightning barked. He had a thing about birds.

"What home?" Emmy asked.

"*Home* home."

"Home home where?"

"Home home on the range."

"That's so funny."

"There's a place you'd like down in Mexico. *Pura vida* down there. Pure life."

"Why do we have to go to Mexico?"

"Eat ice cream on the beach. Sing to the fishes."

"Tell me, Mom."

"Someplace your dad can't find us. Someplace I can figure it out."

"He'll find us."

"You're just a pessimist."

"Hello, Mom. You have a *trial*. The stupid *doctor*."

"Not till September whatever it was."

Emmy looked off toward the broken red cliffs and benches. She puffed her cheeks and expelled a breath. "I don't want to go to Mexico. I want to live someplace real again."

"Why?"

"To take care of you if you get sick."

Oh boy. "Forget about me," Terry said. "I'm nothing. Turkey pucky on the crossing log."

"Not to me, Mom."

Terry kept a Sunday pace, seeing the sights, the pediment and plateau. A VW camper passed them on a downgrade. The bumper-sticker read, "Hayduke Lives!" Along one section every fencepost was topped with an old boot. At the corner a coyote carcass was drying on the barbs. Ravens hopped around. Lightning barked.

"What do you want for *you*, Emmy?" Other than what all kids want—to be totally normal and totally exceptional.

"I don't care, Mom," she said. "I just wish I was dead."

Oh brother. "No way. You're what keeps me going, kid."

Forget normal. These were exceptional times.

What was in Vincent Foster's briefcase, the radio mouth wanted to know. Terry clicked him off. They passed a trading post, pickups snubbed up in a row. None of them blue. Soon there was no one else in sight again. Emmy strapped on her Walkman. She stared off at the red land, bobbing her head to the beat. After a while she slept. Terry drove suspended in space and time, pain eating away. She breathed—in-one-two, out-one-two. She punched in the lighter and got a joint from her pocket. She cracked a window but Emmy woke up.

"Yuck."

"Smoke 'em if you got 'em."

"Why do you smoke if you're not sick?"

"Well, I am a little sick." The joint jiggled in her left hand.

Emmy looked down, played her fingers in her lap. "I knew you were. You shouldn't not tell me things, Mom."

"I know."

"How sick?"

"Comes and goes." She braced. Was now the time?

Emmy bit her lip. "Did the doctor make you sick?"

"No. He didn't make me well."

"I know why," Emmy said.

"How do you know?"

"I saw inside him."

Terry studied her daughter. "What did you see?"

"How mean he is. He wants you to die, Mom. Don't you even care?"

"Sure I care. I think about it." Trying to remember some *fact*, like Peter Moss wants. But in her mind she couldn't even see the doctor's face, just feel him fingering her breast as she sat on the table, on the crinkly paper with her arm in the air. It was cold. His fingers were cold. Maybe her eyes were shut?

Forget facts. She wanted to know how the doctor fit in the big picture. She wanted answers to the big questions. What the meaning of illness is. Why it happened to her.

"It's the same as lying not to tell me things," Emmy said.

"There anything you ever not told me? For my own good?"

Emmy nodded.

"Well, it happens then, doesn't it?"

"Are you going to die, Mom?"

Terry considered her daughter. She wasn't up to it, not yet. "Not if I can help it." She had to do it right. "But let's say I did get sick. I mean bad. And I actually did die on you, way out somewhere in Indian country."

Emmy made a face.

"So here I am, doornail dead. Deal with it."

"This is stupid."

"What do you do?"

"Go home, I guess."

"*What?* Leave me like this?"

"I'd try to wake you up."

"Know how to tell if someone's dead?"

"How?"

"Tap on their eyeball."

"*Mom.*"

"What next?"

"I'd bury you. Then I'd go home."

"How?"

"Well, I'd take your things off like your ring and belt buckle. I'd use your belt buckle to dig a hole."

"What about all my Sugar Beet savings?"

"I'd take off your boot and your sock and put your money in my sock."

"Would you keep my boots?"

"I know where you got them boots. You can't giggle if you're dead."

"Don't bother with burying me, O.K.? Save your strength."

"O.K."

"What then?"

"Hitchhike to town?" Emmy asked.

"Nope."

"Find a house."

"Check."

"Call someone to help."

"Who?"

"I don't know."

"Me either," Terry said. "I'll think about that. Maybe Yellowhorse."

"Then I'd go home. The real one, not the joke one."

"What would you do when you got where your real home was before the bank kicked us out of it?"

"I'd find our lawyer," Emmy said earnestly. "I'd tell him all about it."

"Good," Terry said. "Stay away from your dad. Though Peter would likely be none too pleased."

It rained all through Navajo land but still the desert steamed and glowed, torturing her eyes. The overcast didn't change though the sun moved behind it.

Tucson was full of blue-and-white patrol cars and Terry dialed it down. There were endless tracts of gated communities, and rugs for sale along the frontages, furling on racks with animal faces, a bear, a Mickey Mouse, an eagle. Another eagle on a lawyer's billboard, and the stately cacti looking both indifferent and amused.

South of the airbase the desert bloomed in the clearing light. Cholla and primrose caught the sun. Red-tufted ocatillo wands waved in the roadwash. Sand verbena pooled pink in the flats.

Terry found an oldies station. Sam the Sham. You and Me and Rain on the Roof. Just as lame as when they first came out. She found a *ranchera* station. Emmy put her headphones on.

They entered the wasteland of the Chihuahuan desert, greasewood, tarbrush, thorn acacia on caked caliche soil. Blockfault mountains like die cast on the desert floor. The Chiricahuas' welded columns hovering over the creosote plains.

Geronimo country.

"He had visions," Terry said. "He saw the future like you think you do."

"What visions?"

"Trains, smoking the peacepipe, according to Yellowhorse. He lost but he was never defeated," she said. "Think about it."

By late afternoon they were getting close. Time to start looking for a safe place to ditch the van then mail the keys back to Frank. She drove southwest into the sun. Everywhere she looked there were lights, a tone poem of lights. Glare on vinyl and her watchface flashing. A wash of light in the windshield glass. Light stars in bumper chrome, mica in the aggregate. Glittery ribbons lacing the power towers and cassette tapes stringing the broombush, glinting in the gusts. Foil-wrapped flowers by a roadside cross.

Southern Pacific tracks ran east-west along the highway, and next to the tracks a six-wire fence with boundary monuments, the border, like a hidden drop-off, the waveline of a reef.

"Funky Broadway" on the oldies station.

Then above the desert like a mirage, like Emmy's eye mirroring back, seeing and seen, origin and destiny, the sweeping blue bias of the Mexican *cordillera*. The Sierra Madre, beyond which lay the sea.

SIX

Moss hit *Hands-Free* and Listen. He ran the message on speaker a third time through.

> Hi, yeah, this is Terry, it's—God—two a.m. Saturday morning, and I'm calling to tell you I thought about what you said last night and I realized now was the time to act. Been planning a trip as it was and the county's coming Monday and Warren. We'll be long gone when you get this. I appreciate everything, believe it or not. To everything turn, turn, there is a season . . . Adiós, cowboy. Don't squat on your spurs.

Moss hit the third touchsquare for Delete. She'd actually meant it.

"Singing voice mail? Flake alert!" Crutchfield had stuck his head in, hyena-like, sensing something wounded to sniff out. "What's happening? Case going soft?"

Moss looked up irritably from loading his trial bag for New Hampshire to defend his expert's deposition. "A little light chop is all. Lower cruising altitude, buckle up. We can ride it out." It was in fact a hell of a note to find waiting for him after the first full weekend with his wife in months.

"Settlement offer on the table?"

"I wish," Moss admitted.

Crutchfield smiled, dystopian worldview validated.

"I may have to have a little backup, Crutch. Moral support."

Crutchfield was shaking his head. "My people need me. Adiós, cowboy."

An hour later Moss flashed his boarding pass and bumped his trial bag down the aisle. He compulsively inspected his planemates for cellular phones or laptops in use, unable to shake the conviction that some fool running a spreadsheet would scramble the traffic controllers' vectors and hurl them off on a collision course.

Moss in fact had never recovered from the PATCO strike. How could Ronald Reagan have fired all eleven thousand air-traffic controllers at the same time? Despite the passage of time he continued to fear that the replacements would never be up to snuff. And what about the thousands of pissed-off strikers? Workplace terrorism was no laughing matter. How many would remember the codes and computer locks, the shift times and the hiding places? How many were still out there nursing a murderous grudge?

The plane was a 757, six seats across. A quartet of Beatles look-alikes—a John with sideburns and hat, a moptop Paul, a very short Ringo, and a very tall George—prowled the aisle with instrument-shaped carry-ons. The flight attendants wore businesslike blue slacks and cardigans with white bibs. They were hard at it, cramming and snapping shut the overhead bins. One in black bangs and pigtail, Latin American maybe, had to reach for the bin lids on tiptoe. She had a mournful and captivating look. Moss found himself staring. A last diminutive passenger was helped to her seat, Asian woman, a mine victim with prosthetic feet. Might have been from Quang Ngai province. Might have been from lots of places.

The video of oxygen masks popping out of the ceiling all at once made the big guy with the elbows next to Moss guffaw. An inflatable slide deployed. Leaping passengers thrust their arms out as they jumped. "Wheee," the big guy said.

Soon the plane was bucking down the runway. The G forces, the sudden acclivity, the ailerons snapping in half, the bank and wheeling view of the planet brought demons surging to Moss's temples. To resist the psychotic conviction the plane was flying apart he forced a study of reality. Out the scratched window the square grids of older neighborhoods gave way to curvilinear patterns of newer subdivisions, like contour lines on topo maps. Some things stand out from the air; Moss cataloged them. A parking lot of school buses. Cemeteries. The toxic green of settling ponds. Subdivisions gave way to prairie. Dry farms and grazing country, lightly salted with late spring snow.

Moss's dilemma was this: He must accelerate the trial. He has no choice. His client is dying and the husband wants her claim. But if the trial date is advanced, how can he reach her? She's apparently vanished. Where will she be at the time of trial? There was nothing he could think to do.

Moss became alarmed on realizing they'd placed the mine victim at an exit door. The door was plainly labeled with a sticker revealing it weighed "approximately 53 lbs." This woman's seat was for the able-bodied only! This could be a big mistake!

Moss hit the call button. He'd change seats and sit by the exit. The sad flight attendant took her time. She'd been working the aisles, turning decorously left and right, renting headset connectors for the in-flight movie. *Mrs. Doubtfire*.

"I'm sorry." She smiled sadly at Moss. Filipina? "It is too late now."

Moss protested in the teeth of her sad smile. It violated regulations. How could that poor woman heft the door, engage the slide? Trust me. I'm a lawyer. "I'm sorry," she said. "It is too late."

The flight attendant moved on, cradling a sheaf of headset connectors like one of Millet's gleaners. *Too late now* . . . The phrase raised a terror in him. The terror raised

a memory. Hanging then falling, McGuire line coiling
slackly above him in the flaming sky.

Moss was to meet Dr. Hoover at the Manchester Holiday
Inn, an original Inn it appeared from the carpet stains and
burnholes in the bedspread in Moss's unit. There was likewise an original smell, as of thirty years of Camels. The
block walls in the hallways were crumbling at the base. At
the ceiling there were red metal fire bells and red-lit EXIT
signs with broken glass and exposed bulbs. Peculiar music
was piped in, samba or something, but the steel security
doors seemed more than adequate and Spectra Vision was
offered.

The Manchester Holiday Inn also had a newer wing fea-
turing fun activities in the Holidome, a kind of windowless
gymnasium. The Holidome housed a swimming pool, Ping-
Pong table, miniature golf, a coffee shop area closed for
supper, and a bar, the Front Runner, open but empty. Moss
hurried past to the lobby.

In the lobby Dr. Hoover was waiting. He suggested a
Thai restaurant, Chicken on Fire. It was not the only in-
consistency with Moss's New England expectations. The
doctor's hairstyle was also unexpected. What remained on
top shot back in raked and well-oiled strands gradually
thickening over the downslope to a skirt of curls around
his collar. The whole thing glistened like something from
pre-Revolutionary France, a phenomenon heightened by the
restaurant's flambeau cressets.

In all the dark and ice-bitten downtown of Manchester,
New Hampshire, that night not a soul appeared to be abroad
except the dramatically highlit few dining by torchlight at
Chicken on Fire.

Dr. Hoover philosophized a bit over *pud pug gai*. Family
medicine as a specialty was a child of the sixties, he was
saying. His had been the generation of reformers, dedicated
to bringing primary care to Appalachia and the inner city,
increasingly abandoned by swelling ranks of specialists.
There came a new breed to the fore—intensively trained,

family-oriented people's physicians. Residencies were established and periodic recertification, the first specialty to require it. Dr. Hoover had gotten the call as a Vista Volunteer at Rikers Island. Twenty-five years later the family physicians' moment in history was finally at hand. But respectability has been a long time coming, held back by the holdover G.P.s, the bumblers, the Bondurants.

"I hate medical malpractice lawsuits," Hoover asseverated. "But I hate substandard practice in my specialty more." His curls quivered with conviction.

"I need that said at trial."

"This case will never go to trial. He'll settle."

"In case it does go to trial, I need you there. You're my only expert on the standard of care. The time for substituting someone else is over."

"Your case will be over by tomorrow. I'm sure of it."

"Well," Moss smiled. "Good, but the client's not real settlement-minded. You pretty flexible on flying out to testify?"

"Whatever it takes."

"Anything else I need to know before tomorrow?"

"I think we've covered it."

"Great. Say, this is some chicken."

"You should taste the *gai prig gung*."

The trailer for *Hot Links* promised gorgeous girls ready to play where steamy seduction was par for the course. The fairway scenes were eye-catching though Moss suspected problems in character development. He clicked off, lights out, but his sleep was troubled by the demons. The image of the hovering smile. The choppers slamming and blowing apart. The awful weightless moment, then falling for the paddy. He woke. Lying sweating in the steam heat, he was stricken with a free-floating sense of futility. *Too late now*. Got to be the chicken. Or the presence out there in the boreal night of Don't-Call-Me-Jerry Basteen.

In the morning Moss jogged up the Merrimack to Amoskeag Mills. Ice choked the river and coated the town. The air was laden with corpuscles of ice. Moss passed thousands of rock-busted windows in the factories following the river banks. Most cars in the thin traffic had Massachusetts plates. The elaborate fish ladders at Amoskeag Falls had never serviced salmon. Everywhere, good intentions gone awry. Moss turned back. On one black stone mid-river perched one great black-backed gull.

He was a little late getting to Hoover's office in a converted white-framed cottage with green shutters. When he walked in Hoover had the appearance of someone in custody. He sat in his leather desk chair as though encircled by captors: Basteen pacing, hands clasped behind him. Nikki, the court reporter with the mole, unsnapping the legs of her stenographic stand, threading paper through her key-punch. Bondurant, hands in pockets, pumping a trouserleg, working his keys. Heinz quietly sitting below a wall of framed diplomas.

"Everybody just happen to be in town," Moss asked, "or does ROMPIC believe in safety in numbers?"

"You're late," Basteen noted.

Nikki asked if she could swear the witness. She was fully assembled and looked ready to have a good time. Swear him, Basteen said.

Hoover handled the first question, the one about telling the truth, adequately. It was downhill from there.

Basteen had Hoover's c.v. marked. He was unusually well-informed about the man's career. Family medicine certification was listed as obtained in 1974. But hadn't Hoover scored just two points above the cut for passing? Hadn't his certification expired in 1980? Wasn't that because he failed the recertification exam?

"I notice the defendant isn't certified," was Hoover's answer.

"And it's not on his c.v., is it?"

Bondurant gave Moss a fat smile. He'd recently responded "none" to the request for production of all applications for board recertification.

Hoover had attended Central Tennessee Medical School,

but, Basteen inquired, hadn't he applied and been turned
down at six other medical schools and two schools of os-
teopathic medicine? Hadn't he been turned down everywhere he applied except Central Tennessee? And what was
different about Central Tennessee?

Basteen produced a startlingly insincere grin, Louis
Armstrong with a gunmetal glint.

"The student body is black."

"Ninety-six percent black?"

"Ballpark," Hoover mumbled.

Basteen himself was Harvard. He affected an Ivy League
locution, long traded up from Five Points jive. He sat back
and rustled a bit, sported a little shimmer and strut. He
spoke with a convert's derision. "You didn't get into any
white medical schools."

"No."

"So you went to school with Negroes? White man in a
Negro school? Down south wit de folks? Dat right, King-
fish?"

Nikki started from her machine. "King fish?" she said.
"Is that one word or two?"

Basteen raised an immaculate index finger.

Hoover wrung his hands.

The other board certifications on the c.v. had sounded
good at the time to Moss. The National Board of Primary
Care. The National Board of Preventive Medicine. Diplo-
mate of Family Practice. Margolis had vouched for them
and Moss didn't think twice about it. But Basteen had
marked as exhibits copies of Hoover's applications for each
certifying board. He knew not only that none were recognized by the AMA, but that the entire accrediting body
consisted of one Roman Silberfeld, M.D., Las Vegas, Ne-
vada, who would certify anyone for any purpose for a $600
fee.

A little light chop, Moss observed. Fasten seatbelt low
and tight. Where had the bastard gotten the book on this
guy?

"Dr. Hoover, you have been sued for medical malpractice, have you not? Six times, correct? In two cases the patients died under your care. Two others involved failure to diagnose cancer. In the first of those you testified, did you not, that early diagnosis would have made no difference in the plaintiff's outcome? In the second case you testified that a family practitioner may rely on a negative radiographic report to justify failure to follow up. What were the outcomes of those cases? What did the juries conclude?"

"All of those cases were ultimately dismissed."

"All were settled for substantial sums *then* dismissed. Two only after verdict, correct?"

"That information is confidential."

"What did those two juries conclude, Dr. Hoover?"

The man shot a desperate look Moss's way. There was nothing Moss could do. A jury verdict is a public record. Those particular juries, it developed, had nailed Hoover's hide to the barn door. And so had the New Hampshire Board of Medical Examiners in a private censure proceeding no one was supposed to find out about. But Basteen had found out about it. He implied he had found out a few other things he planned to save for trial. They had the goods on Hoover and they were letting him know. It was Heinz, Moss realized. He looked at the adjuster, a study in pitted and lapidary repose.

"Hey, Jerry," Moss said with sudden bonhomie. "Shall we take a short break?"

"The name's Jerome, Peter. Not Jerry."

"You can call me Pete."

"You can't call me Jerry, O.K.? It's Jerome."

"Jerome."

"Jerome."

"Jerome. How about a break?"

"As you wish."

Nikki stretched, arching her back as she made little fists. The defense team filed out, Nikki bringing up the rear.

SEVEN

W*hy didn't you* warn me?" Hoover was distraught.

"Why didn't *you* warn *me?*" Moss was stunned. Who vetted this guy? How had he gotten past Margolis and everybody else?

"Nobody knows these things. Where did he find Silberfeld? These files are *secret.* Nobody's ever gotten into this before."

"Heinz knows."

"What?"

"Your insurance company sold you downriver."

"My malpractice carrier?"

"Who else could know about the other cases, and about the censure, and probably Silberfeld too? Your insurance company sold you out."

"But why?"

"You betrayed them. You testify against doctors. So your carrier gave your claims files and dossier to Jerome Basteen. Told him where the bodies were buried, because Heinz asked them to. Professional courtesy. Your carrier may want to denut a plaintiff's expert from the Rockies someday. Heinz will accommodate. Why do doctors let insurance companies run their lives?"

Hoover loosened his tie and collar and smoothed his carapace of hair. He shuddered. "What's next?"

"You have to hang in there," Moss said. "Squat and hold."

"I really don't want to go through this again at trial."

"You told me there would be no trial." The prophetic son of a bitch.

What was next was an inquiry into Dr. Hoover's opinions regarding Dr. Bondurant's care. In this portion of the deposition Dr. Bondurant took a keen interest. He pitched his lineman's build forward and settled his elbows on his knees. He hunted Hoover's rabbity eyes. It's not easy to call another doctor a malpractitioner when he's looking you point-blank in the face from three feet away.

Basteen fired off a volley of declaratives for Hoover's nervous assent: Wouldn't you agree that medicine is an art, not a science? That you can't practice medicine out of books? If you want to follow a recipe, you use a cookbook. But if you want medical diagnosis you use clinical judgment.

A bad outcome doesn't mean malpractice, does it? Clinical judgment is easy to second guess, isn't it? Hindsight is 20/20, but Dr. Bondurant was the man on the line, wasn't he? He was exercising clinical judgment. You weren't there, Dr. Hoover. Can you really second-guess what he did based on what he saw?

You don't in fact know what he sensed when he palpated Ms. Winter in clinical exam, do you, Dr. Hoover? Even if his judgment was mistaken and there was a malignancy, an error of judgment does not mean malpractice was committed. Does it?

You have to rely on what the patient tells you, don't you? If there's no clinical evidence of a breast lump what more can you do? You can't biopsy what's not there. Isn't that right?

Hoover was watching Basteen's hands. Basteen's beautiful fingers were working toward him, palms down across the conference table.

"Doctor?"

"That's right."

"The five mistakes you talk about in your report, they were errors of judgment, I guess."

"Yes."

"A judgment call, even if it turns out wrong, is not the same as malpractice, is it?"

"No."

"It would be nice to practice with a retrospectroscope." Basteen smiled at his quip. "But regardless of how his judgment looks in hindsight, Dr. Bondurant did not in fact commit malpractice, did he?"

Bondurant was bearing in like a bird on a worm.

Basteen assumed the baleful cast of one in judgment.

"Excuse me," Moss interjected pleasantly. His fingers fluttered for attention, like Woody Allen.

Nikki held the ready position, fingers bent above the keys.

The poor fuck stammered and spoke. "I can't say that he did."

"I want to break." Moss smiled all around. The flaming poltroon. It was come-to-Jesus time.

"Well, hey." Bondurant addressed Hoover palms out. "Got any Coke?"

Hoover was astonished by the question. "Sorry," he said. "No. I'm very sorry."

"They got Coke over across the street?"

"I suppose they may."

Bondurant stood. "I'm going to look for a Coke," he announced, and out they filed.

It was Moss's turn to work the doctor. "When you called me with your opinions you told me the first obligation of the physician was to do no harm. You're harming the hell out of my case."

"There were five serious errors of judgment," Hoover said. "Serious ones. I can say that."

"*Acts of negligence.*" Moss said. "*Deviations from the*

standard of care. That's what you have to say. Not errors of judgment."

Hoover shook his head. Moss was about to lose it. "What about the fucking diagram?" he demanded. *"He found the tumor.* He drew it and sat on it for three years as it grew and grew. *And grew."*

"That's *right."*

Hoover had acquired a dingy look. His curls were wilting, his bell rung. He'd become so suggestible, he'd entertain a suggestion from Moss.

Bondurant pushed in the door, Coke Classic in hand. "What's wrong with this town?" He stood around grinning. "Talk about dead. Where's your industry?" he demanded of Hoover.

"It was mostly defense."

"Clinton'll get what's left, when he's done with us." Bondurant repositioned his chair. He configured a particular angle of view. His sharp interest in Hoover's interrogation waned somewhat, replaced by attention, clinical perhaps, to the manner in which the court reporter's skirt was inching homeward on her net-stockinged thigh.

Nikki went at it in a spirited manner. With every keystroke a black pen wedged in her machine would twitch. Her quarter-moon earrings would jiggle. She kept an erect posture, elbows at her side. She watched the speakers' lips.

Hoover volunteered a view about the diagram. Now that was substandard. To fail to follow a diagrammed and suspicious breast lesion. Without question that was substandard.

"What diagram?" Basteen affected perplexity.

"The diagram of the tumor. The one that was crossed out."

"What tumor?"

"Ms. Winter's tumor. In I believe 1989. Yes, November 1989."

"Whose diagram?"

Now Hoover became perplexed. "Dr. Bondurant's diagram."

Basteen looked in apparent puzzlement at Bondurant. Bondurant shrugged and looked at Heinz. Heinz looked nowhere and everywhere. The reporter looked from mouth to mouth to mouth, waiting for words to form.

Basteen formed some. "There was no diagram in Dr. Bondurant's chart, Dr. Hoover. Was there?"

"It had been, well, scribbled upon, apparently."

"Apparently? When did you first see this diagram someone supposedly drew?"

He had recently been sent a fax.

"Mr. *Moss* sent you this diagram?"

From Heinz was then heard a short, cynical snort. The team took it as a signal. Basteen began to cackle softly. A grunting rumble came from Bondurant. Bronchial merriment. Nikki joined in. Ha ha, she laughed. The mole capered. Ha ha ha. Something had to be funny. Laughing was funny.

What the hell was this about? They knew where the diagram came from. Moss began to feel very uneasy. It was past time for the airport but Basteen wouldn't let up. Moss's heart sank. A second night in Manchester, and he had a client to find and a case management conference with Langworthy to prepare for.

Hoover had begun talking very slowly and in a strange tinny voice. His curls were limp as seaweed. What he said no longer mattered. He was brain-dead and broken. He'd say anything Basteen wanted; he'd betray his profession, his country, and Terry Winter to get this over with.

The hours dragged on. The process was purely punitive now, deposition as caning. Hoover was being taught a lesson—what befalls the turncoat who violates the code. Bondurant's look of glassy satisfaction was more than Moss could stomach.

In the Holidome on the way to his room Moss passed the Front Runner bar. Nikki waved gaily. She pointed at her margarita, motioned for him to join them. Moss kept walking. Moss bore up. Moss did not hurl his trial bag in the pool. Bondurant was nursing a glass of brown liquor.

Heinz was elsewhere. Basteen, still fully suited, gripped a little bottle of Evian water in one hand. With the other he massaged his court reporter's knee. Before him his cell phone sat cocked like a travel alarm.

In his overheated unit Moss unscrewed the Travelmate plastic vodka bottle, thought better and screwed it up again, and lay back looking at the water-stained acoustic tile. Even if he found his client, no way could he go to trial now. You have to prove medical negligence through expert testimony that establishes the standard of care. His one and only standard-of-care expert had just been shot and plucked. It's too late to find another. He'll never survive a motion to dismiss. *It is too late now.*

Hours later he awoke. The overhead light was still on. He was totally, ferociously lucid. There had come to him in the middle of the night a brilliant stratagem. He scribbled it down on a Holiday Inn telephone pad. Guts ball, à la Junker. Go for it, by God.

It would never work. It was all he had. Moss lay back down and slept as though he'd earned it.

The overcast the next morning had a light spot in it that reminded Moss of the sun. He hunched down the commuter's aisle and prepared for the puddle plop to Boston. He watched with morbid fascination the de-icing of the prop's frail dragonfly wings with what looked like hot water wands from a carwash.

All, certainly, was not lost. Moss had copped an amenity kit from the hotel bathroom, and he had mileage-plus upgrade to first class on the main leg west. Heading out of Boston he felt small in the cool cushiony seat with its superfluities of elbow room. Diminished by the breadth of failed expectations.

Moss declined the liquor unctuously offered, gratis though it was. Across the aisle a cap-backward kid had also somehow made it to the forward cabin. He'd accumulated on his tray table a row of teeny-weeny Jim Beam bottles, a couple of Pepsi cans, and a plastic cup. He had his headphone on and his connector snubbed into the armrest though the in-flight feature, *Manhattan Murder Mystery*, was yet to begin. He was laughing hysterically. Must have been the comedy channel.

The first lunch course was a mixed green salad. Moss unsealed the little cup of dressing and sprayed his shirtfront with Ranch Lite.

With no warning the 757 began to shudder and thrash like a virgin with an incubus. Clear air turbulence. Red alert. The kid grinned like an idiot at a videogame. Moss wanted to retch.

He fixed his attention on the wall-mounted flashlight, the pulse of its light-emitting diode. Like something on a camera. A dashboard. An electric eye. A warning. Don't look down.

EIGHT

J*unker, fingertips on* fingertips in a pose of prayerful concern, had been joined in his office by Neil Wylie. Wylie stayed on his feet. He kept his suit jacket buttoned. He bristled with agitation before a serene west-facing view. Flagstaff Mountain was mantled with new green in the lower meadows and aspen stands. Behind the mountain lay a flawless sky. The view, Moss thought, as he watched from a doorway, must have seemed to Wylie an ominous scene, sparkling with ultraviolet threat. Springtime meant ticks, poison ivy, dangerously swollen creeks. Wylie hitched down the Levelors across the great outdoors. Junker swiveled smoothly officeward and cast his eye upon the prodigal at his door. He lay his long hands atop his barge of a desk in the fashion of the Lord.

"Peter."

"I am summoned?" Moss swayed slightly, still spacey from the flight.

Wylie's agitation accelerated. He apparently felt the need to add something. "Moss," he added. He spoke the name as a command.

Strange bedfellows, Moss observed, who worship at the Church of the Bottom Line. Wylie Coyote, tax attorney,

wise user and sagebrush rebel, board member of Mountain
States Legal Foundation, allied with Junker, Courageous
Advocate, Trial Lawyer for Public Justice, tribune of civil
liberties and giant judgments, who affected a Native American aesthetic. They had made a sacrament of their common
ground, the primacy of the fee—the final measure of human
endeavor.

"Here we are." Junker was moved to introductory remarks. *"Partners."* His hands rose. They expressed in the
air a metaphor for a law office, a capacious shape with sides
and a bottom formed by fingers and touching thumbs.
"Each of us part of *one firm*. We spend more time with
each other than with our wives. Ever think about that? Peter, we're *family*." Junker gave the word a portentous ca-
dence, more Mario Cuomo than Dan Quayle.

Moss sank deeper in the Ralph Lauren couch thinking
about it. He noticed between the imitation Maria bowls and
the rainmaker kachina the case files in *Winter v. Bondurant*
stacked on Junker's credenza, and beside them reams of
continuous-feed green-bar billing printouts.

"What do you want, guys? I've got a lot to catch up on."

"I want to know about settlement in the Bondurant case,"
Wylie said in an unfamilial way. He'd been studying the
file.

"Long gone. Kiss it good-bye."

"I can talk to Basteen," Junker offered.

"No, you can't. We have no authority. Anyway the case
has changed complexion."

"So it appears." Wylie waved a memo from the case files,
Moss's summary of his meeting with Dr. Greenwood.

"I'm dense, Moss. Explain it for me. What's this mean
for case value?"

"Case value?"

"Moss, I'm dense."

"Our client is dying, Neil, is what that means. It won't
be easy for her daughter."

"I understand the woman's terminally ill. What does that
do to the case?"

"If our client dies before trial there's still a case."

"Case value?"

"This is a heartless state, Neil. Dead people aren't worth much."

"How much?"

"Dad claims he supports the kid. If true the kid has no pecuniary loss on the mom's death. So the kid and the dad get noneconomic claims only and they're capped."

"At?"

"Two-fifty combined."

"The economics aren't there."

"Can you strip it down and try it?" Junker wanted to know.

"Could, but she dies and the spouse controls the claim."

"So?"

"Not a friend of mine."

"Befriend him."

Moss laughed. "Don't call Basteen, Junker, but call this guy if you like."

"I'm really dense," Wylie said. "You have a two-fifty max case we're soon to be fired from? Is that it?"

"That is possibly it."

"A case on which you *turned down* four hundred?" Junker circled back to Wylie's point of departure.

Wylie was disconsolate. "Oh shit, oh dear."

"The question is, what do we want as a *firm*, Peter, not as Peter Moss." Junker projected a statesmanlike tone. "A fair outcome and a fair fee is what we want as a firm."

Moss expressed a little surprise. Junker wanting no more than a fair fee was like Gandhi advocating violence.

"So how do we pull it out of the fire?"

"I have some ideas." Moss endeavored to sound positive. "No depositions of defense standard of care experts. That should save major costs."

"How about our standard of care expert?"

"You haven't heard?" Get a pro, Junker had said. Ask Margolis. Go with the tried and true.

"I heard," Junker grunted.

"I'm having him bronzed and planted on a New Hampshire courthouse lawn."

"Peter, how can you go to trial?"

"I have some ideas. You'll like 'em. Case management conference tomorrow afternoon. We'll see how things sit with the judge."

"You're dreaming. Let me talk to Basteen. Get one-fifty, a hundred, anything. Stop the bleeding."

"No authority."

"Get it." Wylie assumed the imperative mode.

"You got client problems," Junker added, "you find solutions."

"How do you do that," Moss asked, "when the client's gone?"

They stared at him.

"Where to, I have no idea."

"Oh shit, oh shit, oh dear."

NINE

The letter that unscrolled from the telefax later that afternoon began with pious, stilted ridicule for the plaintiff's claims and a pledge to seek sanctions for misleading interrogatory answers that concealed the metastasis Moss had only recently disclosed. It concluded with a confidential $200,000 statutory offer of settlement time-limited to the start of the next day's conference with the judge where, the letter hinted, unpleasant surprises lay in store.

Moss's gelid fluids began to trickle again. Basteen knew Moss had no liability expert and possibly only a capped death claim. But for all his swagger Bondurant did not want to face a jury this time.

Moss had to find his client, and, once found, lean hard. He called the Sugar Beat for Yellowhorse, Terry's Lakota friend. He reminded him of the battle of the blue pickup, the calvary rescued in the nick of time. "By the way," Moss said. "Thanks."

"Yeah, you," Yellowhorse said. "I remember you."

"How can I reach her?"

"Can't, man. She's out the chute."

"Know where she went?"

"Somewhere out where the buses don't run. Took off last

weekend in Frank's Chevy. Frank wants his rig back."

"Frank?"

"Owns the bar. He reported it stolen yesterday. How the shitheel found out."

The shitheel, it developed, was Warren, monitoring police communications on his shortwave. Now Warren was out the chute as well.

"And I was watching him good, like a duck on a bug." Yellowhorse laughed hilariously. "Shitheel give me the slip. Catch him, you know how to find me."

Moss was at a loss. He called the police and the skip trace networks. He called the FBI, the Salvation Army Locator Service, Find-Me in Georgia, Friend Finders in Arizona. He called Basteen to ask for an extension of the offer. The extension was denied.

Another summons from Junker was shortly flashing. Wylie's fax room spies had passed on word of Basteen's letter.

"You got to be kidding," Junker said. "She stole a car?"

"Probably some kind of assumed permission. I don't know."

"Reported stolen?" Wylie asked.

"Well, evidently, yes. Look, she was being stalked. There were phony reports to social services. They won't file charges. This will help us find her."

"Stalked? By who?"

"The husband. Ex. Almost ex."

"Our future client." Junker snorted.

"Are you telling us," Wylie said, "the two hundred thousand's dying on the vine while the client lams out in a stolen car?"

"A van, I believe," Moss said. "Maybe a sport utility vehicle?"

"Status of the offer?"

"Basteen won't extend. We have to reject it."

Junker looked pained. "Whose case is this, Peter?" Junker asked. "How'd we lose control?"

"Well, it's her's. She's the client so it's her case."

"Cut the shit."

"No shit. I'm trying to find her."

"Cut the shit and take the two hundred."

Moss stared at Junker. Wylie peeked suspiciously through the Levelors at spring's ascent of the mountain, a hundred feet a day.

"I have no authority." He spoke with deliberation.

"Take it anyway."

"Fuck off."

"Take it and explain later. She'll understand. What does she care? She's run off somewhere to die."

Moss gave them a stony look, for lack of power of speech.

"Do it for her kid. She'll love you. Explain it was the right thing to do. She'll go along, Peter. What alternative does she have?"

"To sue me and you, you son of a bitch, and she'd win."

"Back off, guys." Wylie the mediator.

"Sue you too, Wylie."

The Coyote went rigid. Moss recognized an expression of almost unbearable distaste for litigation. Especially medical malpractice litigation, and especially since his oft-told ordeal of getting stranded in the Bugaboos. Wylie had made the mistake of heli-skiing with a group of doctors in Canada. Great clients; byzantine tax fuck-ups. You'd think that with a half-dozen physicians and millions of dollars of equipment he could feel secure, but the unforecast blizzard blew in, the copters were grounded, and Wylie, shivering at the rim of a hissing campfire, praying for Mounties, endured a dusk-to-dawn dressing down for his partners' willingness to sue physicians. A vividly miserable night, for which he'd always blamed Moss.

"Moss." He spoke sharply, like a master addressing his dog.

"Neil."

"I've gone through the numbers. There have been unauthorized expenditures on this account."

"Not an account. A lawsuit."

"A *receivable*, Moss. That's what this is."

"I don't see it that way, Neil."

"Here's how I see it." When it came to litigation Wylie couldn't pour it out of a boot. How he saw it was beside the point. "This case has meant money outgoing on six months with zero income production. Is that a rational allocation of firm resources? It gets to a question of cutting losses. So, simple. Take the settlement or dismiss the case. What do you think?"

"I think you guys are a couple of cheesedicks."

"Laugh, Moss. We've got a business to run."

"A profession. There's a difference."

"We've got a major receivable."

"We've got a client."

"Not for long we don't."

Moss stared at Junker. Junker shrugged. His narrow shoulders moved independently of his spreading torso.

"You're overlooking something, Junker."

"There's no ethical angle to this. Your girl lied to us. Now she's left us holding the bag. We're done with her."

The phrase struck Moss cold.

"You're pissing up a rope, Junker, if you think I'll withdraw from representing a terminally ill client. You sicken me, man. You could gag a maggot off a meat truck."

Moss was regressing, a product of stress. Verbally, he'd crossed the Red River, headed south.

"Peter, listen. I like the case with a live client. No more do I like the case. That's that."

"That's what?"

"You can advance costs only subject to my approval."

"Partnership agreement," Wylie noted. "Eight point four point two."

"Discretion is mine," Junker said. "I got the big D, Peter. I hold the marbles."

"Subsection b."

"Where do we stand, Neil?"

Wylie went to the credenza. He rifled through the green-bar printouts, watchface reflection playing on Junker's diplomas like Tinkerbell. "Document examination, four thou, court reporters and transcripts come to three, travel and lodging in New Hampshire, L.A., Houston, forty-five hundred plus."

"Houston?" Junker asked.

"Unauthorized," Wylie answered. "Experts are Hoover at fifteen hundred and Epstein at six grand. Six grand? Incidentals, thirty-five. Total, twenty-two five and climbing."

"What was Houston?"

"Epstein. Eight hundred an hour."

Wylie whistled. Junker sucked his teeth.

"The cancer center charges that," Moss muttered. "Epstein gets nothing. He's pro bono."

"It's not where the money goes, Peter, it's where it comes from."

"It comes from us."

"The firm."

"The partnership."

"The family. I got it." Moss adopted a shrewd look. "Listen, I have this thing figured. Dial it down and hold for trial. Long as I have Epstein, I have a case."

"No you don't. You still need the standard of care."

"I have it."

"Moss, I'm dense."

"I call Bondurant in my case."

"In your case as your witness?"

"You can't eat turkey dinner without a turkey."

"*Bondurant* is your liability expert?"

"I don't need another expert," Moss said. "I have the man himself. He admitted to the standard of care in his deposition. It's on record. I prove it up *through him* at trial."

"Bondurant testifies against Bondurant?"

"Sure. He lays out the standard and lies about what he did to follow it. All I need to do is prove he's lying."

"That's insane. I love it. It's a dumb idea."

"Why?"

"Langworthy."

"Langworthy?"

"He'll never let it fly."

"So far," Moss said, "he's let things fly. I've had to duck."

"Moss." Wylie wasn't following. He in fact looked dense. "Tell me the plan."

"Simple. Set Bondurant up, knock him down, then Epstein gives us damages. The fucking Pharaoh of Breast Carcinoma."

"At eight hundred an hour? The economics aren't there."

"Cut him off." Junker was shaking his head.

"No Epstein and I'm dead."

"Call the mortuary. She wants Epstein, she can find the twenty grand more he's gonna cost. His fees are her obligation, not ours."

"Which we advance."

"At my discretion."

"Eight point four point three."

"My discretion's run dry, son. No more costs of any kind will be advanced on this file. You got to make do as is, Peter."

"I can't."

"Then shut her down." Junker kissed his fingertips like a Frenchman.

"Moss," Wylie barked. "Let me see if I've got it now. We're twenty-two five in the hole. Client's dying. When she dies case goes south with the husband. Recovery is maxed at two fifty regardless. But there will be no recovery because we have no expert witnesses and the client's vanished in a stolen car while being investigated for dependency and neglect. No experts, no damages, no claims, no client, no fee, no case. Have I got it now?"

"He'll Rule Eleven you for sure," Junker observed.

"What's that?" Unfamiliar citations made Wylie anxious.

"He'll sanction you halfway home to Texas, son."

"The goddamn doctor *did* it. He malpracticed on her and covered it up and now *she's going to die*."

"So what?"

"So *what*!"

"This is not a congressional investigation, amigo. This is a lawsuit like any other."

"This lawsuit is not like any other."

Junker did a double take, jowl snapping. "And how the fuck is that?"

"It's big. There's a punitives claim. It's not just negligent care."

"What is it?"

Moss threw up his hands. "I'm not quite there yet." Time to blow a little smoke. "I'm close. It may involve the Junius Foundation."

"The what?" Junker studied Moss warily, as though he had a communicable disease. "What this lawsuit is is a loser, pal. We're gonna eat not only thirty-five, forty thou in her costs but fifty or more of theirs because you rejected the statutory settlement offer."

"Oh shit, oh dear."

Moss was reminded of a military dilemma. All routes of honorable escape are closed off one by one. Honor then bids perseverance despite certain defeat. Or, if the choice is between getting shot in the back or in the face, get shot in the face. Or, sometimes a rope is all you've got to piss up.

"I am going to trial and I'm going to win," Moss accordingly declared. "And next time you shave, Junker, take a look in the mirror. You are what you used to hate."

Junker sighed. His face sagged, doughy and gray. "Peter, I sense an element of the personal has confused the question. Am I right?"

"Wrong."

"You bought in again, didn't you? What is it with Bondurant?"

"Bondurant," Wylie barked. His head was waggling like a dashboard dog's. "It's a holy war, you and doctors. It's a political thing."

"Get some distance, Peter. From Bondurant, from this woman, both."

"I intend to do my job. I know what happened here. It was bad. My job is to prove it."

"You've seemed troubled, Peter, ever since you got back from sabbatical. You contract some tropical illness?"

"You sound like I need counseling, fellas."

Moss saw then in Wylie's response, as he glanced down, tucking his head in the affirmative, that there was something else. The son of a bitch had searched Moss's office. He'd found the office bottle.

"Shit."

"Your client's long gone. You'll never see her again, Peter. Apparently, although it would benefit the daughter, you won't settle the claim in her absence."

"Correct."

"There's only one thing you can do, son."

Moss tried to look defiant but defeat dulled his eye.

"Bail."

Moss shook his head no.

"Why not?"

"Because it would be wrong."

"Who are you, Richard Nixon? Mother Teresa?"

Was it time to take a moral stand? Take a stand and get shot in the face?

"Cut her loose, Peter. Let go. Tough love. This case is over."

Moss shivered, partly in anger. He swallowed distastefully. "O.K., Junker. I got the point." He took a couple of breaths. "I'll do what I can."

Junker smiled paternally. "I know you will."

When Moss called home he got their machine. *Here comes the beep*, went Sally's karaoke rendition of the Beatles' tune. *Here comes the beep*.

"Sally, pick up. Pick up, Sally. Sally, are you there?"

He let the tape run noiselessly.

"It's six-oh-five. Let's go out for some mediocre ethnic. You be the designated driver. I'll be the designated drunk."

He let the dead tape run on.

TEN

In *the east* county, en route to the round courthouse for the case management conference, things were picking up. Mountain bluebirds coursed the yucca stubble. Redwings settled in cattails, yellow-heads soon to follow. In the shallows of a groundwater lake a heron was poised, spear-ready as a Chippewa. Meadowlarks were in full throat. Pasque flowers bloomed for his sins.

As required by the rules and promised to his partners, Moss had sent the motion for and notice of withdrawal of counsel certified, return receipt requested, to his client's last known address, the Sugar Beat Saloon, though she was five days gone to parts unknown. An irreconcilable conflict, the boilerplate read, has arisen in the attorney-client relationship. He fax-filed copies with the court for the case management conference and to Basteen. The transmittal letter to Basteen rejected the settlement offer. Rejecting settlement *and* moving to withdraw—let Basteen chew on that a while.

The motion and notice were pleadings without valor. That is all they were. Pleadings. Moss entertained ways to rationalize withdrawing from the case. He'd taken on too much, having to outwit not only Basteen and Bondurant but his own client, his own partners. Terry was a pain. Like Junker said, she ditched the case. Like Crutchfield said, a flake. Like Bondurant said, irresponsible. *Bondurant* . . . Withdraw and he walks again. Though, undeniably, were Moss to withdraw, a burden would lift like a shroud from a departing soul. No more med mal. *Malpráctica no más*.

At the ramped entrance to the ludicrous green building, trial bag in hand, Moss paused to observe Basteen and company debark his BMW and make way along the sidewalk. For a big man Basteen had a mincing step, conspicuously so beside Bondurant's slab-footed gait. Behind Bondurant was a vaguely familiar young woman working a mouthful of gum. Watching them, Moss imagined antipersonnel mines and remote administration of electroconvulsive shock. But Basteen safely minced on inside to the security gate and handed over his gear and gadgets.

The courthouse was a pressure cooker surging with conflict. Heated exchanges were happening everywhere. Clear-eyed cops in erect public postures escorted surly jailbirds in shackles and greens. Lawyers were all over the place parentally lecturing clients, or waiting, vacuous, to take their turns, or phoning in for news. There were signs—Quiet. Court in session—but no one was deterred. Anger, tears, madness, cunning, confusion, fear, shame, indifference, all were at hand down every hallway. Jurors with badges stood around blinking at the sights. Why wouldn't a physician want to leave his practice for a couple of weeks to stand trial here?

At the direction of the bailiff, a bodybuilder in a crisp sheriff's uniform, all rose in the windowless court. The judge wanted this one on the record, explained his clerk, a willowy law student with a vacant look. Then the judge swept in, robe swirling, ready for business.

Appearances were entered and motions taken up with no ado.

"Plaintiff's motion to accelerate trial. Your client's condition, Mr. Moss?"

"Grave, Your Honor. Terminally ill, as Dr. Greenwood's affidavit attests."

"Granted. Trial is advanced to June 27."

"Your Honor," Basteen uncoiled. "That is scarcely two months off. I'm afraid other commitments prevent . . ."

"I ruled, Mr. Basteen."

"If Your Honor would hear me out. My consulting oncologist, Dr. Irizarry Singh, is confident that if Ms. Winter undertook conventional cancer therapies she would survive well past the September trial setting. She is failing to mitigate her damages. I don't see why Dr. Bondurant should have to suffer for the plaintiff's recklessness with her health."

"I told you last time." The judge now addressed Moss. "Basteen's hoping your client will die. Mr. Basteen, I ruled. The next motion is yours for sanctions for misleading interrogatory answers. Your explanation, Mr. Moss?"

"My client has not been under medical care for six months. She is uninsured. She explained her condition as best she could. I supplemented the answer as soon as I learned of the recurrence."

"Explanation accepted. Motion denied."

"May I be heard?" Basteen had assumed the stooped pose of the supplicant.

"I *ruled*, Mr. Basteen. Next. Plaintiff's renewed motion to compel production of records relating to board of medical examiners investigations. Mr. Basteen?"

Bondurant whispered something Basteen dismissed with a shake of his head. He rose to his full height. "Your Honor, the proceedings of the board are confidential by statute. Section twenty-five seven one and two."

"As to the board. But as to Dr. Bondurant no privilege obtains. He will produce all responsive documents in his possession under seal for my *in camera* evaluation of relevancy versus privacy interests. I want them here by the end of the month. Any problem with that, Dr. Bondurant? That gives you a week and a half, Dr. Bondurant."

Bondurant raised his eyes. "Guess not."

"That leaves a final matter. Mr. Moss's motion faxed us this morning. Have you seen this, Mr. Basteen?"

"Indeed." Basteen nodded.

"Has there been a substitution, Moss?"

"At this time, no. I remain counsel of record."

Langworthy examined Moss a long moment. His deep and wide-set eyes were disconcerting, like creatures crouching under a ledge. "Mr. Moss, you want off the case?"

Moss flushed. He indicated something like assent.

"What are your client's wishes?"

"I am unable to communicate with my client."

"Why is that?"

"Her whereabouts are unknown."

The judge hooked on his glasses, glanced at the motion, removed the glasses. He pointed with them like a senator. "Your client is dying, Mr. Moss." The crouched eyes came forward.

"She is, Your Honor."

"Your client is dying and you want me to *accelerate* her trial then leave her with no lawyer? And you don't know where she is?"

Moss said nothing. He had cases on point, an appellate opinion allowing withdrawal when a terminally ill client could not be located. He declined to cite his authority to the judge.

"Mr. Moss, I shouldn't have to advise you of your professional obligations. Your first and last duty is to your client. There may be duties you have shirked in the past. *This is a duty you will not shirk*. Not in my court."

So Langworthy knew about Moss's time in the stockade, his C.O. discharge. A quarter-century passes and still the conflict is fought. Get over it, Judge. The war is over; we lost. Touch the names on the wall and move on. Though Vietnam, Moss knew, would be like the Civil War, still playing out until everyone who was over there and everyone who wasn't was gone from the face of the earth.

"I can assure you," Moss said quietly, "I have the strongest allegiance to my client." What tests had the judge's code of honor survived? What fire had the judge withstood?

"Outstanding, Mr. Moss. Because if you have problems with your case, you don't cut tail and run. Maybe you don't get along with Basteen? Neither do I. Maybe you don't like me. I'm not the point. The point is the duty a lawyer owes a client. Am I making myself clear? You took an oath, Moss. For a lawyer, duty to client comes only after duty to country and to God. *Motion to withdraw denied.* Is there anything else that needs to be addressed?"

Moss had little chance to reflect on the multiple ironies he'd be reporting to his partners before Basteen was standing again, straight and prim as a mortician. He glanced briefly to his rear. Moss turned to see sitting in the gallery a hairless Ready-Kilowatt type in academic tweeds, the bulbhead, beside the young woman. "Indeed there are, Your Honor," Basteen said. "Some very troubling matters, indeed. Extremely troubling."

"Proceed."

"At our last hearing on motions you ordered the plaintiff to stand for deposition regarding her sexual and obstetrical histories. Mr. Moss has not complied with requests from my office to schedule that deposition. In light of his motion to withdraw, I question the plaintiff's intention and ability to comply. In our view the noncompliance is sufficiently serious to warrant dismissal of her claims."

"Mr. Moss?"

Moss stood. The courtesies were wearing. "I will do everything in my power to ensure compliance with the orders of this court. Your Honor."

"Absolutely you will." Langworthy smiled. "Motion to dismiss is denied at this time. Anything else?"

"There is, Your Honor. We just this week learned of the criminal alteration of evidence in this case."

"You have my attention, Mr. Basteen. By whom?"

"May I present the testimony of Professor Crawford?"

The bulbhead stood and buttoned his tweed jacket, homed in on the witness chair in a familiar way and was sworn.

Dr. Crawford, associate professor of anthropology at Stanford, breezed through his credentials, dwelling on a few celebrity trials, the Zodiac killer, the Wayne Williams child murders, the congressional investigation of the King assassination. His specialty was cross-over immunoelectrophoresis, a technique developed to age blood stains that was adaptable to inks. He'd described in *Nature* his use of the process to identify deer killed in the twelfth century from stains on an Anasazi knifeblade unearthed at Chaco Canyon. He'd determined by date and place of drugstore purchase the pen used by the Zodiac in the boasts he mailed to the *San Francisco Chronicle*. James Earl Ray had probably not acted alone, given electrophoretically enhanced diary entries.

Immunoelectrophoresis had, in Dr. Crawford's view, ten times the accuracy of BATF match-ups like those relied on by Lieutenant Moschetti. Dr. Crawford had observed Moschetti's crude attempt to examine the chart in March. It was the kind of performance the sheriff's department had dismissed him for. Afterward, Dr. Crawford reevaluated Terry Winter's chart with state-of-the-art technology. His analysis did confirm Moschetti's opinion that a diagram had been drawn at a different time than the doodling on the crucial page in question. But the diagram was drawn *after* the doodling, not before, as Moschetti had mistakenly concluded. And Moschetti misdated the ink. Dr. Crawford's more sophisticated studies showed the simplistic outline of breasts and a lump had been added *on top of* the cross-hatched scribbles by a Pilot Precise V7 rollingball, fine.

"Dr. Crawford," Basteen inquired. "When did the Pilot Precise V7 rollingball, fine, first enter the market?"

"The court may be interested to learn this particular series of rollingball pen was not marketed until March 1993."

"Signifying what?"

"Sometime during the last year someone with access to Ms. Winter's chart added the breast diagram on to one of its pages."

Moss's cross-examination slid off the bulbhead like beer

off a balloon. The bulbhead was slick. A big boy from California. He'd cost ROMPIC a bundle. Where the hell was this going? Nowhere good, Moss realized, when, as their eyes met, he now recognized the next witness. Patti, Bondurant's front-office girl. She'd left her gum outside.

"I was watching him the whole time," Patti told the judge. "He wouldn't take just copies. He had to have originals. I thought that was funny, so I made him sit there in the waiting room. I thought it was funny how he was acting, and I kept a real good eye on him through the billing window over there. He was weird. He said weird things."

"Please identify who you were watching in Dr. Bondurant's waiting room November 12 of last year."

"Him."

Patti pointed. The bailiff looked up from his crossword. The law clerk crossed her legs and straightened her shift. Moss felt sick. He stared at Basteen. The mortician. Bondurant began to smile, as did the judge, Moss noticed with alarm.

"And what did you see Mr. Moss do?"

"After he got through looking at it is when I saw him go back some pages. He kind of hunched up but I saw it. He got out this black pen? I saw that. I saw him write something real careful. Right on the chart. It looked like it was right there on that page, right on the doctor's doodle. You know that page? Right there on it he was writing like he was making circles. Big circles then a littler one. A smaller littler circle in it."

"What did you do about this?"

"Well, I got the chart back and took a look but I didn't see anything. Just the same doodle it looked like, you know. So nothing. Not until we talked with the professor. Then it all added up, how weird he was."

Moss required a continuance of the hearing. Moss needed to investigate and conduct discovery. More immediately he needed to contain his outrage. Basteen had another idea.

"Shall this matter be referred to the district attorney, Your Honor, for criminal inquiry?"

The judge regarded the ceiling. The bailiff and the clerk sat a little straighter. "I'm retaining jurisdiction, Mr. Basteen."

"In that case, I renew my motion for dismissal of the plaintiff's claims on the ground of egregious and continuing misconduct including criminal tampering with evidence."

"Mr. Basteen." The judge had begun looking emphatic again. "We will proceed to trial on the accelerated date. Mr. Moss may present his forensic documents testimony at trial. You may present yours. *At trial. Understand. This case is going to trial.*" Bondurant darkened. He looked put out. Langworthy then smiled maliciously at Moss and suddenly Moss suspected a thread connecting his rulings: He's setting me up for sanctions. He may be setting up Basteen too.

The judge rose and leaned across the bench. He was pointing a finger at the lawyers. His law clerk looked a little embarrassed. The bailiff was ready for trouble.

"You fellows need to get a few things straight. Mr. Basteen, we've had our differences. I punch the clock for the government now. It ain't easy money but at least it's my show. I am *not* recusing from this case. I am *not* dismissing this case. I am *not* continuing this case. I am staying on this case. Mr. Moss is staying on this case. This trial will go forward. Mr. Moss, do what you need to do to represent your client as best you can. Is that clear? *I am staying on this case and so are you and so are you.* We will all be there at trial. Get used to the idea. See you June 27."

He turned, flared, and vanished in the paneling.

Moss packed up in a hurry. He needed air, but Basteen, waving off questions from his client, was bending Moss's way.

"Let me give you a little advice, Pete. You need a lawyer."

Outside Moss looked west. In the high country another

storm was rolling over the gray-reefed range. Somewhere beyond the stormbank, Moss sensed, was his lost and dying client, while here he had no ropes, no comrades. He was thrown back on mother wit alone. He was free-climbing.

ELEVEN

T*erry walked slowly* into the Sea of Cortez, her wig belted to her waist. She plunged her hands through the surface and bubbles trailed from her fingers. A wavy dappling of sunlight gloved her. She turned and studied her palms, snared in rubbery nets of light.

On the beach Emmy finished the Neapolitan bar Terry bought her from the Seri Indian vendor at the trailer camp. A daily ritual, eating ice cream, La Flor de Michoacán, while Terry took her swim. Twenty years later and it was still her Mexico. Not a Para-Sail or Jet Ski in sight.

Lines of pelicans scaled the laminated water, wingtips almost touching. Blue-footed boobies gathered in quivers then arrowed deep for squid. Frigatebirds glided by in formation and oystercatchers worked the flats. Lightning sat watching like a kid at a fireworks show.

"Earth to Mom," Emmy hollered to her from the beach. "Hello."

Terry waved once then swam away, further out than she'd been before. As she understood it, the Seris believed in three worlds. The world of the surface, and a mirror world under the sea that was identical but reversed, and a third, brilliantly lit underground world that could be seen where the boojum trees grew. Light that glimmered from the cracks in the earth.

Treading water, Terry drew the wig from the belt. She breathed deep and dove, fingers knotted in the synthetic ringlets. She unfurled her false hair and released it suspended, rose and gasped for air. She shook her head and opened her eyes to rainbows.

Terry worked free the prosthesis from the sewn-in pocket of her swimsuit, tossed it and languidly crawled to shore. Behind her, I'm Me Again! bobbed upright on the wavelets like a little lunar module. A bird pulled out of a plunge to snatch it. The blue-foot circled the bay with deep wing-beats, white prosthesis in its beak.

"Say good-bye, hair," Terry said, back on the sand beside Emmy.

" 'Bye, hair."

"It's the real me from here on in."

Weeks on the beach and traipsing through the desert had bleached Emmy blonder and frosted her eyebrows. There was real definition to her tanned features now. Good-bye dog's ears and baby fat. Clear desert, blue ocean, and her daughter growing up—not a bad deal except for Emmy's conviction it was a matter of time before her father found them. A conviction Terry shared. This fatalism thing was catching, south of the border.

That, and what was still unspoken between them, and her headaches and eyes and the pain in her bones, irritatingly constant now, like an overbearing sky, reminding her what was coming down. Provoking the odd gesture of defiance.

Defiance—acceptance. You had to have both, Terry concluded, here where the surface world ended, the mirror world started, and the underworld beckoned, taking a few weeks to get ready for the next phase. And for talking about it.

"What's that?" Emmy asked. She pointed at the bird circling with its trophy.

"Boobie," Terry answered.

Now the Seri ice cream vendor was squatting down beside them. Tiny hands and big splayed feet, a tattoo on his hairless face, a single blue line across his cheeks and the bridge of his nose. Lightning trotted over.

"What's up, amigo?"

A visitor had been looking for them. He waited at their trailer. The Seri chuckled. He was always chuckling, polishing an ironwood carving of a whale.

"He say tell you he come for her."

Like divers they made their way through the desert. They meandered along a white sand bottom, careful not to touch. Staghorn cholla, yucca colonies, agave stars. Barrel cacti like brain coral, tilting southwest, spines dipped in blood. A red rattler retreated like an eel. Emmy didn't flinch. They startled a school of quail. A cardinal flashed, caracaras shadowed overhead. Doves shoaled from their path.

The Seri was hard to stay with. He shot through the matorral like a snake. On a flat rock a raven fed on a lizard. A blacktail deer was coughing. Something moved, wings whistled. In a paloverde a dove nested motionless, shiny black eye all alert intensity.

A cactus wren chorkled like an irrigation pump. A gilded flicker squeaked like a wellbucket handle. But there wasn't any water.

Terry made it to a huge cardon, dropped her daypack, and collapsed in its shade. The brightness had become unbearable. Some while later Emmy ran up. She'd found an arrowhead, glittering obsidian.

On their desert rambles they'd seen many things. They'd found a cow killed by bees, black tongue and eyeballs bubbled with stings. They'd come across two vaqueros breaking ponies Sonora-style, staked by the necks and hind legs, with blindfolds and rawhide nosepieces pulled so taut they bled. The cowboys got one pony untied. Both mounted and spurred him off blindly, jerking the raw nose this way and that. As soon as they were gone Terry freed the other four, yanking away the blindfolds and gitting them off with a whack and a holler. She crouched back in the scrub with Emmy, heart hammering like a bird's.

Emmy had wanted to know what the point was. "They'll just do it again."

"Point is," Terry told her, "there's a standard of care. You have to do what's right."

"Care for what?"

"Life," she said. "Treat no living thing cruelly. Don't hurt animals, don't hurt children, and stop the ones who do just because they can."

Now in the shade of the cardon cactus Terry fingered Emmy's arrowhead. All those weeks getting ready. Now was the time to act. Take care of Emmy and deal with Warren.

"I'm dying, Em," Terry said, but no one heard.

"C'mon, Mom," Emmy called. "He says there's water up here."

At the top of a sculptured rinconada they reached a tinaja, a plunge pool five feet across and, according to the Seri, bottomless. He submerged his face to drink below the surface alive with wigglers. Terry then Emmy did the same. Dozens of yellow butterflies picked and waved at the muddy margins. A vermilion flycatcher watched from a palo blanco bough. There was neither wind nor cloud. Yellow primrose and purple verbena carpeted the bolsón below. Beyond the valley a black mountain and blanching the sky a haze from the gulf. Thirst quenched, it was the perfect place.

Boojum trees were all around. Feel their *icor*, the Seri said. In all things dwelled a lifeforce called *icor*, an invisible hairy bug that flew around the thing whose spirit it embodied. Among the bristly, twisting boojum she could sense a surly and maddened force. The frustration of being a tree. Why cutting a branch will release the blowing wind.

"Emmy, sit down." The right place, the right time—the end of the trail. She was ready. "You need to know something."

A boojum creaked. The ground shimmered and Terry

understood. Illness has no meaning, the boojum said.

"I'm not going to make it through the summer."

"What do you mean, Mom?"

"I'm dying." Illness just is.

"Now?"

"No. Yes. Not exactly this minute, but yes I am. This is it."

Emmy looked stricken, as Terry expected, but also angry. "Tell me the truth, Mom."

"I have a thing about talking about it. I can't tell people." Telling her was like letting her go.

"But I'm me."

"Dying's something Moms shouldn't do," she said. All messed up now with tears, as she'd feared. Blubbering idiot. She hated this.

"Tell me the real truth."

"I shot my wad. Won't get well. Matter of months. There. You're on your own. I said it." What her own mother had never said. "It's done."

Emmy's eyes shone but the grim fury remained, and a dazed look, almost of humiliation.

"You really are really dying?"

Boy, was this complicated. "Didn't you know?"

"I was too afraid."

"It's nobody's fault."

"Yes it is."

"It's my body is all. I got sick. It happens. I'm not even sure how much I blame the doctor."

"He could have made you well."

"True."

"You're dying because of him."

"I guess."

"Get a clue, Mom. *It's his fault.*"

"I suppose it is."

"It's *my* fault too. I want to die."

Oh, brother. "No way. I get to think about you growing up. That's what makes me happy now."

"Can't anybody help you?"

Shaking her head and not trying anymore to control it. "You need to get ready for school and stuff this fall. We have that trial, a lot to do."

"Nobody can help?"

"No, Em, damn it."

Emmy hugged herself. Terry tried to comfort her but she pulled away.

"What's the matter? Emmy, *answer me*."

"I'm not mad at you, Mom." Through clenched teeth.

"What is it?" She reached for Emmy's arm but Emmy wrenched it from her.

"He broke his promise. *I hate him*." Emmy began to sob, now letting Terry hold her. "I knew it was a lie. It's my fault. I wish I was dying too."

Lightning was there licking and nuzzling. The Seri stood off perplexed.

"You can talk about it. You can tell me."

So Emmy did. They washed their faces in the tinaja and drank and sat tailor-fashion on the smooth stones. Emmy worried the dimpled arrowhead. Bit by bit, with a feeling of deliverance, she told her mother everything she'd sworn not to, every detail, for no harm could come of it now.

The blue truck was on the beach near the headlands where the trail led back to town. They'd heard him from a distance target shooting, like firecrackers on a string, at what she didn't want to guess. Now Warren assembled his surf-casting rig, tying on lead and what looked like a PVC popper with a blue jethead skirt. He watered the line with a squeeze bottle. With a two-fisted pole-vaulter's run, he planted and cracked the twelve-foot cane like a bullwhip, kiting the skirted popper all the way out to blue water. He walked it in on the slack tide coming over the rocks. He cast another and let it set, driving the rod upright in the sand by the beach spike on the butt-end. On the third eyelet he hung a little bell. He reached for the mescal.

A wind had come up and spindrift curled from low rollers in the channel. On the beach the dunes smoked in the wind like dry ice. Lightning whined softly. They watched behind a brushy ridge. The trail came out at the Seri village but the way to the trailers and town would be blocked by Warren.

Terry poked through her daypack and found a pen and a postcard. A jackalope—Greetings from Moab. She took Emmy by both shoulders. She would head down the face of the ridge. Emmy should go with the vendor to the Seri village and wait there.

Smiling intently, "This'll go just fine. But just in case, here's what to do." She slipped the roll of bills from her sock to Emmy. She didn't think the Seri saw. The eagle fetish she kept for herself. On the jackalope card she wrote Peter Moss a note: "Stop everything. We missed the boat. *We had it all wrong*. Details to follow." She gave the card to Emmy.

"I'll probably see you in a couple of hours, but if I'm not back by tomorrow morning you need to get out of here. Find a stamp and mail this card, then go to Boulder and go see Peter Moss. Take buses. Say whatever you have to. Hey, tell the truth."

"Don't worry about me, Mom."

"When you get there tell him everything you told me." Terry winked and kissed her. "It'll work out, baby."

"I know it will."

She gave Lightning a head rub and shook the Seri's hand. "Protect her."

"Con mi vida," the Seri said.

Terry eased herself down the cactus ridge. She dropped on to wet sand by the pools in the lee of the headland. She straightened up, breathed a few counts, and set off toward Warren. Blowing sand feathered her ankles. The vein on her temple stood forth.

In an eddy by the rocks the wig had drifted in with other plastic garbage rocking in the backwash. Three chicos jeered and scared each other, poking at it with sticks. It sank from sight then slowly rose, her effigy, long whorls unwinding. The macho of the three pawed it in and fished it out with his stick. Triumphantly he held it speared before his comrades, faceless and dripping, in a charade of conquest.

Part Three

THE TRIAL

ONE

A *charade* . . .

Captain Haas calling in a full Fort Benning night-line sweep on Phu Quan. The hamlet had produced on fire. Nobody would be there but mothers and kids, grandfolks, and the captain wants a night sweep, when everybody's sleeping, so when the tracers flame the palmthatch we maximize the kill.

At LZ Believer, the firebase on the hill, Captain Haas had been red-ass pissed. We will not be taken lightly in this country by these people.

Having no choice he put Moss in charge. A half-strength company of teenagers and Moss at twenty-three who'd come to think, I'm too old for this shit.

Slowly the afternoon lengthened, heat beginning to relent. The shadows spread like bloodstains. Slowly the idea sank in.

The operation had a jinxed feel from the start. Bunkered down two nights before at LZ Believer above a narrow peninsula between paddies and a deep canal. The peninsula led to a bridge to the forest. The forest would be cleared here and there for hamlets, among them Phu Quan. The firebase bunkers above were secure, too secure—ten feet deep and in danger of caving if the monsoons hadn't quit. They'd been bivouacked three weeks without contact. Tired, filthy, strung out, bored. One night they caught a little harmless fire but it jerked the captain's chain. He ordered massive return volleys, but the edgy silence afterward didn't help his mood. He sent Hobart, his last lieutenant, out the slit trench with a patrol. They found a couple of tunnels and smoked them with CS. They flipped a few grenades.

Moss would later own a German shepherd that got into porcupines. Stumbled back at dawn nearly bled to death, fifty quills down her throat. She learned from experience, but not the right lesson. She learned to hate porcupines, to chew into them every chance she got. Sally would hug her caked neck while Moss tenderly twisted out the quills with needle-nose pliers, cursing Captain Haas.

The following morning the captain ordered the company to work downhill where the heat had come from. In a tunnel Hobart blew the night before were two dead VC with thirty-year-old French Mausers. No wonder they couldn't shoot straight. Below the hill the ground funneled onto a grassy strip alongside the canal. Across the canal was a wall of jungle. They probed the water but it was too deep to ford. It was hot out in the open. Moss was on the radio when an incoming M-79 blew a hole in the bank, then another from a different direction. The enemy had U.S. rifle grenades. They were walking them up from somewhere behind the trees.

Moss asked about pulling back but the captain wanted Hobart on the handset: String the company out so they couldn't home in. Double-time down to the bridge and cross it. Get out of the open, split up in squads, and flush the fuckers out.

It was so hot on the treeless strip. All ninety men porting four gallons of water. A few fools with flak jackets open. They formed a column, Hobart in front, Moss at the rear. They shuffled clumsily toward the low planked causeway, no siderails, twelve feet wide. But for the panting and banging of gear, there wasn't a sound. Not a leaf in motion in the triple canopy on the other side.

In those days Moss had great ears, like a sixth sense. The moment the column was reaching the bridge, he suddenly understood the booby-trap cunning that had baited them there—stung them with nightfire on the hilltop, mocked them with their own M-79's, prodded Haas like a quill-maddened dog. His only question was whether the enemy he sensed entrenched behind the treeline would command-detonate by radio or wire.

The whole company went down together from the concussion. The wall of trees shuddered with fire. All four men on the bridge were hit. Men were hit up and down the line. Moss lowcrawled toward the blastcrater at the foot of the bridge. He pulled into a crouch and ran for the bridge. He collared Hobart and dragged him to the crater. With only barrelflash to aim at he emptied his M-16. Then he emptied Hobart's. Then he emptied five more rifles from five more men who were down and struggling to get in the hole. He ran back along the bank, grabbing weapons and raking the trees and when the last round was spent from the last M-16, Moss pulled out his .45 and emptied it and dove then himself for the blastcrater writhing with the wounded.

He called for air support and reported to Haas their dilemma: Cut to pieces from the tree line. Five killed, eighteen wounded. No cover except a hole in the sand. No way to fall back with so many wounded, two still bleeding on the bridge. Worst of all, no ammo. Night coming when the enemy would finish them off.

Son, the captain told him, you got to tough it out.

The gunships rolled on past dark, tracers raining down, and then it was quiet. All night Moss listened, hearing nothing but his own shallow breathing, the beat of his blood, the sounds of the wounded. Daybreak came like an undeserved gift. Medical evacuation got through and they were resupplied by noon.

Moss felt the captain might have second thoughts, the company now down to one-third strength with a radioman in charge. VC wants to play tough, the captain said, we'll play tougher. Move on to Phu Quan.

Upchurch, on point, reported back the obvious: The village had a hundred or so women and children, not a full-sized male in sight, hootches with bunkers where they'd suffocate when the roofs caught fire.

"I ain't going," Catman said. He swung his head between his knees. "It's an evil deed."

The most evil part of the captain's orders—wait until night—gave Moss the time to think things through.

Ambushes aside, Moss looked forward to an honest firefight. It was a change of pace and the enemy couldn't shoot for shit. Village sweeps were another matter. A line sweep at night meant burning the village, killing innocents, and probably shooting some of their own.

Late afternoon they came across a body in the brush, a girl, maybe ten years old, killed by last night's strikes, her bicycle run up in the bamboo. Seeing her—that such things happened to children—and his decision was made. Bury her, he said. And then: We're not taking Phu Quan.

Moss smoked at the time, Pall Malls, one after another. He fingered the rubberband on his wrist. He watched the company waiting as the heat began to lift. Nodding off leaning on trees, hyperawake at a rustle or a lull. Rubbing nightfighter grease under red-rimmed eyes.

Moss told Catman that nobody was going, then went to the rest one by one. Everyone was in. They'd seen him standing under fire by the bridge. They'd take a court-martial if it came to that.

Everybody fell in at the edge of a weedy field that would be visible from the firebase a couple klicks north. They let it get good and dark. Moss hailed the captain on the radio. "We're approaching the hamlet, sir," though it was nowhere near. Pointing to Upchurch, who let off a burst.

"What do you have, Moss?"

"Contact, sir." Pointing; a series of bursts. "Two down trying for the woods. There's another." Pointing. Bursts.

"Gertz is circling left, Burris right." Pointing.

"Line ready?"

"That's a rog, captain. All lined up." He held up his hand up. "Village quiet. Do we move?"

"Move in. Put out all the fire you've got."

Moss gave a conductor's batonsweep and they slowly advanced on the empty field, tracers lacing the blackness; magnesium flares dripping sparks, draping the mahogany; the M-60 shaking and howling; M-26 grenades whomping midfield—a light-and-sound show for LZ Believer with Moss on commentary—nearing the plaza, blowing the well, shooting chickens, flaming hootches, wasting a cow, fire squad securing the road, there goes Victor Charley, Spradley's got him tagged.

They were spirits at his command, ghosts imagined into being. In his swelling sense of mastery Moss felt he could do anything. Lights could shoot from his fingertips. He could cause miracles. Prevent evil. Make a difference.

Slowly Moss raised both palms for crescendo. He covered the mouthpiece. Scream, he told his men. Scream real crazy, scream like you're loving it. He turned the volume knob and held the handset in the air.

"We're putting them down, sir. We're taking it out."

That village had mattered, Moss still thought. Stopping the murder of women and kids had mattered. His Vietnam was mostly flashes of things gone wrong except for what didn't happen in Phu Quan.

A few weeks after Nixon was elected with his secret plan to end the war, Moss got stuck with Calley heading an LLRP team in the Song Chang valley up in I Corps. Ridenhour, another Americal Lurp, would not tip Congress to My Lai 4 for three more months, but down in Chu Lai there'd been rumors. Calley disagreed with Moss on the subject of villages. Greasing gooks, Calley said, is the Lord's work, soldier. What the hell you think we're here for? They don't like us either.

Calley was a fuck-up and a fool, but it kind of framed the debate.

The morning after the night sweep of Phu Quan Captain Haas had addressed the unit at the firebase on their outstanding performance. The enemy has been dealt a heavy blow. Moss reports sixty-seven K.I.A. He was putting Moss in for his first Bronze Star.

The men had cheered with lusty irony. Moss knew it was time to leave line infantry.

What had his client said when Basteen asked her what she'd learned from her travail? To value your life. Moss could get into that at every level.

Now Junker was wanting to see him, the green voice-mail light pulsing indignantly. The case was coming on for trial in a week. What are we still doing here, son? I thought I said pull out.

Sorry, sir. Judge's orders. This is war.

TWO

W*hat was Moss* supposed to make of this?

You think you know your client and your facts, but all you really know is your case—which is to say your own mental constructs. Who was Terry Winter? And if he was so far from knowing her, who the hell was Bondurant?

Moss studied the photographic likeness of a cowboy riding a rabbit with antlers, on the back of the card the message to stop everything, we had it all wrong.

Real good.

Stop everything a week before trial, details to follow from a client who's vanished.

It had been a dissociated couple of months. Walking the halls a pariah, daring anyone to mention the case. Suffering Wylie Coyote's administrative indignities—reassigning his secretary, pulling his paralegal, sticking him with pool typing, loading the retreat agenda with items curtailing contingent fee practice. Nixon dies. Then Jackie dies. Then O. J. takes off in game five of the finals. Trying to get his mind off the fact that he's heading to trial in a week though he has it all wrong, and there's this all-channel deathwatch, cortege of squad cars in warm pursuit of the cryptic Bronco, well-wishers in lawn chairs, choppers worrying overhead.

Please think of the real O. J. and not this lost person.

Moss could feel his moorings slipping. In a way, sobriety made it worse. He'd been on the wagon since the hearing at which the trial date was accelerated. Free-climbing, he needed to marshal strength for the ascent, and he had the feeling, in work and in life, he might not have another chance. Finally his sleep had steadied. The irritability and headaches were gone, and he no longer wondered what to do with his hands. He woke up clear and focused for a day of grim endeavor. Lose focus, though, and he drifted fast, bored and empty, or worse, depressed by intrusive images. Bodies of children and men bleeding on a bridge. Sally's miscarriages. The verdict Bondurant won. Wondering if Terry Winter was alive.

Go, O. J., go.

The week before trial is ordinarily a sleepless frenzy of activity. Moss had time on his hands, trial anxiety concentrated into a paralyzing concern: Where is my client?

Wednesday morning he telephone-prepped Borkin and Moschetti then revised his outlines for their examinations. He went home at two. The office had felt like an enemy camp. Sally was in her studio finishing an esquisse for an intaglio print. He wandered into the yard.

In the old days Moss handled the pretrial whirlies, the intrusions, with a few stiff swacks to stay on track. This trial he didn't know where the track was. *We missed the boat*, the postcard said. *We had it all wrong.* That sounded serious. That sounded like an elemental, Darwinian error, the evolution of a flightless bird.

The yard had reached the season of purples and greens— phlox, iris, violets, lupine and shooting stars, columbines and periwinkles. Lazuli buntings and Stellar's jays. In back along the clear-running irrigation ditch were brighter colors, prickly poppies and Indian plum, wild roses, Harrison's yellow spilling over a fence. Fairy slippers in the meadow where the ditch overflowed. Yucca blossoms like strung shells staked along the bank. A kingfisher ringing like a wire in the wind. A thrush had killed itself against a window and fallen in the grass with flecked breast, curled feet. Moss cradled the weightless corpse and bore it to the flowered ditch, released it on the Ganges.

He evaluated his options. Weeding and shading the lettuce patch. Running the Sanitas Valley trail in the heat of the day. Returning to the office and Junker's voice mail.

The Sugar Beat it was.

Frank, the owner, was keeping the bar. Moss slipped him a business card and told him who his client was. "We spoke by phone a couple months back."

"Terry, Terry." Frank frowned, heavy with regret. He was a little hard to read. Rockies cap and a beard, gray Aggie athletic shorts and, laced-up white and hairless shins, an unsoiled set of in-line skates.

"Birthday," Frank explained. "Only go round once." He braced his way down to the beercocks. The deck was rolling on the *Golden Hind*. "How about a beer? Fat Tire on tap."

Moss opted for herbal tea. Red Zinger in a Beetnik cup.

"I'm looking at more of a sports bar concept," Frank informed him. "What do you think? Six-foot screens, digital sound, country karaoke. Brew pub and a latte unit."

"Hey, it's great like it is. Any word lately from Terry?"

Frank shook his head. He hadn't heard a thing since she mailed him back the keys to his van. Some investigator had been around. Dumb stuff like why she stopped working there. Told him Terry was a good worker but he had to let her go. Came in one day and found her fucking a billy goat. Guy wrote it down, thanked him, asked where might her present whereabouts be at.

"Don't suppose you said."

"No harm. Mexico's plenty *muy grande*."

The postcard was postmarked Albuquerque.

"This investigator. He ask about her borrowing the van?"

"Water under the bridge is how I put it. Horse drove it home. No harm done."

"Say." Moss squirmed a little in his shoulders. "You know just where in Mexico she got to?"

"Way down someplace where the rooster fucks the hoot owl. Talk to Horse. He's the one went and got the van."

Frank hollered and a braided head looked around the poolroom door. Frank motioned. Yellowhorse strolled their way, tightening the Velcro on his orthopedic belt. He chalked a cue, sizing Moss up. "Yeah, you," he said.

"Tell him what you know about Terry."

Yellowhorse blew softly at the blue cuetip. "Why's he want to know?"

"He's Terry's lawyer."

"What's in that cup, man?"

"Tea."

Yellowhorse nodded. "You a lawyer?"

"That's what I am."

Yellowhorse smacked his lips thoughtfully. "Say I got a friend. Like it would have been another D.U.I., you know, except he wouldn't blow in the little thing. So they pulled his license, but he don't have any wheels anyway. What else can they do?"

"That's probably it."

"Nothing, right?"

"Nothing."

"So just keep walking."

"Sure."

"Walk on." Yellowhorse plucked the cue like a bass fiddle.

"Hey," Frank said. "What's the difference between a lawyer and a sperm?"

"A sperm?" Yellowhorse studied his boss.

"At least a sperm's got a one in two-hundred-fifty-thousand chance of becoming a human being." He whacked Moss on the shoulder.

"Whoa, man." Yellowhorse's eyebrows arced. "Two-hundred-fifty-*thousand*?"

Moss reached for an affable expression. He handed Yellowhorse the jackalope card. "What do you think this means?"

"You the lawyer."

"So?"

"You the smart guy."

"Think she went to Mexico, huh?"

"Left the van on the Mexico line but the card says Moab, Utah."

"What do you make of that?"

"I say Mexico. I say she's throwing the shitheel off her trail."

"The shitheel—would be Mr. Winter?" Whose ominous silence the last two months was starting to make Moss nervous.

Yellowhorse nodded. His face darkened and he picked at a tooth. "Won't be sneaking round here no more."

"So what do you guys think? When you expect Terry back?"

They both gave Moss a look.

"She *escaped*, man. They crossed the line. They ain't coming back."

Moss winced and swallowed. He swirled the red tea and watched it settle. "Well, all right then." He raised the red Beetnik cup. "Terry."

"Terry, Terry." Frank doffed his cap.

"She ditched the shitheel and made it across."

Swinging by the office, Moss was intercepted by Junker and Wylie, lurking like muggers at the station where his secretary used to sit. He took one look and opted for a modified, limited hang out.

"Guys."

"Moss. You're going to lose."

"I'm disappointed in you, Neil. The practice of law is not about winning or losing. It's about problem-solving."

"Spoken like a loser," Junker observed.

"Moss. What's your go/no go criterion for this proceeding?"

"We're past that, Neil."

"How can we be past that?"

"We're gone."

"*Moss*. You've lost your client."

"Happens."

"Your client's dead. Your case is dead. You're dead, we're dead."

"From you, Neil? Gangsta rap?"

Junker interjected, "I got something I want you to think about."

"What's that?"

"Keep the case, keep the risk."

"Meaning?"

"You leave and the fee's all yours. You get hit and it's all your hit. Neil can draft it up tomorrow. You get pool typing through the end of the trial."

"Neil?"

Wylie studied his twisting hands. Bad sign—done deal.

"Neil's looked into everything."

Moss didn't even rate a citation to the partnership agreement. "I tell you to fuck off. What then?"

"We don't even like to think of that as within the realm of possibility."

"Expulsion, you mean." In which case Moss is out but the firm keeps his work-in-progress, maybe 80 percent of any verdict, as well as of any liability for costs.

"No one wants that."

"But Junker, we're family."

"Sleep on it, son. We prefer a friendly divorce."

THREE

The partners were avoiding Moss's office like the site of a hantavirus outbreak, but Crutchfield needed an eighth player for slow pitch that weekend.

"I'll be tied up," Moss said.

"Sounds interesting. Mind if I smoke?"

"Yes, I do."

"I'm sorry, Peter. I'm violating your space." He pattered lightly on the window glass. Cut-offs with hiking boots could be seen below, and bright cycling outfits in primary colors shooting the Broadway hill.

The lawyer team, hastily renamed the Slow White Broncos, was taking on the Cunning Stunts of the Women's Studies Department. Judge Langworthy pitched and managed. Forfeiture to the Stunts for failing to field eight might have manhood implications, in Crutchfield's view. It wouldn't help the judge's mood the next day at Moss's trial.

"I'll think about it." Moss went back to his notes.

"So how's life?"

" 'They flee from me that sometime did me seek, with naked foot stalking in my chamber.' "

"I know *all* about that."

" 'That sometime put themself in danger to take bread at my hand.' "

"Wacky guy. What's this?" He had found a trial exhibit, the blue, transilluminated gel model for breast examination self-testing. He gentled the simulated flesh, flicking on and off the backlight to reveal dark wads of different sizes and depths.

"That's not how you do it."

"How?"

"Not cupped fingers but the pads of the tips in circular patterns. Imagine missing an eight-centimeter lump."

"Like this?"

"Crutch, it's not a sex toy."

"It's not?"

"You're sick."

"Oh yeah?"

Crutchfield now had located the 4-by-6-foot foamboard enlargement of the diagram Moschetti found beneath Bondurant's scribblings. He whistled. "Yikes. Giant breasts!"

"Crutch."

"Do they always travel in pairs?"

"Put it down, Crutch."

"You can't go through with this, Peter." Now he looked actually concerned.

"Call it a leap of faith."

"Off a cliff."

"Are you a lawyer, Crutch? Or a sperm?"

"Huh?"

"If you can't bear the cross you can't wear the crown."

"I knew it. Savior syndrome."

" 'The hottest places in hell are reserved for those who in times of great moral crisis maintain their neutrality.' "

"Joan Baez?"

"Dante."

"Bichette?"

"Butt out."

"On my way. You're gonna miss these hills, pardner."

"Ex-partner."

"Game starts at four. Good-bye."

Focus. Stone cold focus. Facts are your friends. Moss stared at Moschetti's huge blow-up with the black oval in the upper outer quadrant. Believe Moschetti and he might have a case. Believe the bulbhead, Professor Crawford, and he might be losing his license.

He opened to the chart page for November 12, 1989— defaced with scribbling, cross outs, interlineations in different-colored inks. Soberly this time, he searched for its secret text.

Bondurant had shrugged off the alterations in deposition. He mumbles when he dictates. He always goes back and corrects the typed draft by hand. He doodles. "All his charts look that way."

Do they?

Other patient's records were off-bounds to Moss, privileged by statute and nondiscoverable. Except for patients who also were his clients.

Fisher v. Bondurant was stored in the basement, at the back of an unlit passageway of transferred files, behind old trial exhibits, a stud gun, a car seat, a respirator, devices that had taken lives, and someone's disassembled wooden bed. He worked free the four banker's boxes and hauled them with a handcart to a bare area on the concrete floor. He pulled a folder at random—*Photographs*—and opened it. Pixie in Danskin, Olga Korbut hairbob—a twelve-year-old burdened with roses, caught between exhilaration and embarrassment, she took his breath away, as she had the judges of the floor exercises. There was another of her muscling the rings, rising like an angel. And a P.R. close-up of her inquisitive, green gaze. Trusting, interested, open. The honesty of her look hit him like a gutshot. An accusation. Jessie Fisher's death had been nothing less than negligent homicide. Bondurant should have lost his license. How had Moss let him win?

Intrusive images surfaced, shame-tinged, inexplicit. The

boy with the hoe, the bicycle in the bamboo. Moss remembered the photographs that came next in this folder. The burn unit—as bad as anything in Vietnam. He closed it and put it away.

At his desk upstairs he lay Jessie Fisher's medical chart next to Terry's and opened them both to office notes. Not his lucky day. The chart was just as Bondurant had testified, typed with handwritten corrections, blue, red, and black ink. No scribbles on top of diagrams and the entries were headed, "w√/pve," which he saw nowhere in Terry's chart, but otherwise the same. Each visit individually charted, with data under, *S, O, A,* and *P*. Visit after visit as he kept having her return. Words added and crossed out by hand.

Spinning my wheels, Moss concluded, and gathered his stuff for home.

In the backyard he envied the peace of the long June dusk. He kept a hold on his water tumbler like a talisman. Sally joined him with a stemmed glass of chardonnay and her esquisse. Brown bats were figure-eighting overhead. Nighthawks swept the upper strata. From treetops robins were sounding taps.

So he was walking away from the firm for the sake of a client he may never see again. Sally felt if anything cheered by the news. No point in talking downsides; they were obvious enough. May need to tighten belts for a while to make do on Sally's faculty salary. May need a second mortgage to repay the costs of trying the case alone. If he lost there were other downsides: A personal judgment for defense costs, maybe a bankruptcy, maybe a career in the ditch.

"So what? So it didn't pan out."

"What didn't?"

"Changing your practice after our sabbatical."

"You could say that."

"I knew it wouldn't." She swirled the golden wine. "Forget Junker and Wylie."

"Babe, I'm trying."

"It's time to make the swerve."

The swerve? "Oh yeah, the swerve."

"So you got too close to it."

"Suppose I did."

"Not all bad, getting too close."

"Like a catalyst, you mean," but he felt uncatalyzed. He felt like he couldn't get up from the chair. The evening was so peaceful it felt uninhabited, threshold to the void. He drank off the rest of his water. He needed her blessing.

"I bless you," Sally said.

Moss smiled irresolutely. "O.K., then. I'll leave the firm, try the case, fall on my sword like a lemming."

"Lemmings don't carry swords. That's precisely the thing about lemmings."

"Like an idiot. Like an asshole."

"You're on. If you're going to swerve, you better do it right. Do everything it takes to win, *everything*, Peter, and I'm happy, win or not." She had that look—very, very earnest. One of his favorites. "Now tell me how you win a malpractice case without a plaintiff or an expert."

No sweat. Just turn it into *Bondurant v. Bondurant*. Assuming he survives pretrial motions, Moss calls the defendant to lay out the standard of care and lie about what he did to meet it. Moss proves he's lying. Cool. The drawback is, by calling the defendant as the plaintiff's one standard-of-care expert Moss has to make him look *good*. Knowledgeable, authoritative, *expert*. Then Bondurant rattles on about all the fine things he did to comply and at that point he's looking golden. It may be the point of no return. The jury's wondering where Moss went to law school. The judge is steamed. Basteen's chilling the champagne.

"Well." Sally took stock. "It's simple, anyway. Simple's a virtue."

"Principle of Occam's Razor. What can be proved with fewer assumptions is done in vain with more."

"The flaw is what you assume."

"How's that?"

"You're staking your case on the assumption that Bondurant is an expert. He knows his stuff."

"I think he does."

"Why would a doctor who knows what he's doing fail to treat a life-threatening disease until it's clearly too late? Implausible. You have to have an answer."

"What level of answer are we talking here? A grand unified theory?"

"Just a little motive. Make me believe."

The robins were getting annoying. The void yawned to the east.

"Bondurant knows he should refer her for biopsy and treatment but he doesn't," Moss said, "because he wants her to keep coming to him instead. He hates to refer. He wants the business. He needs to keep every patient he can so he can recertify without taking the board exam. He's afraid he'd fail it. How's that?"

"No cigar. Insufficient incentive. He act weird around her?"

Moss shook his head. "Perfectly straight, according to Terry. A regular doctor, though her kid thinks he's a jerk. I think he's a jerk."

"What else is there?"

"Pilot project for the Junius Foundation. Some kind of self-referral scam he's cooking up with Dr. Mayhew."

"The what?"

"That's what everybody says. It's not in any directories. Nobody ever heard of it. All the more suspicious, right?"

"What's that doctors say about diagnosing zebras?"

"Not what you look for when you hear hoofbeats."

"The Junius Foundation is a zebra, Peter. Where's the horse?"

"I've got no other angles, Sal." He was losing his faith in the factual.

"Focus on the people involved," she said. "Look for the horse."

Moss picked up her pencil sketch, expecting the expressionistic geometric patterns she'd turned to over the last few months. He was surprised by a face, and by arms limply crossed and trussed beneath it. The background was a darkening cross-hatched sky, rayed light roofed by storm clouds. Hands as strong and striking as Dürer's were bent above the face like talons, working strings that held the arms below. It was a young girl's face with empty Orphan Annie eyes, a look of ambiguous reverie. The sketch was titled *I can dance without you.*

Moss recalled Emmy's Pearl Jam sweatshirt, the sad marionette. "Jesus, Sally," he shivered. He apologized. He had to go back.

The janitorial crew was coiling cords and twisting trashbags. Wylie was still there, studying a printout that piled up on the floor. He gave Moss a dismissive look as he bolted past.

Moss hit the switch for the bank of hall lights. He hit his office switch. The recessed ceiling floods flashed on. It took a while to find the chart, unopened and gathering dust on top of his four-door cabinet since, on some impulse, he'd gotten Morlock to retrieve it months before. With excessive care, as though they might come to pieces in his hands, Moss opened the medical records of Mary Eliza Winter.

It was just as he hoped: virgin pages of typed notes. Page after page, month after month, year after year, not a handwritten word to be found. SOAPnotes full of observations of routine childhood care—school physicals; immunizations; sinusitis, gastritis, roseola, u.t.i. Each entry led off with the letters not present in Terry's chart: w$\sqrt{}$pve. Not only was every notation typed, where there were changes they were also typed, and not only that. They were dated, always contemporaneously with the visit, and initialed "W B."

Of course Terry's and Jessie Fisher's would be the ones he altered; they were the ones with lawsuits. Caught in another big one: Bondurant's routine was the opposite of what he claimed. He only amended typed notes by hand after he was sued.

Moss dictated a supplementation of his exhibit list to include Emmy's chart. He picked up the chart to drop it for copying in his outbox, but stopped midreach. The outside of the chart jacket had a shiny lamination and color code. A label across the front and on the side read "Mary Eliza Winter d/o/b 10-4-81." He angled the jacket to maximize an *S*-shaped glare from the overhead flood. The glare showed the plasticized coating scored with impressions that could not be seen straight on. Squinting, Moss tilted the chart on his palm in the clean white light. Like fracture lines on a lightbox X ray, writing could be made out— "NOT for BME"—and a narrow *U* from the paperclip that had fastened the note to the top of the jacket.

FOUR

T*he judge was* losing it. His seven Broncos could lick ten feminist theorists barehanded and batting left. They'd waive the rules if they had any balls. The Cunning Stunts weren't buying. USSSA says seven or fewer show and you forfeit. So pay your fine, Judgie, and cheer for us in the playoffs.

Langworthy wanted to know who'd screwed the pooch. Not the stalwarts from Junker and Wylie: Lata, switch-hitter from the switchboard. Tina, Crutchfield's paralegal, busting out of her Slow White Broncos jersey. Crutchfield paging glumly through the roster. Moss holding the bat bag, feeling like an idiot. Do everything you can, Sally had said, to win. The D.A.'s office had let the judge down. A couple of prosecutors had just earned a ration at their next sentencing hearings for letting the Stunts off on a technicality.

"Moss," the judge said. "You reported to play the day before a trial. I appreciate that. I value your commitment to the team."

"Anything for the Broncos."

Tina was taunting the Stunts as they swaggered away. "Don't dis the sisters, girl," a gender studies professor replied. Tina flipped her off.

It was working out. Moss got a couple more hours to

think about opening statement. And he didn't have to cringe
at second, watching the judge's double hip-twitch wind-up
from behind.

Someone get that man a robe.

Robed he was the following day in the round green
courthouse, regimental mustache bristling, ready to do business. Langworthy greeted the jury pool being mustered into
the wedge-shaped courtroom with a few remarks on civic
responsibility then retired to his robing room to study last-
minute motions.

The jury commissioner introduced a video. The video
had scenes of elk feeding in meadows, skiers breaking powder, a fly fisherman in the afternoon light. A local news
anchor voiced over, "We live in a country where freedoms
are protected by law. The final safeguard of those freedoms
is trial by a jury of one's peers . . ." The anchor explained
the phases of trial, jury selection, the roles of the plaintiff
and defendant and courtroom personnel, objections, instructions, deliberation, verdict. That they were not to discuss
the case. That they were the last guardians of liberty and
justice in our democratic system.

After the video a few guardians began leafing through
their booklets, *You and Your Courts*. Some browsed the
jury nullification flyer the Patriots had passed out in the
hallway. "You don't have to follow the instructions on
the law if you disagree with them, no matter what the judge
may say." Feet began to shuffle and torsos twist in attitudes
of discomfort. There was a certain amount of sexual ap-
praisal going on. The doughty bailiff and willowy clerk
proctored the situation.

Moss studied the venire. The savvy ones had brought
their own reading materials. *The Celestine Prophecy*
popped up here and there, and a *Women Who Run with the
Wolves*. A Christian Science Reader, an *Utne Reader, Ho-
listic Aromatherapy*, and *Dr. Susan Love's Breast Book*, no
less. The reading list from hell for an M.D. in a cancer
case. There were a few mohawks and male ponytails, co-
eds in clogs and washable tattoos, and a smattering of

T-shirts. Lettered T-shirts asserting allegiances certainly made jury selection easier. Moss noted PEACE; Die Yuppie Scum; BUTTHOLE SURFERS; Semana de la Chicana; Wailers' World Tour; SMOKING POPES; SINGLE PAYER—It's Simple It's Fair; and, Shorty's Place, Amarillo, Texas. Our kind of folks, Moss thought. Nobody in Dockers, gray hair, or a feed cap.

The clerk called the lawyers to the robing room. The judge was ready for motions. Basteen brought Bondurant along by the elbow. The readers looked up from their books to watch them go.

Judge Langworthy had a few questions. "Where's your client?" he asked Moss.

"My client?"

"The plaintiff."

"Mexico," Moss said. "Traveling." As though it were a long weekend in Cabo. "But I have some reason to think she may not still be in Mexico."

"What are you talking about, Moss?"

"I understand she went to Mexico."

"For treatment of some kind?"

"Quite possibly, Your Honor."

Basteen, darkly caparisoned in charcoal and pearl, wrinkled his nose derisively. Bondurant looked from face to face. He wiped his mouth. He didn't get it. Moss blurted out a request for a short continuance.

"May I remind the court," Basteen remarked, "my request for a continuance was summarily denied."

"Sauce for the goose, Mr. Moss, is sauce for the gander."

"I recently received a communication." Moss endeavored to look assuring, informative.

"Yes?"

"It suggests Ms. Winter may be back in this country."

The judge shifted in his studded leather chair. He didn't like trashing a team player. Moss tried to get away with sitting tight. His palm made a print on the glass-topped table. Bondurant's eyes began to silver. He got it now.

"You accelerated the trial date, Moss. I've got a room

full of jurors hot to trot. Wherever she may be, your client's day in court begins in thirty minutes." He frowned, reproach leavened with apology. "Sorry."

Bondurant openly grinned, like B.Y.U. was putting it to State.

Moss nodded. In an odd way it was gratifying. The drama would unfold despite everyone's pitched efforts to prevent it—not just Bondurant, Basteen, and ROMPIC, but Moss's own partners, for a wavering moment perhaps Moss himself, his client's husband, maybe even his client too. The battle would be fought, the truth contested, and the sword of justice fall not in some confidential settlement conference but where it was supposed to. In a court of law.

An elegant finger was tapping for attention on the tabletop. Basteen recalled for the judge that the plaintiff had been ordered to submit to a second deposition. "I've been stonewalled, Your Honor." He gave a wounded appearance.

"Remind me what this is about."

The court, Moss explained, had ordered, over his strenuous objection, Ms. Winter redeposed on her sexual and childbearing history. At the same hearing the court ordered Dr. Bondurant's board of medical examiners file submitted under seal. That was never done. Moss guaranteed his client would gladly sit for redeposition as soon as she was available. In the meantime, what about the defendant's noncompliance with the court's order? Sauce for the goose.

"What's the relevance?"

"There may be documents critical to my case."

"Why?"

"I have to see them to know."

The judge paged through his orders; he pursed his lips. "I'm going to rule. Two parts. Part one. I'm going to do you a favor, Moss." And he was. He could toss the case right then under Rule 37(d). "We recess for her deposition when she gets here. She doesn't get here by the end of your evidence, I'm directing a verdict for the doctor. Understood?"

Bondurant's elation floated him to his feet. "Son of a

gun," he said. The elegant finger motioned him down but Bondurant stood gangling about like a free man.

"Doctor."

"Yo." Bondurant blew through his lips. He resumed his place between the mounted artillery shell and the three-lapped flag.

"Part two concerns you, doctor. You don't turn over to me every single board of medical examiners document in your possession as ordered two months ago by five-thirty P.M. today, I'm entering a default judgment in favor of the plaintiff. Judgment against the defendant, who is you. Is that understood? I'm going to listen to opening statements. I'm going to read the doctor's documents *in camera* tonight. Moss, you'll get a ruling in the morning. Is everything understood? No deposition, the goose gets dismissed. No documents, the gander gets defaulted. Have you got it, gentlemen?"

They did.

"Then let's do it."

Of the hundred or so veniremen in the gallery, sixteen were called and sworn. Of the sixteen the only T-shirts were Shorty's Place and Die Yuppie Scum. Die Yuppie Scum cut a figure as he flipped open the gate and huffed to the jury box, arms bouncing rapper-style—black jeans tucked in Doc Martens, sleeveless black shirt and coiled tattoos, chains and pierce pins here and there—one through a brow, four on an ear—skinhead swathed in a red bandana.

Three were blacks and one Hispanic. Half were women and half small businessmen. There was an Agro-American in a Harold Warp's Pioneer Village cap, a dentist, and an FBI agent with a *Wall Street Journal.* Bondurant whispered in Basteen's ear. He made a face and shook his head. Basteen shrugged, brushing him off. He had a system.

The first cull was for hardship. A woman with multiple chemical sensitivities was near collapse from the windowless room's miasma of perfume, newsprint, and cologne. She was outta there. A commodities trader revealed that

June corn was up 2¼. If he didn't liquidate by Thursday he would eat it big-time. Sorry. A Blockbuster clerk with a D.U.I. had to meet with his lawyer. All right. Mrs. Craver was allowed to attend her family reunion in Estes Park. A palsied fellow wanted to know if an insurance company was paying Basteen's fees. Why did he want to know? Because he despised insurance companies. Adiós. The Agro-American had beets in the ground and the small businessmen all wanted off. Their hardship boiled down to not being able to make money if they were sitting on a jury. Presumptions of indispensability earned tongue-lashings from Langworthy. Sad how the largest consumers of judicial services were least willing to pitch in and make them work. The dentist was most insistent. He offered increasingly inventive excuses. His patients needed him. The community depended on him. He was as motivated as a Deadhead at a preinduction physical. He'd pitch fits and feign infarctions to avoid civic service at six dollars a day. Nobody likes an asshole. The dentist was history.

Replacements were called and sworn. The interrogation called voir dire began. Afterward each side could eliminate four, leaving half to sit for trial, six regulars and two alternates.

The judge was the first examiner. Several on the panel had heard of Dr. Bondurant. Good things only. No one had been a patient but three had friends whose whole family went to him. Two recalled the Fisher case and were quickly struck for cause.

The judge worked his way through a demographic questionnaire the bailiff placed on an easel. Item seven was Favorite Radio Show, a matter of interest to Moss.

Moss claimed the oak podium. He propped a boot on its brass footbar. He struck up dialogues on the subject of responsibilities—personal, moral, professional. Voir dire, he said, means to speak the truth. His client was dying of endstage cancer. To her the truth mattered.

Bondurant mooned at the microphone hanging from the ceiling.

Basteen took his turn. He posed a set of insinuating questions on attitudes toward drug use, abortion, sexual promiscuity, followed by stock rhetorical indoctrination. Does anyone here think doctors practice medicine out of books? That medicine means following rules rather than exercising clinical judgment? That a bad outcome is the same as malpractice? That an error of judgment is the same as malpractice? The doctor has to rely on what his patient tells him, right, Mr. Casebolt? Does anyone think the size of jury verdicts is getting out of hand in this country? That there's too much litigation in our society? Are you saying, Mr. Hinton, that people look at lawsuits as easy money? That people sue every time things don't go their way?

A lot of heads were moving up and down. Basteen was tapping into the "climate." The phenomenon that everybody these days got a chip on their shoulder. Don't come crying victim. Sorry about your life, but hey, life's a bitch. Gut up and get on with it, as Terry had put it herself.

Each side got four strikes. Basteen systematically struck the three members of his race and the Chicana. His thinking was evident: Minorities were less likely to respect authority figures like doctors. It was unconstitutional but Moss would never make a *Batson* challenge for racial strikes stick against a black lawyer. Moss spent his peremptory strikes on tort reformers and dittoheads. He wanted free thinkers, not the doctrinaire. And no jurors with attitude.

Basteen's dream malpractice jury would be composed of healthcare professionals who'd close ranks with a sued colleague. He'd be happy with insurance-burdened businessmen, law enforcement types, or penny-pinching farmers. Moss wanted women and nonconformists. Little Terry Winters. They got the usual perversely mixed bag rather than the law school norm, the jury of peers. Moss had yet to be favored with the norm.

He approached the podium. He took a few seconds to engage each of the eight. The alternates: Mr. Willits of Willits Plumbing and Heating, who was plenty steamed at being there. Ms. Gideon, a graduate student with the *Utne*

Reader. The first team: Heinie Hinton, the Agro-American. Mr. Casebolt, the FBI agent. Ms. Comstock, a pediatric nurse. Ms. Crenshaw of the Comparative Literature Department. Shorty, a beetdigger from the east county. And, sprawled back with the fuck-you-too, fleering bravado that can give nonconformism a bad name, Die Yuppie Scum.

"Terry Winter is dying," Moss told them. "She may already be gone. Her death"—he pointed—"will have been needlessly caused by Dr. Wallace Bondurant."

The defendant's hand moved toward his face.

"Dr. Bondurant. Who knew her life was in his hands but did nothing.

"You are about to hear a story of courage and responsibility. The responsibility of a medical doctor for negligently taking life, and the courage of the mother and daughter he harmed."

Moss paused. He gripped the podium like a steering device. Like those he addressed, he was wondering what the story would turn out to be.

FIVE

Doctor on trial for causing woman's death, the indelicate Section C headline read.

Teresa Winter is dying because Dr. Wallace Bondurant refused to treat her illness over a period of three years, according to Ms. Winter's attorney, Peter Moss, of the law firm Junker and Wylie. "A curable cancer became a killing cancer because of his neglect," Moss said in opening argument.

Dr. Bondurant's attorney, Jerome Basteen, countered that Ms. Winter chose not to comply with medical advice.

"The plaintiff will come to you, saying, 'I'm a victim'," Mr. Basteen argued, "but the evidence will show that she is really a victim of her own lifestyle choices."

Mr. Winter was not present Monday and the condition of her health is unclear. Her attorney stated he hoped either she or her daughter would be able to testify at the trial.

Dr. Bondurant is president of the state medical society. Several of the most distinguished physicians in

the region will testify that Dr. Bondurant's care was
exemplary, according to Mr. Basteen.

In 1990 Dr. Bondurant stood trial for causing the
death of Jessica Fisher, a young gymnast. Mr. Moss
represented the plaintiff's family in that case. Dr.
Bondurant was acquitted of all charges.

Moss pushed the paper away. He must advise the ink-
stained wretch you don't acquit people of civil claims. You
don't argue in opening. His client isn't dead yet. And he is
not of Junker and Wylie. Not anymore.

He had gotten back to his office at seven to find the door
locked, the lock changed, the separation agreement indem-
nifying the firm in an envelope taped to the door. Instructions were given for removing from the copy room case
files and exhibits and a box of personal effects—artwork,
photographs of Sally, of a waterfall, the Gilbey's Travelmate he'd kept in a drawer to demonstrate mastery. Moss
signed the agreement, loaded his car, drove home and com-
mandeered the dining room table. He asked Sally if Art
Hardware was still open for office supplies. He was up past
2:00 A.M. reworking his plan of examination. In the morning, he grabbed a bagel and loaded a cup with extra sugar.
After skimming the story in the *Gazette-Telegraph*, he rifled the closet for his Greeley banking suit, impulse-
selected a West Coast tie, and was off to meet Dr. Borkin,
his first witness, for breakfast at Jake's.

The phone was ringing as the door shut behind him, but
he was late and Sally would get it.

Outside the convivial booths of Jake's 24-Hour Cafe and
Salad Bar, and beyond the Lamb's Loft Christian Book-
store, and Mary Ellen's Bail Bonds, and La Placenta, as
Sand Creek's one Mexican restaurant was known to the
trial bar, the round green courthouse brooded above the
dusky Platte.

Like a couple of drywallers he and his witness soon carried a lightbox and trial bags over the bridged entrance and
ramp to security. Inside, yellow-tiled corridors fed like

spokes to a central hub where children went at it on the floor with coloring books. The floor was original linoleum, 1961. Jurors in badges stood around not looking anybody in the eye. Something about the structure amplified noise. On the wall to the right of Langworthy's courtroom were scenes, for some reason, of Guanajuato, Mexico.

Moss backed through the double doors and entered. In there all acoustics went dead. Sitting on the defense side of the gallery was Heinz, the man from ROMPIC, conning a horizon others couldn't see. Bondurant sat beside him, deep in thought.

Moss took up at the plaintiff's table, next to the jury box. Dr. Borkin sat tidily on a gallery bench. Moss reviewed his strategy. First, don't step on the seal. Woven into the carpet directly in front of the judge's bench lay the golden seal of the state, concentric rings around a shield with snowcapped mountains and miners' tools and a pyramid inscribing the all-seeing eye. Stepping on the seal with court in session was an indignity that would not be brooked. It lay like a Claymore mine directly in the path of a lawyer's approach for the bench conferences this judge was reputed to despise.

The rest of the strategy was less definite. Theoretically Moss could cut and paste a prima facie case with just Bondurant's stating his duty to act on a suspicious lump, Moschetti's proving Bondurant found one and didn't act, and Terry's oncologist, Anita Greenwood, on causation and damages: That the three-year delay meant the difference between life and death. Occam's razor, swift and sharp. But the jackalope said he had it all wrong, and right or wrong it would move too fast. He'd be done with no Terry having shown up for redeposition, and the case would be shitcanned. While he prayed for his client's arrival Moss would have to pad and filibuster to stretch things out, not his style and not a strategy at all.

Basteen prissed in and unpacked a laptop. Bondurant said something to Heinz then got up to join his lawyer. Basteen was then bending over Moss, cupping his hand. "You can't go through this without her."

"Evidently."

"Take our offer."

Moss looked at him. "You're shitting me." But Basteen meant it. "Sorry, no can do."

What was that about?

"All rise."

Judge Langworthy declined to greet the lawyers. He registered the presence of someone other than they. He hunched in his robe between the state and federal flags on staffs tipped with eagles angled carefully out. In back of him, in a repeating motif, the great seal was graven on a disk of bronze.

Langworthy took his seat and cleared his throat. "The board of medical examiners documents." He slapped a manila envelope on the bench in front of him. "The sealed file, we'll call it. I read through it last night: I don't get it, Moss."

"Sir?"

"What's the point? What's anything got to do with anything?"

"Hard to know without seeing it, Your Honor."

He sighed. "Issues are, according to Basteen, one, privilege and, two, privacy keep you from seeing this stuff. Right, Basteen? Three, Rule 403 keeps it out for prejudice if we get to the question of relevancy. Which mystifies me.

"First. Privilege won't hunt. This came from the defendant, not the board. Which leaves a two-step balancing process. The doctor's privacy interest versus the general public need, then the prejudicial effect on the doctor versus the probative value to the case. Am I right? O.K. Moss." He waved the sealed file threateningly, like a rolled newspaper at a barking dog. "Why do we need it? What does it prove? Tell me more or the doc gets it back."

"I have to know what's in it to say."

"I'll tell you this much. I don't see here that the board has ever investigated the doctor's ability to provide competent medical care."

Now that was carefully worded. "Then there has been an investigation of some kind?"

"Don't quiz me, Moss. There has been no disciplinary action at all."

By Club Med? Of course not. But the board was under a statutory duty to investigate complaints. Complaints and findings were what Moss wanted.

"Here's my problem, Moss. What's the connection to your case? This case has to do with evaluation and treatment for breast cancer. I can't see any connection."

"The connection I know about is this. There was an investigation of something by the board. I can show that Terry Winter's daughter's chart was deliberately withheld by the defendant from the board's investigators."

Basteen's eyes widened. The judge jolted erect. He pressed forward. "You can prove that?" Bondurant hadn't moved.

"I can," Moss said.

"Basteen?"

"Outrageous, Your Honor. Completely untrue."

The judge was silent a long time. "Moss. Do you know why it may have been withheld?"

Moss admitted he did not.

The judge sank into silence again. He stared at the defendant. Bondurant had turned to stone. Heinz coughed. Basteen protested: a fabrication by plaintiff's counsel, a red herring, a waste of time. He gave off huffs of impatience and contempt. His strategy would be as direct as Moss's was evasive: Keep things moving. In that he had an ally in a judge famous for detesting cumulative testimony as well as bench conferences, for never sending jurors out to twiddle their thumbs while lawyers pissed and moaned.

"Your Honor," Moss said. "I agree to maintain the confidentiality of these documents unless and until admitted into evidence by the court. That should suffice."

Heinz coughed. Bondurant muttered in Basteen's ear.

"Not yet it doesn't," the judge said. "Prove what you just

told me and tie it to your case. Lay your foundation and
I'll reconsider."

Langworthy rapped on the sealed file. "I read this stuff,
Moss. You got bigger fish to fry. Call the jury. Gentlemen,
on with the show."

Basteen stipulated to Dr. Borkin's expertise but Moss
wanted to dwell on qualifications. Med school and residency at UCLA, a breast-imaging fellowship at Stanford,
the Felix Bloch Award, state director of mammography unit
certification, editorial board of *Radiology*, Rocky Mountain
Chair of the Breast Health Task Force of the American
Cancer Society.

Dr. Borkin beamed at the jury. Die Yuppie Scum beamed
at Borkin.

The witness expatiated next on the history of diagnostic
radiology, from Roentgen's invisible rays to triangulating
lesions with oblique views. Nurse Comstock jotted notes.

Moss wheeled the lightbox in front of the jury. The judge
and Basteen came down to watch. Films were snapped in
place, most recent first.

Moss asked what these pictures would tell a screening
mammographer about signs of Terry Winter's cancer.

"Prospectively, nothing," Dr. Borkin said. "We now
know a huge tumor was sitting in this breast." He tapped
left. "But it is very occult on film. Ms. Winter has, had,
firm, dense breast tissue. Wolfe's classification DY. Very
little fat. You can't see with a flashlight in a DY breast."

Die Yuppie Scum was grooving on the testimony, laughing noiselessly.

"With hindsight, though, we know where to look. We
can home in." He crossed his hands and moved the Ouija
triangle his fingers made over the place where the lump
was found—just as he had for Moss when they met in the
Chapel of Breasts.

"There."

Jurors peered forward and nodded, for there indeed it

was—stippled rings of streaks and dots, like a spiral nebula among Magellanic clouds.

"When was this film taken?"

"April 30, 1992. Six months before biopsy."

"Can you measure tumor diameter along its greatest axis as of that date?"

Borkin produced a ruler and calipers. "Six and one-third centimeters," he said.

"Now show us, please, the earlier films."

Borkin popped two previous sets of films under a bar on the glowing box. He took the jurors to the tumor site with his crossed hands. There on each craniocaudal view it remained, progressively smaller but unmistakable. Malevolent.

"Shouldn't the radiologists have diagnosed it?"

"Almost impossible. No red flags except in hindsight."

"How, then, could it have been diagnosed?"

"Retrospectively, the films show the tumor must have been obvious to Dr. Bondurant. A competent clinician can feel breast lumps one centimeter or so in size. Pencil eraser or a little bigger. In huge pendulous breasts, even large lumps, three, four centimeters, might be missed. Like they say—beware the ample bosom!" He sparkled. "But not in these." Borkin glanced admiringly at the lightbox films. "Excellent size, shape, lift. Physical exam's where you do it with these."

Moss asked Borkin to illustrate how to conduct a physical examination for a breast mass. They moved to the blue gel model on another stand.

"Objection," Basteen said. "He's a radiologist, not a clinician. Beyond his expertise."

"Lay your foundation," the judge told Moss.

"Certainly."

Borkin explained the outreach programs of the cancer society task force he headed. He detailed his instruction of women in self-examination and of general practitioners in physical examination using videotapes and a similar gel model. Langworthy overruled the objection. Borkin approached the model. He showed how to palpate the breast in concentric circles with the sensitive pads of the fingertips. He stopped whenever he found a lump and flicked the switch to show it backlit in the blue gel.

"Would any jurors like to give it a try?"

Over objection, they lined up and did, except for Heinie Hinton, touching, stopping, turning the lightswitch on and off, murmuring and nodding, and stepping aside.

"In the model the largest lump is four centimeters, half the size of Ms. Winter's tumor when Dr. Bondurant was still claiming there was nothing to be found."

At that the FBI agent arched a brow but Bondurant's interest had wandered. He seemed preoccupied with Professor Crenshaw. She turned and folded her arms.

"From your analysis of the films of Terry Winter's tumor, what should Dr. Bondurant have been able to detect on a reasonably careful examination November 12, 1989?"—halfway between the first two annual screenings, and the date of the scribbled-over diagram.

"Objection," Basteen said. "Foundation."

"I'll allow it. Overruled."

"From this film, in my opinion, a hard, irregular, ugly mass, about two centimeters across. It wouldn't have felt anything like a cyst. It would have been something any family doc worth his salt would biopsy in a heartbeat."

"Objection," Basteen repeated. "Lack of foundation on the standard of care in family practice."

"Sustained. The jury will disregard Dr. Borkin's statement that any family physician would have biopsied the lump."

Right, they'll disregard it. Moss went to the easel with a marker. On the top sheet of a butcher pad he wrote:

November 12, 1989

Dr. Borkin: 2 cm., hard, irregular,
               nothing like a cyst

"No further questions."

Borkin turned his glittery look toward Jerome Basteen but Basteen wasn't wading into this one. He'd neglected to depose Borkin, assuming radiology was not in issue. He had no ammo. The cross was limited to introducing the three mammogram reports that Terry's films were negative.

"These radiologists," Basteen said, "were telling Dr. Bondurant they found no reason to suspect that Ms. Winter had cancer."

"Correct."

"Three different radiologists at three different times?"

"Correct."

"Based on the same series of films you just showed the jury?"

"Correct."

"No more questions." Keep it moving.

Moss resumed the podium for redirect. "Could Dr. Bondurant properly ignore physical findings because the mammogram reports were negative?"

"The false negative rate for mammography is seven to twenty percent, depending on the unit. A negative report with breasts of Ms. Winter's density is nondata. It would be like relying on a weather forecast to rule out cancer. You don't find a cancer like this with your eyes. You find it with your hands."

SIX

Y*ou are Terry* Winter's primary treating physician?"

"Yes," Dr. Greenwood said softly. "For cancer care. I was."

Anita Greenwood had hurried through her credentials—nothing on the order of Lewis Epstein's, the M.D. Anderson oncologist axed by Junker to save the cost, but quite strong, though her delivery wasn't. She looked pale and uneasy. Very uneasy and very soft-spoken. The judge had been repeating her answers to make sure he heard them correctly, which was fine with Moss. Bondurant looked pained, like a coach on the sidelines watching a fumble. Basteen projected a magnificent frown.

"Knowing the size and volume of her tumor when it was finally found and removed, is it possible to estimate its size at earlier points in time?"

"Roughly, yes."

"I'd like you to calculate, as best you can, the size of Terry Winter's tumor as of November 12, 1989, three years earlier."

The witness nodded once, hunched forward in the witness box, and commenced to write. Moss suggested she step down to the easel to explain her calculations as she made them.

Although a diminutive woman, Dr. Greenwood's composure was such that standing alone by the easel gave the impression of stature. "When a malignant breast tumor doubles in diameter," she began, quiet and precise, "the number of cells in the tumor, in other words, its volume, increases eight-fold. This relationship is expressed $D \approx V^3$." She underlined it on a butcher sheet with a fat blue marker.

Moss drifted from the podium to the far end of the jury box, outside their field of view, to channel all attention on his witness.

"Ms. Winter's breast was biopsied October 28, 1992," Dr. Greenwood continued, writing the date. "Tumor diameter was found then to be eight centimeters. The volume relationship therefore was eight cubed or five hundred twelve cubic centimeters at that time."

"Dr. Greenwood, if I may interrupt. Dr. Borkin told us mammogram film six months before biopsy showed a maximal tumor diameter of six and one-third centimeters."

"I concur."

"If that was the tumor's diameter six months earlier, how much less was its volume six months before biopsy?"

"Six point three cubed, or two hundred fifty-four cubic centimeters. Roughly half the volume at biopsy."

"If the tumor doubled in volume in six months, what was its doubling time?"

"Well, six months," she said patiently. "I should add that a doubling time of one hundred eighty days is roughly what we would expect with Terry's S-phase, or synthesis-phase percentage of four on DNA studies. Slow-growing but anueploid. Dangerous."

We're losing them, Moss thought, but the women were avidly writing it down.

"Shall I continue, Mr. Moss?"

"Please."

"November 12, 1989, was three years—one thousand and eighty days, to be exact—before biopsy. During those one thousand eighty days the tumor probably doubled in volume at roughly the same rate, once every six months, or six times, if you ignore Gompertzian slowing."

"For the sake of simplicity," Moss said, "let's ignore Gompertzian slowing. What do the six doublings of volume show?"

"They tell us two things. First, they demonstrate that cancer grows exponentially. Because of the three-year delay, there was not six times as much cancer in Terry's breast from the six doublings, but *sixty* times as much. More than *two hundred and fifty billion* new cancer cells."

The judge and several jurors nodded. Basteen evaluated his nails. His frown turned introspective. Bondurant slouched and doodled on a pad.

"Second," Dr. Greenwood went on, "they point us to the likely diameter three years earlier. If you halve the volume relationship at biopsy of five hundred and twelve, times six, you get eight. The cube root of eight is two. So two centimeters—a little less than a nickel."

"Two centimeters in diameter on November 12, 1989?"

"Yes. Two." She completed her chart:

$$V \approx D3$$
$$(V = \text{volume} \quad D = \text{diameter})$$

10-28-92 (biopsy): $D = 8$ cm; $V = 8^3 = 512$ cm^3

4-30-92 (mam.): $D = 6\frac{1}{3}$ cm; $V = 6\frac{1}{3}^3 = 254$ cm^3

$$\frac{512}{524} = 2.105 = \text{roughly double}$$

$\therefore$ dt (doubling time, or 2v) = 180 days

11-12-89
$$\frac{1080}{80} = 6 \text{ doublings of V before biopsy}$$

$$V = 512 \text{ halved x } 6 = 8 \text{ cm}^3$$

$$\underline{D = \sqrt[3]{8} = 2 \text{ cm}}$$

"Dr. Greenwood, back in November 1989, three years before biopsy, would this two-centimeter tumor have felt smooth or rough?"

Nurse Comstock fluttered her hand: Wait. She wasn't finished copying the chart. Dr. Greenwood stood by quietly, hands clasped, until the juror looked up and smiled.

"Not smooth," Dr. Greenwood shook her head. "Rough."

"Round?"

"No. Irregular."

"Would it have been soft?"

"No. Hard."

"Would it have been freely movable?"

"Probably not."

"Tender?"

"Probably not."

"You have given Terry Winter physical breast exams?"

"Many times." She explained how it was done using the blue gel model. Her explanation was the same as Borkin's. Jurors nodded. They appeared at this point well-versed in the subject.

"Given what you know of Terry Winter's physique and breasts, would you expect a reasonably careful breast examiner to have been able to find Terry Winter's two-centimeter tumor on November 12, 1989?"

"Certainly."

"Objection." Basteen was slow on the uptake. "Not qualified to state opinions on a family physician's standard of care."

"I'm not sure she was," the judge said. "Overruled."

"Then I object based on *Hamilton v. Hardy*," Basteen said. The jury was picking up an element of desperation. "Her own practices are not relevant to standard practices."

"Mr. Basteen. Your argument is intellectually incontinent. Overruled."

Bondurant crumpled the page he'd been doodling.

"You're saying the two-centimeter tumor could probably have been easily palpated, or felt, on physical examination in November 1989?"

"Yes, I am."

At the easel Moss flipped back to the top sheet. Under

November 12, 1989

        Dr. Borkin: 2 cm., hard, irregular,
                              nothing like a cyst

he wrote

        Dr. Greenwood: 2 cm., hard, irregular, rough,
                                 nonmobile, nontender

Moss next produced the Giant Breasts diagram with the one black oval and balanced it next to the easel.

"Dr. Greenwood. Assume this was the diagram of Terry Winter's breasts on November 12, 1989."

"Objection. Facts not in evidence. And the diagram is not authentic."

"Overruled," the judge said. "You will be given an opportunity to challenge the evidence."

"How consistent as to size and location is the black oval pictured here," Moss beamed his Art Hardware red laser pointer on the oval, "with what you would expect of Terry Winter's tumor at that time?"

"Very consistent. The oval is exactly where the tumor probably was at that time."

"Your Honor, may Dr. Greenwood return to the witness chair?"

"Dr. Greenwood," the judge gestured. She primly resumed her seat.

"Now, Doctor. If Terry Winter had been sent for excisional biopsy November 12, 1989, rather than three years later, what most likely would have happened?"

"Her cancer would have been diagnosed," she said quietly but firmly. "Knowing Terry, she would have then opted for breast conservation with lumpectomy, or removal of the two-centimeter mass."

"Meaning?"

"Her breast would have been saved. There would also have been an axillary node dissection. Her lymph nodes would probably have been found cancer-free, possibly some replacement of at most three nodes with negligible impact on prognosis. I would have staged her at the worst IIA, very early, but more likely Stage I. She would have undergone a four-to-six month course of adjuvant chemotherapy with adriamycin, five to six weeks of radiation therapy, and that would be it."

"It?"

"Nothing more would have been needed to control her cancer."

"Can you conceive any circumstances that would excuse a physician, regardless of specialty, from proceeding in November 1989 with the treatment you just described?"

"Objection. Lack of foundation on standard of care."

"Sustained."

"I really can't," she said.

"Objection."

"Dr. Greenwood. I ruled you may not respond to that question."

"I'm sorry. I won't again." Smiles cracked in the jury box.

"Jury will disregard," the judge told them.

"In breast cancer," Moss asked, "is there a magic day—a time before which the cancer can be cured if treated, but after which it has spread to the point of becoming a fatal, incurable disease?"

"That is an accepted principle of medical oncology."

"Had Ms. Winter's tumor been biopsied in November 1989, with treatment following as you described, what would be the status and risk of her cancer today?"

"She would very likely be healthy and cancer-free right now, with a high probability of never having her cancer return."

"She would probably have been cured?"

"That's not a term we generally use, but yes. She would have been cured."

"Because her magic day had not yet come?"

"You could say that, yes."

"Now let's look at the reality of what happened. When it was diagnosed October 28, 1992, at what stage was her cancer?"

"IIIB with bad prognostic signs. The tumor was eight centimeters. Ten nodes were positive for cancer. There were ominous skin changes."

"How likely was it then that Terry's IIIB cancer could be successfully treated?"

"Extremely unlikely. The chances of its recurring were greater than eighty percent, in my view, and it did, as we found roughly one year later."

"In lay terms, what did the three-year delay from November 1989 to October 1992 mean?"

"A Stage I cancer was allowed to reach Stage IV."

"Stage IV? Could you explain for us what the change in stages means?"

Softly, but clearly, judge and jury straining to hear, she said, "A curable cancer became an incurable cancer that will kill her if it already hasn't."

"Terry will die because of her doctor's delay?"

Almost inaudibly, "Yes."

Moss asked Dr. Greenwood to explain the progression of the disease. Matter-of-factly she recounted the metastases to Terry's brain and bones. The likelihood over the last six months of palsy, seizures, weakness, depression. The inevitability of progressive organ failure, infections, atrophy, exhaustion. Throughout it all, the accelerating and unremitting pain . . .

Dr. Greenwood stopped. Moss was startled to see her apparently struggle for self-control.

"Dr. Greenwood, how much longer is Terry likely to live?"

"I would be surprised," she said, "if Terry is alive. Is she?"

Moss shook his head. "I don't know," he said under his breath.

"Object to statement by counsel."

"Jury will disregard."

"Although," Dr. Greenwood tentatively took up an answer. "Terry always surprises. Terry has a lot of . . ."

"Guts?"

"Yes." The word itself seemed to fortify her. "Guts."

Basteen settled in at the podium. He locked in on the witness's quick eyes and let her nervousness advance. He'd pull no punches on this woman.

"Terry Winter was not a good patient, was she?"

"How do you mean, Mr. Basteen?"

"She was noncompliant."

Dr. Greenwood considered her answer. "That's correct."

"You recommended treatment. She refused it."

"Yes."

"A number of times."

"Yes."

"The treatment you recommended would have lengthened her life."

"Yes."

"She would be alive today."

"She may *be* alive today."

"Answer the question, please."

"Yes."

"The cancer would be much less extensive."

"Yes, but—"

"Yes or no."

"Object to the interruption."

"Overruled. This is cross."

"*Much less extensive*—yes or no."

"Less extensive, yes."

"If she hadn't disobeyed doctor's orders."

"If you want to put it that way."

Nurse Comstock was scribbling away. Basteen, sensing it, paused, strolling to the front of the podium to let the juror get it all down.

"But Mr. Basteen—"

"Wait for my question." He raised a thin finger.

"Object to the interruption."

"I think she's trying to complete her answer, Mr. Basteen." The judge was curious. "Objection sustained. Dr. Greenwood, continue."

She sighed. "Terry was unique."

"Unique?" Basteen cocked his head and made a disapproving face. "How's that, Doctor?"

Dr. Greenwood bit her lower lip. "Uniquely alive."

His eyebrows lifted. "More alive than you and me? And the rest of us?" Grinning, he indicated the jury.

"Terry was in some ways the most fully alive person I've ever met, Mr. Basteen. She decided to experience her remaining time without treatment and drug-free. I respect her decision absolutely."

"*Drug*-free?"

"Free of chemotherapeutic agents, yes. Radiation, analgesics, other medications."

"But not *drug*-free."

"How do you mean, Mr. Basteen?"

"Are you aware Terry Winter abuses marijuana?"

The judge looked over his half-rims for Moss to object. Moss passed.

"Am I permitted to answer?"

"Please."

"I am aware she *uses* marijuana."

"You are?"

"Yes, and I approved, consistent with guidelines being promulgated for marijuana use in advanced malignant disease."

"And whose guidelines are those?"

"The regulatory working group of the American Academy of Pain Management, on which I serve as vice-chair."

"Really? You *approved* the commission of a crime?"

"What are you implying, Mr. Basteen?"

He shook his head scornfully, overplaying it, Moss observed, when control slipped a notch.

"Dr. Greenwood. Dr. Bondurant referred Terry Winter to you for treatment, correct?"

"Yes."

"You have treated Dr. Bondurant's patients from time to time?"

"Yes."

"You know Dr. Bondurant?"

"I do."

"You have no reason to regard Wally Bondurant as other than an excellent physician, do you?"

"I don't really practice in his field, as you pointed out."

"Oh, I see. Do you recall discussing Dr. Bondurant with me?"

A prohibited ex parte meeting but again Moss passed on objecting.

"I remember."

"Do you recall telling me you regarded Dr. Bondurant as an excellent physician?"

She hesitated, glancing at her colleague. He wet and closed his lips. "Not quite that." She would be precise. "I said I *had* always thought so."

Bondurant's expression sobered. Basteen realized his peril. He popped his notebook shut. "No further questions."

"The delay with Terry," Dr. Greenwood continued. "There must be an explanation. What was Wally thinking?" The jury looked at Basteen and Bondurant, curious like the witness. Bondurant made a low sound in his throat.

"Move to strike the nonresponsive statement," Basteen snapped.

"Jury will disregard."

"Doctor. I have *no further questions*." He grinned and bobbed back to his seat.

Moss half stood for redirect, half sat, half stood, took the flyer. She'd gone to the heart of the matter.

"An explanation. What in your opinion, Doctor, would explain not acting on a palpable breast lump during nine office visits over three years?"

"I can't imagine it." She looked genuinely mystified.

"Mr. Basteen asked about his conversations with you. Did Dr. Bondurant also contact you about this case?"

"Yes, he did."

"Why did he say he was calling?"

"Objection." Basteen was on his feet. "Hearsay. Not relevant. Beyond the scope."

"Overruled. It sounds like an admission to me. Proceed, Dr. Greenwood."

"He didn't want me to testify at this trial."

Moss thought he heard a low whistle from the jury box. "What did you tell him?"

"I said I hoped it wouldn't come to that."

"Did the conversation continue?"

"Yes. Wally was . . . insistent."

"What did you say?"

"I told him since the plaintiff was my patient I should testify if she required it. It's part of the Interprofessional Code."

"Were you reluctant to come here today and testify in a case against a colleague?"

"Of course."

"But you felt a duty to Terry to do so?"

"I did."

"How did Dr. Bondurant react to your saying you would testify if called?"

"He said if I must testify, to try to help him out."

"Your response?"

"I said I was sorry. I would have to tell the truth."

"His response to your saying you would tell the truth?"

"He wasn't happy with me, Mr. Moss."

"How did he express his displeasure?"

She took her time. "I remember his words very clearly. 'Don't make a big mistake, Anita. This could bust your practice.' "

The *Gazette-Telegraph* reporter wakened from the dead. DOCTOR ATTEMPTED TO INTIMIDATE WITNESS, the next day's headline would read. When Moss thought about the testimony, guts was the word that came to mind.

SEVEN

G*od bless doctors,"* Moss said when Sally asked how day two had gone. "God bless the medical profession."

"Don't get too gushy. The calls have started."

"Calls? Oh, Christ."

"Right after you left this morning. I don't like it, Peter. This may be your office now but it's still my house. Why don't you tell the judge this time?"

"Tell him what? Somebody's threatening my wife?"

"I didn't let her get as far as the threat part. And it wasn't just somebody this time. She said she was Genny Bondurant."

"No way."

"Way."

The caller during the Fisher trial had never left a name. Moss flipped through the phonebooks. The only listings under Bondurant were his residence number and a business listing for the Wellness Clinic. Moss called information for Jennifer, Gennifer, Jenny, and Ginger. The number was unpublished. He apologized to Sally. He'd complain to Langworthy in the morning.

Both of them had been absorbed all day in work. To work after dinner both would return. Jury trials and intaglio prints bring out the compulsive. Dinner was a Nick 'n' Willy's pizza warm-up, Weezie's Wishbone, the meatless special.

This new life of theirs, this melding of marriage and work, home and office, was epitomized, Moss offered, by the pizza. Shiitakes, olives, artichokes, asiago—they bubbled and flowed into a single, blended experience. Thus was their life together more than the sum of its toppings.

Sally approached the meal less hyperbolically. "You're right. This is us. Ten minutes together at the kitchen counter. Two greasy slices down the hatch then back at it. No commute so you don't really even *need* a car phone. But a secretary, Peter, you need. Don't look at me like that."

Moss undertook a superficial clean-up. Sally stood and stretched. Two empty Gatorades hit the Ecocycle bin.

"Tell me about your jury."

"Off the wall. Come out and see." Moss sponged smears on the countertop.

"Maybe Thursday afternoon. Who've you got Thursday?"

"The man himself."

"I'll be there."

Sally tied on her work apron, formerly a cooking apron, lined with boneblack from leaning over the press bed. Lettering across the front read "Enough Is as Good as a Feast." She looked good with an apron blousing her waist, skirting her long, jean-clad legs. "What kind of off the wall?" she asked.

"Just weird."

"How? Amusingly weird? Not-with-it-weird? Mixed weird? Darkly weird? Weird Lite?"

"I wanted free thinkers," Moss said. "I got 'em."

"Meaning?"

"Individualists. All shepherds and no sheep."

"Is that good or bad?"

"Could be real good. Could be real bad. Could be run-of-the-mill chaos."

Ordinarily an almost mystical cohesion occurs on a jury, a group personality—a gang of surly guys crossing their arms, a clutch of worried mothers knitting their fingers. The preternaturally bright and attentive. The stupid, the bored, the playful. Solid citizens. Flakes. Rogues and coquettes. This group declined to cohere.

"One guy sits there laughing."

"Jury's the jury. Not a thing you can do."

"Disconcerting as hell when they laugh."

Moss would stand by his analogy of jurors as trout. Wary watchers, skeptics. Hypervigilant for anything sham, but voracious. Sizing up little winged morsels to snap at and savor. Sometimes they were rising. Sometimes they weren't. Sometimes you had to create the illusion of a hatch.

"To work," he said.

"To work."

Moss commuted from the kitchen to the dining room, Sally to her print studio in back of the house by the ditch. He ought now to focus in on examination outlines for Moschetti and his economist. Instead he was drawn back to Emmy's chart. He turned it open on the dining room table, as richly mysterious as an illuminated manuscript. From the chart proceed all things good and evil.

Moss tracked entries for four visits in 1990, looking for patterns and breaks in patterns. Each entry began with similar glyphs. 2/10/90 read: "w√/pve—Tanner stg 1–2. AMEN. H-7, LM-10, Lm-6. BP 111/71. Norm. vel. Ht.-63 Wt.-90." Some system of pediatric baselines.

At the conclusion of each of the 1990 entries were the words, "spec. to lab." Urine specimens, so Bondurant must have been following a chronic infection. Flipping back and forward, he saw "spec.'s" were taken also in 1989 and 1991. Periodically, under *A* for assessment, was the infection diagnosis, "u.t.i.," and antibiotic prescriptions under *P*, for plan—sulfamethoxazole, or Bactrim. Starting in February 1991 "thio." or "thiop." would be noted—probably a medication but the *PDR* was locked away in the office li-

brary. S, for subjective reports of the patient, often read
"dys"—dysuria probably, pain or burning, consistent with
the chronic urinary tract infection he was treating her for.
O, objective, consistently stated "+ bac," for bacteriuria on
urinalysis.

So. It added up. A lot of treatment but right things done
for right reasons. Nothing for a board investigator here.

May as well correlate the data. At the back of the chart
were MetPath computer-generated lab reports. At 2/10/89
a chart entry assessed u.t.i. based on "dys" with "+ bac."
But the MetPath report run for that specimen showed all
values in normal reference ranges, "0" blood cells and "0–
1," or minimal bacteriuria on microscopic high-powered
field. In other words, negative. All of the MetPath reports
for 1989 were negative, as they were in 1990 and 1991.
This was a strange turn. The lab reports in the back of the
chart were invariably misreported in the office notes at the
front of the chart. Meaning infections were misdiagnosed.
Unnecessary prescriptions of antibiotics. With Terry, Bondurant kept not finding a disease that was there and needed
treatment. With Emmy, he kept finding a disease that
wasn't there and needed no treatment. But aside from the
cost of unnecessary drugs, what harm was done? The board
of medical examiners had to have been after something
other than misinterpretation of urinalysis data and over-
prescription of Bactrim.

He got to the cordless phone in the kitchen before the
second ring.

"Peter Moss?" a woman asked.

"Who's this?" He could hear breaths being taken and
released. "Don't hang up," he said. "Who is this?"

"I'm glad I didn't get your wife," she said. "I'm Genny
Bondurant. I saw the article in the paper." Her inflection
rose as though it were a question.

"Well?"

"Wallace Bondurant is my father."

"O.K." Moss braced for a diatribe but she caught him up
short.

"You represented Jessie Fisher? Her parents?"

"Yes."

"I feel bad," she said, "I didn't call you before."

"Why are you calling me now, Ms. Bondurant?"

"I saw the article. Your clients were patients of my father?"

"Why should I tell you anything about my client?"

She sighed. "I probably shouldn't be talking with you either."

"Why are you?"

"I need to see you, Mr. Moss," she spoke quickly. "Nobody can know about it."

"Why do you need to see me?"

"I'm not comfortable discussing this on the telephone." Her voice had sunk to a whisper.

"Does your father know you're calling me?"

"Nobody knows."

"Does his lawyer?"

"Nobody."

"If you want us to drop the case we won't do that."

"I just can't talk about it on the phone. Can we meet Thursday evening?"

"How about Wednesday?"

"No, Thursday." She gave him a time and place, with directions.

"Tell me your phone number," he said, "in case something happens."

"No, I can't. I'm sorry. Good-bye."

Moss thumbed the Off button. He headed out and across the backyard to the print studio, receiver in one hand, Emmy's chart in the other. "Sally!" Moaning like a creature stuck in a well.

Sally was pressed close over a polished plate, carving the copper with a burin. Knuckle hairs of the gnarled fingers of the unseen puppeteer, hair by deliberate hair as orange metal curled from her tool. Moss loved the feel of her studio, the metal plates, French paper, tool drawers, containers of acid, hard-ground, resin, and inks. The great double-cylinder press with levers and felts. The starwheel like something on a bank vault or Nemo's Nautilus. It felt serious, grounded, nineteenth century. A place where lovely things were made. Where without haste or confusion beauty came about.

"I need help," Moss said. He plopped the chart on her copperplate.

"Yes, Peter?" Her smile was a touch strained. "How may I help you?"

"You're a woman."

"Male analysis hits a wall so you need the heavy artillery."

"I need the voice of inner truth."

"This is beginning to sound serious."

"God, I hope I'm wrong."

She turned open the medical chart on her half-worked plate.

"Sally. His daughter wants to meet with me."

She put the burin in a drawer. "Didn't I tell you, Peter? The answer's in his family."

EIGHT

D*ie Yuppie Scum* had a fresh T-shirt. Bad Brains. Shorty had been tagging after Heinie Hinton, but today his body language and break activity aligned him more with the women. The women—the nurse, the grad student, the prof—remained indiscriminate, poker-faced notetakers. Mr. Willits, the plumbing contractor, looked as uptight as ever; Mr. Casebolt of the FBI looked as at ease.

With the first damages witness, trout behavior could be revealing. Failure to rise was an ominous sign; disinterest in damages usually meant you'd already lost on liability.

Throughout the testimony of Moss's economist these fish were hard to read. Except Die Yuppie Scum, who kept nodding off—a bad brains day. The others communicated restlessness, consistent either with boredom or impatience. Moss sensed a threshold had been crossed. He sensed a readiness, an expectancy.

The trial had begun drawing spectators. Drifters off the emergency docket. Hacks hoping for indigent appointments. Bondurant's partisans arrayed in force—office girls, colleagues, the executive staff of the medical society. Heinz, aloof as a cop at a biker bar. None but Churchfield to root for Moss until Yellowhorse swaggered in and stood in the back, striking an Edward Curtis pose. The more the courtroom filled, the greater Moss's look of isolation at the plaintiff's table. His clientlessness.

The *Gazette-Telegraph* reporter yawned. Cut the number-crunching and gimme news.

Moss drifted a fat woolyworm past the jurors' noses.

"Dr. Felstiner. Adding the several elements of economic loss—past wage loss, lost future earnings assuming a work-life expectancy of twenty-two more years, the past and future medical costs of endstage breast cancer, and past and future home services—what is the total net economic impact in 1994 dollars of Dr. Bondurant's delay in diagnosing Ms. Winter's cancer?"

"Greater than nine hundred thousand dollars," the economist said.

Moss wrote it large on the easel pad. He glanced at his jury: Remember that number. Nurse Comstock got it but she got everything that floated by.

"Mr. Felstiner." Now it was Basteen tacking toward the witness.

"Dr. Felstiner," he smiled.

"You're a doctor?"

"A Ph.D."

"All right. Doctor. In forming your opinions, Doctor, did you take into account that the plaintiff's last job was barmaid?"

"Bar manager," he said.

"That she actually lived *in a bar*?"

"I wasn't aware of that."

"The county department of social services had begun proceedings to place her daughter in foster care. Were you aware of *that*, Doctor?"

"I don't believe so."

Murmurs had begun traveling up from somewhere.

"Yet you want these folks to give the plaintiff money for *home* services?"

"Certainly."

"For future wages of over half a million dollars?"

"Correct."

"Were you aware the plaintiff was fired from her last employment?"

"What a crock," Yellowhorse shouted from the back. "What's he talking about?"

Langworthy gaveled hard. The bailiff stood but Yellowhorse was already pushing his way out the double doors muttering.

"That's not the information I was given," the economist replied.

"Given? By whom?"

"Well, by Mr. Moss."

"I see. By Mr. Moss. There's an expression economists sometimes use—garbage in, garbage out. Are you familiar with that expression?"

"I am."

"Nothing further. Doctor."

Moss cringed. He folded and smoothed a page of notes along a central crease. He hated hearing his name come up on a Basteen cross. The economist was out the gate and up the aisle. Moss chugged a mini Dixie cup of water and turned to the gallery. He flipped the *Gazette-Telegraph* reporter a quick glance, a heads up, and called Moschetti to the stand.

Moschetti identified himself as an examiner of questioned documents. At Moss's request he'd studied the medical chart of Dr. Wallace Bondurant for his patient, Teresa Winter. His purpose had been what is known as the restoration of obliterated records.

"Summarize for us what your examination showed."

"A page of notes got changed years after the fact. One— alteration. Four words got added by hand. Two—deletion. Lined through parts of two other words. Three—obliteration. The diagram of the plaintiff's breasts was scribbled out."

The reporter had her lead.

Moschetti briefly detailed his training and experience. There was nothing Moss could do to quell the sidelong grin, head nodding as he spoke, or the Ross Perot cackle. Moschetti explained his equipment and how he'd tested the page from Terry's chart. The microscopy, ESDA indentation analysis, and BATF ink-dating that could not be reproduced in court. The card printing and infrared projection that could.

On a table in front of the jury box he placed the November 12, 1989, original page. He laid rows of fingerprint cards across it, pressed them with a rolling pin, taped the cardbacks together, and held the joined fronts before a mirror. "Voilà." He paraded them along the jury bar. The only markings the mirror reflected were the interlineations "tender" and "comes and goes," the delete lines through "non," and "ir," and the maze of scribbles in the lower right.

"So what does that tell us?" He put the mirror and taped cards back on the table. "Writing and scribbling on top of something else is what." Ms. Gideon the grad student and Shorty the beetdigger were nodding right along. "Let's check out what was scribbled on."

Moss helped Moschetti wheel into place the infrared projector and six-foot screen. The bailiff cut the lights and the windowless courtroom went black.

After a click and warm-up hum a painful white rectangle burned seemingly in midair. It shimmered and filled with the writing and marks of the page from November 12. Moschetti began to work through the series of filters, from ultraviolet to infrared. In the blackened room only a Cheshire-cat bottomlit arc of his face and the bright floating page could be seen. On the page words and lines dropped from sight as filters were successively pulled. It produced a stunning, theatrical effect—forensic IMAX—as the guises were finally all peeled back and infrared breasts and oval hovered in the air like a hologram.

Lights stuttered on to show Moschetti hands apart, with an amazed grin, like a magician completing a trick. The equipment was disassembled and packed away. Moss nodded toward the witness stand. Moschetti obliged. They worked through his exposition of the ESDA indentation studies that confirmed the breast diagram was drawn first then scribbled over later. The BATF ink-dating that showed the diagram was made with a Uniball not sold after 1989 while the cross-outs and interlineations were made with Pentel rollerballs sold first in 1991.

"As of 1989 how did the original entry read?"

"Breast mass: nonmobile, irregular."

"In 1991 or later how was it altered?"

"Someone changed it to, 'Breast mass: mobile, regular, comes and goes.' "

"The black oval, scaled as best you can to real size. What is the diameter?"

"Half inch plus."

"Half inch," Moss said. "Roughly, what? Two centimeters?"

"Two centimeters. That's just about it."

Moss flipped the butcher pad back to his original sheet. He added a third entry to what he'd written the day before:

November 12, 1989

Dr. Borkin:	2 cm., hard, irregular, nothing like a cyst
Dr. Greenwood:	2 cm., hard, irregular, rough, nonmobile, nontender
Dr. Bondurant's diagram:	2 cm., nonmobile, irregular

"Turning back to the diagram, Mr. Moschetti, when was it and the oval showing a two-centimeter lump drawn in Terry Winter's chart?"

"November 12, 1989, is the date of that page."

"When did someone try to obliterate the diagram, scribble it out?"

"Sometime 1991 or thereafter. Couple of years after the fact at least."

"One last thing." Moss brought a multipage Exhibit M to the witness chair.

"Mr. Moschetti, this is Dr. Bondurant's office chart for the plaintiff's daughter, Mary Eliza Winter."

Bondurant watched with a hooded expression.

"Take a look at the jacket of Exhibit M. Can you discern impressions on the front cover of the daughter's chart?"

Moschetti tilted and studied the indentations in the lamination. He cackled softly and nodded. Coated papers, he explained, especially heat-sealed like this, accept and retain ballpoint pressure lines really well. What he sees here are impressions left by writing on a note that was paper-clipped to the front of the chart.

"Can you tell what was written on the note?"

"What it said was, 'Not for BME.' "

"No further questions, Your Honor, except I would like the jurors to view the two original charts."

"Any objection?" Langworthy asked.

Basteen shook his head. Bondurant dug a thumb in his cheek.

"Show the jury," the judge said.

The charts were passed from hand to hand. Jurors craned and squinted at the impressions in the jacket cover, the scribbled-on page from November 1989. The scribbles seemed to meet Nurse Comstock's disapproval.

Basteen collected the charts. He left Terry's at the podium and advanced on Moschetti, rapping Emmy's in his palm. He drew up over the witness, free hand braced on the box.

"You don't know when marks were made on the front of this jacket, do you?"

"Nope."

"For all you know Mr. Moss could have written this note on top of this file last night."

"I don't think so."

"Well, you're being paid not to think so. But you in fact

have no evidence of the origin of the note supposedly paper-clipped on top." He grazed the witness's elbow.

"Evidence? Nope."

"When it was written or by whom?"

"Like I say, nope."

Basteen sighed and gave the judge an openhanded look: Well, what now?

"Your renewed motion for the sealed file, Mr. Moss, if that's what you were after, is denied. I don't call this proof of anything."

"Additional foundation will follow, Your Honor, through other testimony."

"I hope so."

Basteen huffed and returned to the witness. "You used to work for the sheriff?"

"Ran the lab, that's right. Chief documents examiner."

"You were fired, correct?"

"Resigned."

"After an uncomplimentary review of your work in *People v. Bauman?* The mailbomb case?"

"Not of my work, no. I like to chat with reporters." He winked at the one from the *Gazette-Telegraph.*

"And the sheriff fired you."

"We parted ways."

"You've never taught an academic course?" He thumped a fingertip on his palm.

"Nope."

"Don't even have an academic degree."

"AA, Front Range, '74."

"Never been trained in ink-dating by immunoelectrophoresis?

"Whatever that is."

"Never published in the *Journal of Forensic Science* or any other professional journal?"

"I'm not a writer or a lecturer or a professor. I'm a problem solver." He bobbed and grinned.

"Are you?" Their eyes were dueling.

"You want to know who's been dealing off the bottom, I run it down."

"You do?"

"I did." He indicated the defendant.

"Let's see what you did. You showed us your infrared view on the projector. Very impressive."

"Thanks."

"But your infrared view doesn't tell us *when* that breast diagram was drawn."

Moss began feeling a pressure at his ears, eyes, sinuses, like he was underwater. He swallowed. He'd known for months this was coming but it still felt like his head was being squeezed.

"Not the IVS-100, nope," Moschetti said. "ESDA does, and fingerprint cards helps. Ink-dating nails it. The diagram was drawn in 1989."

"If all you had was infrared you couldn't tell whether that breast diagram we all just saw was the first thing drawn or *the last thing* drawn on that page, correct?"

"That's not all I have."

"All we know just from the demonstration here today is that somebody at some time drew a diagram of two breasts and a lump with a different pen than was used anywhere else on the page."

He nodded. "O.K."

"Are you aware of the expert opinion of Professor Crawford of Stanford University based on his immunoelectrophoretic studies that this breast diagram was not drawn by Dr. Bondurant at all?" Basteen's inflection, having climbed to a peak, abruptly plummeted. "Are you aware there is evidence this diagram was in fact drawn by the plaintiff's lawyer, Peter Moss?"

The reporter's lead was quickly amended: Charges of evidence tampering were traded today in the trial of Dr. Wallace Bondurant.

NINE

Trial is an imperfect alternative to bloodshed. The dangerous forces are unreliably contained. The jury is boxed, the public fenced, the witness caged, and the parties drawn up to tables. The judge is elevated at the bar and the combatants in the arena are restrained by rule and ritual. But rules require obedience, and ritual faith. Court is a bell jar. Order is provisional, stipulated. A trial that fails, with truth hidden, or justice denied, can shatter the fragile vessel and set disorder loose.

Moss had lain all night examining a ghost, circling and circling. He woke in a panic. He wasn't ready for Bondurant. Achingly close but not yet there. He had no choice but to push on; no one else was left to call. And then what? If Terry wasn't back the judge would dismiss the case. The truth would be buried. Bondurant would walk. Costs would be awarded. Moss would declare bankruptcy. Terry would die and Warren would take Emmy off to the badlands in his blue truck. A complete catastrophe; all for naught.

Evasive as mist in dreams, in court the defendant looked solid, crudely corporeal. He stood when Moss said his name, pushing his chair aside with the back of his knees. He straightened his suit jacket and shouldered to the stand.

He raised a fleshy hand and agreed to tell the whole truth and nothing but. He sat heavily and turned to stare at Moss, fashioning an open smile, a game expression: Give me your best shot.

"Good morning, Dr. Bondurant."

"Good morning, Mr. Moss."

"Dr. Bondurant. What do physicians mean when they talk about the standard of care?"

The defendant rubbed his nose thoughtfully. "What is expected of a medical doctor in a given situation, is how I'd put it, Mr. Moss."

"What a reasonably careful doctor in the same specialty would do under similar circumstances?"

"Fair enough."

"The standard of conduct it is negligence not to meet?"

"That's right."

"Malpractice not to meet?"

"Yessir." He hunched forward to pull up a sock.

"I want to ask you about the standard of care for family physicians, your specialty. All right?"

"All right."

"You're listed by your lawyer as an expert on family practice standards. Is that right?"

"Well, I suppose." Bondurant's eyes pearled. He let out a self-deprecating chuckle. "If the lawyers say so." Heinie Hinton smiled with him.

"There is a family practice standard of care for following women with suspicious breast lesions, is there not?"

He nodded. "You have to exercise your best clinical judgment."

"Isn't there an accepted standard?"

"Accepted? Not really."

"Do you recall giving deposition testimony under oath in this case?"

"Yessir."

"Your Honor—the original transcript of Dr. Bondurant's deposition." Moss brought it to the judge, sidestepping the great golden seal and eye in the carpet. The judge tore open the gummed envelope with a flourish and handed the bound transcript to the witness.

"Dr. Bondurant, is Exhibit One to your deposition the Flatirons Community Hospital Breast Carcinoma Protocol, a blow-up of which I am holding?" Moss positioned a foamboard-mounted exhibit on the easel and stood beside it with the pointer.

The witness checked the transcript, squinted at the easel. "Appears to be."

"Turn to page sixty-three of your deposition, sir. Beginning at line six did you give the following answer under oath to the following question: 'Does Exhibit One in your opinion set forth the applicable minimum standard for differential diagnosis of breast cancer?' Answer: 'Yes.' "

"That's what it says."

"That's what you said."

"Yes."

"Under oath?"

"Um-hum."

"Verbalize your answers, Doctor," the judge cautioned. "Makes it easier for Shelley." The court reporter beamed gratefully.

Bondurant nodded. "I took an oath."

"Did you understand that was an oath of the same solemnity as your oath to speak the truth to us today?"

"Sure." He shifted his chair.

"According to Exhibit One," Moss pointed, "six weeks is the maximum you can let a suspicious breast lesion go without attempting biopsy."

"Yes."

"It's negligence to let one go longer."

"Objection. Calls for legal opinion."

"Overruled."

"Well?"

"Yeah, that would be negligent, if the lump is suspicious."

"What is the purpose of acting as quickly as possible to biopsy a suspicious lump?"

"We say to do that. It usually doesn't make any difference." He worked his shoulders to loosen his jacket.

"Return to page sixty-three, please. Line nineteen. Did you testify under oath that the earlier breast cancer is diagnosed the greater the chance of cure?"

"Um-hum. Yes."

"And the information you give women in your clinic states exactly that." Moss produced Exhibit L, one of the breast self-examination brochures he'd lifted from the Wellness Clinic waiting room. Bondurant perused it and grudgingly agreed.

"In breast cancer, early detection is the standard of care. Correct?"

He exhaled through his teeth. "Correct."

"What are the characteristics of a suspicious lump?"

"Different from a cyst." He threw up his hands. "You have to exercise your clinical judgment, is what I'm trying to communicate."

"A suspicious lump doesn't come and go. It stays there."

"That's one thing."

"An irregular lump is suspicious for cancer." Moss flipped the easel chart back to the page summarizing Borkin's, Greenwood's, and now Moschetti's testimony. He tapped the word.

"Irregular? Yes."

Hard? Not freely movable? Not tender? Moss tapped and Bondurant confirmed each characteristic as suspicious.

"If you find a two-centimeter lump that's hard, irregular, and neither tender nor movable and it doesn't go away in six weeks, it stays there, what does the standard of care require you to do?"

Bondurant glanced at the jurors intently watching him. He pulled at an earlobe. "Biopsy or refer it out."

"If it's two centimeters. Irregular. Nonmobile. There longer than six weeks, you have to act, correct?"

"In your hypothetical."

"It would be *malpractice* not to biopsy or refer, wouldn't it?"

"Um-hum." His look clouded over.

"Would it be malpractice?"

"Sure, but why didn't she go to Mayhew like I said to? Tell me that. He's the specialist."

"Move to strike."

"Jury will disregard."

"Noncompliant," Bondurant huffed. Basteen was shaking his head in tiny measured movements ten degrees off-axis. "Just like Greenwood said she was."

"Move to strike and request the court to admonish the witness."

"*Doctor. You will not just start talking in my court.* You will answer questions accurately. No more. No less. Do you understand?"

"Yeah. Yeah."

"Dr. Bondurant, I want to turn to the subject of charts."

"O.K."

"Do you always edit by hand office notes the same day they're typed, at most a day later?"

"I said that in my deposition."

"Is that in fact always what you do?"

"Yeah, that's how I do it. Chart is important. Has to be accurate, has to be current."

"Always *by hand?*" Moss indicated a blow-up of the November 12 page. "Edited *by hand* like these notes are?"

"That's right."

"You're sure?"

"That's right."

"Take a look at group Exhibit M. Is that the chart of a patient of yours?"

He opened Emmy's records. An elastic moment passed.

"Dr. Bondurant?"

"She's my patient."

"Any handwritten editing of this patient chart?"

He shook his head.

"Verbalize."

"No."

"Can you explain why not?"

He shook his head again. "I don't know. Lots of them are marked up like hers," he pointed at the blow-up of the page from Terry's. "Who knows."

"What does it mean to doctor a chart?"

"I'm not sure I know what that means." He picked at a thread on his sleeve.

"Doctors have a lot of authority in our society, don't they?"

Basteen stood to object, thought better of it.

Bondurant forced a smile. "Between lawyers and insurance companies, I begin to wonder."

"A doctor can decide whether you can work, or attend school, or travel, or play a sport."

"I guess."

"A doctor can incarcerate you in a mental hospital against your will."

"There are standards."

"Choose who's admitted to a hospital, who gets medicine."

"He has to exercise his best clinical judgment."

"A doctor can literally grant life or take life."

"You said it. I didn't say it."

"In the exercise of all that authority, no one really polices the medical profession, do they?"

"That's not so. We have a board. . . ." He stopped.

"The board of medical examiners."

"Yes."

"What is the board of medical examiners?"

"State agency." He pulled on his collar with a hooked finger.

"The one that investigates complaints about doctors and sometimes disciplines them?"

"Objection. Relevancy."

The judge looked skeptically at Moss. "Subject to a later connection, I'll allow it. Answer, Doctor."

"The answer was yes, discipline, and other stuff, licensure."

"Who sits on the board of medical examiners?"

"Seven M.D.s. Two D.O.s. Two lay members."

"Seven M.D.s? Nominated by whom?"

"Governor appoints. Senate confirms."

"From whose list are appointments chosen?"

"Ours."

"Ours? The medical society?"

"Yes."

"You are the president of the state medical society?"

"Yes, I am."

"When conducting an investigation does the board sometimes audit a physician's practice?"

"Yes."

"What is an audit?"

"Where the board or hospital section or preferred provider group or whatnot does a quality assurance review for something or other. Government regulations more and more. It's a problem."

"A problem?"

"Government regulations are a problem, yessir, Mr. Moss." Bondurant was glaring at his lawyer: Object, his glare demanded. Do something.

"How does the board audit a private practice?"

"Random chart review. Usually."

"Or pulls all charts that deal with a particular medical problem?"

"Sometimes." He cracked his knuckles.

"Or all charts for a particular kind of patient?"

"Sometimes."

"So the board of medical examiners has access to a physician's office records?"

"Yessir."

"No one else has access to a physician's office records?"

"The patient," he said. "Nobody else unless the patient authorizes."

"The chart in front of you, Exhibit M, whose is it?"

"Mary Eliza Winter."

"The plaintiff's daughter?"

"Yeah."

"It has *not* been doctored, has it?"

"Objection."

"Mr. Moss." The judge removed his half-rims. The wide-set eyes came forward. The message was plain: Thin Ice.

"I will link it up, Your Honor." Moss gave Emmy's chart a long, introspective look. He rubbed his lip with the ball of his thumb. Hold back, he cautioned himself. Go slow, build the case for the sealed file, but stick to the game plan, the breast cancer standard of care. Win with facts, fact by fact. Next week when the defense case starts facts will be his friends.

"I'm waiting, Mr. Moss."

On the other hand, what the hell. His client doesn't show soon and next week's already history.

"Dr. Bondurant." Moss stared at the witness as if fishing a hole. He cast. "Why did you direct your staff not to provide the board's investigators auditing your pediatric practice the chart of Mary Eliza Winter?"

"I don't have the slightest idea what you're talking about." Bondurant folded his hands in a complacent pile.

"Why was the board auditing your medical practice?"

"Objection."

"*Mr. Moss.* You must first demonstrate your link, lay your foundation for relevancy." The judge had a stricken smile—at the end of his rope with a naughty child. "Objection sustained." He cracked the gavel. "Court's adjourned for fifteen minutes. Jurors are admonished not to discuss the case or testimony with anyone or among each other."

"All stand." The bailiff barked like a drill sergeant.

With an armload of case reporters and flared hem the judge rose and turned crisply, heel and toe. He disappeared with his law clerk into the false cherrywood paneling. The jury filed out. Bondurant stretched and rolled his head. "Got time for a Coke?" he called. Basteen flipped his client a thumb's up.

The lying bag of shit won't look at me, Moss observed. He can't. The fucking puke. He thinks he's going to skate again. Moss then realized he was scowling at the defendant in the presence of forty people. He closed his eyes and cursed under his breath and turned away. At the courtroom doorway Sally could be seen bouncing on her tiptoes, waving with both hands.

"Hey, Peter." The *Gazette-Telegraph* reporter got his sleeve on his way out. "What's the mystery with the medical examiners?"

"Be here next Tuesday, after the holiday. It'll be worth it."

She looked doubtful.

"It's big," he said as he headed for Sally.

TEN

B*ack on the* stand Bondurant was square-jawed and ramrod straight. Something about how erectly he sat suggested both rigid tension and pliability. A pipecleaner man.

The jury looked a little out of sorts. Heinie Hinton rubbed an eye with the roughened heel of his hand.

"Let's wrap this up, Doctor," Moss said. No more footsy. No more haymakers wild of the mark. Save the big money bets for next week when Basteen calls him back.

"O.K. by me," the defendant said dryly.

"We were talking about your charts."

"What else you got?"

"When you find a breast lump still in the same place as on a previous visit, the first thing you do is diagram it, correct?"

"No, not always."

"Turn to page seventy-two of your deposition, line twenty-one. Did you testify you *always* diagram a lump if it is still in the same place from one visit to the next?"

"That's what this says."

"You *always* diagram a persistent lump?" Moss balanced the Giant Breasts blow-up on the easel.

Bondurant loitered over the answer. "O.K."

"You understand our documents examiner found this diagram," pointing, "on the page of your notes dated November 12, 1989?"

"I heard what he said."

"Ms. Winter's cancer wasn't diagnosed until October 28, 1992."

"Yeah."

"Nearly three years later?"

"Yeah."

"During which you saw her in your office nine times."

"If you say so."

"And performed nine breast examinations?" Moss gestured in the direction of the blue gel model.

"I'm sure I did."

"Doctor." Moss began advancing toward him, a step per clause. "If you found and diagramed a two-centimeter lump in Terry Winter's left breast on November 12, 1989"—pointing at the black oval—"as Dr. Borkin testified you should have done, as Dr. Greenwood testified you should have done, and as Mr. Moschetti testified you in fact did do, but if you then failed to biopsy or refer her out for three years, after nine office visits, and nine physical exams, that would be negligence, wouldn't it?" Moss confronted him point-blank.

"Mr. Moss. That would be gross negligence, but it didn't happen like that."

"Move to strike the latter part of the answer."

"Jury will disregard."

"That would make you liable for malpractice, wouldn't it?"

"If that's what had happened it sure would."

"In your expert opinion that would be below the family practice standard of care?"

Bondurant darkened. "Of course," he muttered, "but that's not what went on with this girl."

Moss let the epithet hang and fade like a struck bell.

"I warned you, Doctor." The judge beetled over the witness.

"That's all right, Your Honor." Moss returned to the podium. "We're going to learn what went on with Ms. Terry Winter in her own words, when she testifies tomorrow."

"Tomorrow?" The judge's gabled eyebrows lifted. "You can assure me of that?"

"I was just informed her flight arrives this evening. We can recess for redeposition tomorrow morning then present her testimony as soon as Mr. Basteen is ready."

"Outstanding." The judge was pleased. Basteen was not. Bondurant looked this way and that like a passenger disembarking at an unfamiliar airport.

"No further questions of Dr. Bondurant at this time," Moss said, "although I reserve the right to cross-examine if he is called in the defendant's case."

"Certainly. Mr. Basteen, your witness."

"A moment, Your Honor. May I confer?" After some pressured whispering at the witness box, Basteen and Moss gathered for a sidebar. "Move for mistrial," Basteen hissed sotto voce. "Moss has melodramatically withheld and is now producing his client at the last minute both to obstruct effective cross-examination and to grandstand the staged entry of this pitiful sick woman. His coy ambiguity about whether she was even alive was completely disingenuous, Your Honor. This was rigged from the start to prejudice the doctor's defense."

"Really? Mr. Moss?"

"I wish."

"Is your client your final witness, Mr. Moss?"

"Correct, Your Honor." The only other possibility was Emmy but he hadn't endorsed her. Emmy would be allowed to testify only in rebuttal and only if there was defense testimony she was allowed to rebut.

"Your motion is baloney, Basteen," the judge whispered. "You were hoping this woman wouldn't show so I'd toss the case. You were hoping she died in Mexico, right? Well, tough titty, like they say. The woman's alive and the trial goes on. She plays cute at her deposition, Moss, you still might hit the shitcan. Understood? Basteen?"

"I want it on the record."

"The defendant's motion for mistrial is denied. Proceed, Mr. Basteen."

On the side of the podium opposite the jury Basteen flipped his client a thumb's down. He smiled pleasantly and set about the reverential rehabilitation of Wallace Bondurant, M.D.

With the gentlest deference Basteen coaxed into view the gems and badges of his client's career, his straight medicine residency, his anesthesiology residency, the Sigma Zeta Community Service Award, the Navy Commendation Medal of 1964, his service on the Advisory Committee on Health to Senator Campbell, as medical director for student health at Rocky Mountain Women's College, as chairman of the legislative committee of the state medical society, as president of the medical society through the crosscurrents of health care reform.

The practice of medicine was patiently explained. Medicine was an art, not a science, the province of enlightened judgment, irreducible to bright-line standards. The standard of care wasn't to be found in rulebooks or recipes. Hindsight may be 20/20 but you can't practice medicine with a retrospectroscope. When you're the one on the line you call it like you see it. Sometimes you're wrong, but a bad outcome isn't the same as malpractice.

Bondurant addressed the jury professorially, enacting the Aristotelian ideal of the reasonable physician, a part no doubt perfected over hours of video playback. Basteen smoothed and polished his client's defects and lapses, led him through every plausible rationale for neglect, left him gleaming as a hood ornament: The Clinician Contends with Noncompliance. One by one the defenses were erected— the Low Index of Suspicion given negative radiology reports, the Judgment Call confounded by fibrocystic disease, the Phantom Phone Call to Dr. Mayhew unrecorded in any chart.

"I think of myself as a patient advocate." Bondurant smiled, a gesture of acknowledgment, as though it were something for which he was modestly famous. "The physician-patient relationship must be one of mutual trust and confidence. I advocate, I counsel, but in this day and age the patient is ultimately responsible for decisions governing her health. What happened here is tragic but Ms. Winter was really a terribly irresponsible patient."

Basteen was giving them the whole enchilada with chile verde. With a sickening feeling Moss saw he may have made a disastrous miscalculation. Basteen might spend next week trotting out docs to praise their president and putting Moss on trial for manufacturing the diagram without ever calling Bondurant back to the stand. Moss might get stuck in place with no way to get new evidence in.

He got a last shot on redirect and hit Bondurant on his lack of boards, how holding on to patients might help him recertify without taking the exam. He did a little harm but the door was closed to new subjects unrelated to Basteen's questioning. Next week would be his only chance and only then if Basteen made the mistake of putting Bondurant back on the stand.

They recessed, scheduling Terry's deposition the following morning in the conference room of the judge's chambers, Moss confessing he'd lost access to his office. Moss had finished frustrated, wanting much more than what he had, wanting in fact no less than to tear Bondurant asunder and devour him in parts. Maybe he wanted more than he should. He had a feeling it showed.

He didn't get home until a little after ten, suffused with secondhand smoke. The Tool, where he'd gone to meet Genny Bondurant, made him feel old, straight, overdressed and underpierced. "I'd like a Virgin Mary," he told the barely legal barmaid. "Hold the Mary." He could still be a fun guy, at least until the band came on. The Psychodykes amplified his alienation. Die Yuppie Scum was backing them up on drums. One of those Jungian sychronicities that seem to happen during trials. What next? Langworthy techno-dancing in cross-attire?

Die Yuppie Scum threw Moss a shaka Hawaiian high-sign. Genny Bondurant ordered a third stinger but Moss said he needed to hit it. Tinnitus, diplopia, cold sweats—the hypersensitivity of an ex-smoker. Ex-drinker. No longer groovy guy. Genny Bondurant was in her late twenties. Round face and big round eyes, gray like her father's. Melancholy eyes, prematurely middle-aged. There comes a time, she said, a little ponderous from the brandy, when you have to stop pretending. I keep meeting women, Moss told her, more courageous than any man I've known.

He opened his front door to three of them looking up. "We don't mind dogs, do we, Peter?" Sally said.

"Hey, man!"

Moss saw at once he'd prepared himself inadequately. "You've—lost weight."

"Weight? What you mean is I look like hell. But we're ready for the son of a bitch. Refried and hot to trot."

"*We* are?"

"You're looking at a team."

"Emmy." If anything, more startling than her mother— taller, it seemed, dark golden skin and eyes the blue of ice floes, of Siberian huskies. Eyes with nothing to hide.

"Hi, Peter," Emmy said.

"Calves today, dogies tomorrow," Terry observed. "I was just finishing telling Sally. Things you need to know."

"I know them," he said.

"We had it way wrong."

"I know we did. God, I'm sorry."

"You don't mean you finally figured it out?" She stood with effort. "Come here and give us some *abrazos*, cowboy. I *knew* you were my lawyer."

ELEVEN

She *was the* best of clients, she was the worst of clients. She wanted to hear about the case, he wanted to hear about her.

Terry was taking something now for pain, Sally told him in the kitchen, and something else for seizures. She had no appetite. Emmy had gotten her to finish a slice of Weezy's Wishbone. Her arm trembled less and she wasn't smoking anymore but the gauntness was almost shocking. Her skin was taut to translucency, ripstop smooth except for sores here and there. She tensed in the Queen Anne chair, gripping the arms, knife-eyed and animated. In a compressed and angular way she looked vital, ardent.

"Case is rolling," Moss said. "We downsized it some."

"Right on. Simplify."

"Tell me about you. Where the hell'd you go? How'd you get here?"

She opened a palm. "I'm a survivor. Not."

"That's a joke," Emmy explained.

"My kid keeps me going. I've got the world's greatest kid."

"I see that."

"I've got the world's greatest mom," Emmy added.

"We're tough and we know it." Terry coughed. The

cough deepened and became racking. Her eyes welled and her fingers lay lightly on her chest as the gasping eased.

"The heart is a muscle, amigo. That's what got us back."

They'd been on the road. Sort of a Thelma and Louise deal, or Bob Hope or somebody, till Warren ran them down. Which took him quite a while, finding the Sugar Beat van on the border, then working from Puerto Peñasco down to Kino Bay, asking about gringo gals at every flea-bag on the coast. Guy's relentless when he wants to be. The big thing was getting him turned around. Once it sank in he hauled ass as far as New Mexico, then stopped. An issue of who'd be running the show, him or Moss. It took some doing but he got with the program. So she called Moss's office. They told her a tale.

"Leave town," she said, "and the whole shootin' match goes right to hell. They moved up the trial on us? Your firm kicked you out because you wouldn't drop my case?"

"Like I said, I am your lawyer."

"The South African woman wants to come work for you, by the way."

"Lata liked you off the bat."

"Sally's who you need, buddy. Clearly the alpha wolf in this outfit." Got them tickets and picked them up at Stapleton and settled them here in a single day.

"Fold-out couch is the best we can do," Sally apologized.

"Putting me up in the *living* room? Is that supposed to be funny?"

"That," Emmy said, "also is a joke."

"All in all, Mexico was a constructive experience," Terry told him. "I figured some things out, too."

"Like?"

"Like it's not, I'm a bad person so I got cancer. It's not some evil influence or the stars weren't lined up right, or I'm being tested, or I didn't have a balanced diet. Like what the meaning of illness is."

"Tell me."

"It's nothing. Illness doesn't mean anything. Illness is

like thunder, or night, or rain, or the moon getting smaller and coming back again. Illness just is."

"You mean—shit happens?"

"That's right. It's not that complicated. Shit happens and mean people suck." She paused. "Mean people," she said, "have no soul."

Moss assessed her earnest look. She had figured things out indeed. But he was curious. How had she gotten Warren to get with the program?

"Enemy of my enemy," she said. "We made a deal."

Warren would be driving up from Albuquerque with Lightning, the dog. They got along better now, but Lightning would be needing a place to stay.

"Why does Warren want to help you?"

"He doesn't but he loves his kid. Sort of. Like a terrorist loves his homeland."

"Terry, tell me. Did he hurt you?" He studied her straightened features for marks masked by the disease.

"Why you want to know?"

"I'll cut off his . . ." Moss glanced at Emmy.

"It's O.K. And Warren won't hurt me."

"Can I believe you?"

She paused to breathe, building her strength. "Sick people don't lie."

"Oh yeah?"

"Not anymore. Truth City, Peter, from now on out." She raised her fingers in the Scouts' honor sign. "I'm not who he wants to hurt."

"You trust Warren?"

"Warren, oddly enough, is a man of his word. I often wished he wasn't."

"What kind of deal did you and he make?"

"He let us come. He gave his word he'd let the trial run its course. Back off and let the system take care of things."

"How," Moss asked, "did you get him to give his word?"

"Reasoned with him."

"I'm so sure." Emmy rolled her eyes.

"Reason and a little of that old what you lawyers call consortium."

Moss shook his head.

"You know me. Anything for the case. But Emmy's the one had her old man's number. Emmy's got the power. Make the blind walk and the cripple see."

The luminous blue eyes were rolling again.

"There's something you have to do tomorrow." Moss said soberly. "You have to sit for deposition again. You can't refuse this. The Terry-Jerry show one last time. Tell me you'll do it for the case."

"No problem."

He stared at her in disbelief.

"I got no problem with it. What's the matter with you?"

"You're too cooperative. It worries me."

"I'd steal the flowers off my mother's grave if it helped take the bastard down."

"Nice building," Terry commented as Moss hurried her up the courthouse ramp ten minutes late. "Who's the architect? Cookie Monster?"

They were shown to Judge Langworthy's conference room by the law clerk. Nobody there but Nikki, Basteen's court reporter. Hi, guy! Long time no see! Mole frolicking, blouse swelling beneath the judge's martial ornament of sword, shell, and battle carnage. Moss drummed on the glass-topped table. He heard something; faint; off. Adrenaline kicked in as it would on bivouac in Quang Ngai. Langworthy's muffled voice could be discerned from behind the door. And other noises at intervals, brief, low, portentous.

Moss slipped to the door, Lurp-stealthy without forethought. He listened, turned the knob, pushed the door a quarter inch then threw it open in mock surprise.

"Peter," the judge said heartily. "Come in. I'll tell you what I was just starting to tell Mr. Heinz."

Nods and smiles all around. Salutations of the day. The

judge in shirtsleeves. Heinz in shirtsleeves. Basteen in a gray double-breasted.

"Guys," Moss smiled. "Jerome—didn't you hear? It's dress-down Friday."

Chuckles.

"This case should settle," the judge declared. "I mean that, Peter. You've done your job and ROMPIC should pay. Pay generously, in my view. I think Mr. Heinz appreciates that." Heinz smiled tightly without wrinkling his eyes. "Your client's finally here, so what are we waiting for?"

All three looked expectantly at Moss.

"Where's Dr. Bondurant?"

"Day off," Basteen said. "I have his full authority."

"Authority for what?"

The judge smacked his lips and took a seat at his desk. He swiveled and stopped, facing Moss, cocked an ankle informally on a knee. Suspendered, in a cardboard-stiff white shirt, the judge gave Moss the impression of a song-and-dance man. He expected a cigar, a boater, a little soft-shoe.

"I want to tell you what I'm presently inclined to do. Both sides should know. It may help guide negotiations. Unless the moon falls out of the sky, I'm not going to dismiss this case. I'm strongly inclined to let it go to the jury. I think Mr. Heinz understands the risk that could present. Today's deposition will go forward. Mr. Basteen may go into the fullest detail, so don't come crying to me about protective orders, Moss. I'm still considering the medical examiners issue with the sealed file." He gave Basteen an arch look. "If Moss presents an adequate foundation I'm leaning toward letting the jury have it." He frowned sincerely.

Basteen grinned back, shit-eating type, and twitched with cognitive dissonance.

"Think about it, gentlemen. There's a lot to be gained by coming to terms."

To Moss's astonishment the judge winked at him: See, buddy, I'm trying to lend you a hand.

"I'll sound her out," Moss said. "She's tired. She's kind of bewildered by everything."

I'm so sure.

"She's going to learn real soon a trial ain't slow pitch, Moss."

Moss shook his head and looked helpless.

"All right, gentlemen, go do your jobs."

In the conference room, Nikki stored her gum in a tiny magnetized box on the undercarriage of her stenographic device. She gave Terry a cheery oath and her fingers pranced before the keys. Heinz drifted down the wall of bookcases and lodged in a folding chair in the corner.

"Good morning, Ms. Winter."

"Jerry." She braced in her seat and grasped the table like a billfisherman in a fighting chair. There was something formidable in her manner, the degree of tension, the way she bore in with her eyes. Such changeable eyes, like the ocean—from dancing sparkle to painful glare, to ink sleek and knowing, to slaty cold, murderous.

"My lawyer tells me—" she said.

"Don't divulge communications with me," Moss cautioned.

"He says nothing'd please you more than seeing me dead. Is that right?"

"Ms. Winter, the judge ordered this deposition months ago."

"Here I am. Deal with it."

"I'm entitled to find out what your lawyer improperly prohibited last time."

"Kind of weird sitting across the table from someone like you. Hoping I was dead."

"The first subject I want to cover is sexual conduct."

"What can I say? I'm a free-range woman of the nineties." She smiled but her eyes had guttered, bleak and hard.

"Terry." Moss touched her shoulder. She untensed a bit. "Just answer his questions."

And she did. Questions about whether she'd contracted venereal diseases, watched x-rated movies, had extramarital affairs, lesbian affairs, been molested, her first sex, frequency of sex, kinky sex; sex, Basteen leered toward her, Nikki flinching slightly away, with animals?

"No," she responded coolly. "Sorry to disappoint."

Basteen had gotten her gynecological history from the medical records. He went through all of it, from spotty discharges to a D-and-C to a live birth in 1967. Moss could bear it no longer. He cursed below his breath and stood. His hands were balling into fists so he plunged them in his pockets, spun and paced, stanching his racing disgust. Ride it out, he told himself. The judge won't stop it and a face-off with Basteen now would only educate him. He paced and cursed and paced. Got to ride it out.

Basteen affected not to notice. Intimidation and suborning perjury were his stock-in-trade. He was as workaday brutalizing women and procuring lies as a butcher filleting a steer. His nonchalance from repetition gave the illusion of deftness.

Since her breast surgery, he asked, did she regard herself as sexually appealing? What did orgasm feel like now? "Have you ever been raped?"

"Yes," she said.

"When?"

"Just now."

Basteen smiled. Moss could have sworn the smile disguised a wince. The court reporter blushed. This was no longer fun. Heinz sat fixed on a middle distance, placid as an owl.

Terry required a breather. She curled on her side on a leather bench. As Basteen and Heinz conferred in the hall Nikki sat next to her. She began massaging her shoulders. What was formidable, Moss saw, was simple enough: She perseveres on guts alone. Heart, as she would have it.

"Ready, Ms. Winter?"

"I hope you have more questions," she said. " 'Cause this is rich."

"How's that, Ms. Winter?" He picked at a cuticle.

"You think my sexual conduct brought this on."

"Just answer what he asked," Moss said, "unless I tell you not to." Moss wanted to stop the provocations. He was beginning to appreciate the breadth of Basteen's ignorance.

"Indeed, I have more questions," Basteen said. "Let me start with your daughter."

"Fire away."

"Hold your fire," Moss said.

"Do you know why the board of medical examiners would have any interest in your daughter's care?"

"Don't answer that," Moss said. She didn't.

"You don't have a problem with how my client cared for your daughter, do you?"

"Or that," Moss said.

"What do your daughter's medical needs have to do with your late diagnosis of breast cancer?"

"Or that. The court's order limited this deposition to *Ms. Winter's* sexual and childbearing history," Moss said. "You're way beyond the scope, Jerome."

"Come on, Peter." Basteen now looked openly frustrated, almost hurt. He didn't understand; he needed help.

Ain't it a shitter, Moss thought sympathetically, when your client's been lying to you.

Terry whispered, "Why not say? What's wrong with truth?"

"Tell him and we'll never see Bondurant under oath again," Moss whispered back.

"I'm sorry, Jerome," Moss said, "it's in the judge's order."

Terry made a sympathetic face—what can I do?

"Look." Basteen closed his notebook. "Off the record." He signaled the reporter to beat it. She sighed and grabbed her purse and magnetized box and swung out of the room.

"I'm going to level with you guys," Basteen said. "I've had investigators working this case. I don't have to ask this stuff. I know already."

Yeah, right.

"I know about your husband. I know what he does for a living. The board of medical examiners file, I know about that. There's nothing in it, Peter. Red herring. You'll see. I'm going to cut to the chase. Our two hundred's there for the taking."

She laughed.

"You're not well," Basteen said, corrugating with false concern. "You could lose this case. You probably will. Go easy on yourself. Think about your kid."

Moss buried his face in his hands.

"Oh, I am, Jerry. I am."

"How much do you want?"

"That sounds so crude."

"How much?"

"You mean, name my price?"

"Name it."

"Life without parole."

"Tell us what it will take."

"I need to talk to my attorney first."

"Of course."

"But, for discussion purposes, what do you guys think of a cool million?"

Basteen looked at Heinz. Almost imperceptibly Heinz nodded, a three-millimeter shift of the head.

"For settlement of all claims and your agreement of confidentiality," Basteen spoke rotundly, "it's a deal. One million dollars."

"No confidentiality," she said.

Basteen looked at Heinz. Heinz gave another delicate nod.

"All right. No confidentiality. Just a mutual release of claims and stipulation today to the dismissal of the case."

"Trial's over, in other words?"

"You won't even have to testify."

"Not interested," Terry said. She glanced at Moss. "Right, counselor?"

"Your call."

"No deal, Jerry. I'm in this for keeps." She leaned forward. "Let me give you some advice. Trying to humiliate me then buy me off—bad tactic. You read me wrong. Always have.

"Let's finish this patty-cake," she said. "First tell Asshole to butt out." She cocked her head toward Heinz. "Asshole makes me nervous."

A nap on the grass and a wash-up, foregoing a pain shot for the sake of clarity, fifteen minutes breathing, in-one-two, out-one-two, gripping her eagle fetish, visualizing the tinaja with yellow butterflies, a vermilion flycatcher on a palo blanco bough, the Seri hunkered like a mudhen, as the boojum creaked and the truth was spoken, and Terry testified. Emmy sat at counsel table with Moss. When Terry was done Moss rested his case. The judge ruled the plaintiff had met her burden. Motion to dismiss denied. The court was in recess until 9:00 A.M. Tuesday when the defense could call its first witness.

Terry's testimony wasn't forceful. How could it be? She was weak and required breaks, questions required repeating, answers trailed away. She clenched and closed her eyes as pain washed over her. She found herself coughing and clutching for breath. She was faithful to the facts. Authenticity was a strength, as it had always been. Her puzzlement about a Dr. Mayhew, a supposed referral, was convincing. No one could think her noncompliant, getting nine breast exams in thirty-two months, so diligent with Emmy's wellness checks.

Basteen never took the gloves off. He did inquire politely after her husband and the trip to Mexico, but he never pushed her around. Not from kindness. Because it was obvious to everyone that she was dying.

Through it all a tension ran—what was unsaid. The jury felt it. Mr. Casebolt squinted. Professor Crenshaw strained forward. Die Yuppie Scum had a far-off searching look, like a surfer. Nurse Comstock twisted her hands. Heinie Hinton kept glancing at the door. Where had the defendant gone?

Moss pushed the envelope on redirect. Why did you return from Mexico? Because of what my daughter told me. What did she tell you? Objection, hearsay. Sustained. I know why my cancer wasn't diagnosed, Terry volunteered. Why? Objection, foundation, hearsay. Sustained. Langworthy graveled hard.

Afterward, in the hall outside the courtroom by the prints of Guanajuato, Basteen was sulking, waiting for the rest of his team. Moss had an idea. He steered Terry toward Basteen. Give him something to chew on over the weekend.

"Hey, Jerry. How's the Minister of Defense?"

"Go home, Peter."

"Your boy's hide just got nailed to the barn door." Moss grinned broadly. "Let's see what you do with him next week. Put up or shut up."

Basteen's disdain took in them both. "My client's got class."

"Class?" Terry bridled. As though she didn't?

Basteen gave her a styptic look. "What do you want, anyway? You don't want money. What is it?" he demanded. "Why do you insist on persecuting my client?"

"Because," Terry said. She closed and opened her complex black eyes. "Your client doesn't have a soul."

TWELVE

The Moss household had a busy Fourth of July weekend. Sally took Emmy on walks in Sanitas Valley in back of the house and the irrigation ditch. A wet late spring had left a huge unstable snow burden still sheathing the Front Range to the west. On the lower slopes of Sanitas Valley the flowers lay like ground fog. Swallowtails bobbed like jellyfish and towhees chittered and screaked in the scrub. Sally carried a yellow personal safety alarm and Emmy was never left alone.

They ate together near Terry's bedside and together worked on the case. They deliberated whether and how Emmy might testify without appearing to be self-serving. Moss explained the need for corroboration. Some think a child will make things up. It was no time to start getting cocky. Everything hung on whether the jury would believe Moschetti when all the evidence was in, and on how Basteen presented his case. He can kill us, Moss warned, if he's smart.

Home, office, client's quarters, hospice—it's convenient, Sally commented, it works. It's very nineties, Terry observed. Terry was worsening. For the most part she tried to rest. But this was her trial. She wasn't going to miss it.

At counsel table Tuesday morning they marked time before court was called to session. Terry, Emmy, and Moss. The courtroom was empty except for the reporter from the *Gazette-Telegraph*. Her Sunday article had migrated up to Section A. Real news. Now she would expect Moss to deliver. Moss snapped his rubberband and jiggled a boot in his banking suit pantsleg.

Basteen managed to make his entry grand, scanting the reporter, flipping the gate, presenting a Brioni-clad back as he pulled out and positioned his laptop and files. He gave the impression of someone alone in his office or study, a personal domain. He would not recognize the presence of others. If his client were there he would recognize him, for he was a physician. He carried a status that merited recognition. But his client wasn't there.

Visitors took their seats. The bailiff and clerk manned the perimeter. Basteen's studied self-absorption continued, his cocked jaw, the unruffled arrogance his careful airs expressed.

Moss recognized the syndrome and was heartened. He pushed back from the table and leaned past the podium toward his adversary. "Ever know a dog that got into porcupines?"

Basteen ignored him pointedly.

Moss clapped him on a richly textured shoulder. "I'll tell you the story sometime."

"All *rise*."

Langworthy presided from the bench as for a military review. He scanned the room gravely. "Ah, here we are." He beckoned, heads turned. Bondurant crossed the doorway and came forward. Moss breathed a touch more easily, but he wasn't there yet.

Bondurant acknowledged Terry with a nod but his eyes were on her daughter. Emmy watched back with a concentrated blue gaze, glowing in her golden aura. Classically beautiful to Moss's mind, and precociously self-possessed, like the young Garbo, Anna Christie, a colorized version. One could see the woman within.

The jury was called. Die Yuppie Scum in Suicidal Tendencies attire, Heine Hinton bolo-tied, Shortie collared and Mr. Casebolt in jeans, the women in summer suits, all sneaking their first looks at the plaintiff. The defendant took his place beside his counsel, the one in sincerity-blue serge, the other in boardroom black. The one looking like a guy's guy, the other like an *esquire*. In his two-thousand-dollar suit, spread collar trimmed with a post-modern tie, Mark Rothko purples bleeding to blacks, his Italian cordovans, and a burgundy silk pocket square to finish it off, Basteen aimed for magnificence.

He stood. He paused to shoot his cuffs. "The defense calls," he paused again. "Dr. Wallace Bondurant."

"Yes," Moss hissed between his teeth. Captain Haas to perfection. To help set the ambush he'd offer not a single objection.

Basteen began with an attempt to humanize the defendant— inquiries about his children, his nickname, Walloper, from lineman days at Brigham Young, his charitable work. Attention Homes for Runaway Girls. The Family Learning Center.

"Why did you decide on family practice instead of a more lucrative medical specialty?"

Here Moss expected the defendant to declaim a few great themes: prevention, wellness rather than illness, helping parents help their kids. Community-based medicine. Not high-tech but the healing touch. In a phrase, family values.

"Preventive care," Bondurant answered. He suppressed a cough. "General medicine you see lots of things."

What, Moss thought, have we here? Not the learned physician and not Marcus Welby either. He checked out the jurors' body language—sitting back with crossed arms. He liked the contrast between the parties. Terry, angled and intense, holding on and bearing in. Bondurant creamy and boneless, soft eyes wandering the room.

Why family practice? Basteen tossed the cue a couple more times like paper airplanes auguring in. Moss declined to object to the repetition, which Basteen took as license. A mood was building, frustration mounting to recklessness, to asking too much, which Moss meant to encourage.

When they reached the subject of Terry's care the witness's distraction planed off. Bondurant was far more at home with professional than personal history. Moss let the dreary lies rain down. Ms. Winter never mentioned a persistent lump, all he found were cysts, he never diagrammed anything, there was nothing to diagram, nothing to biopsy, though from abundant caution he arranged for Mayhew to see her. He assumed she complied with the referral.

"He gets to make things up?" Terry whispered. Moss put a knuckle to his lips.

With a dull witness, no objections, and a pressure to regain lost ground, Basteen's mannered and constipated style was getting unruly. He began leading, repeating, shying off into hearsay. Still Moss gave him rein.

Basteen reared to a theatrical stop. He paced the courtroom once and back like a runway model, then turned, full of portent, to his witness. Moss coiled more tightly.

"Last week the plaintiff's lawyer asked you about the state board of medical examiners," Basteen said. He must have concluded the judge was going to give Moss the sealed file. "You explained all that. Have you ever been disciplined by the board?"

"Objection." Moss could refrain no longer. "He's asking questions that refer to documents I haven't been allowed to see."

"Your Honor." Basteen essayed an innocent look. "Dr. Bondurant has no objection whatsoever to your providing Mr. Moss the board of medical examiners documents. We simply think they lack relevance to any issue in this case and should therefore not be admitted." He smiled copiously at Moss, affecting the suggestion of a courtly bow.

"Offer accepted," Moss replied. The judge handed him the sealed manila envelope. What glasnost this? he wondered. And hoped: may it lead to the opening of the one remaining door.

"Objection overruled. I'll consider admissibility later. Proceed, Mr. Basteen."

"Ever disciplined?" Basteen repeated.

"Never."

"Have you ever been audited, as you described last week?"

"Like most physicians at one time or another I have been through a quality-assurance audit."

"Did that audit result in any adverse findings against you?"

"It did not."

"Any discipline or restriction of your medical practice?"

"No."

"Any unfavorable conclusions at all?"

"None," Bondurant said firmly.

"Did the audit relate in any way to breast care?"

"Not at all. My quality of care has never been an issue to anyone."

"The plaintiff's daughter was also your patient. Please open Exhibit M, her chart."

He perused the contents with, it seemed to Moss, a kind of wistfulness.

"What medical treatment did you provide young Ms. Winter?"

Emmy's eyes comprehended her doctor. Moss glanced over and saw what Bondurant would see, her extraordinary blue eyes. It was as though she lived in her eyes, experienced the world wholly by watching it. She was here to see, and we to be seen by her. Moss considered how terrifying that might be to the man.

"Dr. Bondurant? What did you do for Mary Eliza Winter?"

"Oh," he said. He had a fogged look again. "Typical pediatric. Routine physicals. Immunizations, wellness checks. Minor infections. Regular stuff."

Keep coming, Moss thought. A little closer.

"What did your treatment of Mary Eliza Winter have to do with breast care for her mother?"

Haas had just sent his man onto the bridge. Moss had every touchstone he required. He flexed his toes in his boots. His trigger finger itched. There was no going back.

"Nothing whatsoever," the doctor said forcefully. "I was trying to help them out. Teach how to take care of yourself. I didn't even charge for the kid."

"No further questions, Dr. Bondurant."

"Mr. Moss?" The judge invited him to the podium.

Moss stood. "Your Honor, it's ten-fifteen. Is this a good place for a break?"

"Very well." Langworthy brought down the gavel smartly. "Recess for fifteen minutes. You're admonished again not to discuss the case among yourselves or with anyone else, and not to form any opinions until the conclusion of testimony."

"All stand."

The courthouse retinue departed with clerical propriety. Terry wanted a word with her lawyer. She expected her lawyer to not just sit there when the doctor makes things up. She expected maybe a little more proactive approach. Moss had no time to explain. He stepped quickly down the aisle, sealed file under his arm.

A perfect July day had formed beneath the foothills of the Rockies. A skateboarder glided statuesquely past, click-clocking on the sidewalk seams. A cyclist hummed by like a yellowjacket. A knock-kneed novice on in-line skates wobbled Moss's way. Across the highway a line was forming at Mary Ellen's Bail Bonds. Cottonwoods twinkled in the breeze and willows shimmered silvergreen. Remove the motionless real estate balloon hanging in the heavens like a planet, and with a little imagination the valley of the Platte lay verdant and painterly as the Hudson.

Genny Bondurant sat smoking Kents in her blue Subaru wagon. She required further assurance she would not be asked to speak. If she were she'd deny everything. She'd rather commit perjury, she told him. You'll be a witness in the religious sense only, Moss assured her. She looked at him queerly. She seemed older than her age, and untrusting not of the unknown but of the known too well. An observer, Moss said, a guardian of the word. I promise, no testimony. Just be there.

THIRTEEN

T*he sealed file* held little of obvious interest: A form greeting from the board. Photocopied sets of the Medical Practice Act, the implementing regulations of the Department of Health, an accompanying transmittal letter. A notice of re-instatement, a notice of case-closure, a 1994 good-standing certificate. A no-jurisdiction letter from the attorney general. Not only no sign of discipline, but no censure, no admonition, no record of complaints, no expression of interest in any medical subject.

But the two certified notices warranted a second look. The notice of case-closure read:

CERTIFIED MAIL-
RETURN RECEIPT REQUESTED
CONFIDENTIAL AND PERSONAL

July 14, 1992

Wallace Bondurant, M.D.
The Wellness Clinic
100 Neptune Way

Re: Closure of Case No. 4023BME-A

Dear Dr. Bondurant:

You are notified BME 4023-A is hereby closed under the authority of Revised Statute § 25-10-107(4)(d)(iii) as of the date of surrender. No findings have been made nor evidence formally taken. The Attorney General has confirmed with the Department of Health that jurisdiction to proceed is lacking. All matters under review shall therefore be considered moot, with no records retained at the licensee's request.

Very truly yours,
Lamont Treadwell, M.D.
Chair, Board of Medical Examiners
LT/mb
cc:

Thoughtful of them, Moss reflected after the recess, to have included the statutes.

It was time to come out from the treeline but Langworthy wanted to talk schedule. Basteen listed anticipated witnesses by name and, the jury being present, chief credential—professor of this, chair of that, medical director of the other.

"Mr. Moss. Any rebuttal likely?"

Moss glanced at Terry then Emmy. Turning meaningfully behind him, he caught the somber eye of Genny Bondurant in the third row.

"Yes, Your Honor," looking back at the bench, "rebuttal testimony may be necessary."

Basteen whispered a question to his client, who then also looked behind him and flushed. He turned forward and dropped his face. He pushed at his scalp with the fingers of both hands.

"Proceed," the judge said. "Your witness, Mr. Moss."

"A moment, Your Honor." Basteen and Bondurant exchanged a round of sharp whispers. "Your Honor. Bench conference requested."

Langworthy beckoned irritably with his fingers. Moss

held back, watching Basteen barely skirt the seal. The lawyers and judge hunched gravely together like referees con-
ferring about a personal foul.

"The defendant's daughter is in the courtroom," Basteen
declared under his breath.

"So what?" the judge said.

"This is an outrage. Moss is hailing the defendant's family into court. My client does not want his family involved.
The publicity—" he glared at Moss. "The publicity is
enough as it is without bringing his children into the sordid
little spectacle Moss is trying to create."

"Do you have her under subpoena, Moss?"

"No, Your Honor. She's a spectator. This is an open
proceeding. It's a free country."

"I demand sequestration and removal of Ms. Bondurant."
Basteen was letting his volume swell.

"*You* want sequestration *now*? Very well. Sequestration
is so ordered. Is Ms. Bondurant an endorsed witness?"

"No, Your Honor." Moss said. "By neither side."

"How about rebuttal?" Basteen snapped.

"I can't predict rebuttal until I know what I have to rebut."

"Jerome," the judge said soothingly. "I'm not going to
sequester every potential rebuttal witness. She stays. Any
endorsed witnesses have to leave."

Basteen's nostrils flared. "I want my objection on the
record." He set his teeth.

"So noted," the judge said. "Hey, it's her father. She
probably just cares. Now if you've got any witnesses in
here, run them out." Langworthy's smile broadened. He
loved, Moss observed, to see a lawyer shoot his own foot.

Basteen, to the puzzlement of the jury, began working
through the gallery, tapping three doctors on the shoulder
to leave, then Yellowhorse, who got up indignantly and
tapped Basteen back.

"Dr. Bondurant," Moss began mildly. "You've testified
a couple of times now. You told us quite a lot about your
training and your treatment of Terry and Emmy Winter and

the practice of medicine. Like everybody, I've been listening, and there are some things I'm troubled by. You told us about standards last week, for breast cancer diagnosis. I'd like to talk now about a different standard of care."

"O.K." Bondurant said. There was a distance in his eyes.

" 'I swear by Apollo Physician' . . . what is that, Dr. Bondurant?"

"Hippocratic oath."

"The oath all medical doctors are bound to uphold?"

"Right."

"What is it that doctors swear to do?"

He massaged the back of his neck. "Something like use treatment to help the sick according to my ability and judgment. *Judgment*," he repeated. It was becoming an article of affronted belief.

" 'But *never* with a view to injury and wrongdoing?' "

"Something like that."

" 'I will abstain from all intentional harm.' "

"Yeah."

" 'Especially from abusing the bodies of men and women.' "

"That's in there."

" 'If I carry out this oath may I gain forever reputation among all men.' "

Bondurant nodded.

"Verbalize," the judge said.

"Yes."

" 'If I transgress.' " Moss stopped. He moved to the front of the oak podium and crossed his arms. " 'May the opposite befall me.' "

"Yes," Bondurant said. "Right."

Moss took a while to discipline his feelings. He had to parcel this out. "Dr. Bondurant. Your lawyer asked about your children. They haven't lived with you since your daughters were young. Why is that?"

"Objection."

"Sustained," the judge said, annoyed.

Moss tarried over his notes. He could feel the witness's

discomfort rising, and his own, everyone's. "What is the family plan, Dr. Bondurant?"

"At my office?"

"Yes, the Wellness Clinic."

"Well. The way we lighten the load for folks who need it."

"The load?"

"I treat self-pays, Medicaids, you name it, Mr. Moss. I work with folks, whatever their station in life."

"What is the family plan?"

"Give you an example. Somebody doesn't have dependent coverage, say, or any. Maybe physicals, check-ups, what all, get excluded."

He'd seized on the topic, Moss saw. Talking crowded aside anxiety, the feeling of being watched.

"So what I do is charge one family member office visit and another's a no-charge if they bring her along."

"Two for one?"

"Two for one."

"Terry and Emmy Winter, were they on the family plan?"

"To my recollection."

"They were on the family plan because they were self-pay? Meaning no insurance?"

"Evidently."

"The family plan." Moss tapped a pencil eraser against a front tooth. "You remember that? They were on the family plan?"

"Yes, and it says so here." He thumped Terry's chart.

"They came in together, then? Two for one?"

"Right."

"For example, Terry needs a breast check, you see Emmy too, no charge."

"Mary Eliza? Yeah, that's right."

"Terry was conscientious about bringing her daughter in?"

"I do it gratis. Meaning on me, if you understand what I'm saying."

"Terry always brought Emmy with her?"

He hooked on his gold-rimmed glasses and ran a finger down a ledger sheet. Basteen had begun rustling with impatience. "Either that," Bondurant said, "or, looking at this here, say Mary Eliza came in for an infection, I'd see the mom too. One o.v. charge, two patients, every time. That's your family plan."

"From 1989 through 1992, how often did you see Mary Eliza Winter?"

"Total looks like fourteen."

Basteen hesitated, hands on the table edge, then pitched from his seat with the fall-back, pounce-forward momentum of a dog mounting a pick-up bed. "What is the relevance of treatment provided the daughter?" he demanded.

"The relevance, Mr. Moss?"

"Motive, which has been placed in issue by the defendant," Moss said evenly. "And impeachment. And punitive damages."

The judge's eyes narrowed.

"I will explain if the court would like."

"Not needed." Langworthy's face loosened. He looked up at the acoustic tiles, assessing relevancy in the abstract like a spinning colored ball only he could see. This fateful application of law to fact, Moss knew, was the crux of his case. Its salience seemed lost on all but Moss and the decision maker.

At length the judge slowly nodded. "I'll allow it," he said with undisguised reluctance. This was not a judge disposed to self-doubts or second thoughts. But Moss knew what he'd allow would look less like free rein than enough rope to hang with. "Objection overruled."

Basteen remained standing perplexedly. "Then beyond the scope."

"Overruled. You brought up the girl's care on your direct."

Basteen took his seat with a parochial grunt.

"Dr. Bondurant. You treated Emmy Winter on fourteen separate occasions?"

"Looks like."

"When Terry and her daughter came to your office, what would happen?"

He made a low sound as if clearing his throat. "What do you mean?"

"Who would you see, when? Where?"

"After sign-in I'll see Mom. Then I'll see Mary Eliza. What are you asking me?"

"Mom in examining room A?"

"Yeah."

"Then Mom dressed and waited up front while you saw Mary Eliza?"

"Uh-huh."

"Verbalize," the judge admonished.

"Yeah. That's right."

Moss turned back briefly to check on Genny Bondurant. The gallery was full, the reporter attentive, Patti working her gum, Heinz withdrawn in a marmoreal calm. Genny Bondurant was also sitting motionless, expressionless, as were Terry and Emmy, watching.

"Dr. Bondurant, what percent of your practice is pediatric?"

"Fifty-fifty," he said.

"Pediatric—means what?" Moss shot a look at Nurse Comstock, buried in her steno pad.

"Kids. Boys and girls."

"Boys and girls?"

"Yeah."

"Mostly girls?"

"Your *Honor*," Basteen complained. Moss saw that Basteen sensed something dangerously off though he didn't yet know what.

"Overruled," Langworthy said. "You dwelled on his practice in your direct examination. Dr. Bondurant, answer the question."

"Mostly girls." He was looking at his hands. His hands wouldn't keep still.

"Your license to practice medicine." Moss picked up the manila envelope, now unsealed. He pulled out a copy of the second certified notice, the notice of reinstatement. "It was reinstated July 15, 1992, it says in this letter. Is that right? Reinstated?"

"If that's what it says. What's this have to do with?"

"Why did your medical license need to be reinstated?"

"Objection. Irrelevant. Privileged. Prejudicial under 403."

"Overruled," the judge said again, wagging his head. "You opened the door."

"So I could practice medicine, I guess." Bondurant tried levity, a faltering little chuckle.

"You had been stopped from practicing because you voluntarily surrendered your license, correct?"

He nodded. Basteen twitched.

"Verbalize," the judge said.

"Yes."

"So you surrendered your license to practice medicine." Moss hitched an elbow on the podium. He plucked his rubberband. "Was it July 14, 1992, when you quit medicine?"

"If that's what it says."

"You surrendered your license and the board reinstated you, it looks like the very next day?"

"Um-hum. Yes."

In the jury box Shorty did a full squint-and-blink, come-again? double-take.

"The very next day, back in practice again?"

"Well, yes. Well, sure."

"When you surrendered your license the investigation and audit of your practice ended, correct?"

"I suppose so." He made a noise in his throat.

Basteen flipped open and booted the laptop.

"This statute." Moss pulled a photocopied sheaf from the manila envelope. "Section 25-10-107(4)(d)(iii), provides that when a physician gives up his license all ongoing investigations or actions terminate as moot, correct?"

"I guess."

"Section (e) provides that no documents shall be retained

that would unduly damage the reputation of any person referred to in the record."

"I think so."

"Section (f) provides that unless a case is formally adjudicated, on surrender of license no records related to a case investigation shall be retained if the former licensee so elects."

"Objection," Basteen sputtered. "Statute speaks for itself."

"And that's exactly what it says," the judge ruled.

"You asked the board to destroy the records of its investigation of you."

"That's my right."

"Your medical society legislative committee lobbied for this statute, didn't it, Dr. Bondurant?"

"We did. Yes."

"Thanks to this statute, you started over the very next day with a clean slate, didn't you?"

"It's the law," he protested.

"The law," Moss said pensively. "Known to your committee as the Clean Slate Act?"

"I think that's right."

"The board's audit had been of your female pediatric patients, hadn't it?"

Nurse Comstock started from her notepad.

Bondurant looked up for help then quickly down, his daughter in the line of sight behind his lawyer. "Yes," he said.

"The board asked for charts."

"Yes."

"But some you pulled and told your employee Patti not to send."

"I don't know."

"Doctor." The judge loomed. "Answer, if you know."

"There were some," he said.

"Including Emmy Winter's?"

"Yes."

The judge darkened, profoundly displeased. Bondurant

had testified and Basteen had promised this had not happened. He fingered the gavel like a weapon.

"The board had received complaints against you," Moss asked gingerly, "of sexual improprieties?"

Basteen attempted to object. The judge banged him down before the third syllable.

"Had the board received complaints of sexual improprieties?"

Bondurant raised then dropped his shoulders in a gesture Moss couldn't decipher.

"Doctor," the judge rebuked him. *"Answer that question."*

"This has been years," he said slowly.

"Had such complaints been made?"

"Anybody can say anything."

"Take a look at the notice of case-closure." Moss approached him. "At the bottom it says 'cc:' See that? Then there's nothing. No names."

"I see."

"The original had names of women after the 'cc,' the 'copy to.' "

"Yes."

"Those were the names of those who'd complained about the sexual improprieties?"

"Objection," Basteen shouted and stood, fingers splayed on the table. "These questions invade physician-patient privileges. Mr. Moss has no right to their identities." His control was unspooling fast.

"I agree," Moss said. "That was to be my next question of the doctor, why the names were redacted. Was it because those who complained to the board had been your patients or their parents?"

"That's why they're confidential."

"Yes," Moss said. He let some time pass. "Now, Dr. Bondurant. The board was investigating the complaints but the investigation was stopped in its tracks July 14, 1992, when you surrendered your license. Twenty-four hours later you got it back. Clean bill of health. Correct?"

"I was entitled."

"Entitled," Moss repeated. He nodded. "Dr. Bondurant. *Did you continue seeing Emmy Winter after the reinstatement of your license July 15, 1992?*"

He made some meaningless sounds.

"Did you keep seeing Emmy?"

"Well, I saw her, sure, that year, some more."

"In examining room B?"

"It would have to be."

"Move the admission into evidence of Plaintiff's R, Dr. Bondurant's board of medical examiners file."

"Objection, Mr. Basteen?"

"I . . ." Basteen hammered autistically at his laptop. He exhaled and shook his head.

"Verbalize, please. For the record."

"I guess not."

"So noted. Plaintiff's R shall be received."

FOURTEEN

E*xamining room B,* Dr. Bondurant. Describe it."

"Pediatric."

"Dr. Bondurant?"

"Decorated for children with the wallpaper. Animals, lollipops, stuff like that." He trailed off obscurely.

"When you examined Emmy, it was always in examining room B?"

"Yeah. Probably."

"She was eight years old when you first saw her?"

He checked the chart. "Correct."

"Eleven when you last saw her?"

"Correct."

"You were alone with her each time?"

"What do you mean?"

"No nurse, no physician's assistant, no office girl, no mom, nobody but you and Emmy?" Ms. Comstock had stopped taking notes.

"I don't know." He was rubbing his brow. "That would be usual."

"There's a mirror in room B?"

"Sure. Right."

"With a clown's peaked polka dot hat and ruffles and instead of a face, it's a mirror?"

"Yes."

"That's a one-way window, isn't it, Dr. Bondurant?"

The defendant flashed a look at the gallery. In his eyes, like a phosphorus flare, Moss saw again the incandescent fear he kept shuttered away.

"Dr. Bondurant?"

Basteen said nothing. He closed his laptop and pushed it aside.

"So the girls can look in and tell me when they're ready to be seen."

"To be seen." Moss chewed a lip as if hesitant to go forward.

"Dr. Bondurant. You had Mary Eliza Winter undress alone in examining room B each time she came to your office."

"Routine. Girl tells her."

"Routine?"

"Wellness check."

"You would watch her do that."

"Your Honor. *Objection*," Basteen complained fatalistically.

"Overruled."

Bondurant reddened. "Judge," he accosted Langworthy. "I mean no disrespect," he said through clenched teeth, "but I don't have to sit here and listen to this . . ."

Langworthy silenced him with a raised hand. "I'll tell you, sir, what respect for this court means to me. It means telling the truth. Now tell it."

"You watched her through the clown mirror?" Moss asked.

He glanced again at Genny Bondurant then pressed his fingers in the folds of his scalp. "I can't believe this," he mumbled.

"You watched her, didn't you, then you went inside."

"I went inside."

"Dr. Bondurant, you were treating Emmy Winter for urinary tract infection but she never had an infection, did she?"

"Objection."

"Overruled."

"I don't know."

"Look at the chart."

"It says u.t.i. That means infection."

"But the lab results were all negative. Look at them." The defendant paged deliberately through Exhibit M. It gave him something to do.

"They were negative, it looks like." He had not looked up.

"But you diagnosed infection anyway?"

"I tend to be cautious when it comes to kids."

Moss let the silence settle.

"You would find an infection despite no laboratory confirmation, prescribe an antibiotic, and tell Terry she had to bring Emmy back in four to six weeks."

"I don't know," he said sullenly.

"Do you see that pattern in the chart?"

"Uh-huh."

"You do?"

"It happened."

"You administered thiopental to Emmy?"

"Did I?" His face ticked, startle-eyed. Fight or flight.

"Take a look, Dr. Bondurant."

"Yes."

"Pentothal, it's also called?"

"Yes."

"Starting February 4, 1991."

He studied the chart. "Yes."

"And on each visit after that, except the last three, you gave Emmy Pentothal."

He paged back and forth. "Yes," he said staring at his notes.

"What is Pentothal, Dr. Bondurant?"

"Barbiturate," he murmured.

"Anesthetic?"

"Yes."

"Hypnotic?"

"Um-hum. Yes."

"Knocks a kid out in a matter of seconds."

"Some it will."

"Lasts fifteen, twenty minutes?"

Bondurant looked desperately up at his daughter, his lawyer. Basteen seemed as stunned as everybody else.

"Yes."

"And causes amnesia? Kid can't remember?"

"It can do that."

"But not always." Moss froze to the podium. "Dr. Bondurant, near the end you had a talk with Emmy Winter about the things that happened in room B, didn't you?"

"I don't know what you mean." Bondurant studied his hands.

His hands.

"She was awake for the last visits, wasn't she?"

"Awake?"

"Look at her, Doctor." Moss went to Emmy's side. *"What did you make this young girl promise you?"*

"I don't know what you mean."

"What did you threaten her with?"

"I don't know."

"Objection," Basteen said confusedly. "He said he doesn't know."

The judge gaveled. "Doctor, if you know what the answer to the question is you have to give it. You took an oath. *Answer the question.*"

Bondurant looked hard at Basteen. The lawyer moved his head slightly to the side.

"What, Doctor?"

"I don't know," he whispered again.

The judge glared a dreadful minute. "Mr. Moss, I have to sustain the objection. Move on."

"I understand," Moss said. He exhaled, a breather before loading another clip. He felt a peristaltic pressure building. He tightened his stomach, constricted his throat. He'd

pieced together what happened fact by fact. He'd heard it
from Bondurant's daughter, from his client, from his client's daughter, but he realized he wouldn't finally believe
it until he saw it whole, saw it in Bondurant's eyes.
Stripped away his physician's conceits and command
status, ritual mysteries and royal contempts and scientific
dispassion, and stared into his soul.

"By the last of her visits, Mary Eliza Winter had not
reached puberty, had she?"

"No." Bondurant fled back to the chart. "No."

"Read for us the letters that begin each entry for Emmy's
visits."

He garbled the answer as the jurors strained.

"w√:pve." Moss wrote it at the easel, bold and black on
a clean white sheet.

"Yes."

"The first part means wellness check?"

"Yes."

" 'pve'? What's that? Is that pelvic exam? Doctor?"

He nodded.

"Verbalize."

"Yes."

"Dr. Bondurant. Why were you conducting pelvic examinations of a prepubertal child over and over and over
for three years? *Tell us why. Tell us what you did during
those minutes you had Emmy Winter in steel stirrups. Tell
us. Tell the truth."*

The judge was hammering like a framer. Moss raked the
air in front of him. Basteen bolted forward, calling "Bench
conference." The oversized sole of an Italian cordovan fell
squarely on the inscribed eye of God in the carpet. Basteen
reached the bench, fingers clinging like someone who
couldn't swim to the side of the pool. Moss blew repeatedly
on his fist. He stayed at counsel table waiting for the
judge's invitation. Terry squeezed his and her daughter's
hands.

Langworthy brooded over the defense counsel like a falcon. "Mr. Basteen," he said slowly. "You are an emotional infant."

Terry turned to Moss. "Judge knows his stuff."

Die Yuppie Scum scribbled his first notes.

"Mr. Moss, you may come forward." He did. They huddled. "Another outburst, Moss, and you're in contempt."

Contempt, Moss thought, still breathing heavy. I'm there already.

"I demand a mistrial," Basteen huffed. "This proceeding is hopelessly tainted."

"Tainted?" the judge said. "By what?"

"Any alleged sexual encounters of my client are wholly irrelevant to the plaintiff's claims."

Moss reminded the judge of the subject matter of Terry's second deposition. "Sauce for the goose."

Langworthy stage-whispered to his court reporter, "Mr. Basteen's motion, or demand, for mistrial is denied," and to Basteen, "Jerry, you brought it on yourself."

"I need a break," Basteen said pathetically. "This was . . . unanticipated." He bared teeth at Moss: You tricked me. You fucking sandbagged me. "I need to confer with my client."

"You boys better pull yourselves together by the time we're back in session," the judge said evenly. "I will have order in my court."

The defendant climbed down to join his lawyer. Jurors watched, quiet as fish. Recess was taken. Genny Bondurant said she was doing O.K. She was good for the rest of the morning. Terry was hurting but clear of mind. She saw what lawyers were for, when you can't stop the bastards all by yourself. All eyes were on Emmy. Moss led her and Terry past the meddlesome reporter. By the time they returned to session, Moss standing stiffly at the podium, he'd gone cold and hard, guileless and utterly factual.

Though some facts would be foregone. Some facts were too unspeakable to be spoken.

"Were you seduced by your patients, Doctor?"

The moment lengthened awkwardly. Bondurant shifted and winced terribly under the scrutiny of the women. He raised his head slowly to take Moss in dead-on. The fear in his eyes had burned away. They showed no metal or light, but pooled deep within, in place of a soul, a liquid core of horror.

Moss saw, and believed.

"Doctor?"

At length Bondurant shook his head bitterly, as if grieving.

"Verbalize."

He muttered no.

"Did you sexually molest Mary Eliza Winter for more than two years?"

"Not . . ."

"Not what? Not every time?"

"On the advice of counsel I decline to answer on the grounds that it may tend to incriminate me." His voice was low and brutal.

"Did you sexually molest another young patient, Jessica Fisher, when you were treating her for shoulder pain?"

"No answer on the grounds it may incriminate me."

"When Jessie Fisher was twelve years old, and prepubertal, did you molest her during pelvic exams?"

"No answer."

"Same grounds?"

"Yes."

"How many others, Doctor?"

"Other what?"

"How many other patients? Five? Ten? More?"

"I don't know."

"Did you keep having Terry Winter come back so you could keep seeing Emmy?"

"Can't answer."

"Same grounds?"

"Yes."

"Is that why you wouldn't refer her suspicious lump for biopsy until October 1992?"

"I don't know."

"You let her cancer grow until you knew it would kill her so you could keep abusing her little girl."

"I didn't even think about that."

"About cancer?"

"Yes."

"You just wanted to see Emmy?"

"I can't answer."

"Because the answer may incriminate you?"

He turned toward his daughter. He was asking forgiveness. "Yes," he said. She looked away.

FIFTEEN

Crutchfield *edged around* the reporter calling in her story on a cell phone. DOCTOR TAKES THE FIFTH. He caught Moss by the jacket. The reporter saw Moss and made a circle with finger and thumb: Way to deliver.

"Hey, Crutch," Moss said. "You here to help?"

"Pro bono?" He made a hilarious face.

"Quid pro quo. You can have my office."

"Already got it but you don't need any help." He clapped Moss on the shoulder. "You know I wouldn't have believed this if I hadn't seen it."

"Tell Junker. Tell the Coyote. Circulate a memo. Spare no detail."

"I still don't believe it."

"Well," Moss sighed comfortably. "I do. We're all believers here. Even Basteen. Even Langworthy."

"Langworthy? He'll pat you on the back while he's peeing down your leg."

"Hey now. Keep the faith."

"You keep your guard up."

Moss threw him a flurry of shadow jabs.

"A dead bee can still sting."

• • •

In the epistemology of trials some facts stick, some slip weightless to the floor. Those that stick can build into a critical mass of essential knowledge—the magnetic cohesion of facts called truth, the highest form of which is truth of the heart. The truth that is beauty, as the poet said.

Bondurant wasn't seen in court again. Crutchfield observed his departure in a silver LeBaron. Making tracks, according to Crutchfield. Inside, Bondurant's support system was breaking up. The medical society staff abandoned him, but the office girls stayed true blue. Heinz also kept the vigil, moving to the front row. Heinz was well cut out for vigils, for holding the line when an insured went up in flames. For discouraging everyone within the periphery of his refracted gaze.

Genny Bondurant left just before her father. Moss didn't know how to find and thank her. She'd done a harder thing than testifying, repudiating a parent disgraced before her eyes. Later in the week she called the house and talked to Terry. About Emmy, about what the jury might be thinking, how difficult things remained with one sister terrified, the other angry, and her mother's shame. How she'd blamed herself for so long. What matters, Terry said, is you came forward, you made sure the truth was told. You did it, and everything has changed.

Basteen's witnesses came and went without leaving wakes. A parade of doubtless highly qualified and caring family physicians pronounced Bondurant's care of Terry excellent. To each Moss deployed questions about standards of care. At what age, he would conclude, is it appropriate to begin regular pelvic examinations? Why? Drs. Franzblau and Irizarry Singh, the pricey debunkers of early detection, decried the futility of treatment—Terry's genes were to blame, there was nothing Dr. Bondurant could have done—drawing groans from the jury box. Dr. Mayhew drew overt hostility when he claimed to remember the phantom phone referral. Mr. Willits grunted. Shorty rolled his eyes. Ms. Gideon openly faced away.

Basteen declined to call Patti, the front-desk girl, and

compound his problems with examining room B. Without Patti, Professor Crawford's elaborate attack on Moss for manufacturing evidence fell into confusion. Professor Crawford, it developed on cross, had gotten into a little trouble himself with the Ninth Circuit, altering evidence for John Z. DeLorean.

For the next few days Terry stayed home with Sally. Emmy went with Moss to the trial. He wanted her as comfortable with the room and its inhabitants as she could become.

In the evenings if Terry had the strength she walked with Emmy along the ditch behind the house into the meadow of Sanitas Valley. She walked slowly, holding her daughter's hand, looking at the ground. Reaching shade and resting and then looking up through the leafwork at the late light breaking through.

Terry's skin had acquired a gold burnish. Etch-A-Sketch person, she would say at the mirror, but her thinness seemed less emaciated than ethereal, her measured slowness less a sign of weakness than serenity. Her eyes were preternaturally bright, her gaze tender and intense: How beautiful are the shapes and colors of living things, of loved ones. Thus suspended—past future, inside without—all experience became metaphoric. The smallest incidents had heightened consequence. Nuthatch upsidedown on the tree-trunk shows how easy it is. West wind spinning from the ridgeline, be thou me.

Wednesday after court Moss pulled his car into the shade spot under the silver maple in front of the house. He and Emmy went around back. "Lightning!" Emmy squealed.

Moss made the connection. Inside, Terry lay exhausted on the foldout bed. He touched her arm. "Warren's back?"

"Yeah." Terry looked dreamy and languid.

"I want him kept out of the courtroom," Moss said. "He's the one loose cannon who can sink the ship."

"He gave his word," Terry purled, lips slabby and sticking.

•　　•　　•

Basteen had no talent for adapting to adversity. He stuck with his game plan—to end his case by smearing the plaintiff. But nobody was buying the caseworker he called to impugn Terry as a mother. As a mother Terry kicked butt. Basteen called Yellowhorse to show car theft and drug use. He should have seen it coming. He asked the judge to declare the witness hostile. "You don't get it, man," Yellowhorse continued, braids flying. The judge let him go. "She believes life is sacred. She is a warrior for life. She'll fight you always forever, man. For her kid, other kids, animals, for nature. For life. She'll die but you'll never defeat her."

Thus concluded the defense of Wallace Bondurant. Recess, and Basteen drifted Moss's way, not openly agitated. "Nice job," he said, though he did not extend his hand.

"You didn't know about Bondurant, did you? But Heinz did."

Basteen sat against the edge of the plaintiff's table. "Let me ask you a question, Peter. Why are you doing this?" He folded his arms.

"This? Too deep for me, Jerome."

"Doing this to my client."

Moss thought a while. "No killing, no feast."

"Tell me the truth."

"I hate to lose, Jerome."

"This isn't about winning. It's about ruining someone. It's a vendetta."

"Aren't you forgetting something? Like what he did?"

"He's helped a lot of people. He's a good doctor. He could help a lot more."

"So wipe the slate clean?" For some reason Moss thought of Calley. Calley and Meadlo cutting down that ditch full of women and kids. They were good soldiers, Nixon said. And war's hell.

Moss stood and began loading his trial bag.

"You see everything in black and white, Peter, but there's always shades of gray. Even here."

"I don't think so." Moss looked up. "I think the world's

way more black and white than lawyers like to admit. Gray's easy for guys like us. Gray gets you off the hook. You don't have to deal with right and wrong."

"You proved what you set out to prove. I acknowledge that."

"So let's put this behind us and get on with our lives? Sorry, my client can't manage that one."

"Wally wants to make up for the harm he caused."

Moss paused. "How's he going to do that?"

"The company will do anything she asks."

"What will Bondurant do?"

"For God's sake, Peter, leave him his life."

"His life," Moss said, "is *his* problem." He snapped the trial bag's latches.

"I can't believe you really think that," Basteen persisted, then added, astonishingly, "You're a caring person."

"You know, Jerome." Moss got intent. "I *do* mean that and you're right, this isn't just about winning. It matters what he did. *What he did* to those children and to Terry. He won't get a clean slate this time. This time we're keeping score, because what you do counts."

Basteen gave Moss an indifferent look. "You see it your client's way. I see it mine."

"Your client's way. Know what his problem is? He's drowning in gray. Let's see what he does about it."

Basteen whistled. "Man, have you bought in."

"Man, have you sold out."

Basteen shook his head wryly. "It's a job, Peter. Win, lose, paycheck's the same. I'm not here to save the world."

Not to save it, no. But why not a better world?

"Tell you what, though." Basteen smiled broadly. "I hate to lose too."

The door in the cherry veneer parted and Judge Langworthy appeared, flanked by his bailiff and clerk. He beelined out the low gate and aisle to the double courtroom doors, meeting no one's eye. A little later Heinz slipped also from the paneling into the empty court. He moved like a diver, deliberate, cryptic, with awkward grace and masked eyes. Thus, Moss thought, Heinz comes and fades from view, proof the world one wishes to improve is dense and dangerous. Illusory. Fluid.

SIXTEEN

The *courtroom quickly* filled before the Friday morning session despite the thinning of Bondurant's ranks. The Slow White Broncos arrived in force: Lata, the receptionist; Tina, Crutchfield's gatekeeper; Crutchfield, looking anxiously upbeat. An investigator from the D.A.'s office taking notes. Sally, sketching. The reporter from the *Gazette-Telegraph*. Distending conspicuously from a front-row bench, Junker himself. Moss took fleeting umbrage: It's too late, Captain, you burned your bridge.

Terry held her daughter's hand. "You're up, kid. Be who you are." Her eyes filmed and gleamed like oil. The forked vein on her temple pulsed. This was what she'd come back for from Mexico, from the end of the trail, when Emmy went before the world and became herself.

Emmy was called as the plaintiff's rebuttal witness. She was sworn and told her story. It was so long ago, and she'd grown up a lot, but she remembered. The zoo animals on the walls. The Peter Rabbit. The candy canes. The clown's face you make with the reflection of your own. The giant needle he warned you with if you didn't behave. The metal rods that swung up and locked. The Velcro straps on her ankles and wrists and how she shook. How cold it was.

How he got red. How he looked at her like she wasn't real. A real person. How scary when the light went out and how it hurt. How he breathed like he just stopped running. The rip the Velcro did when he let her loose, and his footsteps.

While Emmy was testifying, indelible eyes locked on her mother's, for an instant another image intruded—the photograph of Jessie Fisher, shy eyes and winning smile with her 9.8's and her roses, who didn't get the chance to take the stand.

"How did it make you feel," Moss asked, "what the doctor did?"

"Objection. Irrelevant."

The judge would hear her answer.

"Like I wished I was never born."

"Did the doctor talk with you about it?"

"The last times he did."

"What did he say, Emmy?"

"What he would say was little girls are good at keeping secrets. Bad things happen when they don't. Nobody would believe me anyhow."

"What did you say?"

"I said my mother would."

Terry nodded explicitly as Emmy spoke, willing courage and declaring belief.

Moss moved to the jury rail. "What did the doctor say then?"

"Then he said no one will believe her. And I said they will too. I said my mother is a force."

"Did you tell your mother what the doctor had done?"

She shook her head. No, she said.

"Why not?"

Because, Emmy continued, he promised he'd hurt her mother if she told. He pinched her arm to show how he could hurt. He got red like he did and mean. He said he was her doctor and he had power. If Emmy told anybody, he'd make her mother really sick. He really meant it. If Emmy told, he'd make her mother die. But so long as Emmy kept his secret, she'd be O.K.

"Were you afraid, Emmy?"

"I was scared for Mom. We stopped going back to him when she got her biopsy so I wasn't scared for me anymore."

Emmy spread her fingers in front of her and looked at them.

"I wanted her to get well so I didn't talk about it. I really wanted Mom to get well but she isn't. So I told her then."

When they went to the beach in Mexico and into the desert to where the trees were, Terry said nobody could help her. She was actually dying, she said, soon, maybe even that summer. Then Emmy knew for sure.

"He lied." She looked at the empty chair next to Basteen as if picturing him there, a dehydrated husk.

"He's just a liar. It was just his stupid secret. He doesn't have any power. He can't make my mother well. So I told her all about it."

Emmy had learned people were different from what she feared. "He's the one afraid. He's afraid of my mother. He's even afraid of me. It never was my fault my mother got so sick." Her eyes swam recalling she thought so once. Terry caught the table edge. "It's not Mom's fault. It's his."

Terry bent, strength imparted, dazed with pride.

After Emmy's testimony Moss moved to amend the complaint to conform with the evidence by joining Emmy as a coplaintiff on claims of battery, false imprisonment, and outrageous conduct. The judge agreed her claims had been tried with the implied consent of the defense and accepted the amendments. Instructions were argued in chambers, Moss barely there, in a trance state, the intrusive images, Jessie Fisher, the boy with the hoe, the bicycle in the bamboo, passing and vanishing from inner view.

Summations were made. Moss's principal argument, followed by Basteen's tired closing—you don't practice medicine out of books; an error in judgment is not the same as malpractice. . . . Followed by Moss's rebuttal.

In cynical times, Moss said, right and wrong can sometimes be hard to sort out. Goodness and truth can seem beyond our reach. But jurors' duties require them to put cynicism aside and exercise the public virtues: To find truth, oppose wrong, protect innocence, promote good, do right. The Latin root of negligence means not connecting. Not connecting actions to consequences, oneself to others. Punitive damages are for something more. For knowing the consequences, but not caring. Acting for oneself alone, as though other lives don't matter. Acting with harmful intent. All lives are sacred. What you do matters. Let right be done.

The judge read his instructions to the jury. Moss couldn't attend. He was nine thousand miles, a quarter-century away, imagining miracles—a night sky domed with flares while mothers and children safely slept.

The jury retired to deliberate. They returned in two hours. "Madam foreman," the judge addressed Nurse Comstock. "Have you reached a verdict?" With one exception they had. She read unanimous awards against the defendant and for Terry Winter and Mary Eliza Winter of $3 million each. Moss made a sound, an ah, an expulsion of breath. No full-throated cry of victory—just ah. Terry sat erect and quiet, enameled eyes shining, Emmy burrowed in her arm.

As to the award of punitive damages, five jurors assessed $10 million but there was a dissent. Basteen wanted the jury polled. To each the judge read the numbers back. "Is this your verdict?" he asked. Heinie Hinton took exception. He had read the jury nullification pamphlet. He understood it to say a judge's instruction could be ignored if a higher law so required. On a separate verdict form he awarded the majority's $10 million in punitive damages against the board of medical examiners. Against Bondurant he awarded Twenty Years in Big Max and Everything He Owns.

Part Four

THE JUDGMENT

ONE

A*fter a trial* Moss usually took a couple days to celebrate or mourn before punching back in at the firm to work through the queue of recorded messages and the harvest of mail, shucking junk from genuine. Slighted clients and past-due bills to the action stack, solicitations to the Ecocycle box—experts-for-hire, jury research services, alternative dispute resolvers, continuing education gurus. How to Give Your Spinal Cord Case a Solid Backbone. How to Value Children in Litigation. Kowloon custom tailor flyers and anatomical model catalogs. The Articulated Hand. The Articulated Foot. The Median-Section Female Pelvis ("Articulated?" Crutchfield might wonder over Moss's shoulder, or, "How do you rate the Victoria's Secret mailing list?").

This time was different. The difference lay in more than the fact that now he had no firm, no workaday routine at which to resume a resting pulse. This case, this client, Moss realized, had done a number on him. Something invasively personal, transforming. The sense of transformation was encompassing and beyond his control, like climate. Like a biologic phenomenon, lasting as pack ice, sudden as an algae bloom.

Then the post-trial ruling pulled to the curb like a truck bomb. The ruling was routed to the Junker and Wiley relay box at the courthouse. It made its way to Crutchfield, who reached Moss at home. Who made a quick pass down the old halls collecting congratulations before slipping into the old office to read the one-page order that collapsed in a flash the multistoried edifice of Bondurant's liability.

J.N.O.V.

Judgment Non Obstante Veredicto. Judgment notwithstanding the verdict. Moss might have known Langworthy would find a way to even the score.

There was in the ruling the touch of a malevolent Solomon, cleaving an infant and serving up portions to the gander as well as the goose. One could picture the judge relishing the lose/lose for the lawyers. The humiliating verdict against Basteen, payback for the Kaiser account the big guy stole ten years earlier. The kick in the nuts to the plaintiff's side when he takes Moss's win away. One could picture yet not quite believe it. Langworthy wouldn't zap an honest verdict, Moss suspected, without awfully powerful incentives.

Like many an off-the-wall ruling, the J.N.O.V. consistently followed an internal logic from an eccentric premise to an absurd conclusion, thus assuming the appearance of cogency. The plaintiffs, wrote the judge,

> elected to establish the standard of care solely through the defendant's testimony. Such proof, while unexampled in the Court's experience, could theoretically satisfy their burden of establishing *prima facie* professional negligence. It remains, however, a most feeble mooring for the oceangoing vessel of a medical malpractice case-in-chief.
>
> During the defense case grave questions arose about Dr. Bondurant's credibility and competence. Indeed, the Court was sufficiently persuaded by plaintiffs' counsel's effective cross-examination that it

must disregard the defendant's testimony in its entirety as unworthy of credence or deference.

The plaintiffs cannot have it both ways. When their counsel attacked the defendant's credibility after offering him as their only liability expert, he cut off the legal legs of their case.

Without competent, credible expert testimony from a physician of the defendant's specialty establishing the specialty standard of care it is well-settled a medical malpractice claim will not lie. Evidence Rule 701. *Greene v. Thomas*, 662 P.2d 441 (Ct. App. 1982). The verdict is accordingly vacated and judgment directed to be entered in the defendant's favor. In light of the defendant's statutory offers of settlement, the costs of defense shall be assessed against the plaintiffs and their counsel on a bill of costs to be taxed within ten days hereof.

DATED this 13th day of July, 1994.
The Hon. John David Langworthy, District Judge

"The judgment," Moss said under his breath. "The judgment is against *us*."

"You knew he'd knock your verdict back." Crutchfield laid a Merit Ultra Light in the rift between his fingers, chopped his wrist and caught the filter in his lips on the second gainer.

"Knock it back, sure." Moss stood at the window over Broadway. "But knock it out?" The town looked parched and empty, between terms.

"Remittitur, minimum, I'd've predicted." Crutchfield flicked his Bic and turned up the dial on his smoke-eating ashtray. His caseload sprawled across Moss's mock-Empire desk: Sore backs and temporomandibular joints, repetitive stresses and multiple chemical sensitivities, postconcussive and thoracic-outlet and carpal-tunnel syndromes. A family

practice in its own way. A high-volume, low-hassle settlement clinic.

Moss opened the window on the still, dry heat. "I figured
he'd throw out the jury nullifier then tort reform it down
to five mil combined." The pain and suffering portions had
to drop to the $250K statutory cap, and punitive damages
under recent legislation couldn't exceed compensatories.
"Six point five with costs and interest."

"I figured cram-down," Crutchfield said. "Remit you into
six figures. But I expect the worst."

"Not this time."

"J.N.O.V." Crutchfield crushed and broke the just-lit cigarette, his way of cutting down. "Ah, Langworthy." His
mouth took a wry turn. "Ah, humanity."

"Piss off, Crutch." Little annoyed like the pessimist tri-
umphant.

"It's how the world turns, Peter."

"No, it isn't," Moss said. "It's Heinz."

"Come again?"

"It's simpler than that. It's specific and not universal cor-
ruption. It's money."

Somehow, some way, Heinz owned the judge. All bone
and stone, bubbled with blebs and defects, stealing som-
berly off-stage, Heinz was the puppetmaster, costuming
Basteen in Brioni suits, burying Bondurant's secrets, buying or bullying the judge.

"You'll never prove that."

"You're right, I won't."

"What the hell. Wrap it into the appeal. Throw in a judicial misconduct issue."

"No way this J.N.O.V. will stand on appeal."

"It shouldn't, I'll grant you." Another Ultra Light was
snagged on the fly. "Junker wants to talk about the appeal,
Peter."

Moss found the idea inexpressibly offensive. "Tell Junker he knows where to find me."

"You need dough. How you going to get your superse-

deas on the judgment for costs? We can bond it for you.
Hey, I'll help on the briefs."

"Let him try to execute."

"You think Heinz won't? You *have* to bond it, Peter."

"Maybe I will."

"Bond costs a fifth of the cost judgment times two for
interest. At least twenty-five grand. You need us. Junker's
willing."

"Second thought, tell Junker to fuck himself."

"I'm hearing a lot of anger, Peter."

"Fuck you too."

Crutchfield sent a white sigh scudding toward the open
window.

Moss fanned his way out then stepped back in. "Let me
use your phone. Never mind." He took off down the hall.
Downstairs at reception he got Lata to clear a conference
room. He shut the door and sat down. It took four calls to
catch Basteen in his car.

"Jerome, Judge screwed me."

"Join the club."

"I have a proposal."

"Propose."

"I sign for the supersedeas bond. We appeal, we lose,
you got my ass to cover your costs."

"Peter, number one, you don't want to be on the hook
for sixty-five thousand bucks of our costs, plus interest."
He had a weary, unfamiliar tone. "Number two, you're not
good for it. No deal. But if you forget an appeal, I'll forget
the costs."

"You're nuts. Don't make me bond this. What do you
care?"

"I don't, actually."

"Well?"

The connection fizzed and hit a dead space—tunnel or
turning into the mountains.

"O.K." he said. "Sign for it. I'm getting off this thing
anyway."

"Off this thing? Bondurant fire you?"

"Heinz fired Bondurant. So I fire Bondurant if he's not paying me, which he isn't. Then Heinz fires me too, is how I read it. So hell, Peter. Sign for it. You owe me one."

Son of a bitch. The judge and the adjuster shafted everybody. ROMPIC must have denied coverage under the intentional acts exclusion of Bondurant's policy because his conduct was proven to be criminal. So clear-cut they yanked his defense. Bondurant's on his own. If Moss loses the appeal Heinz pays nothing. If Moss wins and the judgment is reinstated, Heinz still pays nothing because the claims aren't covered. The ultimate win/win.

But what happens to the policyholder now? Images of their exits came to mind: The speeding silver LeBaron; the adjuster, amphibian, cabalistic, creeping through the courtroom, intruder and lord.

"Son of a bitch." Moss said it out loud. "ROMPIC really cutting you off?"

"It was a big verdict. Heinz is reevaluating. Total quality management. It's a religion."

"What's going to happen with Bondurant?"

Moss thought at first the car hit another tunnel or canyon turn.

"I really don't care what happens to him."

"He's your client." Moss's incredulity was sincere.

"Not for long." The silence continued uncomfortably. "Hey, I'm breaking up." The transmission was getting fitful. "I'm losing you," fizz fizz, "I'm gone."

On his way out the glass doors of Junker and Wylie, LLC, Moss was detained by Lata. "Hold it, Peter. Don't forget your mail and this subpoena duces tecum. The fellow just dropped it off."

"For me?"

"For the files in your case, *Winter v. Bondurant*. We don't have any of those here, do we?"

"Nope. They're all mine."

"Everything's at your new shop?"

"More like garage. Closet."

"Any openings," she whispered, "at your garage?"

"I'm a one-armed, one-man band, Lata."

"I can sing."

"Wait till I can afford you."

The announcement on top of the stack of mail offered employers a new HMO owned and run by doctors. The Mountain States Physicians' Network, a Junius Foundation project. "The new generation in health care."

A zebra, like Sally said. Even bad guys don't lie about everything.

Moss skimmed the subpoena, signed by the chief deputy D.A. on behalf of a special grand jury. Sure, he'd share his work product with a grand jury.

The bad guy, by the looks of it, needed a lawyer more than ever.

TWO

Clouds *were curdling* into a bank up and down the range. Terry beheld the changing sky from a wheelchair where Emmy parked it on the plank bridge over the irrigation ditch. On the other side Sanitas Valley mounted to a saddle from which the historic buffalo range of the Arapahoe could be admired to the east. Scabbed over now with housing developments out to the middle distance, the perspective obliged an ironic stance. As did Sanitas Valley itself, at the head of which lay the remains of a turn-of-the-century tuberculosis sanitarium. Her eagle fetish clutched in her lap, Terry gazed upon the valley of health.

Moss, in the kitchen with Sally, watching Terry and Emmy on the bridge, considered what he would like to say, to his client and to the world. To speak suitably to the world he'd first take a full tumbler of transparent liquor, rinse his innards and sideswipe out the door. Then might he sound off on judgments notwithstanding verdicts.

To his client, he'd like to say, you bring out the best in people.

Sally held to his waist as if to tell him no, you don't need a drink. You don't need the world. I suffice. After he called with news of the ruling she'd penned and left on his pillow Yeats's "To a Friend Whose Work Has Come to Nothing": "Be secret and exult, because of all things known that is most difficult." He crossed his arm likewise around her.

Sally had finished the intaglio of the sad marionette, Emmy cranking the starwheel as Sally adjusted the blotters and felts. She peeled the paper slowly back and clasped it to a wire to dry. The lips had been reworked to show a confident turn, the twine severed, the child freed. *I can dance without you* No. 1/1 was for Terry. Sally framed and hung it by the fold-out bed.

"What's new on the home front?" Moss asked. "No bombshells, please."

"Dr. Greenwood stopped by. She left the wheelchair. Warren Winter was over. He left the heroin."

"Warren? Heroin? In our house?"

"The first time you were still in trial. Where's my daughter? he said. With Peter, I said. Then he told me to tell you things it would not have been smart to tell you."

"For Christ's sake, Sally."

"Don't be a prude," she called after him as he marched out the back to his client.

Moss touched Terry's bare shoulder, silken in the amber light, tacky from mistletoe oil Emmy had applied. She turned his way. Running shirt on a stick frame—Horse Protection League 10K. Emmy sat cross-legged on the bridge, elbows on knees, fists on cheeks.

"Mind if I interrupt?" he asked.

"You're not interrupting." He had to strain to hear her. "Everything's an interruption of something else, I guess."

"Everything's a continuation of something else," she said.

"There you go. Two ways of looking at the world."

"My way's why I'm not a lawyer."

"Me neither," Emmy commented. "I'm bored." She yawned irritably.

"Look at her. All legs and head like a frog. Squeaks when she yawns like a dog. Emmy, go play."

"I don't have anybody to play with."

"Go play with your inner child."

"Who?"

"You and you."

"*So* retardo." She two-finger whistled and Lightning came skidding from the tall grass to a sit on the bridge. In the strange antediluvian light there seemed a greenish bloom to his brindle.

"Is that in fact a green dog?" Moss asked.

"Sometimes." Emmy stood. Lightning stood.

"I've never seen a green dog before."

"He's special."

They were off upon the buckskin meadow, Emmy running with her fists in the air, Lightning wreathing routes around her, sparrows and larks skimming from their path. The season of purples and greens had ripened into yellows and reds—mullein candles and yucca blooming on the saddle, cheatgrass and thistle, paintbrush and currants, feral apples, gaillardia and sunflowers, swallowtails and monarchs. Ponderosas bearded the ridgelines where coyotes were dozing, and probably a lion. A redtail volplaned the length of the valley as the darkening cloud bank lowered and spread.

"What's this," Moss ventured, "about drugs from Warren?"

She closed then opened her shining eyes. "Got a problem with it?"

"It's just, you know, illegal."

"Past that."

"I am your lawyer."

"Anita housecalled on me. Not to worry. How they do it over in England."

"Do what?"

"Die. They're all smackheads over there. Maggie. Charlie. The Queen Mum."

"That so?"

"They got the look."

"Keep it hush-hush, all right?"

"Hush-hush," she whispered. "Old Aunt Terry got into the sherry. If anybody asks."

"Does it help?"

"Helps me think. Pain gets where you can't think and smack carries it off. Eating ice cream, watching the waves."

"Tell me how you're doing."

"I'm losing my mind." She simulated a delirious look.

"Really."

"I'm not supposed to be here. This—" her look took in the valley and sky "—is gravy. Who'm I to complain?"

"You look good."

She huffed. "It's such a good feeling to know you're alive." The singing trailed away. "Mr. Rogers is a nice man but sick people are more honest."

Moss didn't understand what Mr. Rogers had to do with it.

"I'm not some rah-rah, life-is-a-beach people person."

"No, you're not. Life is serious."

"Scare me." She looked at him, breathing labored, without warning full of tears and laughing at herself. "I can't cry," she said. "I don't have the air to cry. But I can laugh, sort of."

"Hang tough, Terry." Moss rocked her shrunken, silken shoulders.

"I fall down if I try to walk to the bathroom. My head feels like Bosnia. I don't know the names of things, like what's on a door. What you open a door with. I keep thinking there must be something, *one thing*, if I just knew what it was, I could do it and they'd take my cancer away."

She rolled her knuckles across her eyes. Her throat pulsed. A swallowtail beat softly up the muttering ditch.

"At least I'm able to think about the end of things. I couldn't really contemplate it until I told my daughter. Since then has been a happy time, really. You can be happy *and* afraid, you know. *Happiest*."

"Terry, I don't care what you take, you know. I care about you suffering." Now he held tears back. "Oh, Jesus."

"There you go again."

"No, I mean it."

"Oh, like, *oh, Jesus!*"

She smiled but a distance came into her look, canted above the meadow where her daughter played, above the pines, toward the bruised sky. "I've prayed for something," she said. "To die well. Matter of attitude, I think."

A big raindrop struck the bridge, an isolated drop, like a tobacco squirt. Emmy was dragging back toward the house. She'd pulled the neck of her oversized T-shirt on top of her head like a monk. The ditchwater galloped away.

"Ship comes in, you said. We need to talk about that some."

"I said, *ship*."

"I know you said ship."

"Well?"

"Good news, bad news, worse news—what do you want?"

"Start with bad."

"The judge threw out the verdict." Moss tried to explain how that was possible. She took it well enough.

"It wasn't about money," she said, "but you don't look so hot, losing my case."

"There's good news, Terry."

"What—Jerry got fired?"

"Well, that too."

"His act was getting old. One-trick pony."

"The good news I want to talk about is the appeal. We can appeal what the judge did and I think we'll win."

"We'll appeal and we'll win?"

"That's how I assess it. The standard of care was undisputed. Bondurant's credibility went to questions of fact, not expert qualifications. Clear legal error to remove it from the jury. Appeal looks so good my firm wants me back."

"What did you tell 'em?"

"To fuck themselves."

"Lawyer talk, huh?"

"Legalese, we call it."

"Lawyers, judges, doctors, what's happening in America?"

"Terry, we need to talk about the worse news. The appeal will take two years at least and—"

"I'm gone. I don't mind. Can you still appeal if I'm gone?"

"You can die, Bondurant can die, the case lives on. But when we get the verdict back, there may not be any insurance coverage."

"There's something we need to talk about."

"There is. I need a will."

"What?"

"I've been writing my will. Does that work, if I just write one down?"

"Not really my line, Terry, but I'll find somebody for you."

"Hell, Peter. Just when I was starting to think you were a halfway shit-together lawyer."

"A holographic will is supposed to work."

She arched a brow.

"Handwritten works. I think."

"Good. I haven't actually gotten past the dog part. I need a little legal counsel. Ship comes in, need to pay Anita, need something for Frank for the use of the van. And I don't want anything going to Warren. And I want you and Sally to step in with Emmy, if you don't mind."

"Terry." He raised a hand.

"She's a nice kid."

"There's a problem, Terry."

"Same problem?"

"Warren has full parental rights. List us as your choice as Emmy's guardians, but Warren's still her dad."

"I was afraid of something like this." She closed her eyes and brought her fingers to the tender lids.

"Not exactly news."

"Listen, I did time with the man. I don't want any kicky stuff for my kid."

"But Terry."

"I'm of the right-to-arm bears school myself."

"Me too. Laid down my sword and shield."

"Different philosophies."

"You never filed for divorce, did you?"

"Violence is not a solution. Violence is the problem."

"Legally Warren has rights."

"Yeah, yeah, yeah. Rights, rights, rights. Shit."

"So?"

"We may have to collect from Bondurant. He'll declare bankruptcy. But damages for acts of malice aren't dischargeable in bankruptcy."

"This is starting to hurt my head."

"So we can object to discharge and ultimately get his assets."

"Assets—like Mr. Hinton wanted?"

"Everything he owns."

"I think that's fair. We at this point means you and Emmy?"

"Right."

"Just don't forget Anita and Frank and Yellowhorse too. I'm writing Horse down for something. Maybe a truck."

"We won't."

"You and Emmy and the case lives on. I can get into it."

Moss smiled. She actually had him looking forward to the next part.

"I want to tell you something, Terry. You bring out the best in people."

"Oh, sure."

"You're the cure for burn-out."

"The *cure?* Take a look. I *am* burn-out."

"But I've never had a client move in on me before."

"Or move out, I bet."

"You did that once already."

"Prepare yourself for twice."

A second raindrop hurled itself at their feet like a challenge.

"I want to tell you something," she said. "When the time comes I want to see daybreak on the plains."

"No hospitals."

"Still up for it?"

"Your call. You're the client."

"Wheel me in, would you? Storm's coming and I feel tired."

Moss nodded a little too gravely, reading too much in her words. He released the brake and swiveled the chair on its rear wheels. She felt almost weightless bumping down the hard July lawn. He suggested a video that evening.

"Just not one where people die a lot. I mean a lot of people die. Hey."

"Yes?"

"Next time you catch up with Bondurant don't let him get away with that right to self-incrimination trick. Oldest trick in the book. I can't believe he got to pull that off."

"Terry, it's guaranteed by the Constitution. It's in the Bill of Rights."

"Yeah, yeah. Rights, rights. Just like Warren. *Wait*."

He braked the chair.

"Will it be in the paper, the J.N.O.V. thing?"

"You bet. Judge ruled yesterday. The reporter's already called. They'll run something in the morning. Radio should pick it up. Maybe Channel Nine."

She began to curse, dropping her head and gripping the chair arms as though to keep from jumping up, and suddenly Moss realized what rough justice the judge had set loose.

THREE

B*etween a floodlit* car lot with banners and flags and beet-digger pickups angle-parked at the Holiday Bowl, Moss turned west off Twenty-eighth Street onto Jupiter. Jupiter wanted to be a boulevard when it grew up. Toward that end trees had been planted and staked for the wind and enclosed bus stops erected. A bike path peeled off into open space toward the biotech plant. To the south the streetlight rows of gated developments followed the doglegs of fairways. To the north everything looked like something else. One-story medical office buildings like a military post. Flatirons Community Hospital like a church. Like a cardiogram the gray limbus of the Front Range scored the starry sky.

There was no answer at his house, no answer from his pager, and he didn't have a lawyer anymore. The recording at the clinic said it was closed. He was either out of town, so no problem, or in town and not answering. No way to get through the electric gate and find the house.

So try the office, Sally suggested.

"Go to a doctor's office on Saturday night?"

Call it a hunch, she said. Be careful.

Neptune Way ended at the out-of-bound fence for the country club. There, illuminated like a cotton gin in a cone of bluish light, were the gray brick offices of the Wellness Clinic. Summer insects circulated under a sodium vapor lamp. Directly below as if showcased was a shiny silver LeBaron. At the penumbra of the bluish cone the blue truck sat idle and solemn as an Edward Hopper object.

Goddamn, Moss muttered. He couldn't remember having passed a phone booth—already becoming anachronisms. No cell phone. No way to call for help.

The truck's antennae looked promising for CB if not more, and Moss knew radio, or he used to. But the dashboard had the look of an AWACS console. He was way out of his league. A water purifier and freeze-dried rations scattered on the floorboard. An empty open briefcase on the seat.

Moss passed a moment in thought. From Neptune Way, a sound, the cushioned footfalls of a jogger thudding past. Heart monitor strap and pepper spray in a nylon sleeve, headed for the golf course. It was Saturday night in northeast Boulder. The jogger shot him a skeptical look.

He breathed deep, breathed in the sweet vapors of clippings and herbicides and airborne water from fairway sprinklers, and let his pupils get large. Moving in at night had been a specialty once. Something in muscle memory must have been retained.

Under one window a screen lay in the gravel. The lock had been jimmied. Moss took another sip of sweet night air and eased the frame open then pulled himself up. From somewhere in the penetralia of the place he heard a sound, like fabric ripping. He heard a voice, like television, like the nightly news.

He made his way to Patti's front-office station from behind. There all the lights were on. An antiquated billing computer, wire cages and plastic dividers for charts, telephone message-slip spikes, file cabinets with letters of the alphabet. Dead flowers in a vase and photographs of Patti with nieces and nephews and one of Kevin Costner. In the softest voice Moss told the 911 dispatcher to get people there quick.

In the waiting room the walls and floor were carpeted in some beige-cream noncolor. Brass coatracks and noncolored furniture. He hadn't noticed the juvenilia the last time he was there—a Mickey Mouse stained-glass window, a blue, molded-plastic rocking horse. The aquarium with a bubbling filter. A little diver and a treasure chest and gaudy, insensible fish.

At the end of an unlit hall light broke from the second of two doors. From inside the far door Moss could hear the high-pitched voice he could almost understand. He edged carefully down the hall, past clipboards hanging on hooks, a stand-up scale with a height bar and sliding weights, a cart on casters. A biohazard disposal bin with an international warning device, and the darkened doorway to examining room B.

Moss clicked the switch and checked inside. There was an Age of the Dinosaurs chart and a photoposter of an elephant sitting on a picnic table. The zoo animal wallpaper. The stuffed Peter Rabbit on a white supply cabinet. A jar of candy canes and Mutant Turtle lollipops. The metal arms and stirrups and Velcro straps were snapped down and locked below the bed. Moss caught an image of himself in the mirror on the back wall. Poji the clown.

What, Moss wondered, would overcome him here? What could convince him this was his entitlement? Was it blind narcotic need that drove his hands, or a ruining kind of love, adoring innocence to destroy it? Did he fight it? Did he despise himself? Did he know the terror and pain and shame he caused? Did causing pain and terror impel him? Or was there no cause and effect; only sequence, and therefore no meaning? It happened, then it happened again, then again, and again. No soul, and so he drowned in the flood of self, the incoherence of acts and consequences.

Moss braced in the doorway, turned away, and looked back down the hall. The door to examining room A was half opened out, projecting a blade of yellow light. The voice continued intermittently and Moss moved toward it. On the inside of the door was a full-length mirror. He inched along the wall until he could see through the mirror into the room.

Bondurant lay on the examining bed, half-sitting against the far wall. Short-sleeved blue shirt, arms at his side. Part of a sink could be seen, a blood pressure cuff, part of a cabinet, a mini-fridge with a tray of disposable syringes in plastic packages. A four-hook IV rack next to the bed with a pale yellow bag hanging upside down. A faint almond odor. A cart with cotton, Q-Tips, Betadyne, tape. A purple bottle of microbicidal soap. A peeled-back syringe package on Bondurant's lap and a vial in his left fist.

From the IV bag a tube ran to a needle to a vein on the top of Bondurant's right hand, held in place with five lengths of tape. A plastic roller clamp was set at zero part way down the tubing. In a cushioned aluminum chair with his blond ponytail to the door Warren Winter, pistol loose in his hand, watched Bondurant eight feet away.

Every once in a while Winter spoke.

"You've got a nice house, sort of. I looked there first, came in the back. You live there alone?"

Bondurant looked away.

"Sort of nice in a nothing sort of way, like a ski-town condo. Your BarcaLounger and your TV set. All those frozen dinners and cartons of Coke. Sort of random."

"Who are you?" Bondurant's voice was slow and husky.

"Just a dad. One of the dads, is all. Your worst nightmare, in other words." Winter rolled his neck. "And you, what you turn out to be is like—some nobody. Some big dead zero. No life." He tapped his pistol against the medicine cart. "You are your job—is that it?"

Bondurant's eyes were crushed and empty, not tracking.

"Look at me, longnose. Explain yourself."

Bondurant's head moved vaguely from side to side.

"I hate that, being ignored. Especially when I'm trying to help." The chair emptied. Winter stood fingering the spent bottles in the tray. "I like your plan, though. Hydrogen cyanide, the tried and true. Diluent was what? Plain old water. What's the solution? Depends on the problem."

Winter chuckled. "But what concentration did you mix? Tell me that."

Bondurant shifted slightly, looked at him and blinked. "Point two percent."

"Mighty damn dilute. You must be worried about the cramping and the puking and the convulsions. Comes with the territory, you know that. You're the croaker." Winter gave the IV a once-over, like a nurse. "How many drops per second?"

Bondurant shrugged weakly.

"Didn't get that far? Well, we'll get her done. But look at this." He took the one-dose vial from Bondurant's fist and squinted at it under the light. "Pentothal parenthesis thiopental sodium. Uh-oh. What you gave my daughter, am I right? So she'd forget?"

Winter frowned sadly. He thumbed the vial into a trouser pocket and leaned within inches of Bondurant's face. "We can't allow that. You won't remember anyway. Dying," he leaned closer still, "is a significant life experience." He lay the black pistol against the doctor's temple. "You want to be *aware*. Now listen to me."

He drew the muzzle down Bondurant's cheek and rammed it against the roof of his mouth. "I am here to lend a hand. Call it assisted suicide. Call me Dr. K."

He thumbed the roller clamp on the tubing to 5. "No sedative. And how many dps you want?"

"Three," Bondurant said hoarsely.

"Too fast. We want to drag this out some." Winter rolled it back to 1 and drew the pistol away.

"It's showtime, longnose."

Winter sat again, leaned back and crossed his knee. He fixed Bondurant with a rapt unblinking stare. The pistol lay in his palm like a remote control.

"Now die."

Moss studied the positions and distances of the things in the room—chair, cart, bed, IV rack, each of Winter's hands. He reversed them in his mind to account for the mirror-image. Standing flat against the hall wall, he listened to

Bondurant's rough breathing, the hum of the minifridge. It occurred to him not to intervene. It *was* Bondurant's life. Leave him his life . . . Let him end it clueless and stupefied, unrepentant. Leave Winter his vengeance. Walk away and leave them each other, allies in a common cause.

Is that what his client would want?

Bondurant made a dry smack with his lips. He closed his blue-rimmed eyes.

"Starting the trip?" Winter asked. "Climbing up to steady state?"

Walk away—a renunciation, as when the McGuire rig fell when the choppers exploded and he lay down his M-16. As he'd been tempted momentarily to walk away from the case. To withdraw. He pressed back, fly on the wall, willing disappearance, the jungle illusion of not being seen.

There was a movement in the mirror. Bondurant's taped and tethered right hand trembling and lifting, his wretched eyes connecting with Moss's in the reflection, a finger rising and pointing at the doorway. Winter's head starting to turn.

Moss raised his hands against the wall and came forward. "Hey, ranger." He entered the room smiling. "Party's over. Shitbag's got daughters too."

Winter looked Moss up and down with intense curiosity. "Snakehead." He tapped a finger on his lower lip. "It's a private party."

"No more. You're looking at a witness. You have to grease us both."

"Not illegal to help a man accomplish his task."

"Qualifies as homicide in this state." A fool's errand— to reason with Warren Winter—Moss saw from the pinpoint lidless eyes.

"Terry talked all about her esquire. As though something was wrong with *me*."

"It won't work, Warren. Help's on the way."

"Work is not the objective of this operation."

"They're about to indict him," Moss said. "Don't give him what he wants. He's better off shamed publicly and sent down as a sex offender." Moss thought he caught a flicker of consensus; same ends, different means.

Bondurant's eyes fluttered.

"I'm appealing what the judge did. I'm going to win."

"We're off the shelf, snakehead. We are in the realm of the absolute."

Different tactics, like with village sweeps. One involved death and the other didn't.

"I'm unplugging him, ranger." Moss flexed his upraised fingers and held a breath. Stopping killing—it was still the right side to be on. He took a step toward Bondurant.

"Ice it," Winter said. He turned the nose of the pistol toward Moss.

Moss took another step. Sirens could be heard on Jupiter. "Too late. You better make yourself scarce."

"I let you turn him off, what's in it for me?"

Without thinking, Moss answered, "I take care of your kid."

"Bullshit."

Moss could sense him calculating. Why should he trust Terry's lawyer? Because he and Moss want the same thing, and for another reason—Terry's will, a felt pressure in the close room, urging them. Because it's what Terry wants.

"You can't take care of Emmy," Moss said. "You've got two minutes before the cops show. The doctor here is going down. You want to go down too? Attempted homicide? Get the hell out now and I'll handle the rest. Emmy, her school, her judgment, the appeal. I'll make sure he gets prosecuted."

Bondurant said something. "Yuh."

"Shut up," Moss said. His hand moved toward the roller clamp. "You were never here, ranger, as far as I'm concerned. No matter what shitbag says."

More inappropriately than ever a sinner at a fiery sermon, Bondurant then yawned. Afterward his mouth remained agape.

Moss jumped to the bed, grabbed the IV tube, and tore it away. A line of poison dotted the wall. Blood pooled and trickled from the center of Bondurant's hand like a stigma. A red reflux traveled the tube and coiled like smoke in the yellow bag.

Bondurant made a strangulated coughing sound. His eyes rolled toward Moss who backhanded him across the jaw. "Pull out of it."

Bondurant looked from his bleeding hand to Moss, and both looked up but Winter was gone. Vanished into the herbicidal night.

"You." Bondurant strained forward then fell back again. The sirens had turned onto Neptune Way.

"Yeah, me. I'm all you've got left."

"Who was that?" Bondurant said. "My head . . ."

"Him? Your guilty conscience. Try any funny stuff, he'll be waiting.

"Now sit up." Moss ran a tall glass of water from the sink tap. Bondurant took it in both hands and gulped it down. "You need a doctor."

FOUR

Jostling up the fire road from the ditch was enough to kill you by itself. Pain so keen and frequent it became one edgeless experience, pain's opposite. How things become their opposite. Pain becomes voluptuous.

They would do this any morning she was willing. They would ask and she would say, keep going. Passing the streamlet hooped in rose-briars. The butterscotch smell of ponderosas. Lightning nosing at her fingertips. And there, Emmy on the saddle waving against the sky.

They were true blue.

From a couch-shaped sandstone outcrop, pink as flesh, where a canyon fell away to the city below and the Arapahoe plains beyond, she would watch the morning though it burned her eyes. Emmy holding her hand. Lightning plundering the countryside. Peter and Sally looking for birds.

There was a Utah juniper at the outcrop, wind-worked like topiary. A catbird perched atop like a finial, mewing. The canyon was a birdy dell with Gambel's oakscrub, currant and kinnikinnick clinging to the cliff face. In winter Moss would see crossbills in the pines and spectral ferruginous hawks. Sally had found among the sandstone a storm-blown rosy finch. That summer towhees took over the valley while the canyon bustled with buntings and siskins and here and there a solitaire or shrike.

All the tiger swallowtails that year put Moss in mind of blue morphos in the cloud forest and the jacamars they'd seen that unrepeatable moment. Darwin showed that chance was in the nature of things. A bird you'd been looking for for years could flash out from the curtained jungle like truth at a trial.

Who says old dogs can't learn new tricks? Dogs are people too. One morning Lightning pursued a squirrel among the ponderosas that lined the rim. He'd bark it up a tree from the bottom while a magpie hectored it down from the top, driving it from a middle limb in a desperate leap to the next tree in the row where the conspiracy of bird and dog resumed.

White prickly poppies bloomed at the base of the sandstone couch. Pollen boles like egg yolks in porcelain cups. Each blossom acrawl with tiny black beetles. Lifespecks. Emmy would hold one to Terry's ear, like Horton the Elephant listening for Hoos.

Closing her eyes in the warm light Terry thought of her dreams for her daughter—for loving parents and a comfortable house with lush meadows and snowy peaks, for eating ice cream on the beach without a care, for when Emmy grew up and became herself, tall and capable and a whole lot smarter than her mother ever was.

She put a hand to her missing left breast and rolled her broken nails across her scar. Here in the daylight came close enough.

Nights were another story. When she shut her eyes then it was as though she could see the tumors pulsing, glowing and dimming as they grew. With the greatest care, she'd turn her head. She'd long for dawn. Every night she was less and less. She could feel strength seeping from every pore. At times it seemed to flood.

• • •

"Look at them brogans."

Moss sat in the one respectable settee, a flared, clawfoot Queen Anne. He crossed his stretched-out legs at the ankle and reviewed the stained and cracked Luccheses at the ends of them. "These ain't brogans. These are boots."

"Boots," Terry said in a whisper. "Bet I know where you got them boots."

"Where's that?"

"You got 'em on your feet." Emmy laughed and hugged her mother's thin knees, like tent poles under the sheet, as Terry caught her breath.

"Let's light incense," Emmy said.

"Let's have champagne," Sally said.

Terry raised her thumb and closed her lustrous, tinted eyes. Emmy lit a stick of En-mei—*Circle*—and flutes were passed around—even Emmy, even Moss, and one they held to Terry's lips.

The progression of symptoms hadn't been all bad. Diarrhea had progressed to constipation. She went diapered as it was. The palsy in her hand and arm had stopped suddenly. Anita had smiled when Terry told her, in a way that hinted that wasn't exactly great news. Terry got dizzy less often though the clanging in her head continued. The paper Sally read announced the find of tiny magnets in our brains. Millions of magnets. Terry heard them clanging.

Sometimes her gone breast felt on fire.

At night everyone came and went. She'd fall in and out of sleep without moving or changing the rhythm of her shallow breathing. She might not know where she was or to whom she spoke. She might speak to someone not there. Sally would reposition the small pillow until her breathing improved. Peter would alternate the hot water bottle with gel packs from the freezer as one cooled or the other warmed.

They'd eat, play music, talk in her presence. She might respond or not. She might hear but not listen, like a wind flowing over. Sally applied hand pressure and Tiger Balm massage. Emmy worked in the mistletoe oil. Moss would do the dishes. Emmy would not want to go to bed. Sally would have her brush her teeth and lie down at Terry's side.

The champagne danced on Terry's welted lips. Peter and Sally weren't there, then Sally was again, with basin and sponge and a towel.

"How you?" Terry whispered.

Sally shook her head. "How you?"

"I feel like a boil all over."

Sally dabbed Terry's face with the towel. "Let's skip the bath." She worked Terry's shoulders. The smell of menthol rose.

After a while Peter spoke. "What are we going to do now?" he said.

What he meant was, after you're gone? He meant, would his aspirations for virtue get snarled again in triviality and compromise, and his and Sally's love for each other constricted by their separate regrets. Would his sense of transformation, of regeneration, last?

"It's a whole new rodeo," Terry whispered.

In-one-two . . . She lacked the air to hold it. She closed her eyes and the pulsing glow resumed.

Some time later Terry opened her eyes. She felt Emmy's fingers softly on her arm. Emmy's soft breathing and toothpaste breath. She remembered that Emmy no longer cried at night but the memory faded and her mind wandered. Where was she? In the dark, spinning. She awoke again later, awash in sorrows. For a mare that died foaling out. For her mother, father, husbands, a son. She tried to speak to keep from seeing horrible things. Photographs of burning monks. A bee-killed cow. A spur-scarred gelding. Emmy in a fever trance, wide-eyed with terror. She moaned and clutched for her eagle. She needed daylight.

"Look at me," Terry gasped. "Don't be afraid."

Emmy put her arms around her mother's throbbing neck.

Peter and Sally stayed talking and drinking coffee through most of the night. Terry fell in and out of consciousness, Emmy dozing then waking to caress her. They played old records. Ian and Sylvia, *Abbey Road*, Otis Redding.

Terry woke again with an urgent look.

"Mom."

Terry struggled to raise her head. "Take me outside."

A sheet of light was spreading in the east. As the light spread the wind rose. At the sandstone couch a moth floated above the last capsules of a yellow yucca spike, its *icor*. What would happen to Terry's *icor*, her invisible moth, guardian of her spirit?

In the foreground each object was as carefully illuminated as an intended creation. In the distance the light was smearing, horizonless. The day was all-destroying, brimming up to the canyon rim and blistering her welded eyes. The west-facing ponderosa slope was cloyed in darkness but coronas formed on the rimrock pines.

She could see the indiscriminate power of the elements, the particular beauty of living things.

A glaze of waxy light lay upon the buffalo plains. Lakes like spills of white paint, the silvered asphalt of east-west streets. Moving windshields sparkled. Crows in flight caught the sun like plastic. Someone's white T-shirt and socks badged the slope five hundred feet below. Shadows javelined from every stem and seedhead around her. A grasshopper turned broadside to be warmed by the light. On the smooth pink sandstone gravel bits cast monolithic shadows. On her knee she watched the glittering of a deerfly's compound eyes.

The light was passing through her. Her skin was coated with a sheen of sweat. The hairs on her arm shone like whitecaps. Like the Sea of Cortez. The pain crested and washed to shore, soaking into the sand. A rainbow formed and faded. The sand dried and she could hear the tumbling of the grains.

The breeze flayed and parched her skin and scattered the grasses' shadows. She felt naked and cleansed. The warm air had a thrilling, icy feel. She heard her daughter's voice and thought to move her head but it wouldn't move. The voice grew faint in a gathering roar. She felt a shivering excitement. Fear had become its opposite. This was it.

The suffering of things in darkness is the suffering of things apart. Terry could neither speak nor move but she could see and feel. She felt her daughter's hand on the ridged scar where her breast used to be. She felt Emmy's tender touch upon her heart, rising and falling as she rose and fell.

Light was piercing every realm. The painbursts in the nightsky behind her eyes. The zigzag light cracking through from the spirit world below. The wind stilled. Sounds stopped. Colors stopped. Distinctions between things ended and everything was light.

CODA

GRAND ISLAND,
NEBRASKA. MARCH 1995.

In her journeys Emmy had acquired a taste for Mexican food. This was not Mexican food. Really not Mexican food.

Everything about this trip—the fancy tractors, the tall blue silos, the big pale sky, not a mountain, not a rock even, the giant highway, the big solemn people—was really not Mexican, but especially the food. What's for lunch? Salad-burgers. What's for salad? Carrots with raisins. What's for dessert? Yellow Jello with marshmallows in it.

None of this would you find traveling in Mexico.

The huge boring drive took forever. Emmy sat next to Lightning in the back seat of their new red station wagon with her Walkman on, thinking. They couldn't fly because Peter got scared. That had been a surprise. At great intervals they'd stop for Big Gulps. That was nice. It wasn't worth stopping for food, everyone soon discovered. Not much changed all day long except the haystacks. For a while they'd look like bread loaves. Then they'd look like tee-pees. Then they'd roll it in cylinders. Then they'd put plastic and tires all over it.

It was hardly worth asking if they were there yet. So she said, how come we have to *drive*?

That got Peter going about airports. A big conspiracy to hide the truth. Sinister coded language—If your boarding pass does not have a red stamp you will not be admitted on the airplane. Flight attendants, arm the doors for departure. Forbidden words such as bomb and boom, unmanned trains with Stephen Hawking voices, sensor-actuated urinals, white courtesy telephones. The truth being you are utterly powerless. You can fall right out of the sky.

This may be eight hours of cornhusker interstate, he said, but it beats flying. Hear that, birds?

Emmy's view was, at least she was traveling again. Even if it was to look for *birds* in *Nebraska on her spring vacation* when everyone *else* was *snowboarding*. Peter and Sally were just different, that's all, Sally being less different than Peter.

Traveling made her pensive. It was her first trip since Mexico. Her mother's eagle was back home on her windowsill on a square of cowhide. A swooping black eagle with bright eyes and tucked-up talons. *Skyward*. On the cowhide beside the eagle was her obsidian arrowhead from where the trees were when her mother said she was dying and Emmy told her everything. Though a Pearl Jam tape had finished she kept the Walkman on and watched the dead fields go by.

The Holiday Inn they finally stopped at had a Holidome with an indoor pool and stuff like miniature golf she did with Sally. They wanted to get up at four-thirty in the morning. Talk about stupid. Whatever. She trudged along with them.

It was pitch black and scary and so cold standing in the frozen mud. What was scary were the gobbling sounds out in the gurgling river.

To take her mind off the cold and the noises Emmy thought about Mexico some more. How homesick she was at first. Playing Indian with her Indian friend. Red snow cones, Neapolitan bars, stepping on cactus and finding the arrowhead. The bugs on the water where her mother told her she would die after her father found them like she knew he would.

Just like she now knew he would leave her alone. She had the notion she could see the future, whispers and clues she could partly understand.

Peter and Sally did certain things well. They had actually sort of trained Lightning. He'd sit sort of still on command. "Bird," they'd whisper, and he'd sit there whimpering and making gestures with his paws. Then they listened, Peter with his supposed Comanche-in-the-wilderness ears. And they stared.

What her mother had done no one could equal. She freed the ponies in Mexico. She kept her father from hurting them. She got them home to Peter and Sally. She showed the truth about the doctor. She always found four-leaf clovers. She always knew what the weather would be better than a television person. No one could take away what her mother had taught her. To live deep, to stand up for herself, and not let mean people break her spirit. That she was someone of worth.

As the gray light rose around them, so she could see they were standing stock still under a huge leafless black-armed tree, a round metal thing to the side, cattails in ice crinkles, Lightning whimpering and lifting his paws, Peter and Sally under the big black tree staring fanatically at the wide river-bed, the muffled shapes stirring on the sandbars, Emmy had the feeling, as she had had before, that she was in her mother's presence. Not in heaven looking down. Here. How else to explain how still water trembled or grasses waved when there was no wind? The leaf rattle in the underbrush, the quiet breathing she'd hear, or how she sensed she was being watched.

Emmy had another notion: Wherever she traveled her mother would be, because when her heart stopped that morning it wasn't like it stopped. It was like it went up through Emmy's hand to Emmy's heart.

• • •

A limb in the big leafless tree made a loud frightening creak and there was a pulling and whipping of air. A huge black eagle swept down almost on top of them. Lightning flattened and Peter and Sally stepped aside. Emmy almost cried out, seeing it so plainly nod its white cowl and turn upon her its giant golden eye.

The eagle bent its fingered wings and skimmed out over the rushes in a wide bank down the river, vanishing like a jetliner toward the just-appearing sun. From the sandbars a clamor went up. Ten thousand cranes took together to the air, lavender gray in the maiden light.

All day the cranes came and went as they had for ten million years. Landing in the stubblefields loose-ankled as paratroopers, hopping and flapping like popping corn. Aloft among snowgeese glittering like tinsel they spread in loose broken lines to the horizons, scrawling intricate messages, secrets of the future, on the empty sky.

ACKNOWLEDGMENTS

This is a work of the imagination. Its Boulder is not Boulder, Colorado (as fellow Boulderites will quickly see). There are no such Flatirons Counties and Sand Creeks in the real world and no real people, companies, or agencies like those in the book. My law firm and partners have as little in common with Junker and Wylie as the practice of law with the practice of medicine.

But there are lots of real people without whom this fiction would not exist. Too many friends and colleagues to name read and cheered the project on. Writers Jeff Long, Marilyn Krysl, and Tom Zigal gave comradeship and technical help. Awesome teammates included Leslie Breed, my dogged and courageous agent; Lisa Drew, my editor and publisher, and her assistant Blythe Grossberg; the irreplaceable Margo Brown; editor Sarah Flynn, a doctor who knows no malpractice; and the guardian angel who made it come together. Though all errors are exclusively mine, I am indebted to the specialized knowledge of Ron Fundingsland, for intaglio printing; Andrew Bradley, for documents examination; Marian Scott, M.D., for medical review; Steve Briggs, for a judicial perspective; and especially Jack Olsen, for his Vietnam and trial experiences. I've been honored by the friendship and examples of Steve Johs, M.D., best breast surgeon alive; the late John Williams and Wallace Stegner; Cinthia Belle and her work with breast cancer survivors; and the doctors who have taken the stand and spoken their consciences.

My family made me write the best book I was capable of creating—my parents, Baine and Mildred Kerr; my children Dara and Baine; and Cindy, whose judgment and patience, tough love and emotional pillowing, kept the damn thing rolling and got her done.

Abrazotes one and all.